Alafair Burke's books include her Samantha Kincaid series, the standalone thriller *Long Gone*, and her highly acclaimed series starring NYPD Detective Ellie Hatcher, the most recent of which, *Never Tell*, was a Kindle bestseller. A former Deputy District Attorney in Portland, Oregon, Alafair is now a Professor of Law at Hofstra Law School, where she teaches criminal law and procedure. *If You Were Here*, her debut on the Faber list, will be followed by a new Ellie Hatcher novel, *All Day and a Night*, in summer 2014.

Praise for *If You Were Here*:

'I absolutely love Alafair Burke – she's one of my favorite authors. I know it's summer when I have one of her books in my hands. *If You Were Here* is her best yet. Highly recommended.' Karin Slaughter

'After finishing *If You Were Here*, I don't feel I can trust anyone ever again, except Alafair Burke to provide a cracking good read.' Linwood Barclay

'*If You Were Here* has one of the strongest openings in recent thrillers . . . Burke also deserves credit for writing crime fiction (urban, pacy, stylistically restrained) so different from that of her father, Louisiana-based James Lee Burke.' John Dugdale, *Sunday Times*

'Outstanding . . . Burke's account of legal and judicial technicalities is impressive although most readers will find simpler pleasures in her sharp writing, well-constructed plot, and dimensional characters.' *Publisher's Weekly*

'Exciting . . . nds her life turned u . . . her college

years who disappeared without a trace a decade before on a video of a near-tragedy on the subway . . . Will engage [Burke's] growing audience.' *Booklist*

'Burke's first class adventure has murder and mayhem wrapped up in an intricate, innovative plot. Gripping from the first page . . . Will keep readers guessing until the end.' *RT Book Reviews*

'Delivers a cleverly nuanced plot that will keep the pages turning. [Burke's] smart writing is fast-paced and engaging, and this book should appeal to most mystery readers, especially those looking for compelling, intelligent story lines . . . a delight.' *Library Journal*

*if you
were here*

*Never Tell*
*Long Gone*
*City of Lies*
*City of Fear*
*Dead Connection*
*Close Case*
*Missing Justice*
*Judgement Calls*

A NOVEL OF SUSPENSE

# *if you were here*

## ALAFAIR BURKE

FABER & FABER

First published in the USA in 2013 by
HarperCollins Publishers, 10 East 53rd Street, New York, NY 10022

First published in 2013
by Faber and Faber Limited
Bloomsbury House
74-77 Great Russell Street, London WC1B 3DA
This paperback edition first published in 2014

Designed by Yvonne Chan
Printed and bound by CPI Group (UK) Ltd, Croydon CRO 4YY

A CIP record for this book
is available from the British Library

978-0-571-30229-1

In Memory of Judge Betty Binns Fletcher

*if you*
  *were here*

# PART I

All around me are familiar faces.

— Tears for Fears

# CHAPTER
## ONE

Nicky Cervantes smiled to himself as two Wall Street boys pressed past him, one reporting excitedly to the other that Apple stock was up six percent with the release of the company's new iPhone. He could tell from their tone that the good news for the market meant a hefty check for the duo.

Nicky was smiling because one might say he was sort of invested in the market himself these days. And those boys in suits and ties might be whistling over a six percent bump, but Nicky's own payback on the brand had nearly tripled in recent days. When demand for the latest gadget was this red-hot, no one seemed to care where the hardware came from. No additional work for Nicky, either. If anything, he felt a little less guilty about it. Anyone dumb enough to buy jack the day it came out deserved to lose it, was how he figured.

In truth, he never had felt much guilt over it. The first time, he expected to feel real bad, like maybe the lady would start crying or there would be pictures on there of her baby that she'd never get back. But when he finally worked up the courage to do it—to just grab that shit out of her hand while she was preparing some text message to send aboveground—the girl didn't seem to care. He still remembered her reaction. One hand protecting the thousand-dollar bag, the other covering the cleavage peering from the deep V in her wrap dress. In her eyes, he was dirt, and the phone was a small price to pay to protect the things that *really* mattered.

He knew he wasn't dirt. But he also knew he wasn't VIP, like those Wall Street dudes. Not yet, anyway.

He was just a kid whose mom needed the six hundred dollars a month he'd been able to kick in to the household since he'd been working at Mr. Robinson's paint store on Flatbush the past year. And he was the star pitcher for the Medgar Evers High School base-ball team with a .6 ERA, an 88 MPH fastball, a .450 batting aver-age, and a sweeping curve and change-up that consistently racked up strikes. With numbers like that, the nine bucks an hour he was getting from Mr. Robinson had to go once the coach told him he was spread too thin. If all went according to plan, Nicky might even be drafted right out of high school. He could donate a thousand phones to charity out of his first paycheck to make up for what he was doing now.

Nicky was already fifty reach-and-grabs in, but he was still care-ful, compared to some of the dudes he'd met who also sold hard-ware. Tonight he was waiting on the N/R ramp at Times Square, six-thirty P.M. Packed trains. High ratio of Manhattanites to outer-borough types. Low odds of resistance.

It really was like taking candy from a baby. But the candy was a five-hundred-dollar phone, and the baby was some hot chick whose sugar daddy would buy her a new one. The standard play was to linger on the platform, like he was waiting to get on the train. Look for someone—inattentive, weak, female—standing near the door, fiddling with a gadget.

Reach. Grab. Run. By the time the girl realized her phone was gone, Nicky was halfway up the stairs. Easy.

He heard the rattle of the approaching train. Watched the lights heading his way. Joined the other cattle gathering close at the edge of the platform in eager anticipation of scoring a New York com-muter's lottery ticket—an empty seat.

Six trains had come and gone without a baby and her candy.

This time, as the train lurched to a halt, Nicky saw what he'd been looking for through the glass of the car doors. Eyes down, phone out.

Reddish blond hair pulled into a ponytail at the nape of her neck. Long-sleeved white sweater, backpack straps looped over both shoulders. Despite the train's lurch, she typed with two hands, stabilizing herself against the bounce with her core strength.

Maybe that should have been a sign.

He stepped one foot into the car, grabbed the phone, and pivoted a one-eighty, like he had fifty times before. He pushed through the clump of angry riders who had followed him into the car and now stood before him, all hoping to secure a few square feet on the crowded train before the doors closed.

Had he known what would happen next, maybe he would have run faster for the staircase.

It wasn't until he hit the top of the landing that he realized he had a problem. Somehow he heard it. Not the sound of the shoes but the sound of surprised bystanders reacting.

*Hey!*

*What the . . .*

*You lost your shoe, lady!*

*Oh my God, David. We have to leave the city.*

Nicky sneaked a glance behind him to see the woman kicking off her remaining ballet flat as she took two steps at a time in pursuit. She had looked sort of average middle-aged through the subway doors, but now she had a crazy look of determination on her face. In her eyes. In the energy of her forearms as they whipped back and forth at her sides.

At the top of the stairs, he spun left and then right, up the ramp toward the electronics store positioned between the N/R tracks and the 1/2. Why were some trains labeled with letters and others with numbers? Strange how random thoughts popped into his head when he was stressed.

He could hear the thump of an old Run-DMC song that his father listened to when he was still around. Nicky was in luck. The break dancers always attracted a dense semicircle of onlookers.

He leaped over a stroller on the near side of the audience, evoking an "oooooh" from viewers who thought his vault across the make-shift stage was part of the act. Picked up the pace once again, gaze fixed on the stairs that would take him to the 1/2 platform.

He heard more shouts behind him. The crowd hadn't stopped her. A kid cried as he fell to the ground.

Girl wasn't messing around.

He sprinted down the stairs, hoping to hear the familiar clack of an incoming train. No luck.

He thought about abandoning the phone, but the platform was too packed. The phone would fall to the ground, unnoticed by her, scooped up by someone whose good luck today rivaled his bad.

He decided to use the crowd to his advantage. He analyzed the platform that awaited him like an obstacle course, plotting out three or four weaves to maneuver his way to the next exit.

He risked another look behind. The woman had gained on him. She was just as fast, maybe faster. And she was smaller, more nimble. She was finding a more direct path than he'd navigated.

Up ahead, he spotted a busker warbling some "Kumbaya" song behind a cardboard sign he couldn't read from his vantage point. The music was shit, but something about the message must have been magic, because a mass of people huddled around the open guitar case.

They were spread out across the platform. No gaps that he could see.

She was still gaining on him.

He heard the distant clack of a train. Saw lights coming on the left. A local train north.

One pivot around the crowd and he'd be fine. He'd keep running until the train stopped. Hop on board at the last second. Wave goodbye to all this once the doors closed behind him.

Almost over.

He dodged to the left, turning sideways to scoot around a pillar.

He saw a lady's long black hair swing like a shampoo ad. He heard himself say "sorry" on impulse as he felt the heavy thud against his right hip. As he fell backward, he saw the object that had bumped him—the brunette's hot-pink duffel bag—followed by the message on the busker's cardboard sign (THE PREZ AIN'T THE ONLY ONE WHO NEEDS CHANGE), followed by a sea of shocked faces as his body hit the tracks.

It was funny what he thought of in the few seconds that passed as he lay there. His right arm. Would his right arm be okay? As the sound of the train grew louder, he wondered whether his mother would find out why he'd been in the Times Square transit station after school instead of behind a cash register at Mr. Robinson's paint store.

Reflexes kicked in. More than reflex: a deep desire to live. Without any conscious thought, he pressed himself flat between the tracks. More screaming.

He closed his eyes, hoping he wouldn't feel the impact.

And then he felt something he hadn't expected: his body being lifted from the ground. He opened his eyes but saw only white. Was this heaven?

The plane of white moved, making way for the scene of the subway platform again. People staring. Screaming. Asking if he was okay.

He looked toward the blurred, fading plane of white. It was her sweater, topped by the strawberry-blond ponytail, still tightly in place. The forearms were pumping again as she took the stairs two at a time, no pause in sight.

She held her recovered iPhone in her hand.

And Nicky?

Nicky was going to live.

# CHAPTER TWO

**S**itting in a borrowed Chevy Malibu outside Medgar Evers High School, McKenna Jordan thought that kids sure had changed in twenty years. Twenty-five, actually, she realized, since she was their age. How was that possible?

The last bell had sounded only three minutes earlier, and the street in front of the block-long brick building was filled with boys in low-slung pants and ball caps and girls in baby tees and skinny jeans. Some lit cigarettes before hitting the bottom step of the school entrance. Public displays of affection ran rampant—full-on make-out sessions, complete with roaming hands. Even with her car windows up, McKenna had overheard just about every obscenity with which she was familiar, plus a couple of new ones. (At least when one girl called another a "dick trap," McKenna assumed that wasn't a good thing.)

It wasn't as if McKenna and her friends had been angels: smoking, drinking, cussing, even a few teen pregnancies at the school, as she recalled. But at 3:03 P.M.? Right outside the school building? In open view of parents, teachers, and administrators? No way. They'd been too afraid of the consequences.

Maybe the kids hadn't changed after all. Maybe it was the adults who were different.

She checked her phone again for messages. Nothing. McKenna hated waiting for the cooperation of fickle sources. She owed the magazine an article for the next edition. One possibility involved the kid she was here to see at the high school. The other was about Judge Frederick Knight, a notoriously offensive judge who should have been thrown from the bench years before. Both stories needed significant work before she could go to print—work that required information from people whose conduct she couldn't control. That saying about letting go of the things you couldn't control? Not McKenna's motto.

She jerked at the sound of knuckles rapping against the glass of the passenger-side window. She clicked the doors unlocked, and Dana Frazier hopped into the seat next to her. The dark colorful ink that spiraled up her left arm was in stark contrast to the rest of her appearance. Standing barely five feet tall with a blond pixie haircut, Dana was one of those people who looked like she might fit in your pocket. She was so compact that her tiny torso was dwarfed by the enormous Canon hanging from her neck.

McKenna reached out and flicked the camera strap. "You had a two-thousand-dollar camera bouncing around you on the F train? Haven't you heard? Apparently people actually *steal* things on the New York City subway."

Dana flexed her tattooed arm. "I've got mad self-defense skills."

McKenna handed her the car keys. "You mind waiting here after the pictures? I want to talk to the kid alone before we go."

"No problem."

When McKenna had called Dana to ask if she could snap some photos down in Fort Greene, the photographer had said she was taking shots of the Occupy Wall Street protestors, hanging out in the Financial District months after the national attention had passed. McKenna had offered a ride in one of the magazine's fleet cars, but Dana declined, most likely because she had been somewhere else entirely, probably working on the avant-garde photographs she took on the side.

Good for Dana, McKenna thought.

"Speaking of theft," Dana said, holding up the iPad that Mc-Kenna had left on the car dash. "I'm putting this under the seat. These ruffians will grab anything that's not bolted down."

The high school didn't have its own baseball field. McKenna and Dana found the team practicing on a square of concrete that served the triple function of baseball diamond, basketball court, and play-ground to the neighboring grade school.

A well-built man with a shaved head and a golf shirt stretched tight around his biceps watched his suited-up team jog laps around the bases. Once the two women hit his periphery, he rotated toward them, hands never leaving his hips.

McKenna handled the introductions. "Hi there. I'm McKenna Jordan, a writer for *NYC* magazine. This is Dana Frazier. We were hoping to get a word with one of your players, Nicky Cervantes."

The coach sighed. "Been doing everything I can to make that boy famous for his right arm. Now he's the klutz who tripped onto the subway tracks and had to be saved by a *woman*."

McKenna threw Dana a warning glance. They were here to make friends, not change gender attitudes.

"Mind if we pull him away for a few minutes?" McKenna asked. "We'll be quick. Who knows, maybe all the attention will help him in the draft come June."

The coach bothered to look at McKenna instead of his team. He smiled beneath the bill of his blue Mets cap. "You know anything about Major League Baseball?"

"Not a damn thing. I texted my husband from the car to make sure I had the right lingo. Oh, and I know Jeter's the one who looks like a Cabbage Patch doll."

That earned her another smile.

"Cervantes!" the coach yelled, holding up a hand. "Five minutes, okay, ladies? Don't want his arm getting cold."

**N**icky didn't seem surprised that a reporter and a photographer wanted his attention. "Already had three newspapers come by my mom's place last night. A magazine now?"

The night before last, a story started making the rounds on the Internet about a teenager saved from a subway splat by a woman's brave heroics. By yesterday morning, a more detailed version documenting the teen's promising baseball career and the mysteriousness of the unidentified woman had hit the front page of every local paper.

The upcoming edition of *NYC* magazine wouldn't be printed for two more days. McKenna needed to find a long-form angle on the fleeting tale du jour. So far journalists had described Nicky as an honor student and star athlete who'd lost his footing on the platform. McKenna already knew from talking to Nicky's mother that the honor-student label was pure spin. The only academic recognition Nicky had ever received was a certificate of perfect attendance the fall semester of his sophomore year. And when McKenna tried to interview Nicky's boss, a storeowner named Arthur Robinson, she learned that Nicky—unbeknownst to his mother—had quit the job three months ago.

There was another angle to the story. McKenna just had to find it.

She watched as a beaming Nicky struck a series of poses for Dana's camera. Hands on hips. Looking earnestly at the sky. Mimicking a windup.

She didn't really need the pictures, but the modeling session had him in the groove, feeling important. She gave a nod to Dana, who took her cue and headed back to the car, supposedly to grab another lens. Once they were alone, McKenna asked Nicky how he'd slipped.

"What do you mean? I just fell."

"But how? Was the platform slick? Did you have a seizure or something?"

The kid shrugged. "Not sure. Just went down."

"I've seen the MTA's incident report. Bystanders said you were running frantically down the platform right before you fell. One said it was almost as if the woman was chasing you."

If the subway Superwoman actually knew Nicky Cervantes, the story would take on new complexity. Why were they running? Had they been fighting? Why did she leave? And why wouldn't Nicky admit he knew her?

"Whatchu trying to do here, lady?"

What *was* she trying to do? She knew this was the kind of story everyone would forget in a month, like most of the garbage she wrote. She'd like to say she was fostering civic involvement through journalism, but she was simply doing her job: blurring the lines between news, voyeurism, and entertainment. The most entertaining stories needed a protagonist. So far the media coverage of the "1 train tragedy averted" had focused on the good fortune of Nicky Cervantes. McKenna wanted to know about the woman who'd saved him only to sprint away.

The MTA's security cameras had failed to capture any footage of the incident, but McKenna had the advantage of time. Her best lead was a comment posted online by someone claiming that his girlfriend had video of Nicky's fall on her cell phone. McKenna had sent an e-mail to the commenter, hinting at the possibility of payment for the clip; she was still waiting for a response. In the meantime, her firsthand contact with Nicky was leading her to believe that her instincts were on track.

"I know you give your mom money, Nicky, even though you have no obvious source of income." McKenna also knew that, despite New York City's record-low crime rates, robberies on the subway system were on the rise. The story of a mysterious Superwoman saving a promising young teen was media gold. But the story of a female crime victim who simultaneously pursued—and saved—her robber? Pure platinum.

Nicky finally spoke. "You know what? Forget about the pictures, okay? I just want to live my life."

"And I'm trying to find the woman who made it possible for you to do so, Nicky."

"More power to you, then. If you find her, tell her I said thanks. And tell her I've changed. Don't forget, okay?"

"Why'd you need to change, Nicky? Was there a reason the two of you were running through the station?"

He gave his right shoulder a quick massage. "Gotta get back to it now." He returned to practice without another glance in her direction.

# CHAPTER THREE

**M**cKenna checked her cell as she walked to the car. No calls but two new e-mail messages, both from the same unfamiliar address, both with the same subject line: Big Pig. She skimmed them quickly.

One of her contacts at the courthouse had come through. Big Pig was one of many nicknames Judge Frederick Knight had earned among the local bar, this one referring to both his massive girth and his blatant sexism. The messages were forwards of e-mails Judge Knight had sent from his judicial address. They must have come from someone with access to the network. If they were authentic, they were tangible proof to confirm rumors that had been whispered for years. She would have enough material to expose Judge Frederick Knight as the lazy SOB he was.

When she took the driver's seat, she could feel Dana staring at her. "What?"

Dana continued to look at her expectantly.

"I've worked with you for two years, Dana. If I've got something funky on my nose, you're supposed to tell me." She rubbed her face with her index finger.

"You're snot-free. I'm just wondering if you want to talk about anything."

"Such as?"

"The article?"

"We work for a magazine, Dana. There are a lot of articles out there."

"Your article. *The* article."

"No. I most definitely do *not* want to talk about the article. No one should talk about the article. I'm starting to think I made a huge mistake writing the stupid thing."

"Tammy told me you got a call from a literary agent. And from HarperCollins." Tammy the editorial assistant always knew something about everything. Those calls had been to McKenna's direct line.

"Stop listening to Tammy. She's a noodnik."

"Can a woman be a noodnik?" Dana asked.

McKenna had no clue. She grew up in Seattle. Went to college and law school in the Bay Area. A dozen years since her move to New York, her Yiddish still couldn't be trusted. "Whatever. Tammy's not exactly an accurate narrator."

"Well, the narrator says you have a book proposal that goes to auction next week. The magazine piece was to start the buzz rolling."

As usual, Tammy knew just enough to get the story wrong. The publishing house had asked about a proposal, and the agent had talked about the possibility of an auction, but a proposal going to auction next week? Not even close. Not to mention, the agent had made it clear that the book would need to be more than an extended version of the magazine article. It would have to be personal. "Intimate." "Maybe even in the first person." "Like a novel but true." "You were barely thirty years old—dating and drinking at night, facing down cops and DAs by day. *That*'s the book!" The dreaded "memoir" word had been raised.

At first, when McKenna thought she'd be reporting real news, she saw journalism as an extension of her original work as a prosecutor. Attorneys and reporters both investigated facts and wove them into a compelling—and often spun—story. Ten years ago, when McKenna was an assistant district attorney, she made the mistake of becoming a character in one of those stories she was supposed to narrate. Two weeks ago, she had repeated that mistake as a journalist by writing a ten-page feature article about the same case. But a *memoir*? What was that saying about the definition of insanity: making the same decisions over and over, yet expecting a different result?

McKenna's phone rang from her jacket pocket. She didn't recognize the number on the screen but answered anyway, eager for the distraction from Dana's interrogation.

The voice on the other end of the line sounded like a young woman. She said her name was Mallory. She talked the way all young women seemed to these days, slowing the pace of her speech and dipping her voice low into a "fry" at the end of her sentences.

"Hiiii. My boyfriend said to call. I was on the subway the other day when that lady pulled that kid off the traaaacks."

"Has anyone else contacted you about it?" It seemed like every witness expected to be paid for an interview or at least to get on television.

"No. After you e-mailed my boyfriend because of that comment you saw online, I told him to delete it. It happened so fast, the video doesn't even really show anything."

"Well, I'd love to see it." McKenna tried not to let her tone reveal her excitement. It was a stupid story, but at least it was a story. First Judge Knight's e-mails, now a video of the subway incident that had the entire city talking. She might have enough material to meet her next *two* deadlines.

"Yeah, okay."

"Can you e-mail it to me?" McKenna rattled off her address, but next to her in the passenger seat, Dana was shaking her head.

"Our e-mail system's for shit," she said. "Won't accept a big video file. Have her send it to my Skybox."

The details that came tumbling from Dana's mouth were Greek to McKenna. Her attempts to repeat them to young Mallory were reminiscent of the slumber-party game Operator, where words lost all meaning when passed down a line of communicators. Frustrated, Dana finally extended a hand for the phone so she could speak to Mallory directly. Whatever had seemed so complicated to Mc-Kenna was cake to the two of them; Dana soon returned the phone with a satisfied smile.

"Thanks for that, Mallory. Do you mind if I ask, have you shown this to anyone else? Put it on YouTube or Facebook or anything?" Nowadays, anyone with a phone was an amateur reporter. The video wouldn't be of any value to McKenna once it hit a public website.

"That's so last year. Social networking is social *not*-working. I'm more into, like, privacy, so just leave my name out of it, okay? It was cool and everything, but I can't believe people are making such a big deal out it. I mean, you're a reporter. Last time I checked, our country was still at war, you know?"

It wasn't the first time McKenna had wondered about the merits of her career choices.

Once McKenna was off the phone, Dana retrieved the iPad she had stored beneath the seat for safekeeping. "Don't want to forget this when you return the car," she said. "You got 3G on this thing? I can hook you up on my Skybox action."

McKenna nodded for Dana to work her magic, marveling at the woman's ability to use the virtual keyboard for real typing. "I told Mallory to send the video to my public directory," Dana explained. McKenna caught a quick peek at two heavily pierced twins hold-ing fire hoses. She really didn't understand Dana's artistic impulses. "And I'm hitting bookmark so you can find it online without having to download to your device."

Within seconds, Dana had tilted the screen toward her so they could watch together. The video was typical cell-phone footage: shaky, staccato, grainy. A close-up of someone's back. The cement platform. McKenna turned up the volume. Voices, mostly inau-dible. Screams. Someone yelling, "Oh my God!" Someone else yelling something about the train.

By the time Mallory had managed to point the lens toward the tracks below her, a woman in a white sweater, backpack secured tightly on her shoulders, was lifting a stunned Nicky Cervantes to his feet. As she grabbed him around the waist and hefted him halfway up the height of the platform, Nicky's body blocked the camera's view of the woman's face. A man in a denim jacket took Nicky by the wrists and rolled him onto the concrete.

The cell phone jerked toward the woman just as she finished hoisting herself onto the platform unassisted. She turned and sprinted barefoot toward the stairs, ponytail bouncing at the nape of her neck, just above her backpack. The footage returned quickly to Nicky before going black.

Dana let out a whistle. "That chick's kickass. Nicky probably weighs one-seventy. Did you see how she dead-lifted him?"

McKenna wasn't interested in the woman's strength. She rewound the video and tried to stop on the brief glimpse of the woman's face before she turned to run away. After three attempts, McKenna managed to hit pause at just the right moment.

She couldn't believe what she was seeing.

She hit replay and watched the entire clip again.

"So much for identifying Superwoman," Dana said. The image was grainy at best. "Don't worry. You'll find another way to hook in the masses. You always do."

But Dana had misinterpreted McKenna's expression. She wasn't disappointed. She was in shock.

She never thought she would see that face again. Susan Hauptmann had disappeared without a trace ten years ago.

# CHAPTER FOUR

**M**cKenna automatically clicked to her computer's screen saver when she felt Bob Vance walk into her office, looming over her.

Her editor laughed. "If you're going to keep doing that, could you get some pictures of something that's *not* food?" Her current wallpaper was a photograph of a fried-egg pizza. "When are you going to realize that one of the advantages of being a journalist is that you can look at whatever the hell you want and call it research. If you believe Walt, he's been working on a big exposé of the porn industry for the past seven years."

Stanford undergrad. Boalt Law School. A federal judicial clerkship. Four years at the district attorney's office. It had been a decade since she'd left those uptight surroundings, but old habits died hard. McKenna was a natural rule follower. Even as a child, she would lecture her parents for parking in loading zones.

Today, though, she had a reason to hide the screen from her supervisor. She had spent the last hour searching for current information about Susan Hauptmann. There was nothing. In a sadly familiar pattern, Susan's disappearance had consumed the media for a few weeks, with coverage steadily waning in the ensuing months. Now a search for her name pulled up only isolated comments from bloggers and true-crime addicts asking, "Whatever happened to that girl?"

"I hear there's talk of a book," he said.

She rotated in her chair to face him. "You were the one who suggested the article, Bob, and you know how I felt. I don't think I'm up to writing an entire book about it, so don't make me do it."

"I'm not your daddy, Jordan. I can't *make* you do anything, especially when it's not for the magazine. I'm just saying that if the rumors are true—if there's that kind of interest from publishers—something like that happens once in a journalistic career, and only if you're lucky. And this is real news, not the kind of stuff we usually get to do around here."

When McKenna had left the district attorney's office nearly ten years ago, she had vowed not to do any further damage to the people and institutions she had harmed. But somehow, the career moves she'd made in the aftermath had managed to alienate her even more from a job that once was the core of her identity.

It was Bob Vance who had given her a start at a new one. After McKenna had published one not so successful legal thriller and a few pieces on spec about city crime issues, he'd brought her on as a full-time writer. She had fantasized about specializing in local crime and courts, but had come to accept that it would be hard to provide legitimate coverage of the criminal justice system when almost every cop in the city hated her. Instead, she was a features reporter. Given the increasingly silly tone of the barely afloat magazine, she felt more like a paparazzo.

The saving grace was that Vance was a real journalist at heart. The recent article had been his suggestion: a retrospective of the case that had ended her career at the DA's office—a police officer's shooting of a nineteen-year-old named Marcus Jones.

"It's a bad idea," she'd told Vance when he'd proposed it. "Honestly, no one will be interested in Marcus Jones all these years later."

"Ten years. It's an anniversary, so there *will* be interest. People like anniversaries. They distract themselves with the controversies of old rather than fight the battles of today. In my humble and not so ignorant opinion, I think that if anyone's going to tap in to whatever you might have to say, it should be you. You can control the story."

"I tried to control the story ten years ago, and look where it got me." It wasn't only McKenna's prosecutorial career that had taken a hit. It was her general credibility. After her first big feature for the magazine, online commentators gleefully celebrated the irony that a woman who'd made false claims at the DA's office was supposed to be a journalist. The criticism had been so intense that she'd stopped reading the comments before she broke down at her desk.

Although McKenna had written the ten-year anniversary article reluctantly, Vance's instincts had been right. There had been interest, so much that McKenna was getting calls from agents and publishing houses about possible book deals.

"Look," Vance said now, slapping a hand against the desk for emphasis, "all I'm saying is that if I were you, I'd jump at the chance. As your boss? I guess I'm here to tell you that anything you write for the magazine belongs to the magazine. A book's got to be on your own time. You know what I'm saying?"

He didn't wink, and he didn't nod, but he may as well have. Writing for a magazine wasn't a nine-to-five gig, so they both knew that her time was fungible. Just like Dana—working on her artistic photography when she was supposedly photographing Zuccotti Park—McKenna could easily sneak in a few pages of a book during her daytime hours.

"Got the message, boss."

"So you going for the book?" When she didn't respond, Vance held up both palms. "Fine, I tried. I still need four thousand words from you by end of day tomorrow. You working on this subway mystery gal or what?"

Was it work, or was it personal curiosity? Was she seeing things in that grainy cell-phone video? She wasn't ready to talk about it yet.

"I was hoping to find a different angle on the story, but there may not be much more to it."

"I thought you told me someone might have a video."

"It didn't pan out."

"Did you get the video or not?"

Sometimes McKenna wondered whether Bob Vance should have been a lawyer instead of a magazine editor. "The girl sent it, but it was just a bunch of shaking and bumping around."

"Better than nothing. Let's pop it on the website and see where it goes."

"I promised the girl I wouldn't post it," she said, stretching the truth. "Trust me, it's so useless that people would scream at us for wasting their time." At a time when print media was still trying to find its way in an online world, the specter of anonymous Internet vitriol was enough to make Vance back down.

Her first big feature as a journalist had happened because Bob Vance had taken a chance on her. He'd given her a paycheck and a new start. Now she was looking the man straight in the eye and lying to him: "The subway story's not going anywhere."

**A**lone again in her office, she pulled up the video on her screen and hit replay to view it from the beginning. She hit pause at just the right moment to freeze on Susan's face. Maybe Susan's face.

One thing she hadn't lied about to Vance: the quality was crap.

But there was something about the face that was so distinctive. Susan was one of those naturally beautiful women with clear skin, wide bow-shaped lips, and a knowing smile. Her bright green almond-shaped eyes always glinted with the humor of a silent joke. Her appearance gave off alertness and intelligence. Somehow, despite the video's poor quality, McKenna could make out all of this. Above her left eye, right by her hairline, wasn't that the same small scar?

Or maybe she wasn't seeing anything. Maybe she was projecting the resemblance. Had all this talk about the ten-year anniversary of the Marcus Jones shooting pulled her memory back to the time when she left the DA's office? Was that why she was thinking about Susan? Missing her. Wondering about her. Seeing her ghost in grainy images.

She let the video play and watched the ghost turn from the camera and sprint up the stairs. Even the sprint was familiar. While many women ran with arms swinging side to side as if rocking a baby, the ghost pumped her arms like an Olympian, fingers outstretched like knife blades. How many times had Susan lost McKenna with those effortless dashes? She would wait patiently outside the subway entrance until McKenna emerged from the darkness, slightly out of breath.

McKenna paused it again. There was something in the woman's right hand. Something black and rectangular.

She hit rewind and watched from the beginning. There. Pause. It was right after the woman had hoisted her weight from the tracks to the platform. Both palms were braced past the platform's edge. She swung one leg up to the side. As she pressed herself to standing, she reached her right hand along the cement. Grabbed something.

McKenna had her suspicions that Nicky Cervantes was not the honor-student athlete the morning papers had made him out to be. Now she thought she might know why this woman had been chasing him.

She dialed Nicky's home number. When he answered, she said, "Nicky, it's McKenna Jordan. I talked to you today during baseball practice."

"From the magazine. The lady with all the questions."

"I need to know something very important. And I promise not to tell anyone."

"There's nothing else to tell. I fell."

"Just listen, okay? I need the *real* truth, Nicky. And I won't print it."

"Right. 'Cause reporters are all about keeping things on the down-low."

"I'm also a member of the New York bar." She wasn't. Not anymore. "That means I'm licensed as a lawyer. I will get disbarred if I repeat anything you say to me."

"Will you give me legal advice for free?"

Sure, why not? "I need to know the truth. You took that woman's cell phone, didn't you?"

"Why you asking me that?"

"I need to know." She realized she sounded desperate. She tried to calm herself, but she knew her instincts were right. That rectangle in the woman's hand. The city's familiar warnings to commuters not to use their handheld electronics on the train. "You took her phone, didn't you? And she was chasing you to get it back."

She knew from his pause that he was about to come clean. "Yeah," he finally said, his voice quiet. "And then when I was down there, thinking about that train, she jumped in like Jackie Chan. Threw my ass to safety."

Fast. And strong. Like Susan.

"Now what?" he asked. "What's your advice?"

"Keep it to yourself, Nicky. Don't tell a soul. And don't *ever* do something so stupid again. Snatching a phone from a distracted commuter might seem minor to you, but the state of New York views it as robbery in the third degree. It can land you seven years. Bye-bye baseball, hello prison yard."

"I'm done with all that. Told Coach I need to go back to the paint store. He says we'll work something out on practice. Like I said today, I changed. Laying there next to the rats, the sound of that train—I changed."

Though McKenna had heard so many defendants say the same two words at countless sentencing hearings, she actually believed Nicky. She gave him her number in case he ever needed a favor, then she wished him luck with the season.

She watched the video one more time. There was no way to be certain, but the woman in the video looked more like Susan with every viewing. If Susan were alive, where had she been all this time? Why did she leave? Why didn't she tell anyone? And why was she back now?

McKenna thought about the wealth of information stored on her own phone. Text messages. To-do lists. Voice mails. Call logs. Notes to self. E-mails. Whoever Superwoman was, she had gone to tremendous lengths to get that little black rectangle back.

# CHAPTER
# FIVE

**A**n hour later, McKenna gave up her surfing efforts, no closer to learning anything about Susan's disappearance than when she'd started.

McKenna used to think about Susan constantly; then, with time, for only a fleeting moment per day. Like she'd pass the bar where Susan had been asked to leave after breaking multiple strings of Mardi Gras beads on the impromptu dance floor she had created. Or McKenna would see a trailer for a new comedy aimed at teenage boys and think, Susan will see that with me. Or her phone would ring a little too late for any polite caller, and she'd expect to hear Susan's voice on the other end of the line. In retrospect, McKenna struggled to pinpoint the last time her mind had really focused on a memory of her friend.

If forced to guess, she would have to say it was five years earlier—on a Sunday morning, two days after McKenna and Patrick's wedding. She remembered because she hadn't meant to think about Susan that day. She hadn't meant to cry. Even five years ago, the tears had been less for the loss of her friend than for her guilt at having moved on without her.

The morning hadn't started on a heavy note. She and Patrick were next to each other on the sofa, opening the wedding gifts their friends had given them, despite pleas to the contrary. She could still picture Patrick blushing as he pulled a hot-pink rabbit-shaped vibrator from its beautiful wrapping.

"All righty, then. This one's clearly for the wife," Patrick announced, wiggling the rubber device in McKenna's direction.

Husband. Wife. After five years of playing other roles in each other's lives, boasting that marriage was only a piece of paper, McKenna and Patrick had pulled the trigger. As a lawyer, she should have realized earlier that papers mattered. Papers created rights and responsibilities. Papers defined families.

Today, she couldn't imagine a world in which she wasn't married to Patrick Jordan, but that morning she and Patrick were just beginning to enjoy their new spousal titles. She'd shaken her head and pursed her lips like a stubborn child refusing a floret of broccoli. "But I would never stray from my husband," she'd said in a Scarlett O'Hara voice. "Not even with a battery-operated bunny."

The pink toy was from Emily and Glenn. McKenna could barely imagine reserved, preppy Emily perusing the aisles of a tawdry adults-only shop.

McKenna and Patrick hadn't wanted a wedding. Just a couple of rings, a few nice words, and a great party. No walking down the aisle. No puffy dresses. No white tulle vomit. And no gifts.

As a pile of wrapped packages accumulated in the corner of their private dining room at Buddakan, they'd realized that their friends hadn't complied with the request. "What part of 'no gifts' do our friends not understand?" Patrick whispered. "There better not be a toaster oven in there. Where in the world would we put a toaster oven?"

As it turned out, their friends may not have obeyed the stern no-gifts admonition, but they'd known better than to clutter the overstuffed apartment with nonsense like crystal vases and bread makers. Instead, they had conspired to find the tackiest gag gifts imaginable.

The rabbit wasn't the only X-rated toy. There were the his-and-her G-strings. The bubblegum-flavored massage oil. The "just married" condoms. Especially creative: the pasta shaped like boy parts.

That Sunday morning, their two-day anniversary, Patrick and McKenna were showing their gratitude in a similar spirit, giddily opening the presents while sipping champagne and taking turns writing ironic thank-you notes. *Dearest Emily and Glenn*, McKenna had written. *Thank you so very much for the delightful personal massager. Its rabbit-like shape is at once both whimsical and bold. We would be remiss, however, if we did not ask: where is our fucking tea set? Lovingly, McKenna and Patrick.*

McKenna had saved a special present to give to Patrick last. She reached over the edge of the sofa and lifted a shoebox-sized gift from the floor. "The final one."

"Feels pretty hefty," he said. "If it's another one of those"—he gestured toward the personal massager—"you're going to be walking funny for a week."

"This one is for the husband from the wife."

He tore away the elegant white-and-silver wrapping paper, opened the box, and removed a tight mass of bubble wrap. Beneath the transparent layers, the shape of a glass beer mug was visible.

"Is this like when Homer Simpson gave Marge a bowling ball for her birthday?"

McKenna was the beer drinker in their household. Patrick was strictly a Scotch and wine man.

He placed the beer stein on the coffee table. Pint-size. Thick handle. A shield insignia on the side, embossed with Westvleteren, the manufacturer of a Belgian Trappist beer.

"So what gives?"

For the first time, McKenna told Patrick about the night she and Susan wound up with that mug. And then she felt guilty for not thinking more often about Susan over the years. And then she cried. And then she apologized for ruining the last day of their wedding weekend with silly drama. Then she blamed it on too much champagne.

That was five years ago. How could she have gone five years without thinking about Susan?

Susan and that stupid mug. The night McKenna met Patrick. The year Susan left. The year her job fell apart. The stories all belonged together.

She heard once that a novel was really a collection of fifty to seventy scenes that could be woven together at the author's will. The agent wanted McKenna's book about the Marcus Jones case to read like a novel.

She opened a file on her computer and typed: "Chapter One."

# CHAPTER SIX

*I*t was a Thursday, right around the time when single, childless city dwell-ers had labeled Thursday "the new Friday," meaning it was the night to go out, get drunk, and forget that one more day of work—albeit a casual-dress one—still awaited us.

It wasn't just any Thursday but a first Thursday of the month, meaning it was the night of a Susan Hauptmann happy hour.

I arrived late, even relative to the obscene hours we all kept back then. I had been burning the midnight oil that entire week. I told my colleagues I was taking the extra step of preparing written motions for all my upcoming trials. Their deadpan looks were the silent equivalent of "Whatever, nerd." But I'd been in the district attorney's office for four years and was still trying drug cases. I had vowed that this would be the year when I got some attention.

By the time I made it to Telephone Bar, it was well past ten o'clock. The party was in full swing, meaning fifty or so friends and at least three times as many drinks consumed.

Susan raised her arms in the air and reached across two guys from the usual crew for a long-distance hug. "McKenna! You made it!"

Vocal exclamation points were a sure sign that Susan was getting her drink on. The girl worked her ass off at one of the biggest consulting firms in the world. She deserved to cut loose every once in a while. Back then, we all did.

"Pretty good turnout," I yelled over the thumping soundtrack. That was the year when you couldn't help but Get the Party Started with Pink everywhere you went.

Susan was beaming, which made her even more gorgeous than usual. She was always so proud when the happy hours went well, as if they somehow validated all the steps she'd taken in life to lead to all those friendships. Now some people were leaving the city. Others were getting married and having children. They couldn't stay in their twenties forever. That night, though, everyone seemed to be there, just like the old days.

"McKenna, this is my friend Mark Hunter." He was one of the two guys I recognized next to us. "McKenna was my roommate the first year I came to the city. She went to Stanford for undergrad and law school at Berkeley. Mark just left a dot-com, but his MBA's from Stanford. You guys could have bumped into each other at a Stanford-Cal game."

And then off she went to introduce some other solo attendee to another friend. That was Susan's thing. She collected friends. Back before random strangers "friended" each other online after a chance meeting, Susan was that person who found something interesting about every person she met, then pulled out her cell phone with an easygoing "Give me your digits. I'm getting some friends together in a few weeks. You should join us."

Unlike most of the people who do those things, Susan would actually cultivate the friendship. As a result, her happy hours brought together an eclectic crowd that mirrored the divergent pieces of Susan's impressive life: military friends, business school friends, gym friends, "just started talking at the bookstore one day" friends, childhood friends from all over the country, thanks to her army-brat youth. Her capacity for socializing had earned her the nickname Julie the Cruise Director, at least among those friends who remembered The Love Boat.

Unfortunately, Susan didn't always recognize that she was singular in her ability to connect to people. To her, my non-overlapping undergraduate years at Stanford should have been common ground to bond with Mark the former dot-commer. Instead, the two of us stumbled awkwardly through a series of false conversational starts before Mark pretended to recognize a friend farther down the bar. I let him off the hook before he felt pressure to pay for the Westvleteren Trappist I had just ordered.

As I took the glass from the (of course) scantily clad bartender, a small wave of foam made its way over the rim onto my hand. I was licking away the spilled beer—and not a sexy, titillating, "I'm coming for you next" lick but a spazzy kid with jam on her hands kind of lick—when a girl yelling "Woooo" bumped into me. A second, larger wave of beer foam cascaded onto the man next to me.

"Sorry. Oh my God, I'm so sorry." I patted at his sweater futilely. Again, not a sexy, titillating, "I'm taking my time" pat, but a clumsy, ham-handed, "this might really hurt" pat.

"Ah, beer and boiled wool. That'll smell great in the morning." Another person might have made the comment sound prissy or even cruel. Thanks to the friendly smile that accompanied the words, I found them comforting. It also helped that my beer-soaked victim was six feet three with wavy dark hair and hazel eyes. After getting a better look at him, I registered how firm his stomach had felt beneath that wool sweater.

"Seriously, I'm really sorry."

"It's not a problem," he said, accepting a bar towel from the bartender, who apparently noticed the needs of this kind of man without request. He wiped the beer off my hands and shirtsleeves, ignoring the drops of ale on his own clothing. It sounds corny, but there was something familiar about the feel of his skin against mine. "You're here with Susan, right?"

"Um, yeah. I guess you are, too?"

"Patrick Jordan." He offered a firm handshake. "Susan's pointed you out a couple times at these things, but we've never managed to meet."

"Oh sure, you're Patrick from West Point."

That's right. Susan's wildly diverse and impressive background included college at the United States Military Academy at West Point. According to her, the predominantly male student body might not have treated her as well if it hadn't been for a popular trio of supportive cadets led by Patrick Jordan.

"And you're—"

"McKenna Wright. Susan and I lived together for a while a couple of years ago."

"Wait. Are you the one who calls her Bruno?"

Yep, that was moi. "The first time we met, she said her name—'Nice to meet you, I'm Susan Hauptmann,' like any normal person. And then I go and blurt out 'Bruno!' It was the first thing I thought of."

"Of course, because doesn't everyone know the name of the kidnapper of the Lindbergh baby off the top of their heads? Basic knowledge, really."

He raised a finger toward the bartender and I soon had another West-vleteren Trappist in my hand. The truth was that I usually dreaded Susan's parties. I'm neither a mixer nor a mingler, so a night of serialized chitchat, yelled between casual acquaintances, was my version of being poked in the eye with a needle for three hours.

But that night involved no further mixing or mingling. I barely noticed as the crowd thinned and familiar faces paused for a quick shoulder grab or a "Sorry we didn't get to talk more." Before I knew it, the bartender was announcing last call.

Patrick and I paused our conversation only when Susan showed up and squeezed between us, throwing an arm around each of our shoulders. "Yo, I've been sippin' on gin and juice."

Yes, the song was already old by then. It didn't matter to Susan. It was newer than her other hip-hop standby—"Rapper's Delight" by the Sugarhill Gang, the long version if she was wasted on mojitos. She gave Patrick a peck on the cheek. "That's your prize for keeping this one here so late. She's not usually a closing-time lady. Let me get you guys another round."

The bartender shook her head and made a cutoff motion. Susan made an exaggerated sad face. "Party pooper."

Patrick patted his hands against his pant legs. "Well, I guess that's a sign that we're out of here. Any interest in sharing a cab?"

The words were spoken to both Susan and me, but his gaze was directed at me.

Susan made a loud buzzing sound. "Not tonight, Patrick. She's heading downtown. And not in the dirty way, like you're thinking," she said with a devilish tone and an accusatory index finger. "You can get to the Upper East Side on your own."

"All right, then. Very nice to meet you, McKenna." We ended like we began, with a handshake, but this time I didn't want to let go.

Susan hugged me as we left the bar. "Aw, you look like a puppy who got left at the shelter. Don't worry, girl. I just did you a favor."

"How's that?"

"You don't get out enough. You don't know the rules."

"What rule was I about to break?"

"You put out on the first date, and a guy never respects you. And don't you go looking at me with all that virgin-y indignation. If you'd left with him, you totally would have dropped those drawers. Knowing what a dry spell you've been in, they're probably granny panties, aren't they?"

All I could do was laugh.

"Ah, see? I did you a favor. Don't worry. He knows how to find me, and I know how to find you. He'll call."

As crass as Susan could be, she always managed to do it in a silly way that was never threatening or offensive. When we were roommates, I had hoped that her brand of infectious directness might rub off on me, but no such luck. She told me once that her sense of humor had gotten her through army culture. Susan was by no means the first female West Point cadet, but even now women made up only a tenth of the class, and cadets still referred to military-issued comforters as their "green girls."

As one of the most attractive women on the West Point campus, Susan could have had her choice of boyfriends. But she was the daughter of a general. All eyes were on her. She had to choose her company carefully. For the most part, she stuck with the "Dykes in Spikes," as the female athletes were called, but got along with the men by joking around like a kid sister.

I thought Susan had fallen asleep in the cab, her head resting on my shoulder, but then she reached into her briefcase and handed me something wrapped in a white cloth napkin. She pulled out a Westvleteren beer stein.

"You stole a glass? That's a Class A misdemeanor, I'll have you know."

"Then you're about to commit receipt of stolen property." Her speech was slurred. "Because I saw how you were with Patrick. And I saw him with you. And neither of you is ever like that with anyone. Someday you're going to marry that man, and you're going to want a souvenir from this fateful night."

Five years later, on my two-day anniversary, I gave that glass to my husband as a wedding gift.

I saved that beer stein for five years, through three moves, two changes in profession, and countless on-and-offs with Patrick. I saved it because I wanted more than anything for Susan to be right.

When the cab stopped that night outside my apartment on Mott, Susan *tucked the beer stein into my bag as I kissed the top of her head. "Drink some water when you get home. I love you, Bruno."*

*I made sure the cabdriver knew Susan's address, and I covered the fare plus a generous tip before hopping out.*

*I was too distracted to take seriously Susan's prediction about Patrick and me. At the time, my entire focus was on making this the year when I finally got the attention I deserved at work.*

*Both Susan and I turned out to be right.*

McKenna stopped typing and read the last sentence again. *Both Susan and I turned out to be right.* Neither McKenna nor Susan had been prescient enough to realize that 2003 would also be the year when Susan would disappear without a trace.

Now McKenna wondered if Susan was finally back, resurfacing to pull Nicky Cervantes from the tracks of a 1 train.

# CHAPTER SEVEN

**M**cKenna was sitting on a stool at the kitchen island, hunched over her laptop, when she heard keys in the front door. Patrick maneuvered his bicycle into the apartment, careful not to let the tires bump the walls, a practice that had taken months of training after the building had sacrificed the bike storage room for an expansion of the laundry room.

"Hey, you're home!" Patrick said, surprised at the sight of her there.

Theirs was one of a growing number of households in which the female half tended to work later than the male half. Patrick was almost always home in time for the six P.M. episode of *SportsCenter*. He was not only fine with a routine, he liked it. If every single day could be the same for the rest of his life, Patrick would be happy as could be.

But today she was the one who had wrapped up work early, wanting to be alone with that video from the subway platform.

For as long as she had known him, Patrick had insisted on riding his bicycle to work. Another part of the routine. The very idea of riding a bike in Manhattan—the fumes; the horn blasts; the texting, Bluetoothing drivers—scared the bejesus out of McKenna. But Patrick insisted he was safe. Helmet. Side-view mirrors. And though his office closet at the Metropolitan Museum of Art was stocked with conservative suits, for the commute, he donned the look of a badass bike messenger, complete with fake tattoo sleeves on his arms. According to him, drivers were less likely to mess with a cyclist who looked like he might slit a throat over a near miss.

As Patrick carried the bicycle to the far corner of their open loft, he paused behind her for a quick kiss on the cheek. "You started cocktail hour without me?"

She let out a distracted "Huh?," then realized he was referring to the beer stein resting beside her computer on the granite counter- top. "No, it's empty. I was just looking at it."

The mug had felt like such a special possession when she'd given it to Patrick, but five years later, McKenna had located it at the back of a kitchen cabinet, blocked by a panoply of coffee mugs and the cheap glasses that emerged only when they had more guests than good stemware. The beer stein deserved better placement, but a lot had changed since they got married.

"Why would you—" His bike propped safely against a wall of bookshelves, Patrick turned his full attention to her. "Oh, it's *the* mug. That was sweet." He wrapped his arms around her waist and gave her a kiss on the neck, letting his breath graze her ear.

She spun around on the stool to face him. "Actually, I was think- ing about this mug because I was thinking about Susan."

His expression went blank. Apparently McKenna wasn't the only one who hadn't thought about Susan in a long time.

"*Susan*. Susan Hauptmann. She's the one who stole it from Tele- phone Bar that night."

"Oh my God, that's right. I always thought of it as the mug *you* stole." He took a seat on the sectional sofa, extending his legs in front of him. "Why were you thinking about Susan?"

She carried her open laptop to the couch, scooting next to him. The video was cued up. "You know that story about the woman who pulled the high school kid off the subway tracks?"

"I believe you tried to bet me twenty dollars yesterday morning that the kid wasn't really an honor student. I didn't take the bet. Plus, we're married, so it doesn't matter. Besides, twenty dollars in this city would barely fill that beer mug."

"Well, a girl on the platform managed to get it on videotape." She hit play.

Patrick chuckled as the scene played out on the screen, a subtle twitch in his face each time the cell phone jerked in a new direction. "You can't use this, McKenna. Did you try the MTA? They have cameras in the stations."

She held up a finger to cut him off. Listening to the now-familiar audio, she prepared to hit pause. The high-pitched scream. The "Oh my God." The something-something "train!" A thump as another passenger bumped into the amateur cinematographer. The "Don't go down there." "Grab him." "Get his wrists." "I've got him, I've got him." "Is he conscious?"

And . . . pause.

"Look. Do you see it?"

"I can see why everyone's calling her Superwoman. Takes a lot of strength to lift a person like that. Hard to tell, but the kid didn't appear to be helping any. Probably suffering from shock."

"Look at the woman, Patrick. Look at her face."

He leaned closer to the screen and shook his head. "I know the MTA's video coverage is spotty, but really, did you at least check? Maybe you'll get lucky."

"Yes, I checked. Just look at her face, okay?"

He raised his brows at her snappish tone. At least he hadn't called her shrieky, as he was prone to do when her tone became too strident for his tastes. "I'm not sure what I'm supposed to be seeing here, McKenna, and I'm obviously frustrating you. Just tell me. You said something about Susan." He looked at the image on the laptop screen again. "Oh, McKenna, no. There's no way."

"The face. The face is the same."

"You can't even *see* her face."

"The shape, like a heart. The lips. And the arch in her brow. Plus, look." She pointed to a spot just beneath the woman's hairline.

"You can see that scar, from when she fell running across campus— during the Maharathon or whatever."

"The Mahanathon," he said, correcting her. The cadets called the sprint from the West Point gym to Mahan Hall the Mahanathon. Despite Susan's usual speed and dexterity, she had managed to trip on a curb and wipe out face-first. "You can't tell that's a scar. It could be a loose hair or a splotch or something. This woman could be anyone. Seriously, the MTA must have better footage."

"They don't, okay? The guy said an entire hotspot or something crashed. This is all I've got, but look at it. You said yourself the woman would have to be incredibly strong to lift a kid like that. Fast, too, to be chasing a high school athlete. You should see her haul ass up the subway steps. Susan is strong and fast. The only female cadet in your class to get that prize—"

"The Commandant Prize. Because Susan *was* fast. She *was* strong." He placed a hand on her knee and gave it a squeeze. "And she's been gone for a really, really long time."

"People aren't just gone. They never found a body. I don't even think she's been declared dead legally."

He pulled his hand away and shook his head. "You're contradicting everything you've ever said since Susan disappeared. 'She'd never just leave.' That's what we *all* said. It's what we *all* told the police. That somebody must have done something terrible to her. Now you're saying she's alive and well and living in New York after all these years?"

"I didn't say she was *well*. Maybe, I don't know, you hear these stories about people with head injuries who don't even know who they are. They eventually start life all over again."

"McKenna, amnesia? Come on." He walked to the refrigerator and grabbed a bottle of water. When he returned to the sofa, he didn't sit quite as close to her.

"She's just *missing*, which means she's somewhere. She could be back in New York. You can't ignore the fact that the woman in that video looks exactly like Susan."

"We haven't seen her in ten years, McKenna. And that picture—

it's like a blur. You went through all of this before, all those years ago. You cried every day for a month. You stopped eating. You were walking around Hell's Kitchen at all hours of the night, trying to find her."

She remembered those nights. She had wanted so desperately for Patrick to comfort her. He was the only person McKenna knew who was also close to Susan—they never would have met if not for Susan. They had taken very different paths to New York City. Patrick had attended West Point and served in the army before going to work at the museum; McKenna had gone to school on the West Coast and was working downtown as a prosecutor. They had tried the game of tracing six degrees of separation between them, but the one and only direct route was Susan Hauptmann.

So if anyone could help her through the grief of Susan's disappearance, she had assumed, it would be Patrick. And McKenna knew that Patrick felt a sense of loyalty to Susan.

She had heard both versions of the story about the beginning of their friendship. According to Susan, she had pulled the old West Point trick of stuffing her bed, tucking laundry beneath her blanket for bed check so she could celebrate her twenty-first birthday in Chelsea. Nights in the city with the friends she'd made outside the army were an escape for her. They helped remind her that she had a life beyond the one she'd chosen in order to please her father. She used those nights to doll herself up and blow off a little steam, to nurse a side of her personality she could never show the other cadets. That night, she wasn't the only cadet who'd left the grounds. When Patrick Jordan walked into the same city bar at one in the morning, she was sure her reputation was done.

In Patrick's version, the only reason he ever walked into a club like the Limelight was because he had a two-day leave from campus for a cousin's wedding, and the bride and groom decided to go bar hopping after the rehearsal dinner. His ears were beginning to adjust to the thumping music when two of the bridesmaids began gossiping about the girl "slutting it up" on the dance floor with two different men. When he looked at the woman grinding against her dance partners, something about her seemed familiar. He recognized Susan just as she made eye contact with him.

He was aware of the whispers about her on campus—the General's Daughter, they called her, or sometimes Hot Lips Hauptmann—but he knew that cadets routinely exaggerated their sexual accomplishments where the female cadets were concerned. Now it appeared that in Susan's case, the whispers might be kinder than the real thing. And as the son of a mere colonel—though a full one, a "bird"—he could only imagine the panic going on behind his classmate's mascara-laden eyes.

The two versions of the story converged from there: Patrick turned around, left the club, and never said a word to anyone on campus about the encounter. Not even Susan. Back at West Point, popular, trusted Patrick found subtle ways to bring outsider Susan—female, attractive, last name Hauptmann—into the fold. Susan knew she had a real friend.

So when Susan disappeared, McKenna knew Patrick cared. They had been friends long before McKenna was in the picture. But he had been almost angry about it. Not angry at Susan or even about her disappearance. Angry at McKenna. At her reaction. At the crying and the sobbing and the picking at food and the inability to sleep. At what he saw as overly dramatic displays of emotion. At her expectation that it was up to him to make her feel better.

"What you're doing right now isn't about Susan," he said to her at last. "I'm worried about her, too. So is her father. So is everyone who knows her. But you're making this about you. Things suck for you at work, and you're using this as an outlet."

That statement—and the hour-long yelling match that followed—marked the first of many offs in their relationship. Ten years later, he was clearly worried that she would unravel once again.

"I'm not doing any of that now. I just— You know, even if the woman on the subway wasn't Susan, it doesn't matter. She's been gone all this time, and I haven't even *thought* of her in years. I want to know what happened to her. She deserves for someone to still be looking."

He started to push back but thought better of it. "So what should we do about it?"

*We*. Patrick was like that. He could play devil's advocate. He could try to convince her to pursue another path. And then just like that, he could climb aboard and support the mission. That was probably how he'd been able to make it through the army. It was why he was still at the Met—his first civilian job out of the military—after all these years. What were *we* going to do about it. She didn't give him enough credit for that loyalty.

"Her dad started getting sick years ago, and he was the one putting pressure on the police. For all I know, no one's been looking for her. Maybe her loser sister knows something. What was her name again?"

"Gretchen."

"Right. Maybe you can contact the army crowd. See if they know anything?"

"I think I would have heard—"

The expression on her face stopped him. "I'll call around."

"I'll start with the basics. Public records. Credit reports. We can play it by ear."

Playing it by ear sounded so simple. No promises. No rules. Just following intuitions on a lark. As though, if the melody didn't work, you could simply walk away from the piano. But searching for answers wasn't like fiddling with notes on a keyboard. Once you started asking questions, it could be impossible to stop, even when you knew you should.

# CHAPTER EIGHT

**T**he man behind the reception desk at the Four Seasons was oily. Not literally. He wasn't shiny or glistening or greasy. But the way he peered out and up beneath thick black eyelashes, not even bothering to lift his chin despite speaking to a man six inches taller than he; the way he smiled without parting his lips; the way his clenched jaw failed to hide the grinding of teeth behind the forced smile—all of it reeked of unctuousness.

"No reservation, sir?"

"I'm afraid not. Thought I'd be back on the train to New Canaan tonight—deal sealed—but I guess the lawyers had other plans. Guess that's what happens when you let these firms bill you by the hour. How can you tell when an attorney's lying? His lips are moving." He dropped an American Express card on the counter. The name read Michael Carter. That would be his name for the foreseeable future. Until he needed to be someone else. "I'll take whatever room you have available. Beggars can't be choosers, right?"

There was that sealed-lip smile again, as if the request didn't bother him a bit. The clench in the jaw told a different story while he tap-tap-tapped away at his merry keyboard.

"Our standard rooms are all sold out tonight, sir. We do have a city-view executive suite. This would be your rate, exclusive of taxes, of course."

The clerk pushed a piece of paper discreetly across the counter: $995 per night. Exclusive of taxes. Of course.

Carter nodded his approval and watched the black card swish through the reader. Beneath the name Michael Carter was the name of a company: Acumen Inc. The company was real, incorporated as a shell, permitting him to funnel untraceable money through a series of offshore accounts. Panama was popular these days.

"How many keys, sir?"

"Just the one, please." One was the right answer for a business-man unexpectedly stuck in the city for an evening. It struck Carter that two was probably the more typical request, given the liaisons he'd observed so many times in high-end hotel lounges. But a re-quest for two keys by a solo traveler was interesting. It provoked curiosity. Carter made a very nice living—with unplanned and unexplained expenses part of the package—by being completely, entirely, and utterly uninteresting and unprovocative.

He returned the clerk's smile while accepting the room key. Throughout the entire transaction, Carter remained angled away from the security camera that hung on the wall behind and to the right of reception. Now he pivoted to his left, depriving the lens of any look at his face.

Not that it mattered. Just habit.

His fib to the reception clerk hadn't been too far from the truth. He was, in a sense, a businessman with an unexpectedly long detour in New York City.

Compared to the work that had gotten him here, Carter's current position was practically a desk job. His job was to watch. To moni-tor. To stand to the side and make sure there were no problems. He thought of himself as an auditor hired by people who didn't want the audits discovered.

He had mastered the language used to describe his line of work. People paid him a lot of money as a *precaution*. For *peace of mind*. For *comfort*. They paid Carter to watch for *red flags*. *Alarms*. People used these terms to describe what they believed to be a feeling of gut instinct. Carter knew there was no such thing. Facts raised flags. Events sounded alarms. Carter knew how to articulate the subtle culmination of facts and events that caused lesser people to experience an inexplicable "feeling."

Usually he could tell when a target was going to be a problem. Living a life filled with secrets required highly choreographed management of both time and physical location. It meant sneaking away for a supposed bathroom break but placing a brief phone call from the men's room. It meant telling your coworkers you had a headache and needed to turn in early, then driving to a rest stop thirty miles out of town for a clandestine handoff of a package.

He had no problems locating the subject of the audit, thanks to the GPS tracker that she didn't know she was carrying. Carter had been hired because the GPS tracker had traced the woman to other parts of the New York metropolitan area. Carter's boss wanted a better idea of what those side trips entailed.

The first two days had been like punching a clock. No gut feelings. More important, no facts to raise red flags or alarms. Just a lot of time out in Suffolk County, where she was supposed to be.

On the third day of observation, she hopped on an Amtrak to Penn Station. He followed. She didn't seem to notice.

But he noticed her. He noticed that she was using a second phone. Not the one with the GPS tracker in it. A different one.

She'd been typing away on it when that boy had grabbed it from her hands. And then she was gone, barely making it past the subway doors before they slammed shut, sealing him inside that crowded tube. Unknowing. Without eyes or ears. Utterly useless for a moment.

**H**e had hopped off at the next stop, Herald Square, then headed north to Times Square. Clipping through the station, he could overhear the leftover rumblings of commotion. *Did you hear? Some guy fell on the tracks! Someone saved him.* It hadn't taken him long to find the two EMTs at the foot of the platform stairs, one flashing a penlight in the kid's stunned eyes.

The kid was fine. The woman he had robbed was gone.

Carter called his boss from aboveground.

Yesterday morning the papers had called the woman the 1-train heroine—an unidentified mystery woman. She had Carter to thank for her continued anonymity. It had taken some persuasion, backed by cash, for Carter to render the MTA's security footage unavailable. What seemed like a lot of dough to an MTA technician was chump change to the kind of people who hired Carter.

He knew what the mystery woman called herself. And where she was supposed to be. He did not know why she had come to New York City or why she had been so desperate to recover her second telephone. But he had a very strong, and very bad, feeling.

And if Carter had learned anything in his forty-two years, it was never to accept the unknown.

# CHAPTER NINE

**M**cKenna went to the office early to sneak in some work on her book proposal. As much as she had been telling Dana and Bob Vance and the agent and the editor that she was on the fence, she was beginning to think of it as *her book*.

Vance's advice the previous day had gotten to her. This could be a once-in-a-lifetime opportunity, a chance to make something of her time at the DA's office. A chance to write something other than marshmallowy fluffs of city gossip. She had to admit, she'd felt good writing those few pages the previous day, even though she had no idea what role they'd play in the end product. Her plan was to jot down a few more sample scenes here and there. Just enough to figure out whether she wanted to go all in.

She had written a book before. She was a published novelist, after all. But that was different. She'd started writing her novel after she was forced to leave the district attorney's office. She had taken two years off to write it, and she hadn't even begun to try selling it until it was completely finished.

According to the agent, the nonfiction book that she couldn't bring herself to call a memoir could be sold off of a proposal. It should have a "jazzy"—she hated that word—overview, a table of contents, and a summary of each chapter.

She had no idea how to outline the events that had led to the end of her legal career. So far, she had been working on the overview, but instead of jazz, it was turning into cacophony.

*I*t was the gun. Not the gun itself—not at first—but Tasha Jones's insistence that her son, Marcus, didn't carry one. She never vouched for Marcus's character. Neither did I, not once. The case was never a matter of character. Marcus Jones was only nineteen years old, but he had eleven juvie interactions with law enforcement and was out on bail pending felony theft charges when a bullet from Officer Scott Macklin's gun killed him.

"My boy stole," Tasha told me when she cornered me on the courtroom staircase. "Always did and always would. The schools said his IQ was only seventy-eight, but he knew robbery was harder time than theft, and armed robbery, more trouble still. He didn't have no gun. He didn't have no gun, because he never wanted to be in a position to be pointing one, let alone at the po-lice. He went to the docks that night to meet his girlfriend. What he need a gun for?"

Police never found any evidence of a girl. They did, however, find eighty bucks in Marcus's front pocket, despite the fact that the kid had no lawful means of income. I truly believed I would find evidence connecting Marcus to that gun.

I never thought of myself as the most talented trial attorney in the office. It always seemed to be the lawyers from the local schools who were labeled real naturals or geniuses in the courtroom. But I was a hard worker. I was thorough.

And so I traced the gun, hoping (and expecting) to prove Marcus's mother wrong. Hoping (and expecting) to strengthen Macklin's claim of self-defense. Hoping (and expecting) to make the grand jury's job that much easier.

But the gun had another story to tell.

**T**his wasn't working. McKenna was supposed to write about the case from her own perspective. Her excitement as a relatively junior lawyer to be working on her first homicide—and an officer-involved shooting, at that. Her loyalty to the officer involved: Scott Macklin. The stress of being in the middle of a news story that had taken on unmistakable racial tones. The gradual onset of doubts about his side of the story. Her decision to come forward.

And her utter shock when that decision nearly tore the city apart. How could she do that in a synopsis? She could never pull it off.

She closed the file. The truth was, she couldn't look back on that time in her life without thinking about Susan. And any thought of Susan pulled her back to the infuriating video. She opened the video again and hit play.

Bob Vance gave a cursory tap on her office door before entering. "Four thousand words. You promised yesterday. Whatcha got for me?"

"I'm going with Judge Knight."

"He's the fatty, right?"

"More important, he's lazy, offensive, and—according to the smoking-gun evidence I now have—disdainful of the public he's supposed to serve."

She handed him printouts of the two e-mails she had received the previous day. "Frederick Knight has been on the bench for five years. From the beginning, there were questions about his intellectual heft—no pun intended. Last week, I got an anonymous call from a woman claiming to have been a juror in one of his recent cases. She said he was rolling his eyes and cutting off witnesses. He'd go off-record, but she heard him tell a domestic-violence victim that she was *too attractive* to get beaten. And he spent most of the trial fiddling with his phone and laptop. I've heard these kinds of things about him before, so I decided to put out some feelers at the courthouse to see if anyone might come forward."

"And?"

"Those appeared in my in-box yesterday."

The messages were short but damning. One, sent by Knight three days earlier: "Can't stand these people. Dirtbags hurting dirtbags. Lock them all in a cage together and give them bats and chain saws. The world would be better off." And the other, sent just yesterday morning: "Going out on a ledge here because I feel like I'm on a ledge. You guys have space for special counsel? I go on civil rotation in two weeks and can throw your firm some bones until the transition's official. I'm serious: I can't take this anymore."

"Can this be four thousand words?" Vance asked.

"No question. Knight came to the bench after practicing only two years as a law firm associate and then serving for nine years as the judicial clerk to Chief Judge Alan Silver. Clerks are supposed to be clerks, but it's become common practice for judges to grease the wheels for lower-level judicial appointments as a reward for their most loyal clerks. Knight was on the criminal court for two years and then got bumped up to felonies. I can have a section about other clerks who found their way to the bench with questionable credentials. I've got a pattern of Knight always siding with the state against criminal defendants, sexist comments—even on the record—and resisting the appointment of defense counsel to the indigent. These e-mail messages would be the nail in the coffin."

Though the smoking-gun e-mails would be the bait to sell magazines, the story was substantive. It was the kind of thing she'd hoped to do full-time when she'd accepted the job.

"They're legit?"

"That's what I wanted to talk to you about. I knew it would be hard getting anyone to go on record about a sitting judge, so I reached out to a network of potential sources and promised anonymity. Unfortunately, instead of trusting me to protect their identity, someone opened a free e-mail account and sent these to me. They deleted the address information of the recipients, so I can't look there for confirmation."

"Stands to reason that whoever sent you these was probably the original recipient, right?"

"It could be one of his clerks or his secretary. Or, because he was stupid enough to use his public e-mail account, a public employee with auditing abilities could have lawfully obtained access. Or someone could have hacked in."

"I get the point. You're making me nervous."

"I'm trying to nail it down. I confirmed through the court system's directory that the e-mail address listed on the two messages is in fact Judge Knight's. I did some digging, and three days ago, when the 'dirtbags hurting dirtbags' comment was sent, Knight was hearing a bench trial of a shooting arising from a drug deal gone bad. I got the attorneys on both sides to confirm that Knight pressured the prosecutor to come up with a plea because it was a—quote—'who cares' case. I also confirmed that Knight is indeed scheduled to start hearing civil cases in two weeks, where he'd be in a position to help big-firm lawyers."

Vance smiled. "Jeez, Jordan. It's like you're a real journalist or something. The messages are self-authenticating when you put them in that context."

"That's what I was thinking. I figured I had enough to call Knight. All he gave me was a 'No comment.' "

"All right, then. Let's run with it."

She was relieved when Vance left without further mention of the subway video.

# CHAPTER
## TEN

When McKenna was in the zone, she could write almost as quickly as she could talk. Two hours after getting the go-ahead from Vance, she had transformed the notes she'd been keeping on Judge Knight into a full-length article. Although block quotes from the e-mail messages in 28-size font would be the red meat to pull in readers ravenous for easily digestible scandal, she had used Knight as a case study to delve into the cronyism that perverted the court system and a culture in which lawyers were too afraid of retaliation to blow the whistle on bad judges.

She hit the submit key on the article. The modern publishing process moved so rapidly that the article would be online by afternoon.

She turned her attention back to the video. She had seen it so many times, she knew where to stop for any single moment that interested her, but she was still at a loss as to how to confirm that the woman was Susan Hauptmann.

Her eyes were beginning to cross from squinting at the screen, as if that could make the images any clearer. This time, when she hit pause, it wasn't to study the mysterious woman's blurry face. Mc-Kenna was focused on the very end of the video, pausing as Nicky's rescuer sprinted up the stairs.

There was something attached to the woman's backpack. A button. Round. About four inches wide. Some design on it, maybe a few letters at the bottom.

She pulled out her cell and sent a text message to Dana.

Before I give up on that video from yesterday: Looks like there's a button pinned to Superwoman's backpack. Can you try to get a better look?

The phone pinged a few short seconds later.

You know it ain't like TV, right?

McKenna smiled. Recently, she and Patrick had tried to watch a series about a hotshot security team at a Las Vegas casino. Only half an episode in, Patrick had flipped the channel when the security team, suspicious of a drop-dead-gorgeous woman at the nickel slot machines, enlarged the house camera's glimpse of the woman's unzipped purse to zoom in on a perfectly legible handwritten note inside—all in about five seconds.

With Patrick incapable of tolerating shows about security, the military, or law enforcement, and McKenna refusing to watch anything about lawyers, they were on an eternal search for television shows they could enjoy together. Most recently, they had tried watching a show about zombies, but Patrick kept interrupting with surefire plans for battle. Note to self, McKenna thought, scythes are apparently the key to surviving a zombie apocalypse.

She sent a return text to Dana:

Got it. I'll take whatever you can give me.

When McKenna didn't receive an immediate response, she used the wait time to cull through her in-box, under constant attack by an ongoing assault of unwanted messages. Vance had just fired off a reminder about the importance of filing deadlines. Human

Resources was admonishing the staff once again not to abandon food in the refrigerators. Then there were all the irrelevant mass mailings she received by virtue of being listed as a retired member of the New York State Bar: the American Bar Association's report on electronic discovery, a continuing legal education session on accounting for lawyers, a last-chance offer for a personalized plaque to commemorate her fifteenth year as a lawyer—now, how in the world was *that* possible? Delete, delete, delete.

She'd paused to check out a book recommendation e-mailed to her from a friend when a new message arrived from Dana.

> This is what I have for now. Try running it through Google Images. And don't say you don't know how. I showed you myself. I'll work on your girl's face tonight—an image of it, not a makeover. You know what I mean.

Dana had warned McKenna not to expect a miracle, but the snapshot attached to the e-mail wasn't too shabby. McKenna's guess had been correct. Pinned to Superwoman's backpack was a round button, the background plain white, the abstract design a blue circle with a series of lines inside it. Two lines formed a cross in the middle of the circle, dividing the circle into four quadrants. Three of the four quadrants contained curved lines, creating the impression of half circles.

The image on the button meant nothing to her. That was where Dana's suggestion of Google Images came in.

McKenna pulled up Google Images on her computer. Inside the bar where she was used to typing search terms was an image of a small camera. She clicked on it and was prompted with "Search by Image," followed by "Upload an Image." Dana had walked her through these steps last month when McKenna was trying to locate the driver of a delivery truck outside the townhouse of an actress constantly rumored to be planning another march down the aisle. By searching for the logo printed on the side of the truck, they managed to find the name and phone number of a bakery in Brooklyn.

Turned out the driver was delivering tasting samples for a wedding cake. It wasn't the kind of scoop McKenna was proud of, but the magazine tripled its newsstand sales that week.

She uploaded the digital image that Dana had extracted from the video and watched Google work its magic. She immediately got a perfect hit: PEOPLE PROTECTING THE PLANET. The picture on the backpack button was Planet Earth behind crosshairs. The three semicircles had transformed the straight lines of the crosshairs into three P's—an acronym for the organization.

She ran a separate search for information about the group. According to a sympathetic website, PPP carried out "direct actions to defend the planet by liberating animals, disrupting the activities of polluters, and depriving predatory corporate entities of their ill-gotten gains." Another website called the organization "ecosaboteurs." Another claimed the group was on the government's ecoterrorist watch list.

Whether People Protecting the Planet were saviors or a domestic threat, they didn't sound like Susan's crowd. She was from a military family and had gone to West Point. Even after leaving the army for business school, she'd kept a toe in the water through the reserves. She was deployed for nearly a year in Afghanistan through the Civil Affairs Brigade, completing her service as an economic development officer, helping the Afghanis stabilize their banking system.

After all those years in uniform, Susan had enjoyed her freedom from a dress code. She was more of an Armani-suit-and-Prada-handbag woman than a button-adorned-backpack type.

The observation sent McKenna's mind back to one of her last memories of Susan, teetering on sky-high Jimmy Choos. A few years earlier, the heels would have set her back close to a month's take-home pay. Even on a consulting firm salary, they were a splurge, but Susan was so proud, strutting around the store while other women marveled at her ability to maintain balance. "I'm taking these bad boys home. And for the right bad boy," she added with an out-thrust hip, "I'll wear them with nothing but a thong."

The other customers hooted their support. Susan had that way about her.

Those shoes—along with the rest of her belongings—were found in her apartment after her disappearance. It made no more sense today than it had all those years ago.

McKenna dialed a number she had looked up an hour earlier but hadn't had the guts to call.

"Scanlin."

Even ten years ago, McKenna had figured the guy to be close to his twenty-two years of service. Some cops couldn't leave the job.

"Detective Scanlin, this is McKenna Jor—McKenna *Wright*. Please don't hang up. It's important."

"As I recall, everything you believe to be true is always so . . . darn . . . *important*."

"I'm calling about Susan Hauptmann. Can you meet me in person?"

# CHAPTER ELEVEN

**M**cKenna scoped out the landscape at Collect Pond Park. The good news was that the city was experiencing a warm, bright, beautiful October day. The bad news was that the unseasonably pleasant temperatures had brought out the masses. The place was hopping.

She opted for a bench holding one other person. His one person managed to occupy more than half the bench, but there was enough room for her to sit, and he was far too preoccupied by his newspaper to give her a second glance.

Scanlin was the one who'd chosen the park for the meet, placing her smack-dab in the middle of a strip of action below Canal Street that was the heart of the Manhattan criminal court system. This territory used to feel like her heartland, too, pumping blood through her system. How many times had she carried a yogurt down to this park, or a bit farther south to Foley Square, just to breathe some fresh air and enjoy a brief respite from the courthouse's fluorescent lighting?

She used to know all the hot-dog vendors—not by name but by face, cataloged mentally by the characteristics that really mattered. Good mustard. Softest pretzels. The guy who stocked Tab.

She knew which homeless people were regulars on the civil commitment and misdemeanor dockets, and which were harmless enough to become part of the daily banter. Back then Reggie was one of her favorites. "Whatchu gonna use to eat that salad with, my dear?" "I'm going to use this here fork, Reggie." "Well, go on, then. Fork yourself!" Reggie would laugh and laugh and laugh, even though he used the same line four times a day, every single day.

She looked around, wondering what had become of the man. She didn't see him. She didn't recognize anyone.

She felt like an outsider. She *was* an outsider.

When she'd caught Scanlin on the phone, he was just leaving the squad room to give testimony in a motion to suppress. "If it's so important," he'd said, "why don't you meet me downtown?"

He initially suggested meeting in the courtroom where he'd be testifying. But while she used to be able to whisk past security, asking the guards about last night's Giants game, giving a self-satisfied wave to the defense attorneys waiting to enter, McKenna now had to line up with the rest of the citizens to be cleared for entry. Wasn't there a more convenient place to meet? she had asked Scanlin. She'd been hoping for a coffee shop near the precinct, but he had insisted on a location by the courthouse, finally selecting the park. "You said it was important. I'm just trying to make sure you see me as soon as I'm done testifying."

She knew he took a certain pleasure in beckoning her to hostile territory that once was her home.

She wouldn't have recognized him if he hadn't looked directly at her from the courthouse steps and made a beeline to her park bench. "You need to be here, guy?" Scanlin asked. From behind his open newspaper, McKenna's neighbor on the bench threw her an annoyed look. She shrugged, but one glance over the paper at Scanlin sent the man shuffling in search of a new spot to crash.

"Well, how about you? You look pretty much the same. Not too many people can say that after a decade. You should be proud of yourself, ADA Wright."

McKenna didn't know what to say. Scanlin had to know she

wasn't proud. She wasn't an ADA anymore. She wasn't even a Wright anymore. When she and Patrick married, she picked up on his preference that she change her name. In his world, that was what wives did. In her world, the whole thing seemed ridiculous, but she made the change anyway. Maybe her name wasn't the only thing she was trying to change at the time. Her writing name would be McKenna Jordan. Not McKenna Wright, the disgraced prosecutor.

She couldn't return Scanlin's compliment. She'd met him in person only twice, right after Susan disappeared—once when she'd shown up unannounced at Susan's apartment, insisting on speaking to the detective in charge; and a week later, when she appeared unannounced at the precinct, accusing him of avoiding her phone calls based on what she'd considered a conflict of interest.

The man she remembered had been close to fifty years old, with a well-groomed mustache that matched his dark hair. She remembered that he wore cuff links and a subtle cologne that smelled a little like pine. He was the kind of man who made the effort.

Now he took up nearly as much room on the park bench as its previous resident. No mustache, just the graying stubble of a skipped day or two from shaving. No cologne or cuff links. His tie was loose, and the wool of his navy sport coat was beginning to shine from too many cleanings. No, she couldn't say that he looked pretty much the same.

"Thanks for meeting me, Detective."

"What detective doesn't want a face-to-face with a member of the illustrious media?"

She could tell from his smile that he was enjoying his barbs. "I'm not here as a writer. Or as a former prosecutor, for that matter. Is Susan Hauptmann's case still open?"

"It was never cleared, so it was never closed. Last time I checked, not closed means open."

"But is anyone working it? Is anyone looking for her?"

"Not my case anymore. I'm in homicide at the Twelfth now."

"You never considered the case a homicide even when she was in your jurisdiction."

"I know *you* did. You made that clear the day you came storming to my lieutenant accusing me of stonewalling you."

"I'm not trying to relive the past, Detective. I'm asking you why you were so sure that Susan up and left when everyone who knew her said otherwise."

"We never found evidence of foul play. I guess you didn't need much in the way of evidence to go around making claims."

McKenna ignored the superfluous dig and tried to focus on Susan. She could feel the stirrings of all those old frustrations. "To the people who knew Susan best, her sudden disappearance was the strongest possible evidence. She would never put her friends and family through that kind of uncertainty."

McKenna remembered the few basic facts she'd been able to glean from Susan's father and her own queries: Susan's gym card had been scanned at Equinox on the Saturday morning after Thanksgiving. One of the trainers remembered waving hello as she cranked away on the treadmill, seemingly lost in the beat of the music pumping into her headphones. She had RSVP'd to a friend's Sunday card game as a maybe, so no one gave her absence any thought. It wasn't until Monday night that a coworker dropped by Susan's apartment building, assuming she must be incredibly sick to miss work and not call in. At the end of Tuesday, the building superintendent unlocked the apartment door at the request of Susan's father. The police took two hours to show up, and only after ADA McKenna Wright made a phone call.

Though there was no point in rehashing all of the details with Scanlin, McKenna highlighted the key points. "She left her purse, her passport, her wallet."

"You don't have to remind me, Ms. Wright. I know that you, of all people, don't hold the police in the highest regard—"

"That's not fair—"

He waved a hand, not to concede the point so much as to signal his unwillingness to debate it. "I remember my cases. I can tell you the life stories of missing people—men *and* women—that I still wake up wondering about. And I can tell you that I believe I failed by moving on without them, without answers for their families. But I never felt like that with your friend. You know why? Because you and I view the same facts in a different way. Every single thing was in its place at her apartment. You see that simple fact the way you see it. But I've been a cop for over thirty years, and I know that a woman who goes somewhere takes her pocketbook with her. She takes her wallet. Hell, she at least takes her damn *keys*. And there was no sign of disruption to the apartment, even though, by every account, Susan Hauptmann was an athlete. A trained soldier. A fighter."

McKenna thought about the woman in the white sweater, pulling Nicky Cervantes from the tracks and sprinting up the subway staircase. Fast. And strong. A fighter. She knew where Scanlin's reasoning was headed.

"No blood. No knocked-over furniture. Not even a pillow out of place. No sign of a struggle means that no one harmed a fighter like Susan Hauptmann in that apartment. We've got no evidence of harm *inside* the apartment. We've got no evidence that she was surprised on some normal kind of outing *away* from the apartment."

"People don't just evaporate."

"That's where you're wrong. Not physically, not like abracadabra. But that's exactly what they do. Or at least *want* to do. Evaporate. Susan Hauptmann left behind her passport, her wallet, her pocketbook, her keys. She left behind her life. She . . . *left*. You didn't want to believe that."

"I didn't *want* to believe it because I couldn't believe it. I *knew* her."

Scanlin said nothing, but his gaze, though focused across the street at the courthouse, grew sharper. For a moment, behind the razor stubble, sloppy tie, and extra layers of fat, McKenna recognized the intensity she'd sensed in him so many years ago.

"Why are we talking about this now?" he asked.

"Because I think you were right. I think Susan's still alive. I saw her."

"I'm glad to know it. It's too bad her father didn't live to hear the news." Susan and her father always had a difficult relationship, but he was the one who pushed the investigation and worked the media, even though he had just been diagnosed with cancer. McKenna had seen his obituary in *The New York Times* two months ago.

"Aren't you even curious about what I just said?" she asked.

"I don't need to be. I know if you ran into her at the movies and caught up like old pals, you wouldn't be here talking to me. Why don't you go ahead and get to your point. What do you want from me, Ms. Wright?"

She opened her iPad and pulled up the link for the public drive of Dana's Skybox to play the video clip. She hoped that Scanlin had studied enough pictures of Susan back then to recognize her now.

The connection was timing out. Maybe Dana had changed the settings. Or maybe the iPad wasn't getting a good enough data connection to access the Internet. Or, more likely, McKenna the Luddite had managed to do something wrong.

"I'm sorry. I have a video here. I want to show it to you."

"Just tell me what I need to know, all right?"

She started to speak but realized how ridiculous it sounded. He needed to see the actual image.

"I'm so sorry. I'll go back to my computer." The only still photograph Dana had e-mailed her was of the button on the woman's backpack; Dana hadn't yet created a still version of Susan's face. Maybe once she did, she could enhance it for better clarity. "If I e-mail it to you, will you please just look at it?"

His gaze moved to the distance again before speaking. "Yeah, sure. Send whatever you want."

He handed her a business card, and she automatically responded with one of her own. "Thank you, Detective. Really. I know what you must think of me, but I always cared about Susan, and I need to know what happened to her."

He fingered the edges of her card. "I noticed the name change when you started at the magazine."

She held up her left hand, ring forward. "Five years now. To Patrick Jordan. You might remember him from the investigation. He was another one of Susan's friends."

"Seems like you've got a good thing going for yourself now. The writing thing. A husband. I would've thought, of all people—after everything that happened—you would've learned that some things are better left alone."

Scanlin pushed himself off the bench as he stood. She watched him walk to his fleet car, parked just outside the courthouse.

Scanlin resented her. He still had the same conflict of interest she'd raised with his lieutenant ten years earlier. He looked at her and saw his friend Scott Macklin on the front page of a newspaper, beneath the headline COP HERO OR MURDERER?

But Scanlin was on the job, he remembered Susan, and McKenna had gotten somewhere with him: he'd look at the video. That was all that mattered. It was a start.

She was about to walk to the subway when she looked again at the courthouse. There was another conversation she needed to have in person.

# CHAPTER TWELVE

**A**ssistant District Attorney Will Getty rose from his desk to greet her with a warm hug. "McKenna Wright." Everyone from the DA's office—at least the people willing to acknowledge her existence—called her by her maiden name. "Speak of the devil."

She returned the hug and took a seat. This was the same chair she sat in a little over ten years ago, when Getty called her into his office to offer a chance to work with him on an officer-involved shooting. A cop named Scott Macklin had shot a thug named Marcus Jones at the West Harlem Piers.

"Was someone speaking of me?" she asked.

"The chattering classes are very excited. Rumor is you've been asking for dirt on Judge Knight. You can't possibly expect me to help you with that hot potato."

His conspiratorial smile brought out lines that hadn't been there when she'd first met him, but he was still handsome—more handsome than he ever wanted to let on. Neat haircut, but not too fashionable. Respectable suit, but not showy, and probably a size bigger than the salesperson recommended. Will Getty was the kind of trial lawyer who knew that jurors were distrustful of men who were too good-looking.

"I am here about a hot potato—just not that one."

"I saw the article. I was wondering if I might hear from you."

McKenna had thought about calling him before the Marcus Jones article went to print. But he was her superior ten years ago. She was a journalist now and didn't need his permission to publish a story.

And yet.

"I don't know if you noticed, but your name wasn't in the article."

"You don't need to explain anything, Wright. And not that my opinion means squat, but I happen to think that you handled it very professionally."

Her article had focused on the protests following Marcus Jones's death and the eventual exoneration of Officer Macklin. She had disclosed the fact that she—the author of the piece—was the junior prosecutor who had raised doubts about Macklin's self-defense claim. There had been no reason to bring Getty's name into the piece.

She knew Getty well enough to get straight to the point. "I've been asked to write a book. Not write but propose. Who knows what will happen—"

"A book about the Marcus Jones case?"

"Not about the case itself but my place in it. It would be a more personal account than the article. A thirty-year-old woman who, for a couple of months, was in the middle of—I think at one point we agreed to call it a shitstorm?"

The problem boiled down to the gun. Scott Macklin claimed Marcus Jones pulled one, and the gun was found resting in Jones's limp right hand. Jones's mother insisted her son did not own a gun and accused Macklin of planting it. The pistol was a Glock compact with a filed-down serial number. McKenna had recently read an article about the ability of crime laboratories to restore obliterated serial numbers. Eager to prove herself, she'd filed a request with the local field office of the ATF, which was able to determine the last four digits. A search of the ATF's database scored a match, meaning that the gun was used in a previous crime.

McKenna remembered the adrenaline rush that had come with the news. She wanted Marcus's mother to be wrong and Scott Macklin to be right. A boy was dead, killed by a good cop. Mc-

Kenna wanted proof that Marcus was the bad guy. She wanted proof that he had left Macklin with no choice. The gun in Marcus's hand had been used in a previous crime. Marcus, at only nineteen, was a longtime criminal. She knew she'd find the connection.

But the connection between the Glock and that night at the West Harlem Piers wasn't the one she'd expected to find. The serial number of the handgun was in the ATF's database because the gun had been seized by the NYPD in 1992 after it was found in a garbage can. It was slated for destruction in accordance with the NYPD's weapons disposal policy. As part of a public relations campaign called Safe Streets, the police department would make a show of feeding that gun—and hundreds of other seized weapons—to a smelter, subjecting them to three-thousand-degree temperatures until liquefied. But the gun never made it to the smelter. It wound up next to Marcus Jones's body eleven years later.

Eleven years before his death, Marcus Jones was only eight years old. There was no reason to believe that he could have come into possession of the gun back then, and certainly no explanation for how the gun could have made its way to him from an NYPD property room.

But eleven years earlier, Scott Macklin was already a police officer, two years into his service. More notably, he was one of the young, enthusiastic, telegenic officers who had served as the face for Safe Streets. A *New York Post* article about the program showed Macklin delivering a truck full of guns to the smelter. *Officer Scott Macklin said that more than four hundred guns would be destroyed. "Any day we can take guns that might be used in crimes or accidental shootings and turn them into manhole covers and chain-link fences is a good day for the citizens of New York City."*

All these years later, she remembered the sick feeling in her stomach when she'd learned that Marcus's gun—Marcus's *supposed* gun—had a direct connection to Scott Macklin.

Macklin was third-generation NYPD. His grandfather and father and uncles would have told him about the days when every cop carried a "drop gun," an unregistered weapon to toss at the side of a suspect to justify a shooting, if needed. Macklin was a newer breed of police, but tradition in blue families could be deep, as if passed by blood. It would have been easy to slip a gun from the Safe Streets pile.

She'd taken the evidence to the prosecutor in charge, Will Getty. He was one of the most respected lawyers in the office. He had become something of a friend after accompanying her to one of Susan's happy hours. She trusted him.

But as she explained to him all the work she had done—the serial-number recovery, the ATF database search, the old newspaper article connecting Macklin to Safe Streets—she realized how ridiculously eager she sounded. After all, she was a mere drug prosecutor, and her special assignment of second-chairing this investigation was a glorified term for carrying Getty's bags. She had been hoping to be rewarded for taking the initiative, but instead, she'd made herself look like a total freak by pursuing a side investigation into a politically and racially sensitive case without any input from the lawyer in charge.

She could remember what he said to her. "We don't want to do anything rash. But good work, Wright. You've got a good eye for detail."

He told her he would recess the grand jury for a couple of days while he looked into it.

Days went by. Then a week. When she asked him for an update, he explained that things took time and that he was working on it.

And then she'd heard nothing. Hearing nothing wasn't Mc-Kenna's forte. With each passing day, she became more convinced that Getty was finding a way to steer the grand jury in Macklin's favor without her.

At the end of the second week, she met with Bob Vance at a dive bar in the East Village and told him everything she knew. The papers depicted her as a whistle-blower. She declined offers to appear on cable news and at protest rallies, but the people who accepted those invitations made a point of crediting her for revealing the "truth" about Marcus Jones's shooting.

And then Will Getty figured out how that gun really had gone from Safe Streets storage to the right hand of Marcus Jones's dead body, and McKenna wasn't so beloved anymore.

Ironically (or maybe predictably), Will had always been supportive of her. He was the one who told everyone who would listen that she'd been trying at every moment to do the right thing. Even as it was becoming clear that McKenna had to leave the DA's office, he had gone so far as to write an essay for the *New York Law Journal*, arguing that she epitomized the ideal version of a prosecutor who was doing justice. He called her at home and conceded that if he'd communicated with her better after she'd gone to him with the Safe Streets connection, he could have prevented the "tragic misunderstanding."

"Have you ever stopped to think," he asked her now, "that in a weird way, that case helped you find your true calling. You were a good lawyer, Wright, but do you know how many lawyers would kill to write? I don't care how much trash the people around this place were talking. They were all reading your novel, they were all loving it, and they all would have given their left nut to be in your shoes."

Her first career move after leaving the DA's office was almost accidental. After two months of wallowing on her sofa, she had started tinkering with a short story on her computer. As the story slowly blossomed into a book, she lived off her modest savings, supplementing with credit card debt as necessary.

The book was her escape from the real world—pure, unabashed, relentless fiction. When *Unreasonable Doubt* came out, her former coworkers nevertheless chose to see the book as an attempt to cash in on her platform as a scorned ADA.

As it turned out, there was no real profit involved. Despite every lawyer's fantasy of writing a novel and retiring, she'd earned barely enough on the advance to pay off the debt she'd racked up while writing. But she had written a novel. It had gotten good reviews.

She felt better about herself. She let herself be happy for a while, which seemed to stabilize what had been an erratic relationship with Patrick.

Then she took another two years to write a second book, and by then the publishing industry had changed. Stores were closing. Sales were down. Apparently the legal thriller was dead. That book was sitting on her hard drive, unpublished.

By then she was a thirty-five-year-old lawyer with a five-year gap in her résumé; well educated but with only one real interest: in crime.

No prosecutor's office would have her. Even defense firms didn't want her because they believed prosecutors would blacklist her on plea bargains.

She'd written a novel (two, if an unsold book counted), so she knew she could write. And she knew how to tell a story. She wrote a few pieces on spec, and then Bob Vance gave her a chance at a full-time job. That was career change number two. She despised the fluff pieces that dominated her work, but at least she had a paycheck until she figured something else out.

Back in Getty's office after all these years, she felt herself gripping the worn upholstery of the chair arms, knowing she was doing the right thing but wanting to get it over with. Getty was a good lawyer. She could see him processing the information. Considering his words carefully.

"Do you want to do it? The Marcus Jones book?"

"I think so. If I can find a way to do it that is respectful of the people who deserve respect." She patted his desk.

"What you're saying is that the article didn't mention my name, but a book would."

"I wanted you to hear it from me first. And I promise to treat you fairly."

"Okay, then. Can't ask more than that, can I?"

The hug he gave her when she left wasn't quite as warm as the one she'd received when she arrived.

# CHAPTER
# THIRTEEN

Two hours later, Joe Scanlin was back at the Twelfth Precinct. The estranged wife of a suspect in yet another drug-related killing had agreed to come in for questioning.

He knew the history. Six 911 calls made from their shared address just in the last four years. Three arrests of the husband for domestic violence. One time she went to the hospital with a broken jaw. No charges ever filed.

She moved out two months earlier when Child Protective Services threatened to take her kids if they continued to witness the violence against her.

But "separated" and "separate" weren't synonymous.

"Kenny don't sell," the woman insisted. "He don't even use. No way he'd have something to do with *that*. His no-good friends always dragging him down. That's all that is. They the ones did this. Don't you listen to their noise."

Scanlin walked out of the interrogation room while she was talking. He didn't need to hear the rest. Been there too many times. She wasn't under arrest, but he knew she'd stay there in the box until he told her she was allowed to leave. No one ever tried to leave, certainly not a woman who'd gotten used to being beat on.

Back at his desk, Scanlin found himself fiddling with McKenna Wright's—Jordan's—business card. Since she'd called that morning, he had felt off his game. Like he was walking and listening and talking through a filter, smothered by a layer of dust. He was trying to pinpoint the reason why. The moment she'd said her name, he had been pulled into this cloud.

Even as he was insisting that she meet him downtown—at the courthouse, near the courthouse, anywhere that would remind her of her former existence—he had known he was being transparently vengeful. But there were legitimate reasons to remind that woman of the past. She was a vulture. A user. A one-lady wrecking ball. Like so many lawyers before her, she had tried to build a career on the backs of decent men. Everyone knew that most prosecutors worked the job as a stepping-stone to the bench or elected office, and the fastest shortcut was across the back of a dirty cop. If you had to make up corruption where none existed, so be it.

Even with the disappearance of her friend, she never seemed as interested in the truth as she was in telling Scanlin how he should do his job. For a moment down there at the park, he had let his guard down. He'd felt the hardness that he'd readied in the courthouse elevator begin to soften at the sight of her business card. Changed job. Changed name. She was a woman who cared about her friend after all these years.

Now he found himself wondering whether her phone call had anything to do with Susan Hauptmann. All those years ago, she was so convinced that something horrible had happened to her friend. Now she pulled a one-eighty: not only had Scanlin been right back then; now she had a firsthand eyewitnessing of the long-missing woman. No details, mind you. Just the promise of a video he was never shown.

He wouldn't put it past her to dangle the promise of photographic evidence as a carrot. She could pretend to be tracking down Hauptmann as a pretext to talk him up. That was how users like her worked. They saw people as chips that could be cashed in for a favor.

Scanlin knew that Susan Hauptmann was out there somewhere,

hopefully living a happier life. Regardless, Scanlin could die satisfied if he never heard her name or McKenna Jordan's again.

Scanlin had been all too aware of his age the moment McKenna Jordan recognized him across the park. He saw himself through the younger woman's eyes. It wasn't just that years had passed since she'd last seen him. He had changed.

There was a time when Scanlin worked the job a hundred percent, knowing that at the end of the day, Melissa would be waiting—makeup on, hair curled, dinner either on the stove or ordered from one of their favorite Italian places on Arthur Avenue. They weren't rich, but they managed to make their life glamorous. His life was different now, and those differences had manifested themselves in his appearance.

He'd seen the Jordan woman's big article, of course. The story meant nothing to the new cops, but the guys who'd been around for a while paid attention. Scanlin had read it online for free, refusing to shell out six bucks at the newsstand.

He was too smart not to wonder whether her phone call had something to do with her newfound interest in rehashing the past. For all she knew, Scanlin could get her access to the man he suspected she was truly interested in—the man whose career she'd ruined, the man she could use to help sell more magazines.

Scott Macklin was an old friend in both senses of the word. Over a decade had passed since Mac decided to cut off ties with his NYPD buddies. He was an aged friend because—well, because they both went and got old.

Scanlin checked his e-mail. No video from McKenna Jordan. Not even an e-mail. Maybe she had imagined seeing her friend and come to her senses. More likely, the woman was working an angle. The less he thought about her and the trouble she brought down on those around her, the better.

# CHAPTER
# FOURTEEN

**M**cKenna never voiced the opinion aloud, but she believed that she excelled at everything she did. Even thinking it, she realized how narcissistic it sounded. She didn't mean it in a boastful or arrogant way.

To say that she was good at everything she did wasn't to say that she was good at *everything*. The assertion said very little about her natural talents but spoke volumes about something she wasn't good at—taking risks. McKenna excelled at everything she did because she'd spent her life avoiding the things she could not do.

She remembered returning her flute to that tiny old music store in Seattle. Her parents had bought the instrument used, on an installment plan. They were only on the fourth payment by the time it was clear McKenna was no longer interested, deciding that she had a better chance of mastering the violin. The sympathetic owner agreed to rent the family a violin. Then a viola. Then a saxophone and a trumpet. McKenna wound up in debate club instead.

She was no more tenacious as a grown-up. One of her female law professors led a series of golf lessons for the Woman's Law Association, plugging the sport as a way for women to spar with the boys in law practice. For three weeks, McKenna watched as, one by one, her peers got the hang of the swing plane, the cocked wrists, the release of the club, the follow-through. When it was McKenna's turn, the ball would roll forward a pathetic ten feet, as if felled by her wood-chopping swing. No more golf for her.

Her predilection for favoring skills based solely on mastery had almost led her into a math major. She couldn't imagine a life crunching numbers, but they came easily to her, so she'd stuck by them. Lucky for her, she had also been a good writer, a good arguer, and a pretty decent speaker. Even luckier, she happened to live in a world where good writers, arguers, and speakers could usually find a place for themselves.

As a result, even while her career had taken turn upon unpredictable turn, McKenna had always believed that everything would turn out okay because she had been good at enough things to patch together a facade of effortless talent. She was still waiting for that faith to prove well placed.

It seemed these days that her natural talents for breaking down facts and weaving them into a story collided increasingly with her fundamental inability to understand computers. To break down facts, one first needed to gather them. And where gathering facts used to involve questioning witnesses, subpoenaing documents (as a lawyer), or talking her way into file cabinets that were meant to be off limits (as a reporter), now it seemed like every time she needed a piece of information, technology got in her way. McKenna was barely forty years old, but with a librarian mother and an English-teacher father, she was one of those rare young people who was more comfortable with microfiche and dusty notebooks than WAV files and thumb drives.

Today it was this stupid Skybox program, or website, or app—*whatever*—that was making her crazy. She had watched the subway video from the link Dana had given her at least a hundred times, but now all she was getting was an error message informing her that the link was invalid.

She had seen Scanlin's skeptical look when she promised to send him the video. Now hours were ticking by, and she had bupkes.

So much for her credibility—not that she had any with the man.

She had rubbed Scanlin the wrong way from the minute she badged her way into Susan's apartment, insisting that the police brief her on the status of the investigation. It had been a rookie move, but she'd bought in to the idea that her position as an assistant district attorney for New York County entitled her to a certain amount of respect as a law enforcement officer. She hadn't been around long enough to realize that the general maxim didn't hold true with the other half of the equation—cops.

To make matters worse, Scanlin had spent four years in a precinct with Scott Macklin. It hadn't taken Scanlin long to make the connection between the nosy ADA pushing her way into his investigation and the bitch who was accusing his old friend of lying about an officer-involved shooting. She remembered the way Scanlin had raised the issue. She had called him the day after storming into Susan's apartment. The point of the call was to apologize for her heavy-handed approach, but she never got the words out. Instead, she got an earful from Scanlin about the honor, integrity, and courageousness of Scott Macklin, followed by a warning that she was "nobody" as far as Susan's case was concerned, followed by a prediction that karma would catch up with her, followed by a *click*.

She remembered her response to the click in her ear. She had run to the ladies' room down the hall at the DA's office and held her hair back while she vomited. Susan was missing. McKenna had publicly accused a police officer of homicide and perjury. And now the Marcus Jones mess was keeping her from helping Susan.

She had wanted to call Scanlin back. She wanted to explain to him how hard it was to come forward with her suspicions about that shooting. She wanted him to know that she liked Scott Macklin. He'd been a regular in her office at the drug unit. He had shown her the pictures of his new wife, Josefina, and her eight-year-old son, Thomas. He had talked to her like a friend.

So, yeah, she wanted Scanlin to know that she didn't need a lecture about honor and courageousness and karma. All she wanted was to do the right thing, but locked in that bathroom stall, sobbing into a ball of toilet paper, she had known that the Scott Macklins and the Joe Scanlins of the world would forever see her as a back-stabbing, ladder-climbing careerist.

Now Scanlin would think she was yanking his chain once again with the promise of a video that McKenna could no longer find. Another fucking error message on the computer.

McKenna had called Dana twice, and both times got voice mail. She normally approved of Dana's ability to disappear from the reservation with no accountability, but now she was beginning to understand Bob Vance's frustration with her freelancing ways. It was four o'clock. Where was Dana?

She hit redial on her cell. This time she recognized Dana's ring tone—a snippet of the Blondie song "Call Me"—chirping from the pool of desks beyond her office.

"Dana?" she yelled, hitting refresh on her keyboard in a futile attempt to pull up the link. "Is Dana back?"

She was answered with the blurt of a "fuck"—Dana's voice—followed by an explanation from Pete the junior assistant: "You might want to lay low. She's having, like, a meltdown or something."

McKenna found Dana bent over the computer in her cubicle. "I can't *believe* this. It's gone. Every freakin' thing is gone."

"Your Skybox? That's what I've been calling about. I can't pull up that subway video."

"Screw the video. My photographs. My entire backup account. The entire thing is wiped out."

"It's not just the link?"

Dana looked at McKenna as if she were a child asking why dogs couldn't talk. There was no need to provide a response. Instead, she continued ranting to herself. "I'm going to have to call them. You know there won't be a live person. Fuuuuck!"

McKenna could tell it wasn't a good time to press the subject of the video. She turned to Pete. "Do you know anything about this stuff? Why would her account be down?"

"It's not down," he whispered. "It's deleted. It's like someone logged in as her and erased the entire thing. That was her *backup*. She's totally screwed."

# CHAPTER FIFTEEN

**C**arter was situated comfortably in the second-to-last row of the PATH train, by all appearances deeply interested in the *Wall Street Journal*'s analysis of the latest tech-industry initial public offering. There had been a time when Carter followed the markets, squirreling away his few extra dollars in an IRA, hoping that sensible choices would create slow, steady gains that would lead to a comfortable retirement long down the road. That was when he bought in to the idea that if you were a good person and tried hard enough and kept your head down, everything would work out in the end. That was back when he believed in institutions and loyalty and hierarchies. That was back when he believed in . . . anything.

Carter was a different person now. Now he was the kind of person who stayed liquid.

He knew that most of what was covered in this newspaper was irrelevant to the way the world actually worked, but the paper served its current purpose of helping him blend into a sea of commuters departing Penn Station.

The woman's *People* magazine served a similar purpose. It was four o'clock, and commuter traffic was already getting heavy. She could be calling it an early day after a long presentation at her job in marketing. Or heading back after those part-time classes she was taking to get that advanced degree she was always talking about. Or going home to her kids from her monthly mommy day in the city for a facial and a haircut. She looked like any other woman. You'd never know that three days earlier, she had chased a kid onto the tracks of the subway only to rescue him seconds later.

Carter had to hand it to the woman. She was good. The casual observer would think she was genuinely engrossed by the latest celebrity baby bump or ongoing love triangle involving a teen mom. But he could see her eyes sweeping the car, monitoring the platform at each stop. So far, she hadn't noticed him. She was good; he was just better.

What was she looking for?

He almost missed it. The man stepped into the train right before its departure. He sat in the seat behind hers, so they faced opposite directions. He sported earbuds blasting metal that was loud enough for other passengers to hear from a comfortable distance away. He even threw in an occasional mock air drum. He didn't seem like Miss *People* Magazine's type.

But then Carter saw the woman's left hand move ever so quickly to her side, just as his right hand swished down from the drum solo playing in his head. He had given something to her, as if they were two grade-school children passing notes. Very skillful grade-school children.

When the heavy-metal guy stepped from the train at Thirteenth Street, Carter stepped off, too. When he walked up Sixth Avenue, Carter followed. The earbuds stayed in. The metal kept playing.

Carter pulled his cell phone from the breast pocket of his cashmere sport coat. Pretended to send a text but zoomed in and took a quick snapshot once the man's head was turned to the side.

Carter watched the man enter a residential building. He noted the address. He watched through the glass as the man stopped to retrieve his mail from the wall of boxes.

Other people would have called it a gut feeling, but Carter knew it was all about facts. He did not like the facts he was gathering.

He waited for the man to leave the lobby and then entered. He approached the doorman with a friendly smile. "Hi, there. I'm looking for a rental. Wondering if this is a rental building or only ownership?"

"Ownership. It's a co-op."

"Ah, okay. Thanks." He turned to look at the building's mailboxes. Four rows over, three boxes down. That was the one the man had opened. Apartment 602.

It was time to call the client.

He knew by now that the preferred reporting style was to use as few words as possible. Train. Man. Address. "I have his picture."

"Send it. You know the number."

That cell phone number—untraceable—was pretty much the only thing Carter knew about his client. "Sure thing."

He texted the man's photograph.

Two minutes later, Carter's phone rang. The client used the same crisp style—no extraneous words. A minute after, Carter hung up, knowing that his mission had just changed. So much for the easy life.

# CHAPTER SIXTEEN

It was four o'clock, and Scanlin still had that funny feeling in his head. He had to admit that his annoyance with McKenna Jordan was just part of the reason. Her reappearance had not only reawakened his antagonism toward her and his memories of Scott Macklin; it had also triggered a look back at his life.

When he caught the Hauptmann disappearance, he was no longer that hundred-percent detective at the top of his game. Oh, he looked the part. He was physically fit, with the clothes and the watch and the swagger. But on the inside, he realized now, the change had started, because Melissa's changes had started.

At first her problems were hardly noticeable—little verbal tics. In their circle of fast-talking New York friends, Melissa had been the most manic chatterer of all, but he started noticing occasional uncharacteristic pauses. Proper nouns that once were as familiar as her own name were replaced with descriptions like "that restaurant you like with the squid-ink risotto" or "your partner from back when you worked in the Bronx."

Initially Melissa attributed her "offness" to sleep deprivation. Or sometimes to one too many glasses of Chianti. They used to joke, after all, that a bad hangover temporarily suppressed twenty points worth of IQ.

The doctors would tell him later that it wouldn't have mattered if he'd gotten her to experts earlier, but sometimes he wondered whether they said that in a failed attempt to make him feel better.

The pauses in her speech got longer. Her extensive descriptions to compensate for the loss of proper nouns became more vague: "That place—the one where you—have food." A restaurant? "Yes, the one with the—small white food, but dark." Squid-ink risotto? "Right! That's the one." By then she would have forgotten why she was trying to remember the restaurant at all. Was she remembering their second date there? Craving a dish they served? Interested in the dress shop next door? Whatever it was, the moment was gone.

And before he knew it, so was Melissa. The fast-talking friends were polite at first, pretending not to notice that she could no longer follow the conversation. And then pretending not to mind. And then pretending to support his efforts to maintain some semblance of normalcy in their marriage. But his patience for Melissa had outlasted theirs with him, so then they were gone, too.

He could look back and see it all so clearly. A beginning, a middle, and an end to the arc in their lives together. Ten years ago, when Susan Hauptmann disappeared, he had no idea what would happen later and how it would affect him—was already affecting him.

As he recalled it, Susan disappeared just after Thanksgiving. Scanlin got Melissa's initial diagnosis on October 24. Every week she had appointments with specialists. The doctors were constantly changing her medications, trying to wean her from the antidepressant/antipsychotic cocktail they put her on before realizing that frontal-lobe changes were to blame.

And Jenna. Oh God. Jenna. Scanlin loved Melissa more than he could ever love another woman, but no one loves a woman the way a child loves a mother. Maybe in some families, one parent's illness brings the healthy parent closer to the children. That wasn't how it worked for the Scanlins.

Scanlin remembered the initial interview of Susan Hauptmann's sister. What was her name? Gertrude? Gwendolyn? Guinevere? G-something, if he had to guess. See? He couldn't remember. At the top of his game, he could remember the name of a victim's sister. Somewhere right between her last high and the next one, the sister had been a font of information, motivated by concern for her sister but probably also the hope of getting on the good side of a police officer.

As she'd droned on and on about the pressures their father had placed upon Susan—no sons, only one "good girl" to count on— Scanlin had felt himself coming to conclusions. If Scanlin's own daughter, Jenna, could push him away, why wouldn't a woman like Susan, with an SOB father like that, make a clean break of it and start over again?

And then he was getting pushed in a different direction by the likes of some cop-hating prosecutor. Not to mention constant phone calls from the pushy father who had pushed his daughter to the brink and was now pushing him.

All that pushing at a time when Scanlin was in no mood to be pushed.

The truth was that, back then, the only way he found the time to deal with Melissa, her doctors, and his pissed-off daughter was by phoning it in on the job. Susan's father obviously had enough money and connections to pull out all the stops for reward offers and private detectives, so what more could Scanlin do? Writing off Susan Hauptmann as a grown-up runaway made his life easier.

Now his mind was in a fog because seeing McKenna Jordan was forcing him to ask whether he'd rushed to judgment. He could think of only one way to be sure he could stand by the choices he'd made so long ago. He made a call to the Records Department. "It's Joe Scanlin, Homicide, Twelfth Precinct. I need an old case. The name on it is Susan Carol Hauptmann."

He'd take a quick look. Just for peace of mind. Just to be sure he hadn't missed anything.

# CHAPTER SEVENTEEN

**D**ana was still freaking out in the pool reporter room. At one point, she began to screech like a stepped-on cat until Bob Vance stuck his head out of his office and threatened to remove her vocal cords with a letter opener if she didn't shut up.

Her meltdown had sent McKenna into a panic, futilely opening windows on her own computer, hoping that the video had cached itself somewhere in the computer's memory. As if McKenna even knew what "cached" meant.

That video was the only proof—if she could even use that word—that Susan was alive. Even after seeing the video, Patrick had been dubious. Now she had nothing.

She was starting to wonder if she truly remembered what Susan looked like. She had pictures, of course, but pictures were never the same as the real thing. They were a more perfect version—images that were saved for a reason. Photographs were never enough to catch the facial expressions, subtle reactions, and other idiosyncrasies that defined a person's appearance.

McKenna had first met Susan through an e-mail forward. Susan had found a two-bedroom in Hell's Kitchen but needed a roommate to split the rent. Her e-mail blast about the rental landed in the in-box of an ADA who knew that McKenna's tenancy on the sofa of a college friend was wearing thin.

When McKenna went to see the apartment, she couldn't believe her luck. The condo was clean and bright with floor-to-ceiling closet storage and a tiny slice of a Hudson River view. And her new roommate was smart, nice, and hilarious. What could be better?

But just as cameras failed to capture a person's real appearance, first impressions usually didn't reflect real character. Over the next twelve months, McKenna's opinion of Susan evolved. At first she was drawn to Susan's boldness. She was beautiful and magnetic and always spoke her mind. When the man who lived upstairs listened to a Dave Matthews CD on repeat one too many times, Susan managed to sneak into his apartment and swipe the offending disc. She wasn't just funny; she was a good person. Not in a flashy show-off way; she was someone who constantly thought of others. Reaching down to help a fellow subway rider carry a stroller up the stairs. Bringing a flashlight to the widow on the third floor during a power outage. Carrying an extra umbrella on a rainy day in case a coworker forgot one. Answering the door for unannounced visits from her screwed-up sister, despite the hour. She had a big heart and a big sense of humor. It wouldn't be an overstatement to say that McKenna idolized her.

Then one night McKenna found Susan—always so busy, always buzzing with energy—sitting alone on the kitchen floor, a bottle of wine in one hand, the cordless phone in another. Her father had called. There had been a fight. He was the one person who could shut Susan down with nothing but a stern glance. This time he'd gone much, much further. Joining her on the cold tile, McKenna knew she was seeing a side of Susan rarely shown to anyone.

Which side of Susan was McKenna remembering? Did she really remember her, or only snippets of time, artificially frozen in the recesses of her brain?

If she couldn't trust her memories of Susan, how could she possibly begin to recognize the ghost on the 1-train platform, whom she'd seen only in grainy, shaky footage? She had to find that video.

She called Patrick to see if he knew anything about Skybox storage. No answer on his cell, and his secretary said he'd left work early. Just her luck to need him the one day he skipped out before five.

She heard Vance yell another warning at Dana, this time to shut up before he choked her with her own tattoos. With Dana momentarily silenced, McKenna realized that, unlike her photographer colleague, she had a backup plan. She flipped through her phone, found the incoming call from the previous day, and redialed the number. "Is this Mallory? It's McKenna Jordan from *NYC* magazine. You were nice enough to send me a video clip yesterday."

"Sure. I remember."

"I hate to bother you, but we're having some computer glitches on my end. Is there any way I can get it from you again?"

"Same thing with the Skybox account?"

Apparently everyone understood cyber storage except McKenna. "No, that's where the glitch happened. I know it's an imposition, but can I meet you somewhere in person? I'll upload it to my laptop directly, just to make sure I don't mess something up."

There was a pause before Mallory responded in her low drawl. "I guess that would be okay. I'm at work. There's a Starbucks at Forty-fifth and Sixth Avenue. Call me when you're there, and I'll come down."

"I'll be there right away."

McKenna was pulling her jacket on when her cell phone rattled against the desk. This time she recognized Mallory's number.

"I'm just heading out, Mallory. See you in a bit."

"Don't bother."

"What do you mean?" McKenna heard her own voice jump an octave and hoped Bob wouldn't appear, letter opener in hand.

"The girl in the next cubicle overheard the call and wanted all the details. I went to show her the video, but it's gone."

"What do you mean, it's gone?"

"I don't know. It's just not there anymore."

"Is your phone working?"

"I called you, didn't I?"

McKenna could tell that her persistence was irritating the girl, but she didn't understand how Mallory could erase the video and not know about it. "I'm sorry, but I really, really need it. Is it possible you overlooked it?"

"No. I'm positive. I only took one picture since then, and it's gone, too."

"Did you erase them?"

"Not intentionally. I think some dipwad I lent my phone to must've deleted them."

"What dipwad?"

"My friend Jen and I were in line at Margon. Line's always halfway down the block at lunch. Some dude said he needed to call his wife and left the office without his phone. Maybe he accidentally erased it or something."

McKenna was certain that nothing involving this video file was accidental. "What did he look like?"

Another long pause. "I have *no* idea."

"Anything at all that you remember would help, Mallory. Anything."

"Jen was telling me about her douchebag boyfriend, who tried to justify cheating because she gained seven pounds when she quit smoking. I wasn't paying attention. Honestly? I couldn't pick the guy out of a lineup if my life depended on it."

Whoever "borrowed" that phone probably planned that, waiting until Mallory was completely distracted.

"Wait a second. Is this really such a hot story?" Mallory asked. "Is this like some rival reporter stealing the video so you can't have it? That totally blows for you."

McKenna thanked Mallory for the sympathy, figuring there was no harm in leaving the girl under a mistaken impression. Mallory had already served her purpose to whoever had erased the video from her phone. There was no need for her to know the bigger picture.

Not that McKenna had any idea what the bigger picture was. As she hung up, she realized she was in way over her head. Someone had wiped out Dana's media storage account. Someone had tracked down Mallory's phone. Someone definitely did not want that video to be seen. She found herself wondering whether the malfunction in the MTA cameras might be related, before she realized how insane that idea was.

She rushed to her desk and e-mailed a file on her computer to her three different e-mail accounts, saved it to a thumb drive, and then hit the print key. She watched the photograph churn from the printer.

A picture of a button pinned to a backpack. The logo for a group called People Protecting the Planet. This was her only image of the woman on the subway. It was all she had left.

# PART II

Girls, you've got to know when it's time to turn the page.

—Tori Amos, "Northern Lad"

# CHAPTER
## EIGHTEEN

**W**hen Scanlin took the Hauptmann file home, he wasn't entirely sure he would even open it. As he drove to Yonkers, the box from the Records Department filling his passenger seat, he scolded himself for letting McKenna Jordan into his head. Thanks to budget cuts, he had enough work to fill his hours. He didn't need the added burden of dusty files detailing a perfectly capable adult's voluntary disappearance.

*I'm a good cop.* He had repeated that phrase mentally like a mantra, all the way up the West Side Highway onto the Henry Hudson Bridge. I went through hell back then, but *I was a good cop.* I've always been a good cop. Even then.

Now that good cop's dining room table was covered in paper. The DD5s documenting each witness interview. The crime lab reports. Inventories of items seized during searches of Susan's apartment and office. The file from the investigation had been organized by type of document. Scanlin had rearranged the documents in strict chronological order, refreshing his memory of the case from beginning to end.

When he'd told the former prosecutor—emphasis on "former"—that he remembered the case well, he'd believed his own words. But he'd learned through years on the job that memory was a fragile thing, more like a crime scene that had to be protected and preserved from alteration than a fixed, permanent object that was impermeable over time. Usually the evolution of an eyewitness's memory helped the prosecution. He'd seen it so many times. The witness, reluctant and uncertain as she perused the six-pack of suspect photographs. A tentative finger moving toward a candidate, the witness searching for some kind of affirmation from police that she had the right guy. "I think he's the one."

"Good job" was Scanlin's standard response. A small reward, but he could see immediate effects in the relieved witness: a nod, a small, satisfied smile. By the time the prosecutor asked the witness how sure she was of the identification, she would be "extremely confident." And when she pointed that accusatory finger at the defendant—in person, at trial—it was as if the suspect's face were emblazoned on her visual cortex. "I'm absolutely certain."

Say something enough and it not only sounds true, it becomes memory.

Everything he had said to McKenna Jordan about the disappearance of Susan Hauptmann had come from memory. It all sounded true. It all *was* true. And he had been able to recall those facts effortlessly—to pull them from memory—because he had repeated them so many times to General Hauptmann in those first years after Susan disappeared.

Susan Hauptmann was last seen on a Saturday, following her usual routine of a long workout, even on Thanksgiving weekend. No one had any inkling of a problem until she failed to report to work the following Monday morning. When Scanlin was called to her Hell's Kitchen walk-up on Tuesday night, he found the one-bedroom apartment in what her friends described as its usually tidy condition. Neighbors reported no known visitors, noises, or other noteworthy observations. It was as if, as her friend McKenna said so sarcastically, Susan simply evaporated.

But in less obvious ways, Susan had left behind evidence that pointed Scanlin to his eventual conclusion that she had disappeared of her own volition. Her consulting firm's managing partner reported that the firm recently notified Susan that she was underperforming, not living up to potential, and unlikely to be a serious candidate for partnership. After her "noble" service in the Middle East, she had failed, in her boss's estimation, to transition from her military background into the culture of a private firm, where billable hours were more important than efficiency, and the most successful associates understood they could forge their own version of a chain of command.

At the same time, according to Susan's sister, their father was pushing her back into that familiar culture. "The General," as the girls had learned to address their two-star father, had been temporarily appeased by Susan's following his footsteps to West Point, but he had never accepted her decision to go to business school. He'd hoped that her stint in Afghanistan would persuade her that life was better spent in service to her country than as yet another corporate lackey. His words, recited by Gretchen, were right on Scanlin's dining room table, staring at him from her DD5: "Our father would always say, 'The only thing lawyers and consultants have ever created is more work for lawyers and consultants.' "

After a full career in the military, George Hauptmann was launching his own firm to do contract work for the government. One of Susan's friends from West Point had already signed on, and the General was pushing Susan to make the move or, at the very least, go back on active duty. Scanlin had his fair share of problems with Jenna, but he could not imagine wanting to send his daughter to war—especially the two wars that were raging when Susan Hauptmann disappeared.

She had a million friends, but none of them close. She dated, but no boyfriends. Two careers, but no successes. She was a woman who had nowhere to belong. How many times had Scanlin restated these facts, cementing them into his memory with each new recitation? No sign of a struggle. No sign of foul play. A woman in a time of "emotional and professional crisis"—those were the euphemistic words Scanlin had used gently with the father when what he'd really wanted to say was "You drove your daughters away, the ways fathers can. Now one's a junkie, and one has run away from you."

All those facts were true. But memory was malleable. It was selective. Some facts hardened, and others fell away. As he relived the course of the investigation from beginning to end, he found his present self arguing with his former self. How did she leave New York? There were no plane tickets, bus fares, or car rentals on her credit cards. No large cash withdrawals. She'd left behind her driver's license, passport, and every other possession. When did she leave? Perhaps most important, if she really did leave of her own accord, why had she never resurfaced? Runaways, whatever their age, eventually returned, but even after the death of her father, Susan remained missing.

MISSING.

That was the header on the flyers plastered on telephone poles and parking meters across Manhattan as November turned into December. Basic data: thirty-two years old, white female, five feet seven, 140 pounds. In the photograph, shoulder-length blond waves encircled her wide face, marked by a broad smile and gleaming green eyes. She was beautiful. And she was a missing young white woman with an impressive background and influential father. The case had gotten attention.

He remembered all the wack-job calls to the tip line: spottings at bodegas, bookstores, Knicks games. None of them panned out. Well-intentioned but mistaken tipsters believed she was a current coworker, classmate, fellow yoga aficionado. As he leafed through the old notes, he saw that one guy (anonymous) had claimed to have had sex (anonymously) with the missing woman six months earlier in a restaurant bathroom. No information about her current whereabouts.

The tip—viewed in the context of a fresh look at the entire file— reminded Scanlin of another piece of paper he had just seen. He pulled the DD5 of one of Susan's colleagues, Jared Klein. Like most everyone else who knew her, he was utterly perplexed by her disappearance. Scanlin remembered prompting Klein, as he always did, to think of anything—*anything at all*—that might have been unusual. Klein had shaken his head, but Scanlin could tell he was holding back.

"Now's not the time for secrets," Scanlin had warned.

"It's not a secret. It's just— You know, maybe I misunderstood."

"Misunderstood what?"

"Last year, we were working late, as usual. We had a couple glasses of wine at dinner. Everyone else left, and it was just the two of us. She leaned in and—I don't know, it was like she was going to kiss me or something. I stopped it. Last thing I needed was a sexual harassment suit or worse. I expected her to brush it off like a stupid late-night moment, but she got—well, I guess I'd say aggressive. Like, who was I to reject *her*? The next morning she seemed totally normal, and I've always thought maybe it was me who had cloudy judgment that night. But now I'm wondering if maybe I saw a hidden side of her. Jeez, I feel bad saying this about her now."

It had seemed like a stretch at the time. And the anonymous tip about the anonymous sex had seemed like nonsense. The neighbors' observations about all of the people—mostly men—coming and going from her apartment had seemed totally consistent with the depiction of a woman who socialized regularly and operated in male-dominated work settings. The half-empty box of condoms in the nightstand had seemed like a standard precaution for a heterosexual adult woman.

But all of it together? Maybe there had been a side to Susan Hauptmann that her friends and family didn't know.

His thoughts were interrupted by a knock on the door.

# CHAPTER NINETEEN

**M**cKenna looked at her watch. Five-ten P.M. Patrick would be leaving work soon. She sent him a text.

> Guess who pulled a pop-in on the Upper East Side? Meet me in
> the modern wing.

He responded immediately.

> You're here?

> Yes. Modern. Electric chair.

> Bike gear or no?

He was asking whether he should change into his usual commuter wardrobe, or if they would be going somewhere that required proper attire.

> Cleaned-up version requested, por favor.

The Metropolitan Museum of Art was almost a quarter mile long and occupied over two million square feet. When McKenna first moved to New York, she would roam the hallways, thinking about Claudia Kincaid, the runaway preteen heroine of one of her favorite childhood tales, *From the Mixed-Up Files of Mrs. Basil E. Frankweiler*. She would imagine what it would be like to live in the depths of this huge museum, as Claudia had with her little brother, scrounging coins from the fountain and sleeping on the historic beds.

Now McKenna was one of those locals who hopped into the museum a few times a year to see a special exhibit or favorite sections—or, in her case, favorite section, the modern wing. On this particular day, she was taking in one particular piece—Andy Warhol's silkscreen of an empty electric chair. A friend had published an entire essay dedicated to this little silkscreen's implications about humanity's fascination with death.

Of course, her visit had nothing to do with art. She was here for Patrick.

When Patrick first told her he worked at the museum, she was so jealous. She also came to realize how much his continued employment revealed about his values. About a quarter of West Point graduates opted for lifelong military careers; those who didn't had their choice of lucrative professions. Corporate headhunters jumped at the chance to land the kind of leadership skills found in junior military officers. Private security firms paid top dollar for ex-military types willing to provide protection work in dangerous locations. One of Patrick's army friends insisted he was a makeup importer and exporter, but when McKenna asked about the merits of mineral foundation, he looked at her as if she'd asked about soaking her hair in gasoline. When she pointed out his lack of cosmetic expertise to Patrick, he gave her a list of friends who probably shouldn't be questioned too closely about their work. CIA, perhaps. Maybe sensitive cultural liaison work for the State Department? she wondered. Hopefully not hired mercenaries, but she kept her distance just in case.

Patrick, on the other hand, had gone directly from the military to security management for the museum. She'd heard him justify the choice to his wealthier, faster-living friends more often than he would have liked. He felt good working for a nonprofit. He enjoyed the diverse cast of characters who filled the building. He was surrounded every day by some of the most impressive art on the planet. But what had struck McKenna the most about Patrick's employment when they first met was its stability. He wasn't one of those people always trying to climb to the next step, who saw the present as a bridge to the future. He wasn't like her.

On the other hand, she hadn't realized that ten years would go by without even one change.

"We do have other collections in this museum, you know." Patrick took a seat next to her on the bench across from the Warhol.

She rested her head against his shoulder. "Good day?"

"Fine. We had a close call this afternoon with a girl who fell into a Matisse, but luckily there was no damage."

Thanks to films like *The Thomas Crown Affair*, the average person believed that museum security was all about high-speed, high-tech heist prevention. Little did they know that the most significant losses came from damage, not theft. The water delivery guy rolls a flat of Poland Spring bottles into a Renoir. A fresco is hung on too small a hook. A Rodin sculpture's pedestal simply gives out one day. And every year, a big chunk of damage was inflicted by girls who drank too much, ate too little, and insisted on tackling the city in five-inch heels. One little topple and suddenly Philippe Bertrand's sculpture of Lucretia is missing a foot.

"How about you? I've overheard a few people in the museum talking about your Big Pig article."

McKenna had filed her article about Judge Knight with the title "Should This Man Be Calling Balls and Strikes?" It was a reference to the confirmation testimony of the current chief justice of the United States Supreme Court, who had stated that a good judge was like a neutral umpire. To jazz it up, *NYC* magazine had gone with a close-up photograph of Knight's bloated face, the words BIG PIG stamped across him like a USDA beef rating.

The response to the story had been swift. A spokesperson for the chief judge had promised a thorough investigation. Reacting to speculation about his resignation, Judge Knight had issued a statement attacking the tabloid culture of the media and promising full vindication.

But McKenna wasn't here to talk about Frederick Knight. "You too tired for a little outing?" she asked.

"No, I'm good. What were you thinking? Dinner? A celebration?"

While Patrick's moods were ever constant, hers were frustratingly tied to external achievements. In light of the Knight article, he assumed she'd want to spike the football.

"Dinner does not count as an *outing*. Dinner is just . . . dinner. This is an actual *outing*." It dawned on her that she'd never asked him why he had left work early the previous day. "Speaking of which, what was your outing yesterday?"

"What do you mean?"

"I tried calling when Dana's Skybox imploded, and your office said you left early. It was right after four."

He gave her an exasperated look and shook his head. "Incredible. I leave my desk to walk the floor, and they tell people I'm gone. One of our trustees nearly stroked out when he thought I stood him up." He got up from the bench and held out his hand. "Now, what is this about an outing?"

"You're not going to like it, so I'm officially cashing in a chip." She had no idea whether chips were currency in their household, or how she might have earned one, but it seemed like the right way to ask for a favor. "It's about Bruno."

"Uh-huh."

Not mad. Not annoyed. Just processing the bad news.

"I can't let it go, Patrick."

"Yeah, I've been getting that impression."

"I keep seeing her face. Not that I can actually look at it anymore. You have to admit, it's pretty bizarre that the original and the copy of the subway video both got wiped out yesterday."

"Well, if I have to admit it, then . . ."

She smiled. That piece of banter was a staple in their repertoire. "I'm serious about cashing in a chip, Patrick."

"And I was serious when I told you I'll do what I can. I already sent out an e-mail to the West Point crowd. No one's heard anything. I got the impression they were kind of freaked out that I was even asking. It probably seemed a little out of the blue."

"I got an address for Gretchen." Susan's sister was two years older than Susan. A quick search had turned up a marriage license and an address. "She's living out on Long Island. Nassau County," she added quickly, distinguishing it from more distant parts of the island. "Barely past Queens. It's only an hour by train."

"Gretchen's a junkie, McKenna. We go to her, and there's no telling what she'll try to drag us into."

"I know. She's also Susan's only living family member."

She knew he didn't want to go. She also knew he wasn't going to fight about it. Fifteen minutes later, they had purchased their Long Island Rail Road tickets and were ready to roll.

**W**hen the cabdriver completed the short ride from the Roslyn train stop to the address she'd given him, McKenna checked the house number against the slip of paper in her hand. "You're sure this is it?" she asked.

"I guess that would depend, miss, on your definition of the word '*it*.' If what you mean is whether this house is the place you want it to be, I guess that's for you to know and you to find out." He was obviously amused by the choice of words. "But if what you're asking me is whether this house is the property located at the street address that you provided upon entry into my cab, why, then, I can say definitely that yes, this is *it*. Now, are you going to pay the fare or keep asking me silly questions?"

Patrick answered before McKenna readied her verbal retort. "We're going to need you to wait," he said.

"As long as the meter's running."

"What an ass," McKenna said as they stepped out of the cab.

"Suck it down, M, or we'll end up stranded here. Can't exactly hail a taxi on Long Island."

He was not happy to be here.

They took in the house where Susan's sister supposedly lived. Two-story brick Tudor. Manicured lawn. Volvo sedan in the driveway. Unless Gretchen was stealing this family's mail to fund her drug habit, McKenna couldn't imagine the connection.

Patrick gave the heavy brass knocker on the walnut door three sturdy raps. They heard a child's voice inside. "Mom. Moo-oooom. The dooo-oooor."

"Did that video game somehow bust your feet, Porter? See who it is. And if it's those Bible thumpers again, tell them even Jesus had his limits."

"Mo-om. It's not funny to make jokes about Jesus."

The boy who answered the door was about nine years old, give or take. He seemed frightened by the sight of a man on his porch but then softened when he saw McKenna. She spoke up first.

"Hi, there. No Bibles here, we promise. We're looking for a woman who used to be a friend of ours. Gretchen Hauptmann?"

"My mom's name is Gretchen. And her dad's name was George Hauptmann. But now her name is Henesy, just like mine."

McKenna had been so thrown off by the suburban perfection that she'd forgotten that the state's record of Gretchen's marriage to a man named Paul Henesy had been the item that led her to this address in the first place.

"Porter, who is it?" Gretchen was folding a towel when she arrived at the bottom of the stairs. Most people looked like a worse version of themselves after ten years. Not Gretchen. Gretchen looked the way she should have looked but couldn't a decade earlier. Her long dark hair was tied into a loose bun at the nape of her neck. She was dressed comfortably in a pair of blue jeans and a long purple T-shirt, but she still had the trim, athletic body she'd had in common with her sister, even as she tried to destroy it with drugs.

Patrick was the one to say it first. "You look good, Gretchen."

Her nod was barely perceptible. "I've got a phone number. E-mail. Hell, even a Facebook page."

"It's about Susan," McKenna said.

She stepped aside to invite them in.

# CHAPTER TWENTY

**G**retchen led McKenna and Patrick into a brightly lit living room but did not take a seat or invite her guests to do so. "The house is a mess right now. If I had known you were coming—"

McKenna had to search for any signs of imperfection. A few toys littered the floor. The throw pillows were scrunched into the corners of the sofa. Pizza crumbs were scattered across the glass coffee tabletop. An open box next to the corner bookshelf was half packed with CDs.

What was more apparent was the care that had been put into the room. The vase on that same bookshelf was color-coordinated with the unfluffed pillows. Silk rug. Leather chairs. Nice place.

"I can tell you want to ask," Gretchen said, "so I'll give you the short version. I'm clean. Have been for some time now—eleven years this December. I met Porter's father—my husband, Paul—in a program. He was more a recreational coke guy, not the garbage can I was."

McKenna ran the math in her head, wondering about the age of Gretchen's son, the timing of the pregnancy, whether it had been the thing that finally kept her clean.

"I was sorry to hear about your father's passing," Patrick said.

"Thanks, but we weren't exactly in touch anymore. Not like you two, I guess. Even after all these years?"

"Married," McKenna said, holding up her ring. "Five years already."

"Susan always said the two of you were meant to be." Did McKenna imagine the sarcasm?

"I've been thinking about Susan a lot lately," McKenna said. "I want to finally find out what happened to her, Gretchen. You see all these cases solved decades later. New DNA evidence. New witnesses. I want to look."

"You're not exactly the FBI."

"No, but I still have some contacts. And I learned a lot about investigations at the DA's office and as a reporter. Patrick will help."

"Will Scooby and Shaggy be there, too? Maybe get yourself a little Mystery Bus?"

Nope. Sarcasm was not imagined.

"McKenna's not asking for much," Patrick said. He was using what she referred to as his military voice. The one he used with the uniformed guards at work. The one he occasionally invoked at home if frustrated with her. Now he was using it to defend her. It was a voice that quietly projected command in the culture that he and Gretchen knew. McKenna understood that world better now than most nonmilitary people, but she would never be an insider.

McKenna tilted her head, trying her best to appear sympathetic. "I figured you'd be the one the police would have called with any new information."

"Well, I haven't heard squat. Not that I'm confident the police would even tell me."

"You're her closest relative."

"You know what I was like back then. Not to mention whatever my father probably told them, which would've been even worse."

Susan had filled McKenna in on the Hauptmann family dynamics that night on the kitchen floor, one hand still gripping the phone after the call from her father. The General used to joke openly that he'd wanted to name the girls George and Mercedes. George for

Gretchen, because he'd wanted a namesake son over a daughter; and Mercedes for Susan, because he'd wanted a new car over a second girl.

Their mother, Carol, had done her best to protect them from his poison, at least in the beginning. Susan had early memories of dark looks across the table, followed by screaming matches behind her parents' closed bedroom door. But the General wasn't a man who could be reasoned with. He listened to complaints, in the sense that he could repeat them back—word for word, usually to mock the sentiment—but he lacked the empathy to truly understand another person's perspective.

One summer Susan had taken to calling him General YB and refused to explain the significance. Her sister knew that YB stood for "Yes, but." Each of the girls at various times in their lives had steeled themselves to have a true conversation with the General. They would strategize their talking points, searching for the softest possible expression of the deepest emotions. No matter how well— and how tactfully—they articulated a perspective, being careful to say nothing that might make the General feel judged, their father would always respond with a quick "Yes, but—."

Susan had all her reasons for wanting to go to a private liberal arts college. "Yes, but nothing prepares you for leadership like a military education." Her sophomore year in high school, she wanted to spend a semester as an exchange student in Denmark. "Yes, but it's the pinnacle of privileged indulgence. You should be at home, working."

The way Susan told the family history, for her first twelve or so years, Susan and Gretchen had been bonded by their shared experiences in the Hauptmann household. But when Gretchen hit high school, that bond began to tear. It started with the death of their mother. For whatever reason, the girls developed different ways of responding to their father's solo parenting.

Susan was the more rebellious one, at least initially. She was a good student but had no interest in history, world events, American exceptionalism, or any of the things that engrossed her father. She broke curfew to hang out with her friends and spent the rest of her time looking at fashion magazines and watching reruns of 1970s sit-coms.

Gretchen, on the other hand, tried to please their father. She was one of the few girls in their high school's JROTC, the junior version of the Reserve Officers' Training Corps. She was at the top of her class, both academically and athletically. She took her father up on every opportunity to know his work and his colleagues, practically deposing them about the details of military life and the doors it could open for a promising young person. She was gunning for a spot at West Point, not that anyone doubted she would get it. She was the heir apparent.

"It used to drive me crazy," Susan had confessed the night Mc-Kenna found her in tears in their apartment. "The way Gretchen kissed up to him. When Mom died, it was supposed to be the two of us against the General. He'd have to learn how to take care of us. But then she took his side. It was like she abandoned me. And he didn't have to try anymore with me because he had *her*."

Then the high school principal found a plastic bag of pot in the heir apparent's locker. The General had been so convinced of his daughter's innocence that he insisted on a fingerprint test of the bag. The lab found not only Gretchen's prints but also cocaine residue. The drug test that the General forced on his daughter revealed not only pot and cocaine but also speed and LSD.

A year later, the ex-boyfriend who tipped off the principal mysteriously had all of his college applications withdrawn and twelve thousand dollars of credit card debt racked up in his name.

Revenge was probably sweet, but it hadn't saved Gretchen from her first trip to rehab, nor had it made that trip her last.

"I used to give Gretchen so much shit for trying to suck up to him," Susan had told McKenna that same night. "But look what it did to her. It broke her. And the minute she was out of the picture and he set his sights on making me the golden child, what did I do?"

Off to West Point she went.

Though McKenna had gathered that life with General Hauptmann wasn't easy, Susan always seemed to bring an annoyed but ultimately optimistic eye to the relationship with her father, choosing to believe that the tough, gruff, antiquated geezer had a softness that only his daughters knew. Gretchen fostered no such fantasies.

"Did Susan tell you about my arrest?"

McKenna could tell from Patrick's blank expression that he hadn't known, either.

"Oh yeah. Got caught in Alphabet City with enough crack that they accused me of intent to distribute. I used my one phone call to ask Dad to bail me out. You know what he said? 'I accepted a long time ago that you would wind up in jail or dead. It's time for you to go your own way, Gretchen.' And then he just hung up, leaving me there to get strip-searched, not to mention ogled and pawed by the guards and one of my new roommates. I remember every word of that call, because it's the last time we spoke. But you know what? It's true what they say—you've got to hit rock bottom. I was looking at ten years in prison, but I got lucky. The case kept getting pushed over for trial, and in the meantime, I cleaned up—started working a program. Finally swung a plea deal for rehab and probation at the state level. Two months before Susan—before she was gone. Guess she didn't want you guys knowing about her jailhouse sister. Those cops who investigated her disappearance sure knew. I'd been clean nearly a year by then, but they never treated me as anything but a junkie. I guess that's what I was."

The next half hour felt more like a therapy session than an unexpected drop-in from two old acquaintances as Gretchen devolved into a monologue about the dysfunction in the Hauptmann family. How her father could be kind to everyone except the wife and children he saw as nothing but an extension of himself. How his love—if you could call it that—had always been conditional. How the estrangement from him had finally been her key to getting clean.

"Susan did everything she could to become the child he'd always wanted. It was never enough. He at least talked to her—unlike *moi*, the bad-seed daughter. But she could never really please him. No one could."

"I'm glad you've found a better life for yourself," McKenna said. She gave Patrick an apologetic look. Coming here had been a mistake. Hearing the details of a broken relationship between a dead man and his daughters was the kind of psychological drama Patrick hated. Searching for a way to end the conversation, McKenna pulled a folded sheet of paper from her purse. "Do you recognize this? It's a logo for a group called People Protecting the Planet."

Gretchen shook her head. "Susan wasn't much of an environmentalist. Why?"

"I'm not sure. Just something I'm working on."

In her periphery, McKenna noticed Gretchen's son craning his neck around the corner of the hallway, eavesdropping. He tucked his head back like a surprised turtle, then poked it out again. "Mommy, is Daddy coming to see us tonight, or is he staying at his new house?"

"We'll talk about that later, Porter." Gretchen offered an embarrassed smile. "Paul and I are going through some changes right now. I'm afraid I need to ask you to go. The truth is that I know nothing more about what happened to my sister today than I did ten years ago."

She led the way to the front door, but only Patrick stepped outside.

"Sorry," McKenna said, "but just one more thing. What happened to Susan's stuff?" She immediately recognized the irony of saying "sorry, but" to a woman who had been raised by General YB.

"What stuff?" Gretchen asked.

"Your dad waited six months, I think, and then packed her apartment up."

"I don't know. Ask Marla, his nurse. She took care of him at the end. She also got a huge inheritance, unlike, oh, his daughter. Like I said, the old man could be kind to people who weren't related to him. If anyone would know, it would be her."

"You were really that estranged?" McKenna asked.

"Jesus, did you not listen to anything I just said?"

McKenna asked for Marla's full name and number. Gretchen didn't hide her frustration but excused herself to the kitchen and returned with a document whose pages she was flipping through. "I was served a copy of the will as a courtesy. Nice, huh? Here you go." McKenna jotted down the information—Marla Tompkins, a Manhattan phone number—and thanked Gretchen once again.

Patrick was waiting for McKenna on the porch. As she joined him, she promised Gretchen she'd call if she learned anything more about Susan's disappearance.

"Don't," Gretchen blurted. "I mean, I wish you wouldn't. I wish you wouldn't call, but mostly I wish you wouldn't do any of this. Just let it be."

"Don't you want to know what happened to your sister?"

"You don't get to say that to me, McKenna. Who are you? You were roommates for, what, a *year* before you decided that even the good Hauptmann girl was a little too wild for your taste. You thought you were some hotshot DA when Susan disappeared, and where did that get any of us? You don't think I know what happened to you at work? You think you can solve this like some cold case on television and try to get your career back? And, Patrick, don't even get me started on you. I'm her only family now. I'm the one who gets to say that it's okay to move on. And I've moved on."

Patrick was the one to speak up first. "We didn't handle this well, Gretchen. Try to enjoy the rest of your night."

McKenna could tell he was speaking to her just as much as to Gretchen. She couldn't let it lie, though. "Back then you told the police she wanted to get away from your father. To start another life. I think you were telling yourself that because you wanted to believe she was okay. If she is, don't you want to know that? Don't you want her to see how well you're doing and to meet her nephew?"

"See, you just don't get it, do you, McKenna? If you really knew my sister, you'd realize that if she were alive—if she were here— she'd know exactly where I was and how I was doing. She would know about her nephew. Hell, she'd probably have Porter's schedule down to the minute. She'd know that you were here right now. And yet I haven't heard one thing from her in ten years. Either she's dead, or she's got a damn good reason to keep her distance. Do you seriously think that, after all these years, you can take care of something that Susan Hauptmann couldn't? Please. Don't."

As they walked toward the cab, they heard the bolt lock behind the closed door.

# CHAPTER
# TWENTY-ONE

Scanlin should have anticipated the knock, but it annoyed him all the same. "Come in," he called out, trying to hide the frustration in his voice.

Jenna had lived in this house for twenty years. When Melissa was home, their daughter had walked in and out as if it were still her home, too. Now she insisted on knocking, no matter how many times he told her not to.

"Sorry I'm late, but we better get moving." She looked at her watch. "They won't let us in after eight."

The nursing center had told them four months ago that it "would be for the best" if Scanlin timed his visits to see Melissa with their daughter. He had read somewhere that architects considered triangles the strongest base of support: something about symmetry aiding in the distribution of weight. He saw that in his own family. His visits to Melissa depended on all three points of their family triangle. Melissa no longer remembered him as her husband. But she remembered Jenna and understood in their daughter's presence that Scanlin was Jenna's friend. Without Jenna, he was a stranger to Melissa. And without Melissa, Jenna wanted nothing to do with him.

He realized that the scenario was a triangle only from his perspective. From theirs, did he matter at all?

"Dad, are you coming?" While he was pulling on his jacket, she had stepped into the dining room. "Big surprise. Work. Well, at least the table's being used for something. God knows you never had dinner at it."

She laughed, but he knew that the joke was based in the ugly truth. He had been a shitty father. He'd been always working or trying to live the hotshot life he enjoyed more in his imagination than in reality. Nice suits. Cologne. Beautiful wife. Dinners at favorite restaurants, talking up the waiters who'd worked there since he first trotted in with Melissa on his arm.

He hadn't left any time for Jenna. He'd seen the parenting duties as Melissa's domain, something to be done while he was at work.

Now his daughter's comment made him self-conscious about the files sprawled across the table. He did a quick tidying of the documents, putting the coworker's DD5 on top as a reminder. He was a good cop. He'd always been a good cop. Even then.

But he hadn't pulled at every thread. Given where he was in his own life ten years ago, he had seen Susan Hauptmann primarily as her father's daughter. One daughter was a drug addict, and the other daughter was a runaway. But she was an adult woman with no boyfriends and yet an open box of condoms in her nightstand. Maybe Jared Klein—the co-worker who'd said Susan had put the moves on him—really had seen another side of her. Maybe that was the side that had put her in danger. Maybe Scanlin had missed it.

He had been so convinced that Susan left town to get a fresh start away from her father. Even if he'd been right, what if it had been Jenna? What if Jenna—instead of pretending he did not exist when she first learned of her mother's diagnosis—had walked away in disgust, leaving without a trace? He would want someone to find out what happened to her.

Susan Hauptmann's parents were both gone. Her sister was a screwup. If someone were going to search for the girl, it would have to be Scanlin.

# CHAPTER TWENTY-TWO

**M**arla Tompkins had a broad caramel-colored face. Deep lines were beginning to set in, but the retired nurse's most noticeable features were the dark freckles across her nose and the warm smile that greeted McKenna at the front door.

When McKenna had called the woman from the train back into the city and asked to meet with her, she had jotted down the address without realizing it should have been familiar.

She noticed the wedding ring on the woman's finger. "Thanks for seeing me, Mrs. Tompkins. I came here once with General Hauptmann's daughter Susan. I was very sorry to hear about his passing."

Susan's father had lived in the family's home near West Point, but kept a one-bedroom Upper East Side pied-à-terre in the city.

"Your friend's father was a very generous man. He knew things weren't easy for me after Harold—my husband—passed away. He always told me I had nothing to worry about, but it never dawned on me he would leave me an apartment of my own. Well, it's not mine yet. But it's going to be, and the executor of the estate saw no point in evicting me in the meantime."

"I'm wondering where I can find any of Susan's belongings that General Hauptmann may have had. Susan's older sister, Gretchen, suggested that you might know."

"By the time I started to care for the general, he had already packed up most of his things, preparing for the end. That's the way he was. Very unsentimental about death. Stoic. He kept the basic necessities—a television, pots and pans and dishes. A couple of pictures of his wife on the nightstand. His personal belongings were already in storage."

"And after his death?"

McKenna remembered Susan's breakdown over the news that her father had cancer. They had spent nearly four hours downing every variety of vodka on ice at Pravda. McKenna could tell that Susan was unwavering in her commitment to get obliterated, but she had no idea why until Susan held up yet another shot glass: *To the General. He's human after all.*

McKenna had tried consoling Susan with the usual clichés about advancements in medical care, but she soon realized that Susan was crying more from anger than fear or sadness. She was angry because her father had managed to use his cancer as one more way to pressure her to join his firm. News of his illness would kill the effort before it was off the ground. The firm had secured respectable work for a new player, but it would never land the more lucrative government contracts without assurances that the man himself—or his daughter—would be around for the long haul.

And she was angry because she cared. Despite it all, she cared about her father and did not want him to die.

Mrs. Tompkins offered McKenna a seat in a leather recliner. "I was very surprised when he left it all to me. Not the entire estate, of course. He had his charities and whatnot. But I'll get this apartment and a bit of cash to help cover the maintenance."

"What about the things he put in storage? Are they available? I'd be happy to go through it to see if anything of Susan's—"

"I don't know precisely, but Adam would. Adam Bayne. Do you know him?"

"Of course." Adam was one of Susan and Patrick's classmates from West Point; he had been the closest thing Susan found to a boyfriend among the army crowd. Despite attempts to make their relationship work over the long haul, the two were strictly platonic by the time McKenna came on the scene. Susan used to joke that her relationship with Adam had been doomed the minute her father decided to call Adam "son." "If he's the General's son, that makes him my brother. Which means no more playing with his pickle." That was Susan.

Adam had stayed friends with Susan but had found a true mentor in her father. Unlike Susan, he had signed on to work at his firm. Adam may have been the one to extinguish any chance that she might join him there when he told her about pulling "tub monkey" duty in Afghanistan—peering out with an M-60 from behind hill-billy armor, playing rear guard for a private convoy in the exposed bed of a pickup. Susan had heard too many stories about the deteriorating picture on the ground. She had no interest in heading back to the Middle East, even to help her father.

Now McKenna was wondering whether George Hauptmann's special relationship with Susan's ex-boyfriend had been one more step in the man's search for a legacy—from Gretchen to Susan to Adam.

"Adam's the executor. He was so close to the general; plus, they worked together and such. He took responsibility for going through the storage unit. I believe he kept a few mementos and some records from their business but got rid of most of it. He could tell you more."

McKenna thanked Mrs. Tompkins for her time and said she'd follow up with Adam Bayne. The woman stopped her before she left the apartment. "You saw Gretchen? How was she?"

"Very well," McKenna said. "Healthy. Happy. She has a beautiful son." She saw no reason to mention that Gretchen's husband was in the process of moving out.

"She visited him. Just once, shortly before he died. He was in terrible pain by then, but he was so happy to see her. I gave her his diary. He wasn't writing in it anymore, and it seemed like she should have it. I was hoping she'd come back. That maybe they'd made peace. But she never returned. Not even an appearance at the funeral." Mrs. Tompkins shook her head. What a shame.

It was just like Gretchen to not want anyone to know that she had found a single moment of softness for her dying father. Despite the estrangement, at least she had made one exception to say goodbye.

No one ever had that chance with Susan.

# CHAPTER TWENTY-THREE

**C**arter watched the house from the curb in his rented Chevy Malibu. He had watched the house before. He knew the woman shared it with three other people—two female, one male. He knew that one of the women was currently at work as a desk clerk at the local U-Haul branch. He had seen a second woman leave fifteen minutes earlier on her miniscooter. That left two at most inside— the woman and the man who had recruited her. Or at least, according to Carter's client, the man had been led to believe he was recruiting her.

Because Carter had done independent research, he also knew about the house. He knew from property records that it was a three-bedroom, two-bathroom split-level ranch built in 1954. It belonged to the grandmother of Hanna Middleton, the girl on the scooter. Hanna had spent a year at the University of Oregon but now lived in this house in Brentwood with three of her friends. The grandmother had gone into a nursing home last July, perfect timing for Hanna to drop out of college and pursue other passions on Long Island.

Because Carter had already been inside, he knew the place was just how the grandmother must have left it, except for the attic's acquisition of agricultural fertilizer, diesel fuel, and a mess of chemicals that shouldn't be under one roof together.

He got lucky. The last remaining occupants of the house—the woman and the man—walked out the front door, got into an early-model Honda minivan, and drove away.

When he'd seen the woman yesterday on the PATH train, she'd been on alert. She had pretended to read her gossip magazine, but he was certain she knew precisely the number of people on that train with her, where they were sitting, and what they were wearing. Today she walked straight from the house to the car, her eyes only on her companion. Yesterday she hadn't wanted to be seen with the heavy-metal guy on the train. Today she was on home turf. She wasn't worried.

Once the minivan turned the corner, he moved quickly. He walked to the front door, duffel bag in his right hand. The bottom lock slipped easily with a pick. It was probably the same one Grandma had, back when no one bothered. Though the top lock was a more sophisticated bolt, they'd left without securing it. Easier entry for him, but their carelessness could be a sign that they'd be returning soon.

Thanks to their own handiwork, rigging the place for explosion was relatively simple. They'd lacked a couple of key ingredients, but he had what he needed in the duffel. The technical name for the fuse was an anti-handling device, but it was essentially a booby trap.

He took one last look at his masterpiece as he started down the attic steps. He knew he was crossing a line. He was no longer a mere observer. He was using tactics learned in another world.

They had crossed a line, too. He'd seen the evidence with his own eyes. If they didn't go into the attic—if they didn't handle the anti-handling device—they'd have nothing to worry about. And if they did? That was their decision, not his.

# CHAPTER TWENTY-FOUR

**P**atrick was waiting for her with two seats at the bar at Union Square Cafe. Their favorite bartender asked if she wanted the usual. She gave him an enthusiastic yes. A minute later, Bombay Sapphire with a twist appeared in front of her.

While McKenna had been visiting General Hauptmann's nurse, Patrick had gone back to the apartment to change out of his suit into his usual weeknight fare of button-down shirt and blue jeans. She noticed he was already eating a salad.

"Sorry, I was starving. Your errand go okay?"

She updated him on her visit to Marla Tompkins. "I feel like I missed something. Like there was a question I should have thought to ask but didn't. I guess all I can hope for is that Susan's father held on to some of her things and that Adam might have them. Would you mind calling him in the morning to check?"

"No problem. Is that it?" he asked. "You seem upset."

"Sorry. It's just that you know you've had a bad day when Gretchen Hauptmann, of all people, looks at you like *you're* the selfish one."

"She didn't say you were selfish."

McKenna hadn't wanted to talk about their visit to Gretchen's house while they were in the cramped quarters of the train. She had hoped that the view of Nassau County whizzing past them to the steady rhythm of the car against the rails would calm her. Instead, the hour-long trip had given her time to fume over every aspect of the conversation.

"She accused me of looking for Susan to advance my own career. She can try to convince herself she's moved on and has her whole Volvo-driving-mommy life now, but I remember what she was like. She'd call Susan at all hours of the day and night, and Susan would never know what she was going to get when she picked up: Gretchen bitching about their father, Gretchen strung out and barely able to talk, Gretchen so manic that Susan could set the phone down to go to the bathroom and her sister wouldn't even notice. And now *she's* judging *me*?"

McKenna initially had felt bad for not telling Gretchen what she'd seen on the subway video. But her instincts had been right: Gretchen wouldn't have believed it. What she hadn't expected was Gretchen to make her doubt her own loyalty to Susan. The accusations weren't entirely misplaced. The truth was, McKenna and Susan had been roommates for only a year, and McKenna had been the one to initiate the split. She had told Susan that it was because she was about to turn thirty and thought she should live by herself for the first time in her life. But the reason McKenna had splurged on her own place was to avoid admitting to Susan that she just couldn't live with her anymore. She was too frenetic. Constantly buzzing around. Always planning the next outing. Staying out until three in the morning or not coming home at all. She couldn't sit and watch television or read a book. She couldn't be alone. She couldn't just . . . be.

"Fine, she came off a little self-righteous, but is it really a surprise that she doesn't want to dig all this up again?" Patrick asked.

"A *little* self-righteous? And what was that comment about you?" Patrick said nothing, but McKenna could remember the acidic tone of Gretchen's voice. " 'Don't even get me started on you'? What was she talking about?"

"Who knows, and who cares? Gretchen's the kind of person who isn't happy unless everyone is as miserable as she is. I could tell the first time I met her. On campus visits, families would bring care packages and games and stuff, and Gretchen would just sit there and run Susan down in front of her classmates. She's a button pusher. She may be clean, but she's probably still totally fucked up. Maybe that's why her husband's bailing on her."

Such a cutting comment was out of character. Patrick was annoyed about the wild goose chase.

They were cut off by their bartender friend asking if they were ready to order. McKenna didn't need to look at the menu. Patrick might be starving, but she was too stressed out to eat. A half serving of pasta would be more than enough for her tonight.

Unfortunately, her dinner order said more than she'd meant to reveal. "You need to eat," Patrick warned. "And don't even try to convince me you ate lunch, because I know you never do when you're obsessing."

"I'm not obsessing."

"Um, hello? Train ride? Long Island? A sudden drop-in on Susan's sister? And then Susan's father's *nurse*? How far are you going to take this, McKenna?"

"It's only been two days," she said.

"Three. Three days when you've done nothing but read old newspaper articles about Susan and look at pictures of her from a decade ago. You don't think I noticed that you got up in the middle of the night to pull out yearbooks from my storage trunks? You haven't slept, and you're not eating, but you seem to have no problem drinking."

She didn't like the sound of the pissy sigh that escaped her throat, but she also didn't enjoy getting lectured.

Patrick placed a hand gently on her knee. "The woman on the subway was fast, and she was strong, and with your mind on the past lately because of the Marcus Jones anniversary, it's not surprising that you thought about Susan. She was a big part of your life when you were at the DA's office. But I saw the video, McKenna. And I knew Susan a lot longer than you did. It wasn't her."

"What about Dana suddenly losing all her files?"

"Computers crash all the time."

"The same day the girl who took the video had her phone tampered with?"

"She *thinks* it was tampered with. How many times have you accidentally deleted something from your phone? And you said yourself the girl sounded like a ditz. Try and take a break from this, okay? Eat a little. Get some sleep. Stop tearing the closets apart in the middle of the night." She returned his smile. "Things will look different in a couple of days."

Everything Patrick said made sense. As she watched him finish his salad, she made a point of nibbling some bread, just to prove she could.

**P**atrick was already removing his coat in the elevator.

"A strip tease? All for me?" She feigned a seductive tone.

"Nothing sexy about it. I'm exhausted. And I need to drop a—"

She held up her palm. "No. Don't even say it." She was well aware of his many sayings for what it was he needed to do in the privacy of their home, and she didn't try to hide her disgust. When they first got together, she was mortified by Patrick's comfort with physiological realities. Peeing with the bathroom door open. Smelling his underarms on a hot day. Farting, no question. When she found him fanning what he called his "undercarriage" in front of her air-conditioning unit after a bicycle ride, she finally had to say something. "How in the world do you expect someone to put up with this? Where's the romance? The mystery? You mean to tell me you'd still find me attractive if you walked in here to find me doing something like that?"

"I don't believe in being anything but myself. Besides, I like the idea of walking in to find you doing all sorts of things you never planned on anyone seeing." It was a good line, and it had worked. For a while. For a few years, she had found his frankness charming. Now she was rolling her eyes.

As previously announced, Patrick was tired. He crashed as soon as they hit the bed. But she was high from running around all night. She was also more than a little buzzed from her martini and the bottomless glass of wine that had accompanied her pasta.

Patrick reached for her as she slipped out of bed. "Don't. You promised."

She hadn't promised, but it wasn't Susan's case that she wanted to work on. Her book proposal wasn't getting anywhere. Maybe if she made some progress on it, her thinking would be clearer. She didn't bother turning on the living room lights as she flipped open her laptop. She worked best this way. She'd written at least half of her novel while drunk between bouts of crying on the sofa, just her and the dim illumination of her computer screen.

She reread what she had written the previous day. *It was the gun.*

No shit, it was the gun. She had been so damn proud of her investigative skills for tracing that stupid gun. The serial number. The hit in the ATF database. Hell, even when she realized the eleven-year-old connection between Scott Macklin and the gun, she hated the implications but felt certain she had uncovered a truth that would have remained buried without her industriousness.

Only problem was, she was wrong. How in the world had she been wrong?

Her fingers flew above the keyboard as she recalled the story of that damn gun.

*The serial number was a match. The Glock next to Marcus Jones's body had been seized by the NYPD eleven years earlier and scheduled for destruction as part of the city's Safe Streets program. Only four of the NYPD's 34,800 police officers had been assigned to that year's gun destruction project. And one of them was Scott Macklin.*

*Coincidence? Impossible.*

*I brought the information to my supervisor, Will Getty. We had to take the evidence to the grand jury. It was a no-brainer.*

*But the funny thing about odds is that even if it's one in a million, there is a distinctive one, apart from the 999,999 others. There's always an ex-*

*ception. Some poor schmuck golfer gets struck by lightning in his backswing. A lucky waitress actually wins the Powerball. And eleven years after Scott Macklin worked the Safe Streets gun destruction program, he looked down the barrel of one of those guns that was supposed to have been liquefied.*

*For Macklin, the odds of being one of the cops who had unmonitored access to the guns scheduled for destruction in 1992 weren't one in a million. They were four in 34,800. Macklin was one of the four. That left three others.*

*I never stopped to think about the other three. Will Getty did.*

*One of the other cops on gun-smelting duty in 1992 was Don Whitman. By the time Macklin shot Marcus Jones, Whitman was already serving six to eight for selling tips, favors, and other forms of support to the Crips in their effort to dominate the Latin Kings in a deadly turf war during the late 1990s.*

*A cop on a gang payroll had been given access to truckloads of weapons slated for destruction. That at least one went missing no longer seemed shocking. It was inevitable. From a dirty cop to the Crips to the streets to Jones's hands over a decade later.*

*When Will Getty finally found James Low—the kid in the neighborhood who admitted selling the gun to Marcus—the truth became clear: I had accused a cop of murder and sent the city into race-based tensions and protests, all over a coincidence.*

**M**cKenna always wondered what would have happened if she'd stopped to think about the other three cops who'd had access to that gun. She could have been the one to prove that Marcus Jones had carried that Glock to the docks that night. She could have cleared Macklin of any suspicion in front of the grand jury, instead of running to a reporter with specious claims.

Those two weeks—after she'd gone to Getty and before she'd gone to Bob Vance—had been wasted. Instead of checking out the other Safe Streets officers, or at least pushing Getty to update her, she had treated his silence as conspiratorial. She had assumed that he was burying the evidence.

By then McKenna had known Patrick for three months. She considered asking his advice before going to the press, but he had worries of his own. It had been six months since a banner on the deck of an aircraft carrier declared mission accomplished, but Saddam Hussein hadn't been captured, and a suicide bomber had attacked the UN headquarters in Iraq. There were rumors that the army—struggling to fight two wars in the Middle East—was pulling retired officers back into active duty. McKenna's problems had seemed minor in comparison.

She pulled her thoughts back to the book proposal. She knew the facts cold. She suspected that she always would. But this book was supposed to be more than facts. It was supposed to be the human story behind the events. She needed to focus on the *people*.

While writing her novel, she'd thought of the characters as living, breathing, sentient beings and had let them drive the narrative. If she were going to write a book about the Marcus Jones shooting and its aftermath, she would be a character, though not the only one. Perhaps not even the main character.

She needed to write about Marcus, initially labeled a thug based on his criminal history but who had been known in his neighborhood as Patches—the sweet but strange boy whose face was spotted from a skin condition called vitiligo. She needed to write about Marcus's mother, who once chased members of the 137th Street Crew down Madison with a broom when she found out they were pressuring thirteen-year-old Marcus to join their gang. McKenna needed to write about Will Getty, of whom she'd assumed the worst but who was simply being cautious with the investigation of a politically sensitive case.

And she needed to write about the man she had accused of perjury and murder. She pictured Scott Macklin's face and began to type.

# CHAPTER TWENTY-FIVE

*I* *never wanted to be the prosecutor who brought down a cop. If anything,*
*I needed Scott Macklin to be vindicated. I became a prosecutor because I be-*
*lieved in a firm line between right and wrong. I wanted to help crime victims.*
*I wanted to punish bad people who did bad things. But a prosecutor is only*
*a lawyer. Though I had the legal knowledge and training to help the truth*
*navigate its way through the justice system, every single one of my cases relied*
*on police officers to educate me about the truth. They were the ones who*
*questioned witnesses, interrogated suspects, and gathered physical evidence. If*
*I couldn't trust them, my job meant nothing.*

*And this wasn't just any cop. It was Scott Macklin. He was a member*
*of the Drug Enforcement Task Force of the Narcotics Division when I*
*was trying drug cases. That meant I saw him more than other cops. He'd*
*been in the grand jury room with me at least thirty times, testified in five*
*of my trials, and come to my office for search warrants and legal advice*
*dozens of times. And it wasn't only about the work with him. He perused*
*the frames on my office walls—the college and law school degrees, the cer-*
*tificate commemorating my time as a clerk for a federal judge, the absence*
*of any personal photographs. One day he asked if I was married, quickly*
*apologizing if he was being inappropriate. I assured him it was fine, but*
*no, I wasn't married. He told me that love had changed his life. It became*
*a running joke. Whenever he was at the courthouse, he'd pass my office*

*door: "You're. Still. Here. You need to leave this office if you're going to find love."*

*He talked to anyone who would listen, including me, about his gorgeous wife, Josefina, and his new stepson, Thomas. Then one day he came to my office to tell me he was moving out of Narco into a new federal-state team formed through Homeland Security. He might not be around the drug unit so much.*

*I made some lame joke about him movin' on up to a badass Homeland Security gig with the feds. Then he abruptly changed the topic. He asked me, "speaking of the federal government," if I had learned anything about immigration law during my judicial clerkship. When I said that I hadn't but had taken a course in law school, he closed my office door and told me that he was worried about some "complications" with Josefina's legal status inside the country.* Complications. *I remember that word in particular because his voice broke when he said it. Her young son was at risk of being deported. He looked away from me, trying to regain his composure, but his emotions failed him. He shook his head in frustration and wiped away the tears starting to pool in the corners of his eyes. I offered him a Kleenex from my purse. I also wrote down the name and number of an immigration lawyer I knew from school.*

*Neither of us ever spoke of that day again, not even after I accused him of lying about Marcus Jones.*

*He trusted me. He talked to me like a friend, and he trusted me. I needed to believe cops, but I really needed to believe this one.*

**D**ammit. Now she was the one wiping away a tear. That moment in her office had gotten to her. Her memory of the details was fuzzy at best—something about Josefina entering the United States lawfully but her son being brought into the country later—but she remembered Macklin breaking down. He didn't want to lose the family he'd only recently found. He didn't want Josefina to get in trouble. He made too much money to qualify for free legal aid and not enough to retain a private lawyer.

She'd never seen a man cry, let alone a man like Macklin. He was at least fifteen years older than she was. Six-one, probably 220, he had a square head and thick hands like two baseball gloves. She had wondered whether he might resent her later for witnessing him in that state. She felt like she had emasculated him in some way. That night after work, she had talked to Susan about it, thinking that she must have seen men in vulnerable moments during her time in the army.

Susan had told her that men moved past their emotions. Though McKenna was sitting in the bar that night, reliving and questioning every second of that brief office interaction, Macklin was a man, and men, Susan explained, didn't pore over every millisecond of every human encounter. Just then McKenna's cell phone had rung—an incoming call from a lawyer she had just started seeing. When she rejected the call, Susan reiterated her point: "See now? If the tables were turned, and you had been the one calling him, you'd spend the rest of the night wondering why he didn't pick up, what he was doing, and what you'd done wrong. A man won't do that, not even a wussy man like Nature Boy. Nature Boy will just hang up and assume you'll call him back later. We could stand to learn a few things from men."

Nature Boy. Susan never seemed to approve of any of McKenna's potential suitors—except Patrick, of course. She called poor Jason Eberly "Nature Boy" because he was a lawyer for an environmental nonprofit. A noble choice by any measure, but the nickname did manage to sum up Jason's penchant for reminding everyone that he was more benevolent than they. He'd openly note that it was only through a loan forgiveness program that he was able to work for a nonprofit. When private lawyer friends would complain about an unreasonable client or nightmare partner, he'd say things like "That's why I'm glad I work for a cause." McKenna had nothing against his chosen cause, but Susan was right: Jason reeked of do-gooder-ness.

Jason. Benevolent, noble, earth-loving Nature Boy. If he was still working for environmental causes, he might know something about the organization whose button had been on the subway woman's backpack.

She opened Google and searched for Jason Eberly. Up popped a slew of information about an up-and-coming teen singer. Who knew? She tried again, searching for "Jason Eberly attorney." She found a hit at the website for the law firm of Walker Richardson & Jones. It was one of the ten largest firms in the country.

She clicked on the link. Gone were goatee and shaggy hair. From the looks of his closely shorn head, he'd lost most of his hair entirely. According to the bio, he was a new partner at the firm and had counseled clients on hundreds of transactions and litigation matters across all industries, nationally and globally, including chemical refining, oil and gas, mining, heavy manufacturing, and toxic torts. So much for saving the planet.

She jumped at the feeling of a hand on her shoulder.

"Patrick. Sorry, you scared me. Did I wake you?"

"My alarm went off. You've been up all night?"

She hadn't noticed the sunlight beginning to make its way into the living room. "I was writing."

"Looks to me like you're surfing the Internet. Who's Jason Eberly?"

"A lawyer I used to—"

"Oh, wait. That's the guy you were dating when we first met, right?"

She knew how it looked. How many stories had she heard about extramarital affairs that began with an innocent "I wonder whatever happened to so-and-so" Google search? First comes Facebook, then comes Betrayal.

But her husband's expression wasn't jealous. He looked tired. And worried. And at least a little angry. He was looking at her and remembering all those nights when she drank too much, ate too little, and couldn't sleep. She didn't want him to think she was going back into the dark place that had kept them apart for so long.

"I really was working on the proposal. Then I realized I need to produce something for the magazine. I thought I could do a story about these people who are trying to reduce their carbon footprints to zero. One guy even stopped using toilet paper for a year. I thought Jason might know something about the movement. Turns out he's gone to the dark side." She rotated the laptop in his direction, making clear she had nothing to hide.

He took a quick look at the lawyer's head shot. "Guess I don't have anything to worry about there."

"Never," she said, arching her neck back and giving him a soft peck on his navel.

"Cold face," he said, giving her hair a quick stroke. "I need to get to the museum a little early today. The queen of Jordan is supposed to be in. Can you grab a little more sleep before work?"

She nodded. She was tired, and the reception desk at Walker Richardson & Jones wouldn't pick up until nine.

"You'll remember to call Adam Bayne today?" she asked. "See if he still has Susan's father's stuff?"

"I really wish you'd rethink this. Last night it was Gretchen on Long Island, then the old man's nurse. Look at you. You're already exhausted. Just give it a rest, okay?"

"I just want to see if Adam has any of her things. If there's nothing there, I'll let it lie." At least for a while, she told herself.

He assured her he would make the call, but she could tell he wasn't happy about it. She climbed back into bed, working her way into the warmth Patrick had left under the blankets.

When Patrick kissed her on the cheek before he left, his lips felt soft and he smelled like toothpaste. She kept her eyes closed, pretending to have found sleep.

# CHAPTER TWENTY-SIX

The slam of Scanlin's coffee mug against his desk was harder and louder than he'd intended. One desk over, Ricky Munson—always trying to earn a reputation as the squad's funny boy—couldn't resist a comment. "Whoa, whoa, whoa. Stop the clock. Haven't you heard that it's 'be kind to dishes' day?"

There was a reason Munson hadn't yet achieved squad-comedian status.

Scanlin had slammed the mug for a reason, and the reason was that people were stupid. They were stupid, and they were assholes. Sometimes they were both. He'd just gotten off the phone with some finance guy whose in-home chef was found dead in the family townhouse the previous day. Odds of homicide were low, but thanks to an ambiguous bump on the woman's head, Scanlin had to wait for official word from the medical examiner before releasing the crime scene.

It had been under twenty-four hours since the woman's body had been wheeled away—a woman who'd cooked for this d-bag's family for sixteen years. And the man wasn't even in the city. He was calling from East Hampton, natch.

Didn't matter. He insisted on a guarantee that his caterers would have access to the kitchen the following weekend. The best part was when he tried to defend himself against Scanlin's suggestion that his priorities might be a bit *off*. "I'll have you know we treated Rosalyn as family, Detective. She even stayed overnight in the pool house when she cooked for us in the summer."

When Scanlin slammed the cup on his desk, maybe he was picturing the guy's skull.

Now he welcomed the distraction of the delivery he had just received from the Records Department. He had reached out to Jared Klein, Susan's former coworker who had mentioned her late-night attempt to turn work into pleasure. Klein remembered little about the night beyond what he'd said during the original investigation, but after some pressure, he repeated his suspicion that he had seen an entirely different side to Susan's personality. "She was always such a—" He stopped himself from using the word he was undoubtedly thinking. "She was, you know, hard. Tough. Obviously came from a man's world. She was fun, always trying to fit in, not like a feminazi or anything. But not a *seductress*. More like a raunchy kid sister. That night? God. I admit I still think about it sometimes."

Maybe Klein realized it was more than a tad creepy to be fantasizing about a missing woman, because that was all he had to say about Susan.

The documents on Scanlin's desk were copies of any and all reported incidents within a block of Susan's building in the three weeks preceding her disappearance. It was the kind of step he should have taken at the time, but he couldn't swear that he had. Neighborhood canvass, yes. A search for incidents involving her or her apartment, yes. But a three-week record search? Maybe not. Neighbors occasionally saw male guests coming and going at Susan's apartment. Maybe one of them had gotten a parking ticket or had witnessed a neighborhood altercation.

As Scanlin flipped through the pages, he realized why he may have skipped the step ten years earlier. In densely packed Manhattan, a whole lot of podunk idiocy went down in a three-week period. A shoving match at Taco Bell when two customers simultaneously reached for the same root beer spigot. A couple of graffiti cleanups, courtesy of AmeriCorps, because the complainants had uttered the magic phrase "gang symbols." One week must have seen particularly good weather because reports of ranting homeless people skyrocketed. A whole slew of noise complaints but remarkably few parking infractions. Were meter maids slacking, or had people figured out that even sky-high garage rates were better than the city's $265 parking tickets?

Scanlin flipped back to two noise complaints that had originated from Susan's apartment building. They were both called in by the same tenant—Vera Hadley, apartment 402. Same floor as Susan, who was in 406. The first complaint was about a loud stereo from the apartment downstairs at 10:40 P.M. Twenty minutes later, Hadley called back to say that the music had stopped, "no thanks to you people." The second complaint came in two days before Susan was last seen at the gym. According to Hadley, a man and a woman were screaming inside apartment 404. For reasons that weren't clear, the call was logged in as possible DV—domestic violence— triggering a response from patrol officers. When police arrived, the hallway was quiet, no one answered the door at 404, and Hadley had no further information to offer. Call closed.

Scanlin shifted his attention to a separate pile of documents: summaries from the neighborhood canvass conducted after Susan was reported missing. No response at 404 over the course of four different days, at four different times. The tenant on the lease was a man named Paul Roca. According to the mailman, Roca had left "last week," and his mail was being held for a month.

If the blockhead patrol officer talking to the mailman had thought to ask whether Roca had left before or after the next-door neighbor had disappeared, he hadn't thought to make a note of it. A stupid mistake. And yet Scanlin had let it slide.

He did a quick search for Paul Roca. Still at the same address. Arrested six years earlier for hitting a girlfriend. The charges had been dismissed without prosecution but were enough to pique Scanlin's curiosity.

Mr. Roca was worth a visit.

# CHAPTER TWENTY-SEVEN

**M**cKenna's love life had never been noteworthy until she met Patrick. Two college boyfriends. A shack-up for the last two years of law school, more to save rent than as an audition for marriage. She was starting to get into a relationship with Jason Eberly, aka Nature Boy, when Patrick came around and ruined her for anyone else. Until she met him, breaking up meant exactly that. No polite holiday cards. No phone number stored in the cell. No staying friends. She and Patrick kept going back to each other until they finally got it right.

When she called Jason that morning, it was the first time she had spoken to him in over a decade. She used her maiden name, and even then, there was an awkward silence on the other end of the line. Too composed to ask, "Who?," Jason obviously needed a moment to place the name. There was another long pause when she asked to see him. "McKenna, I'm, um—I'm very flattered, but I'm married. Two kids. I don't know how my wife would feel about—"

She resisted the urge to blurt out, "In your dreams!" She was the one who'd broken it off. "Oh, I should have explained. It's about a group called People for the Preservation of the Planet—for a story I'm working on. I work at *New York City* magazine now."

"Given that you called me at the firm, you probably know I'm not at the epicenter of the conservation movement anymore. I sold out to the man."

"Really, I just want to pick your brain. Fifteen minutes. You can bill me if you want."

From the looks of his office, she was thankful he hadn't taken up her offer of payment. His sleek glass desk was the size of a queen bed. Floor-to-ceiling windows offered an unobscured view of Central Park. He greeted her with a quick hug, more a pat on the back than an embrace. "You look great, McKenna. Getting out of the hellhole that is legal practice must be the secret to the fountain of youth."

"The law thing seems to have suited you well." She was telling the truth. Where he'd been a bit shy and goofy-looking as a younger man, he now appeared confident and comfortable in his own skin.

"You're interested in the P3s?"

"Is that what they call themselves?" she asked.

"Guess it's supposed to sound more hard-core, reminiscent of a gang name like the 18th Streeters. They're an offshoot of the Environmental Liberation Front, or ELF. Even ELF is considered an eco-terrorism group, but the rumor is that P3 was formed by a couple of guys who found ELF's practices a bit too . . . tame."

She couldn't imagine how Susan could be connected to such a group. "How big are they?"

"I don't know a lot about them," he said. "The groups I associated with stayed away from ELF. And we were just beginning to hear whispers about a more radical offshoot. These days, the only time I give groups like that any thought is if they're causing problems for my clients."

"What kind of problems?"

"Protesting a nuclear power plant, trespassing to collect water samples they hope will validate some conspiracy theory about toxins. But some of these groups go off the deep end. Bomb threats. Chaining themselves to trees scheduled for a chainsaw. Burning down new construction. Breaking animals out of research laboratories."

"Are they national or located in a certain region?"

"Like I said, I'm no expert. Are you focusing specifically on the P3s, or is your article about ecoterrorism in general?"

She tucked her hair behind her ears—an action that Susan once called her "tell" when trying to teach her poker. "Ecoterrorism in general, but I've found that focusing on one example, then placing it in a broader context, can be really effective."

"Ah, right, like your article on Judge Knight. Excellent job, by the way. Well, if the People for the Preservation of the Planet are going to be your next Big Pig, I think I've got the right contact for you. I had to hammer out a document subpoena with an FBI agent last year when one of our cosmetic clients was targeted by activists for testing mascara on rabbits."

McKenna knew that her face revealed her disgust.

"Never gave any thought to where your makeup comes from, huh? Anyway, the agent knew this ecoterrorism stuff backward and forward. I could give her a call and grease the wheels. Maybe you can get a sit-down."

He dialed a number and put his phone on speaker. Four rings. "You've reached Special Agent Jamie Mercado."

At the beep, he picked up the handset. "This is Jason Eberly. We worked on the . . ." He said the first half of the name of a well-known cosmetic company, then smiled at McKenna. "That matter involving the rabbit research last year. I have a friend here—McKenna Jordan with *New York City* magazine. She's been research-ing a group called People for the Preservation of the Planet. She was hoping to get some background information, and I thought of you." He left his number and asked for a return call.

McKenna was thanking him for his time when his phone rang. "Well, that was quick," he said, looking at the caller identification screen. "This is Jason. Thanks for calling me back so quickly, Agent Mercado. I've got McKenna right here. I'm going to put you on speaker, if that's okay."

"Ms. Jordan, this is Jamie Mercado with the FBI. I'm going to need you to come into the field office to see me. We're at 26 Federal Plaza. You can check in on the twenty-third floor."

McKenna could tell by the tone of the agent's voice that she was not offering a friendly sit-down for assistance with an article.

"I appreciate the offer, Agent Mercado, but would tomorrow work for an appointment? I want to make sure I'm thoroughly prepared so I can make the best use of your time."

"Am I correct that you have been investigating the People for the Preservation of the Planet? Known as the P3s?"

"I wouldn't call it investigating. I've been researching an article."

"And how exactly did you end up focusing on that group?"

"I don't know what you mean."

"I can play back Jason's message if necessary. He said you were interested specifically in the P3s."

"Is there something wrong, Agent?"

"Like I said, Ms. Jordan, I'm going to need you to meet me at the field office. And just to be clear, I can get a grand jury subpoena if one is required. There is no privilege that protects journalists from testifying."

McKenna couldn't imagine what this FBI agent thought she could possibly offer. It looked like she would find out soon enough. "I'll be there in fifteen minutes."

# CHAPTER TWENTY-EIGHT

**A**s Scanlin approached apartment 404, he heard the repetitive thump–thump–thump of generic dance music. He rapped the base of his fist against the front door to the beat, then heard the volume drop. A voice behind the door yelled, "Wrong apartment, man."

"Police. Just a couple quick questions, Mr. Roca."

Roca was tying his black silk robe when he opened the door. Scanlin was overpowered by the oaky smell of cologne.

"Sorry," Roca offered as he turned to primp his hair in a full-length mirror just inside the entrance. "Running late for a date. The smell fades fast. I swear."

Roca didn't seem interested, but Scanlin flashed his badge out of habit. A quick look around the studio apartment revealed more tasteful choices than Scanlin would have expected, given the first impression. Natural wood floors. White walls. Neutral furniture. What Melissa would have called "pops" of color from matching pillows and accessories. Had to be either a girlfriend's or a decorator's touch.

"You sure you're at the right place?" Roca asked. "Can't think of anything police would need here."

"It's an old case. Taking a new look. You remember Susan Hauptmann?"

Roca shook his head immediately, then paused as the name sank in. "Oh yeah. That's the girl from next door. What happened with that?"

Scanlin shrugged. "That's why I'm here. We never talked to you back then."

Roca laughed nervously. "You're kidding me, right? That was, like, eight years ago."

"Ten."

"Talk about taking your time." Roca walked to a double-wide closet and began flipping through a row of neatly hung dress shirts. "What do you need to know?"

"Did you know her?"

"No. I mean, by sight, yeah. Exchanged pleasantries in the hallway, that kind of thing. But I didn't even know her name until after everyone was looking for her."

"You were out of town when that happened."

Roca squinted, searching his memory. "That's right. Got sent to L.A. on a client project for over a month. When I got back, the posters were still up. That kind of thing."

"Susan was a pretty girl," Scanlin said. "*Really* pretty. Liked to date, from what I heard."

"Yeah, I'd see her come and go with guys. Girls, too. You know. Social, like that."

"How about you? She never came or went with you?"

"This has to be a joke. Seriously, is someone punking me?"

Scanlin took out his badge again so Roca could get a better look. "No joke. Just crossing all the T's. Making sure we didn't miss anything. Turns out one of your neighbors heard you arguing in here with a woman two nights before Susan disappeared. Sounded to her like domestic violence. Lo and behold, after Susan disappears, you up and leave for a month. Then there's that pesky arrest you had for assaulting a woman a few years ago."

"That girl was crazy. She found lipstick on some cigarette butts in my garbage and started trashing the place. I was trying to calm her down, and she called 911 on me. You can't think—"

"I'm just trying to make sure the lady you were fighting with two nights before your neighbor disappeared wasn't Susan Hauptmann. So why don't you give me a name, and I'll be on my way."

"It was ten years ago. I have no fucking clue."

"So *think*, Roca. And I'll make it easy for you. It was November twenty-seventh, on Thanksgiving."

"Dammit. Fine, okay. Um, wait. I was gone by then. Figured I was starting the L.A. gig December first, I might as well make it down to Santa Fe to see my folks for Turkey Day. I left the day before. Hold up. Who called the police about this supposed argument at my place?"

Scanlin didn't respond.

"Was it that crazy bird in 402? Had to be. Now she's nearly deaf, but yeah, she was still calling the cops constantly back then. She was always getting the apartments mixed up. Apparently directional hearing wasn't a real strength."

Scanlin gave closer thought to the layout of the small complex. Four apartments on one floor. Five floors total. Two voices fighting inside an apartment. The echo of the stairway running floor to ceiling through the center of the building like a fire pole. Thanking the man for his time, Scanlin left Roca to his primping and crossed the hallway to apartment 402.

**H**er neighbor had been right: Vera Hadley was nearly deaf. She was also a hoarder. What probably began as small stacks of magazines, newspapers, collectibles, videotapes, out-of-season clothing— just waiting for the right moment to be sorted through—had grown into layers of padding throughout the apartment. From what Scanlin could see, the poor woman had enough free space to navigate from the entrance, to one empty spot on her sofa, to the kitchen, and—God willing—to a bathroom.

They'd been making progress since Scanlin had given up any semblance of speaking in a normal voice and begun screaming into her hearing aid. Yes, she remembered Susan Hauptmann from down the hall (followed by a saddened *tsk* and a shake of the head). Yes, she remembered frequently calling the police over the years. Yes, she supposed it was possible that if an argument had erupted in that "nice woman's" apartment, she might have attributed it to the "carouser" across the hall.

When he gave her the date of the noise complaint and asked what she recalled about the incident, he expected either a blank stare or a long recitation of every dispute she'd ever overheard. What he did not expect was the woman to stand up from her cubbyhole on the couch and say, "Let me get my notes."

# CHAPTER TWENTY-NINE

"Too familiar. Recast." McKenna remembered her editor's comment, red-penciled in the margin of the manuscript for *Unreasonable Doubt*. The note was in response to McKenna's depiction of an FBI agent who appeared at the local police precinct to exercise federal jurisdiction over the investigation.

But McKenna had met a few FBI agents in her time at the district attorney's office, usually when the feds were cherry-picking her best drug cases, and they'd all been straitlaced, clean-cut, and rigid. They had deep voices, didn't laugh, and favored midpriced suits from places like JoS. A. Bank. Just because it was a stereotype didn't mean it wasn't true.

But Jamie Mercado didn't fit the mold. She was petite, with long, dark, wavy hair and a full face of makeup, complete with cherry-red lipstick. Like agents McKenna had worked with in the past, she wanted answers, but instead of resorting to legalese and bureaucratic officiousness, Mercado leaned across the table toward McKenna, raising her voice in obvious anger. These were moves McKenna associated more with the NYPD than the FBI, and she had experienced them only from the other side of one-way glass.

"For a full-time reporter with a reputable magazine, you don't seem to know much about a topic you're supposedly investigating.

Not the name of a single person associated with the group. No information about the organizational structure or geographic focus. Not the details of even *one* of their suspected anti-industry missions."

"I told you," McKenna said, "I just started looking into it."

She knew that any false statement to a federal agent—even outside a courtroom, whether she was under oath or not—was a felony. She was not required to offer information, and she could refuse to answer, but she had to ensure that every utterance from her mouth was true—at least technically.

"Yes, you've said that so many times, you're beginning to sound like a windup doll. So, fine. I went to college. I remember what it's like to write a paper. You think you have an idea, so you dig around a bit to see if you're interested, if there's enough material to merit a deeper search."

McKenna nodded in agreement. No falsity there.

The college Mercado was referring to would have been the University of Idaho. In a quick briefing from Jason Eberly, McKenna had learned that Mercado was a good and thorough agent who treated her hunt for ecoterrorists as a personal calling. With the resources of a large law firm and their corporate clients behind him, Jason had done some digging into Mercado's background to get a better sense of the woman who had been his bunny-blinding client's best ally against the protestors. After two years of full-time college, she took another four to graduate because she had to help raise her younger sister. Her father, a logger, went on disability after his chain saw hit a railroad spike that activists embedded in the trunk of a western red cedar in the Nez Perce National Forest.

"But from what I remember," Mercado continued, "you still have to get the idea from *somewhere*. A newspaper article. A comment made by a friend. A report on the radio. How did you come to hear about the P3s? They're one of the lesser known militant environmental activist groups."

"I don't always remember where ideas come from." Technically true.

"When you say you've just begun your research, what do you mean? What precisely have you done?"

McKenna could refuse to answer, but there was no privilege to avoid testifying if Mercado got a grand jury subpoena. And this was her opportunity to learn more about the P3s and why an FBI agent was so determined to talk about them.

"I'd be more comfortable sharing my work product if I knew you had a real need for it, Agent. My understanding is that the FBI is prohibited from engaging in general information gathering about political groups."

McKenna's lawyering skills weren't entirely rusty. The statement was perfect. An offer to cooperate. The reference to work product, suggesting she had something of value to offer. The not so veiled threat to expose the FBI's activities if they ran afoul of federal restrictions against domestic spying.

"You can rest assured that we don't gather intelligence against American citizens based on their exercise of First Amendment rights. Maybe if we did, I wouldn't need to question a private reporter for essential background information after a bomb comes close to wiping out an entire residential block."

McKenna felt the air leave her throat. She couldn't breathe. A *bomb*? When her mouth finally opened, she felt herself wanting to tell Mercado everything. The subway video. The P3 button on the backpack. McKenna's suspicion that the woman carrying the backpack was Susan Hauptmann. What had Susan gotten herself into? What had *she* gotten herself into?

Then she remembered all those interrogations she had watched from behind the one-way glass. Just as McKenna had chosen her words to convince Mercado to reveal her motivations, a good agent might say anything to test McKenna's resolve. How many times had she seen detectives lie to get a confession?

"What bomb?" she asked.

"An explosion in Brentwood—out near Islip—last night. We've managed to keep it quiet so far. The Long Island papers are calling it a suspected gas leak." Mercado pulled a photograph from a file folder and slid it across the table toward McKenna. The second level of the house was gone, replaced by shards of wood and drywall.

"The next-door neighbor's air-conditioning unit blew out of its casing. The expert tells me anyone within six feet of the epicenter would've evaporated into a 'pretty pink mist.' Those were his exact words—the kind of juicy tidbit you'd like for an article. It'll be a while before we can identify them or know the number of bodies."

McKenna had no way of verifying Mercado's story. Was the agent holding up her half of an information-exchange bargain, or laying on the details to give a lie more credibility?

"What about the neighbors?"

"Got lucky. We found some other bombing materials at the site, but those didn't ignite. Looks like the bad guys were building something and set it off accidentally. One of the surviving residents is a dumb little thing—barely drinking age, searching for an identity. Maybe thirty years ago she would've ended up with the Krishnas. Now she's a so-called 'environmental activist.' She shacked up with a group of older P3s. Denying any knowledge of the bombing materials, but . . ." She trailed off, as if everyone knew that denials were predictable, false, and temporary. "They had enough fertilizer to take out an entire warehouse when mixed with the right ingredients. We don't know the intended target, the date of the planned attack, or who else might be out there to complete the job. So I'm thinking that for a reporter who wants to do the right thing—a former prosecutor, to boot—that might be a good enough reason to answer a few questions."

McKenna slid her iPad from her bag. "You remember last weekend a woman pulled a teenager from the subway tracks at Times Square?"

Mercado nodded.

"A girl on the platform tried to get a cell video of it. The video's been deleted, but I managed to get this still shot of the woman's backpack."

"That's the P3 insignia," Mercado said.

"I didn't know that at first, but yes. I read a few articles online about the group and then went to Jason this morning to see if he could point me in the right direction."

"So you were just looking for the subway woman?" Mercado was clearly disappointed that McKenna didn't have a more ambitious research project in the works.

"That's all. I went to the kid who got rescued. I tried the MTA's security cameras. This was just one piece of a wild goose chase. If it makes you feel any better, I won't be writing about the bombing. Unless something goes down in the city, our magazine treats it like it didn't happen." McKenna didn't know the area well, but Brentwood was out in Suffolk County, forty-plus miles from Manhattan.

"And you still don't know who the woman with the backpack is?"

"No." The denial was legally permissible, since McKenna didn't *know* anything, but after the word came out, she wondered if she had done the right thing.

She could tell that Mercado believed her now. "When you were looking for your mystery girl, did any of these names come up?" The agent pushed another sheet of paper across the table.

McKenna didn't recognize any of the four names—three female, one male. "Who are they?"

Mercado heard the question but didn't answer.

"I told you, Agent, this isn't on my magazine's map. To be honest, most of what we print these days is what we call 'lifestyle.' What you'd probably call gossip. You won't see a story from me on the bombing."

"Doesn't mean I need to share my sandbox, though, does it? You mind showing yourself out?"

McKenna could tell there was no point in arguing. She wished the agent the best of luck with the investigation and made her way back to the reception area.

She knew from her time as a prosecutor that the federal building was closely monitored. Her descent in the elevator, her march through the lobby, her traipse to the next block would all be on screens for Mercado and her pals to view, if they were interested.

So McKenna gave them no reason to be interested. She did her best to appear calm. Indifferent, even. But mentally, she was repeating the four names Mercado had asked her about, over and over again, committing them to memory.

# CHAPTER THIRTY

**M**cKenna ducked into a deli two blocks from the Federal Building and quickly jotted down the names from Mercado's piece of paper. She had just finished scribbling when her cell phone rang. She recognized her editor's number.

"Hey, Bob. I'm just on my way in. I should be there in fifteen—"

"Where are you now?"

"Not far. Downtown. I'll be right—"

"Don't come in."

"You've got something for me?"

"No, I mean, we've got something of a shit sandwich here." He sounded strange. Panicked. Vance didn't panic. "Look, I can only say so much."

"Why, Bob? Are the aliens listening?"

"This isn't funny, McKenna." Usually Bob Vance could find anything funny, and he wasn't the one who'd spent the morning being grilled by an FBI agent. "I can't say much because the magazine's counsel doesn't want me to."

"Counsel like an attorney?"

"Attorneys. Multiple. There are—some issues."

"Issues?"

"Jesus, please stop repeating everything I say. These obviously aren't my usual word choices, all right? Our lawyers got an affidavit this morning from the state court's tech people. They inspected the primary e-mail database for the judicial system, and those Big Pig— The e-mails we ran in your piece about Judge Knight didn't come from his account."

"I don't understand. I thought he was a no-comment."

"Well, after he gave you a no-comment, he called a lawyer who was able to do what we couldn't. The judiciary keeps complete records of all e-mails sent through its systems. They checked the dates and times when Knight supposedly sent those messages, and there was nothing. And they did a text search for the content of the messages. Nothing."

"But why would someone—"

"It gets worse, McKenna."

"I published forged documents. I have New York State's court system saying I got a story wrong. I'm not sure how it can be worse, Bob."

"Knight's attorney used the affidavit from the court system to go to the free e-mail service that was used to forward you the supposed messages. They have IP addresses. That kind of junk."

"Okay. And?"

"Jesus, McKenna. If there's something you need to say, tell me now. I can still fight for you. If I'm in front of it, I can control the damage. I mean, did I push you too hard? Were you spread thin with the pressure to write a book?"

"Bob, I swear to God, I don't know what you're talking about."

"I can't believe I'm saying this. The IP address. The 3G connection or whatever used to access the anonymous e-mail account that sent you those messages about Knight? Your so-called anonymous source e-mailed you from your own iPad, McKenna."

"No. There's no way that's right. I'll take a lie detector right now, Bob. Tell them."

"It's ironclad. Your IP address. Your iPad."

"I'll find some tech geek to fix this. There's no way—"

"It's not going to be that simple. I was on the phone, weighing the options with counsel. I thought I could hold them at bay, but there's some serious shit going down here. I've got an FBI agent searching your office right now, McKenna. They're saying that opening an account like that to forge e-mails could amount to a felony—"

"Wait, Bob. Who's saying that? Is it an Agent Mercado? Female? Dark hair?" Mercado would have to be Wonder Woman to have gotten to the magazine with a warrant already. She must have applied for it the second she got the call from Jason Eberly.

"No, the agent's a man, and he's not saying a word. It's the lawyers who are calling the shots."

"Listen to me, Bob. The FBI thing has nothing to do with Knight. It's a story I was working on about environmental terrorism. There was a bombing or something late last night." As she tried to tell him about her call to an old friend who was an environmental lawyer, and the road to her interrogation with Mercado, she realized how crazy it all sounded. So much for Mercado pretending to believe McKenna when she said she didn't have any information.

"There's nothing I can do, McKenna. The lawyers are going into bunker mode in case Knight sues. They were saying it was worse than Jayson Blair and Stephen Glass." Given the kind of fluff work the magazine had steered her toward, she never would have expected to be compared to two of journalism's most infamous liars.

"So what are you saying?"

"You're terminated immediately until further notification. Your entry card into the offices has been deactivated. Your press credentials are revoked. Your log-in to our databases will no longer work."

"Bob, my work. My e-mails. All of my data—"

"I'm sorry, McKenna."

She could tell that he was, in fact, sorry, but it was the kind of regret that came from trusting a person only to be disappointed. Bob Vance didn't believe her.

# CHAPTER THIRTY-ONE

Everyone was a liar.

Carter had no shortage of examples. The Bible-belting, Jesus-loving politicians who got caught with hookers and rent-a-boys. The fat housewives who swore they kept a reasonable diet and a regular exercise regimen but breezed through the McDonald's drive-through three times a week when no one was looking. The spoiled trust-fund kids who held themselves out as writers and artists and "entrepreneurs."

Most people didn't really mean to lie. But the story they told themselves and the world was a better version of the truth. It was as if they implicitly measured themselves against a bell curve of human behavior created in their own minds. By imagining others as worse, everyone could say they were above average.

As a result, Carter knew that what people believed to be true about themselves was rarely the absolute truth. It was the relative truth. Carter's own identity—these days, at least—was very much about the tricks he had learned in the positions to which he'd been trusted. Tricks like explosives.

Carter thought of himself as one of the best in his line of business. He certainly knew more than the average bear. He was smart. He was ambitious. He was willing to sell his skills to the highest bidder.

The actual skills? His talent was understanding people. Including the people who had started hiring him once he realized there was money to be made on the skills he had acquired. But when it came to his knowledge of explosives, he may have exaggerated. Sure, he knew more than the average person, but the average person could barely light a match. And he hadn't set up explosives since 2007.

He had moved to the Marriott after one night at the Four Seasons. The Marriott sucked, but it could be counted on to forget its guests. Given the change in mission, he needed to be forgettable.

Now he was sitting at the built-in desk in the corner of his room, with those stupid outlets at the base of the lamp that never worked. He was checking the tracker on his laptop again, hoping to get an update on the woman's location. Nothing.

He checked the news reports again, too. The explosion had definitely taken place. Two women were in custody. No reports about the other two occupants, in particular the one he was interested in.

He shouldn't have driven away. He should have waited nearby. Watched the explosion. Made sure no one walked out alive.

But any decent emergency response to a bombing would have been quick and overwhelming. And if he'd gotten stopped? Toast.

The time estimates varied by news report. Ten-thirty P.M.? Ten-forty? Eleven?

He hadn't made the explosion big enough. He'd wanted to make sure the investigators found evidence that the people who lived there had been stockpiling bomb materials—that they were the ones who had done this.

She must have seen the detonator. She could have leaped from a window at the last minute and escaped the blast.

All he knew for sure was that her phone somehow made it out of that house. The woman—Carter didn't know her real name, so he just called her "the woman"—didn't know it, but his client had installed a GPS tracker in her phone.

Carter knew he had a problem when the woman's phone moved from the house, down the block, to the left, and then to the right. It was a route toward the Long Island Expressway, 1.6 miles. It took about ten minutes. She was probably running. Fast. And then she stopped. And then she turned off the phone. Twenty-two seconds later, she realized that killing the power wasn't good enough.

The tracker went dead. Maybe she threw the phone under the tire of an eighteen-wheeler. Or pulled out the SIM card and lit it on fire. Whatever, the tracker was now dead.

The woman wasn't. She was alive. And she knew she was being hunted.

This had gone very, very wrong.

Carter set aside any inch of doubt he had allowed to creep in and replaced it with the confidence that had come with fifteen years of work, training, and specialization. There was a reason he had his job.

Because he was an expert, he knew that the tracker in the woman's phone had been put there by his client, which meant his client would be monitoring it, which meant his client would know what Carter knew.

He called the special number.

"We have a problem," he said. "She's alive."

# PART III

You stepped out of a stranger.
—Kate Bush

# CHAPTER THIRTY-TWO

**T**hough she'd admit it only to her closest friends, McKenna had a Google Alert. A million years ago, when "Google" still sounded like a masturbation euphemism, McKenna was publishing a debut novel. In awe of the fact that newspapers, magazines, and trade reviews would weigh in on the value of her wee little book, she had set up the ongoing search service. Every time her name appeared on the Interwebs, she got an alert.

Today the Google Alert was going wild. If only her novel had brought so much buzz. Since *New York City* magazine had posted its retraction of the Knight story, her name had gone viral. Print media. TV. Blogs. Twitter. It was a weird feeling to be sitting at her familiar spot on the living room sofa, knowing at only the most abstract level that her name was rapidly becoming a part of the zeitgeist outside the bubble of her home. The first telephone call was from the literary agent who had been so damn hot to see a book proposal about the Marcus Jones shooting. *Needless to say, the timing's probably not great right now. If anything changes, I'll be sure to give you a call. But until then— Well, I wish you all the best.*

No bueno.

She finally closed her e-mail to avoid the incoming Alerts. She was interested in an entirely different news story. Word of the ex-

plosion in Brentwood had gotten out, as Agent Mercado had predicted. Although details were fuzzy, multiple media outlets were
reporting that the FBI had two people in custody on suspicion for
possession of weapons of mass destruction.

When her cell phone rang, she was tempted to ignore it but
checked the screen to see if she recognized the caller. Patrick. She
had tried to sound cool when she left a message earlier, but he had
probably heard about her firing.

"Hey," she said.

"So it's true?" They'd been together long enough that apparently
"hey" could say everything.

"How much have you heard?" she asked.

"Someone burned you on the Knight e-mails, and the magazine's
throwing you under the bus."

"That's— Well, no. It's worse. It started when I went to see Jason
Eberly this morning—"

"Your secret boyfriend?"

He was trying to cheer her up, but he had no idea how much her
world had changed today. That was her fault. She hadn't even been
honest with him about her reason for contacting Jason. "He called
an FBI agent for background information about that environmental
group." She didn't bother to say "the group I thought Susan might
be part of." She knew his thoughts on the issue. "The next thing I
know, the agent was hauling me in for questioning because they're
a bunch of ecoterrorists. There was an explosion at a house where
they were storing bomb materials. Then the FBI showed up at my
office with a search warrant, right when Knight was bringing down
the hammer on those e-mails. Plus, the magazine is saying there's
evidence that I was the one who fabricated the e-mails. Bob actually
asked me if I was under too much pressure. They think I'm going
crazy."

"I'm coming home."

"Are you sure?"

"Of course. I'll be right there. I know it's bad, McKenna, but
everything's going to be okay. I promise. We're going to be fine."

Those words brought more comfort than McKenna ever could have predicted. She found herself watching the clock on her computer, counting down the minutes she had to sit here alone. She needed someone with her right now. Not any someone—Patrick.

She finally forced herself to pull her attention back to the real world. *The New York Times* seemed to have the most detailed coverage about last night's explosion. McKenna recognized the names of the two women in custody—Carolyn Maroney and Andrea Sanderson—from the list that Agent Mercado had shown her.

That left only two more names, one male and one female. She typed the man's name, Greg Larson, into Google, but the search brought up too many results to be helpful. She narrowed it down to "Greg Larson and People for the Preservation of the Planet." She found a few hits quoting Larson at various environmental protests. According to several reports, he was the de facto leader, even though the group eschewed any hierarchical structure.

The remaining female name on Mercado's list of names, Pamela Morris, also proved too common to be of use. Even when McKenna coupled it with the environmental movement, she found nothing.

She called a homicide detective she knew at the Thirteenth Precinct. Female. Youngish. Most important, Detective Forbus owed her a favor for running a story three months ago about a gang killing that no one cared about until it consumed four full pages of a widely circulated magazine.

Forbus picked up on the second ring. "Forbus."

Though McKenna started in with introductions, but Forbus remembered from the earlier case. "Tough break about the magazine," Forbus offered. "If it helps any, everything you said about Knight is a hundred percent accurate. If he didn't write those e-mails, I guarantee you he thought every last word."

"Put it this way," McKenna said. "If you framed a guilty man, would his guilt really matter?"

"Nope, but like I said: *if* it helps."

"What would help is a search. Greg Larson. Forty-six years old.

Has at least one arrest, for criminal trespass at Oregon Health and Science University in Portland in 2007."

"Yep, got him. And that's one of many. All misdemeanors—petty stuff. Trespassing. Vandalism. Public disorder. Disobeying the order of a police officer. Oregon. California. Arizona. Montana. Illinois. D.C. D.C. D.C. D.C. Texas. D.C. Busy guy."

If Larson was running the movement and had been willing to face arrest so many times for his beliefs, he was unlikely to divulge any information. McKenna had to hope that the last person on Mercado's list might know something—and had lived. "One more name?" she asked. "Pamela Morris."

"And?"

"That's all I've got."

"Date of birth? State? Something?"

"Nothing." She thought about the age ranges of the other residents in the house. The youngest was Carolyn Maroney, twenty-two. Greg Larson was the oldest. "Between twenty and fifty," she offered. "And probably in New York, at least until recently."

"Very helpful," Forbus deadpanned. McKenna waited as she heard fingertips against a keyboard. "Yeah, what I thought. I've got fourteen driver's licenses in New York alone. And just to be clear, this counts as a favor—an actual call-it-even favor, whether it helps you out or not."

"Fine. Um, narrow it down to criminal histories."

More typing. "Yeah, okay. Down to one, but it's way back. Pamela Morris. Thirty-nine years old. Two prostitution pops in the late nineties. Nothing since. Maybe got out of the life. Happens sometimes, even outside of Hollywood fairy tales."

"Can you run her with the date of birth in the general databases? See what you find?"

"Look at you, little Miss Jessica Fletcher." More typing. "Yep, I got her. Huh."

Huh? *Huh* was usually bad.

"'Huh'?"

"Well, it could be anything. But your girl's very low-radar. No driver's licenses. No car registrations. No NCIC hits." Meaning no involvement with law enforcement. "Very minimal. Like, off the grid."

"Does she have contacts in the area?" Pamela Morris might be able to confirm that Susan Hauptmann was the woman from the subway platform.

"All right. Let me see." More typing. "I've got a mom here. Arresting officer called her after one of the two prostitution busts. Loretta Morris." She rattled off an address in Jersey City. More typing. "From what I can tell, the mom's still at the same address. That's all I've got, Jordan."

"What about a booking photo on the prostitution pop?"

"*Pop*. Listen to you with the cop talk." More typing. "Looks like she was cited and released on her first arrest, but yeah, she got booked on the second *pop*. I'll shoot it over to you. E-mail okay?"

"I'll take it." McKenna started to recite her work address out of habit, then caught herself and provided her Gmail account instead.

"I'll make a note of it. And best of luck. Because if you ask me? Whoever Pamela Morris is, she doesn't want to be found."

# CHAPTER THIRTY-THREE

**S**canlin wasn't usually the type to cheer on members of the judiciary. Judges sat behind their benches, literally elevated above the courtroom and clothed in antiquated garb to remind the world of their superiority. Yet they knew nothing about the real world affected by their rulings. (Even the word played into the myth of judicial superiority, as if they actually "ruled" over others.) How many times had Scanlin seen routine consent searches bounced, all because some lefty judge who had never been north of Eighty-sixth Street believed that no one who was carrying would be stupid enough to let a cop check his pockets? Judges were glorified lawyers who didn't know the unwritten rules of the streets. Even the judges who tended to rule for the state—judges like Frederick Knight—did it more for political popularity or disdain of criminal defendants than respect for police work.

But what was that saying about the enemy of my enemy being a friend? The maxim must hold water because, on this particular day, Scanlin found himself hoping that Frederick Knight was out there somewhere, treating his gluttonous self to all the fried eggs and bacon in lower Manhattan.

Just that morning, *New York City* magazine had issued a retraction of a hatchet job they'd run against Knight the previous day.

The language on the website was formal but apologetic, explaining that the contemptuous e-mails supposedly authored by Knight were apparently fabricated; offering sincere regrets about the story; and promising a thorough investigation and complete transparency as additional information was gathered. Scanlin's favorite line was the final one: New York City *magazine has terminated its relationship with the author of the article, McKenna Jordan.*

In the cutthroat world of New York City media, the circling sharks smelled fresh, oozing blood. Several other media outlets— the *Daily News, New York* magazine, Gawker, Mediabistro—were comparing the emerging story to other journalistic scandals, but it was the *New York Post* that went furthest, not only digging in a knife but giving the blade a vengeful twist.

*Although* NYC *magazine promises its readers a thorough investigation into the events that led to the fabricated article, critics will argue that the scandal should be anything but a surprise. The reporter in question, McKenna Jordan, née Wright, made headlines a decade ago as an assistant district attorney. Wright was the junior prosecutor who went to the press with evidence that she claimed would prove that a twelve-year police veteran's shooting of nineteen-year-old felon Marcus Jones was not justified. Her allegation poured fuel on a fire simmering between civil rights activists and supporters of the NYPD. She resigned from the district attorney's office when an investigation revealed further evidence to back the officer's self-defense claim. She subsequently published a novel that was a thinly veiled depiction of her former life as a prosecutor. And the reporter who ran with her claims all those years ago? His name was Bob Vance. That's right: the same Bob Vance who now sits as editor in chief at* New York City *magazine.*

Scanlin wondered if the demise of McKenna Wright Jordan would provide any kind of karmic justice to his old friend Scott Macklin.

Scanlin couldn't remember the last time he'd seen Macklin. It must have been about six years ago, after Mac heard that Melissa finally had to go to the home. He stopped by with a casserole from his own wife. Scanlin didn't mention that he already had a freezer full of Pyrex dishes. Apparently Scanlin was going to be treated as the neighborhood widower, even though Melissa was very much alive—at least to him back then.

Even six years ago, Mac's decline was obvious. It had been fast. If anything, age had taken hold of him even faster than it had Scanlin. Before, when Mac announced that he was marrying Josefina, he was like Benjamin Button, aging backward, whistling like a giddy newlywed. He insisted that life with Josefina's young son, whom he treated as his own, only made him feel younger. The guys who sported bags under their eyes from trying to keep up with their own growing broods begged to differ, but no one begrudged Mac his happiness. How could you carry one ill thought about a man who'd do anything in the world for his family and the fellow officers he treated as such?

But then Marcus Jones pulled a gun, and Mac became the white cop who killed a black teenager. Throw in the reckless, grandstanding antics of McKenna Wright, and Mac's miraculous reverse aging reversed itself again and then some. By the time Mac came to see Scanlin with the casserole, he just seemed old and sad.

Now Scanlin opened the second drawer on his desk and pulled out a Rolodex that had been made obsolete by electronic databases. Miscellaneous business cards were stuffed randomly among the yellowing notes. He skipped to the tab marked M and flipped through the entries. MAC. It was the only name the man needed.

Josefina picked up the phone. She sounded distracted but happy. Harried but not annoyed, like maybe she was balancing the phone between her cheek and shoulder while unloading a bag of groceries. He wished Melissa were still around to answer their phone that way a busy woman does. Before the diagnosis, Melissa had gotten crabby, snapping at the mildest irritation. He chose to think it was the dementia setting in and not the changes between them, but there was no real way to know.

Mac wasn't home. His wife asked if she could take a message.

"I was hoping to talk to him. To, I don't know . . . catch up."

"He's helping Tommy move a mini-fridge into his dorm room. He should be back in an hour or so."

"That little rug rat's off to college already?"

"Freshman at Hofstra. He wants to be called Thomas now, but I can't help it. Mama's always going to call him Tommy."

"I'll give Mac a call later, then. I don't know if this is a touchy subject, but it's about that prosecutor who tried to jam Scott up back when—you know, when he was still on the job."

Her end of the line went silent. He pictured her freeze, momentarily distracted from the groceries. Her voice was lower when she spoke. "I don't know who you're talking about. Scott— You know how a man is. He shielded us from the details. We don't like talking about that."

Scanlin regretted mentioning it. He should have ended with the polite chitchat and a routine message. "Sure, I totally understand. Trust me, this is a good thing. Karma's biting the ass of someone who deserves it big-time." He felt uncomfortable about using profanity with her. "I'll let you get back to what you were doing. I'll give Mac a call later."

He hit the print key on the *New York Post*'s delicious massacre of the reporter and former prosecutor in question. He'd bring it to Mac in person. It was even better than a casserole.

# CHAPTER
# THIRTY-FOUR

**M**aybe if Patrick had come home at that moment—right when McKenna ended the call with Detective Forbus—everything would have been different. But that wasn't what happened. She was left there in the apartment, alone with her thoughts.

And when McKenna was alone with nothing but time and energy, she had to stay busy. She stayed busy by opening the box that had arrived via messenger, courtesy of Adam Bayne, while she was talking to Agent Mercado that morning. According to what Adam had told Patrick, George Hauptmann had one box in storage marked SUSAN. Adam could never bring himself to dispose of it.

The box was small. If Susan's father were alive, McKenna could ask him why he had chosen to keep these six cubic feet of his daughter's belongings. Photographs, school merit certificates, the West Point degree—those items made sense. But as McKenna unpacked the box, she also found a commemorative plate from the Mount Vernon estate, a wine opener from Napa Valley, and a pink plastic Slinky. Were these items from special moments they had shared together? Or had the best intentions to preserve treasured memories collided with the last-minute realities of packing up an apartment?

McKenna set aside the bulkier items and made a stack of photographs—some framed, some bound in albums, many thrown haphazardly into the box. Flipping through the completed pile provided an escape, a reprieve from reality, while she waited. Waited for what, she didn't know. For Patrick to come home and make her feel better? For someone to realize that the Knight e-mails were legit? For the mysterious subway woman to emerge, bearing only a superficial resemblance to Susan Hauptmann? For the FBI somehow to *un*search her office? There wasn't always an end point to waiting.

She almost missed the picture. So many of them were of people she'd never seen. Or they were old, old, old pictures of the Hauptmanns—George, Carol, Gretchen, and Susan, looking like any other 1970s family in polyester shirts and flared pants. But McKenna paid slightly more attention to the pictures from the college years. West Point. Those beautiful, rolling hills next to the Hudson. The tanned, hard-bodied, buzz-cut men in tank tops and shorts, arms around shoulders, wrestling, tackling each other to the ground. How many times had she teased Patrick that the U.S. Military Academy was the gayest place on earth?

Of course, the entire campus wasn't all young men. Some of the cadets were tanned, hard-bodied young women. Women like Susan, far outnumbered by her male colleagues.

It shouldn't have bothered her. The photograph was taken twenty years ago. But the look on Patrick's face. The smile. The twinkle in the eyes. The joy. She loved seeing that look, which she had always thought was reserved exclusively for her.

The way his hands rested so comfortably on Susan's stomach as he hugged her from behind. Susan's lips on his neck. McKenna's mind filled with other images of the two of them together. Laughing. Kissing. Removing clothes. Her own intimate memories of her husband, but with Susan.

Those weren't the only thoughts pulling at her. From the minute she had shown him the video of the woman on the subway, Patrick had been steering her away from looking into Susan's death. He had insisted that the woman didn't look like Susan, even though the resemblance was so clear.

She felt her fingers shake as she scrolled through her contacts list, searching for Adam Bayne's phone number.

He sounded cheerful when he answered. "McKenna, I'm so glad you called. I wanted to make sure that you got the box we sent over. I'm not sure what you were looking for, but that's all the General kept from Susan's things."

"Yes, it's here. Thanks for sending it."

"Look, McKenna. I—I heard about your situation with the magazine." She wondered whether there was anyone in America who hadn't. "Our firm has investigators, computer experts, that kind of thing. Let me know if we can do anything to help."

From what McKenna gathered, it was no surprise that Susan's father had invited Adam to work for him. Adam had been a West Point "Star Man," a cadet entitled to wear a small star on his uniform collar, signaling his place in the top five percent of his class. Other cadets called them "star geeks" on the assumption that all they did was study, but Adam's skills went beyond book smarts. He was fearless and decisive, traits that would later serve him well in the Special Forces.

General Hauptmann's contracting firm had never lived up to the man's goals, but Adam had managed to land on his feet. After winding down the General's active work in the Middle East, Adam returned to New York to launch his own private security firm. Adam's clients tended to be sports teams, celebrities, and other "high-value" clientele.

"Thanks, Adam. I appreciate it. I actually have a question for you. And I feel kind of weird asking it, but were Susan and Patrick ever . . . together? I found a picture of them—"

"I thought you were trying to write about what happened to Susan. I'm not sure how old flirtations could have anything to do with that."

"So they were a couple?" McKenna tried to block out the mental images.

"If you can even call it that. I guess I assumed you knew. I mean, *I* certainly knew."

"No, I didn't. I thought she was with you in college."

"She was. Mostly. But we were on and off. We were young. You know how it is. Didn't you and Patrick go through the same thing? Sometimes being together isn't as clean as we'd like to think. Things worked out for you guys. Not that it's my place to give advice—we don't know each other well, and God knows it took me long enough to settle down—but it's never helpful to start thinking about your spouse's exes. Isn't that the whole point of being married? You're there for each other from that point on, and the past doesn't matter."

"I was with Patrick for *five years* before we got married. Were they together even after he met me?" She thought about the weeks that would go by when they were taking a break. How stupid she felt sitting at home, wondering whether he would call. Wondering whether she should call. Where had Susan been all of those nights? She remembered Gretchen's comment to Patrick at her house: *Don't even get me started on you.*

Adam sighed loudly. "Look, McKenna. You know how Susan was. I loved her, but she had problems, and needing the attention of men was one of them. It was a big part of the reason it didn't work out for us. She couldn't be with one guy, so yeah, sometimes she was with Patrick. She was with a lot of guys we knew. But it was never serious. It was just— Well, you know."

"If the sex didn't matter, how come neither of them ever told me?"

"I should've gone through that stupid box myself before sending it over. No offense, McKenna, but if you ask me, you've got bigger things to be thinking about right now. Again, let me know if we can do anything to help. You take care, okay?"

# CHAPTER THIRTY-FIVE

**M**cKenna had heard the sympathy in Adam's voice before he'd hung up. She could imagine him thinking, Poor thing. Poor, pathetic thing.

She was pathetic, sitting here alone on the living room floor, frantically sorting through old photographs, wondering how long Patrick's relationship with Susan had lasted. How happy they had been together. What trips they may have taken.

She looked at the clock. She had time for a quick walk before Patrick got home. She needed to clear her head before she saw him.

She headed up toward Madison Square Park. This stretch of Broadway, between Fourteenth and Twenty-third, once was so congested that you literally had to press yourself sideways against adjacent buildings to pass another person on the sidewalk. A few years ago, the city had closed most of the street to car traffic, forming a pedestrian walkway complete with tables and umbrellas for shade. It was all part of the ongoing campaign to make the city more *livable*.

Her mother always said to her, "I love visiting you, but how long are you going to continue *living* there? The crowds and the honking. All that noise. It's so *stressful*." But Manhattan's packed sidewalks had always been a kind of comfort to McKenna. Losing herself in a crowd allowed her thoughts to roam free. Some of her best ideas—whether for a closing argument, her novel, or story concepts—came when she meandered anonymously among the thousands of other tiny specks of humanity occupying this little island.

She still felt shamed by Adam's admonishment. He was right, of course. Everyone had a past. She certainly hadn't been a virgin when she met Patrick. When they started dating, she began the whole "what's your history" conversation. When she asked about his last girlfriend (first name Ally, last name unknown), he described her as "a big-boned girl. Not in a strong way, either. Soft. Smushy, if you will. With red frizzy hair. Lots of brown freckles. Moles, too. Big ones, on her nose and chin. Not the brightest bulb. And a voice like a horse. A real doll."

Point made. There was nothing to be gained by hearing details about former lovers. No one else mattered once they met each other.

At the time, it had seemed like such a sweet and simple solution to avoiding petty jealousies. Now McKenna wondered if, at some level, he had been avoiding the truth about his past (present?) with Susan. But why did any of it matter? Like Adam said, she had bigger problems to deal with.

Yet there was a reason the picture of Patrick and Susan had shaken her. If he and Susan had been that close, they could still be in contact. He may have known this entire time that Susan was out there. He could be making sure that McKenna didn't search for Susan—or publish the subway video.

He had seen her log in to Dana's Skybox account, which meant he could have signed in to wipe it out. Once she thought of that possibility, she realized he also had access to her iPad, which meant he could have been the one to send the forged e-mails about Judge Knight. Without the video, no one would believe she'd seen a woman who'd been missing for ten years, and the Knight e-mails had put the nail in her credibility's coffin.

Okay, she was seriously losing it. If she said any of that out loud, the listener really would call the nice men with the butterfly nets and a white van.

She was at the park now. She smiled as she looked at the long, winding Shake Shack line, extending from the hamburger stand, across the south side of the park, and turning north toward the dog run. If Patrick were here, he'd have something funny to say about New Yorkers being like cattle, standing in lines only because they existed. Two summers ago, he had nearly thrown a woman out of the five-hour line for the Alexander McQueen exhibit when, two hours in, she said, "Wait. You mean it's dresses?"

She gave herself a mental pep talk before heading home. She liked to say she'd been with Patrick for ten years, but becoming a couple was never as clean as you liked to remember. They were different people ten years ago. Neither was ready to do the work that came with a real relationship. They took breaks. A lot of them. She spent nights with other men. He was with other women, and Susan might have been one of them. It didn't matter.

But that picture had taught McKenna one thing: she didn't know Susan very well. They were friends. They drank together. Giggled. Partied. Commiserated over their jobs. She'd known Susan had no problem with one-night stands or "no commitment" hookups, but Susan had always given McKenna the impression that her relationship with Adam was stable and monogamous before they broke it off. Similarly, McKenna had known about Gretchen's drug problem, but Susan never told her about Gretchen's arrest, even though McKenna was a prosecutor when it happened. What other information had Susan been keeping to herself?

Then it dawned on McKenna that she might not be in this mess if she hadn't been playing so close to the vest herself. She should have posted the subway video to the Internet immediately, asking people to identify the mystery woman. She should have told Scanlin, Vance, and Gretchen about the sighting. Even that morning, she should have told Mercado about the link between Susan and the P3s.

Instead, she had held back. And where had all the secrecy gotten her?

It was time to try a different route.

She pulled out her iPad and opened her Twitter app. She typed as quickly as she could before she lost the nerve:

> Contact me w/ ANY info about disappearance of Susan Hauptmann ('03). There's a connection b/w past & present. Help me find it.

She ended with an embedded link to her e-mail address. Thanks to her active efforts, nearly ten thousand people followed her personal Twitter account. Still, the odds of one of them knowing anything helpful about Susan were minuscule. She needed an even bigger audience. Then she realized she probably had one.

She switched accounts and logged in to the official *New York City* magazine feed. She watched as the little thinking wheel at the top of her iPad turned, a sign that it was processing the request.

She was in. They hadn't thought to change the password.

> NYCM changed its locks but not Twitter password. Please RT any & all of my messages before they delete & change PW.
> —McKenna Jordan (fired)

She included a link to her e-mail account, hit send, and began typing a second message.

> NYCM not telling full story. Help me do it. Contact me w/ ANY info about disappearance of Susan Hauptmann ('03). RT b4 they delete! McK J

In the abbreviated world of Twitter, with its 140-character limitation, she had asked her fellow Twitter users to "retweet," or repeat her message to their own followers, before the magazine could delete it. She wished she could be a fly on the wall when Bob Vance gave the magazine's lawyers the news.

She made her way back down Broadway, feeling confident that she had her head on straight. She didn't know why someone had gone to such lengths to erase the subway video. She didn't know how the video was connected to this morning's explosion on Long Island. And she was still unemployed and disgraced, thanks to someone's efforts to make sure she looked like a total loon.

But at least she was doing something about it. She wouldn't stop until she answered every last question. And Patrick would help her.

She was about to slip her key in the front door when she heard Patrick's voice inside. He'd beat her home.

Maybe the internal pep talk to quell the paranoid voices hadn't worked after all, because she didn't insert the key. She paused. She paused to eavesdrop on her own husband in their own home.

"I don't know where she is," Patrick was saying inside the apartment. "I told her I was coming home."

Silence.

"I'm about to call her. I just walked in. She's not here. Her purse is gone."

Silence.

"I *know* it could be nothing. But she's got a bunch of your old stuff scattered all over our living room floor. Is there something in here that could be an issue?"

Silence.

"Fine. I'll let you know when I find her. But don't worry. I have it under control. Problem solved. Just take care of yourself."

Silence. Silence. Silence.

# CHAPTER THIRTY-SIX

**M**cKenna was frozen in the hallway, the apartment key hovering one inch from the lock.

She had to get out of here. She took the stairs one floor down, to be sure Patrick wouldn't hear the elevator ding on their floor, and then she headed straight to the Union Square subway station to lose herself in the nearest crowd available.

*I have it under control. Problem solved.*

There was only one person who could have been on the other end of that phone call. Those paranoid voices were making more sense.

*I have it under control.*

She made her way into a pack of subway commuters standing just inside the turnstiles to watch a guy playing an electric violin on the makeshift staging area at the southwest corner of the station. McKenna had seen the performer before. He favored recognizable rock anthems, punctuating the high notes with eccentric moves like side squats and karate kicks. She knew he'd draw a large enough crowd to keep her concealed. She also knew she could get a phone signal this close to the station entrance.

She checked Twitter. Her blasts were working. The magazine had deleted her posts from its official feed, but there had to be nearly a hundred retweets already. Those people's friends would continue the pattern, and then theirs, and so on. She also had eight hundred new followers to her personal account. If the trend continued, she'd have a healthy platform to communicate directly to the public as more information came in.

She checked her e-mail next, in case any tips had come in. There was a message from Detective Forbus. The attachment was a booking photo for Pamela Morris from a prostitution arrest in 1998. Morris would have been twenty-four at the time but looked at least thirty. Three inches of roots revealed her to be a natural brunette, but the rest of her hair was bleached and processed to the texture of straw. Her face was simultaneously drawn and sagging. Although she'd clearly tried to put on a tough face for the camera, black smears around her red eyes revealed that she'd been crying. It looked like she was recovering from a fat lip.

That was fifteen years ago. No arrests since, but that morning an FBI agent had mentioned her name in the context of a weapons explosion at the suspected site of domestic terrorists. McKenna reminded herself that she had no way of knowing whether this Pamela Morris was the same Pamela Morris.

This particular Pamela Morris had been—in Forbus's words—keeping a low profile. Plus, Mercado had said that the college student who owned the house had been shacking up with a group of "older" P3s, and this Pamela Morris was closer to Greg Larson's age than to a college student's.

McKenna's cell phone rang. It was the home number. She almost answered it. Maybe Patrick would have an explanation.

But she knew what she'd heard. And now she was hearing those voices in her head again. The picture of him with Susan. All his attempts to talk her out of looking into her disappearance. The afternoon when he left work early but denied it later. The worst-case scenarios.

She waited for the voice-mail alert to flash on her phone and then checked the message. "Hey, babe. I got home as fast as I could, but now you're not here. Let me know where you are, okay? We'll figure this out. Try not to worry."

How could his voice sound so different than it had a few minutes earlier? When she'd heard him inside their apartment, his voice had been crisp. Stern. The way people sounded when they were alarmed or angry or frantic but struggling to maintain control. His military voice.

And now? When he called her? *Hey, babe.* Like, Hey, let's go grab some enchiladas and margaritas and make everything better. Even the tone of his voice was a lie.

She thought about calling Adam Bayne. He did private security. He had offered to help.

But he already thought she was nuts for asking about Patrick's past with Susan. If she started talking about erased Skybox accounts and forged e-mails from her iPad, he'd think she was certifiable. And he'd known Patrick a hell of a lot longer than he'd known her.

She was on her own.

# CHAPTER THIRTY-SEVEN

The address McKenna had gotten from Detective Forbus for Pamela Morris's mother turned out to be a brick duplex south of downtown Jersey City. Two symmetrical halves. Fifty-fifty odds.

The east side of the porch was adorned with an array of well-maintained potted plants. A plaster frog sat next to a teak rocking chair. The welcome mat read, HI. I'M MAT. The west side of the porch was . . . a porch.

McKenna was looking for the mother of a middle-aged former prostitute. She played the odds and rang the west bell.

The woman who came to the door fit the role. Probably only in her mid-sixties, but hard years. She wore sweatpants and a New York Jets T-shirt and smelled like an ashtray. Despite the age difference, she bore a strong resemblance to Pamela Morris's booking photograph. Pale eyes and thick eyelids. Wide bridge of the nose.

The look she gave McKenna made her feel like she was supposed to give the woman something.

"I'm looking for Loretta Morris," McKenna said.

"You can stop looking, because I'm right here."

"My name is McKenna Jordan. I'm trying to find an old friend of mine, and I think she might be connected to your daughter, Pamela. I'm afraid it's a bit of a long story, ma'am."

"I've got nothing if not time, and you look harmless enough." She stepped aside to usher McKenna in.

The house was dated and cluttered but otherwise well maintained. Linoleum entranceway. Fake brick fireplace. Brown carpet in the living room. Probably typical of the homes built in the neighborhood in the 1970s.

Loretta let out a small groan as she lowered herself to the sofa. McKenna took a seat next to her. "Is there any way I can get in touch with your daughter? That might be the easiest way to find my friend."

"Is your friend in Pamela's church?"

McKenna couldn't imagine trying to explain: *Well, you see, I think I saw my long-lost friend, but the only lead I have is a button for a batshit-crazy environmental group that blew up its own house this morning. And someone named Pamela Morris—who may or may not be the same Pamela Morris as your daughter—had something to do with that bombing. But now the house is blown to bits, and the people inside—including maybe your daughter and maybe my friend—are now pink vapor.*

Instead, she lied. "My friend is missing, and I'm trying to find her. She told me she was doing some kind of work with a woman named Pamela Morris. It might not be your daughter, but I figured if I find every Pamela Morris in the area, I'll eventually find the one who knew my friend."

"Sounds sensible enough, but my Pamela's not in the area."

"Is that right?" Her one lead was fizzling out.

"She travels. Found herself a nice man some years ago. He's a preacher. They're sort of like missionaries, I guess—going around the country, converting people or whatever. I was never much for religion, but I guess it works for them."

If Pamela were tied up with the head of the P3s, she could have sugarcoated it for her mother. In the fictional version of Pamela's life, the lead organizer for an ecoterrorist group became a preacher. Attacks on research laboratories and oil refineries became missionary work. Protests became proselytizing. "Do you know where she is now? It would be helpful to contact her."

"No. We don't check in day-to-day. She mostly sends me Christmas cards. Mother's Day. Just to let me know she's doing all right."

"Maybe I can give her a call?"

Loretta shook her head, as if realizing that a mother should have her daughter's telephone number. "I've never been much for the phone." She waved a hand for emphasis.

"I see. The Pamela Morris I'm looking for had a couple of police interactions back in the nineties. For—" She struggled for a euphemism. "For being a lady of the evening." She cringed at the sound of it.

Loretta's gaze moved to the fake brick fireplace. "That was a long time ago. Pamela's doing better now. Turned her entire life around. This area was a bad influence on her. When she left, everything changed. Has a man. Has her church. No more police. No more— lady of the evening." She returned her gaze to McKenna with a twinkle. She'd known it was a corny phrase.

"So, I'm sorry . . . when did you last see her?"

"It's been a while."

The woman did not want a stranger to know she never saw her daughter and didn't have her phone number. "I'm so sorry to press, ma'am, but my friend is missing. It's important."

"I haven't seen her in person since—I guess it would be fall of 2003. Doesn't seem that long ago, really."

"That's—um, that's quite a long time not to see your daughter."

Loretta's breezy tone became stern, and her face darkened. "Maybe in some families. Not this one. Pam started running away when she was fourteen years old. Dropped out her senior year. Moved out right after. Seemed the only time I ever saw her was when she needed money. Or bail the one time. I guess I suspected the kind of life she was living, but at least when she got arrested, she came clean with me. I let her move back in while she tried to get her act together—went to counseling for girls trying to get out of that . . . lifestyle. It would last a few weeks at a time, then she'd be gone again and we'd start the cycle all over."

"That must have been hard for a mother to see." McKenna didn't know what else to say.

"You have no idea. I just kept thinking every time the phone rang, it would be the police telling me my baby girl was dead. At one point I let her stay with me even when she was in the life. It was a terrible compromise to make, but at least I knew every night that she was alive and in one piece. And because she didn't need as much money, she promised me she'd only see her regulars, not the kind of guys who would beat her up. She told me a couple of the guys were married with sick wives and told themselves that being with her wasn't the same as cheating, since it wasn't emotional. One guy was a funny-looking dude—and a little slow—but she said he'd bring her flowers and love notes and stuff. One guy paid her just to talk to him and watch movies. That kind of thing."

"How did you go from that . . . arrangement to her leaving?"

"She was getting a little too comfortable telling me about the work. I lost it one night and told her it was still— Well, that's not what I said. I told her *she* was still a whore. It would've been better for me to just slap her across the face. She walked out, and that was the end of the—arrangement, as you called it. Frankly, the cards she sends a couple of times a year, that's about as much as I heard from her when she was living two miles away."

"Did you ever hear her mention a woman named Susan Hauptmann?" McKenna pulled up a picture of Susan on her iPad, the same one that her father had used for the reward posters.

Loretta shook her head. "Nope. Pam never had many female friends. Or male ones, for that matter—at least I wouldn't call them friends."

"How about the People for the Preservation of the Planet?"

Loretta chuckled, then covered her mouth. "Sorry, but that's quite a tongue twister, isn't it? Nope, never heard of that one, either."

"Would you say Pamela was an environmentalist? Or passionate about animal rights?"

"She had a hamster in the fourth grade and traded it to the boy next door for a Popsicle. You sure you've got the right Pamela Morris? You might want to try the other ones."

But McKenna left Jersey City with a feeling in her gut that she had the right Pamela Morris. Happy talk in holiday cards might keep a mother at bay, but the fact remained that Loretta hadn't seen her daughter since 2003, the same year McKenna last saw Susan Hauptmann. Something had happened. Something to explain both of them leaving. Something to explain their shared connection to the P3s. Something that had changed life for both of them forever.

# CHAPTER THIRTY-EIGHT

**C**arter lit yet another match. Dammit. That was the problem with these enormous hotels. The windows didn't open. Too many concerns about liability.

No open windows meant no fresh air. Which meant that Carter's room at the Marriott smelled like vomit.

Three times on his knees in front of the toilet bowl. The last time had been dry heaves, but still.

He had even given himself the talk, the one from two years ago, when he'd made the decision to go private. He saw what was happening. Other people were doing the same work for ten times the money and without all the bullshit.

Since then, the line had gotten blurred. What had been a government job became private. Some of the things he couldn't do then he was allowed to do now, but other things he was authorized to do then were now off the table. The geography changed, but the skills were the same. Usually the same cast of characters, too. Different theaters but somehow still all connected. Working for the same people. Playing the same angles.

The explosion out in Brentwood was a perfect example. He'd killed people before. In Kandahar, he'd started thinking of it like a video game. They had all signed on to the game. Some people won, and some people . . . didn't.

But in Brentwood, he'd screwed up. The woman who was part of the game had won. She'd made it out of the house before the explosion, run 1.6 miles in ten minutes, and now she was in the wind.

In response, the client had tweaked the mission once again. The client had new, undisclosed information. There was a third party in the picture. He was a threat, too.

This time, Carter's usual pep talk wasn't doing the trick. This latest mission wasn't the war zone come home. It wasn't a situation where everyone had signed on to play the game.

He wasn't sure why he had puked. Was it the realization of what he'd already done? The pressure of what was expected of him next? The fact that, as hard as he had tried to become the man who'd accomplished what he had in the past two years, he'd been given an assignment that he couldn't bring himself to execute? If this job crossed the line, where was the line? And how many times had he already blazed right over it?

He had lived the last two years in a lie. Lying to the clients. Lying to himself. He wasn't the man who'd earned all that money. He wasn't the hired gun who could carry out this next job. He wasn't . . . Carter. And he had no idea what he was supposed to do next.

He walked out of the hotel without checking out. He went to a cash machine and withdrew the maximum amount of four hundred dollars. He had a foreign bank account under an untraceable name that he could get to later. He had saved about four hundred grand so far. It wouldn't last a lifetime, but it was enough. Enough for him to walk away.

In about ten minutes, the client would figure out that a man who was supposed to be dead was still alive.

He passed a thrift store and remembered a book he'd read about an ex-military drifter who traveled the world with nothing but a toothbrush. Five minutes later, he paid twenty-eight bucks for a pair of used Levi's, a white canvas work shirt, and a pair of Timberland boots. He stuffed his own clothing in a trash can on Forty-fourth. He'd learned that GPS devices could be planted anywhere. He wasn't taking any chances.

A bus was heading his way on Seventh Avenue. The advertisement plastered across the side promised a new beginning through weight loss.

He threw his phone under the front tire as it passed. Heard the crunch. Looked down over the curb to make sure it was in pieces.

A kid stepped out of Chipotle shoving a football-sized burrito in his face. "Dude." He spoke through a full mouth. "Your gear is toast. Bummer."

As Carter passed a pay phone, he thought about calling in an anonymous tip about his client and the man Carter had been instructed to kill. But they wouldn't believe him. And they'd trace the call. Police response in midtown could be fast.

It was time for him to walk away. Carter was free.

# CHAPTER THIRTY-NINE

**B**y the time McKenna got back to the city, it was after nine o'clock. She felt like she'd been awake for four days straight. Had it really been only that morning that Agent Mercado had summoned her to the Federal Building?

Patrick had called her eleven times and had left three additional messages.

*Hey, it's me again. Where are you? Call me at home, okay?*

*McKenna. You're starting to worry me. You had a shitty day. I know. I want to help. Call me, okay?*

*All right, I'm trying not to lose it here. But you call me at work telling me you were questioned by an FBI agent about some ecoterrorism group and had your office searched. Someone's setting you up at work. And now you're gone? For hours? Maybe you're working on something. I don't know. Just call me. Even a text. Something. I'm still home. Okay. Bye.*

She would have to face him eventually. She stepped outside to make the call. There was no answer at the apartment. When she tried his cell, she heard a ring, followed by a long tone, a ring, followed by a long tone. He was on the phone.

If he were home and on his cell, he would have picked up the apartment phone when it rang. At this time of night, he would know it was McKenna. He'd want to know where she was.

Which meant he wasn't home. Maybe he was looking for her? But that wouldn't make any sense. If he were so worried, wouldn't he be glued to the apartment, waiting for the phone to ring? But he wasn't, which meant that he was doing something besides waiting for her. He was doing something that he'd lie to her about later.

He was probably talking to Susan again. She tried to tell herself there must be an explanation. Maybe Susan had a good reason for leaving, and he was doing the right thing by helping her now. The fact that Susan had jumped in front of an oncoming train to save Nicky Cervantes suggested that she was the same kind person at heart. Her instinct to rescue others was ingrained.

But to leave like that? To let missing posters go up all over the city? To watch as her friends and family mourned her? To keep that a secret for ten years?

McKenna could still hear the coldness in Patrick's voice. *I have it under control. Problem solved.* And then to call her moments later with *Hey, babe.*

Maybe he and Susan were spies. Maybe Patrick was a national hero. Maybe he had a secret storage unit filled floor to ceiling with war medals for saving the country from alien invasion time and again. But to bifurcate his life that way? To know her for ten years—marriage for five—showing one face to her and one to Susan and whomever the hell else who knew whatever secrets they were carrying?

It didn't matter why he had lied to her. She was afraid of him. She was afraid of her own husband.

She was so tired. She couldn't think straight anymore. She needed to sleep. Where the *hell* was she going to sleep?

She was checking out last-minute hotel offers online when she realized she wasn't sure how she would pay for it. All of their credit cards were in both of their names. Patrick would be monitoring her charges.

She had friends, but they were all "couple friends" at this point, which meant making up a story to explain her need for a crash pad, then having to explain why she'd lied once Patrick started calling around for her.

Fuck!

She scrolled through the contacts on her phone. Who the hell could she call? And then she knew.

Dana picked up on the second ring. "Holy hell, woman. All hail the renegade! Who knew you could go all gangsta?"

"I know," McKenna said. "It's absolutely insane."

"That stunt you pulled with the magazine's Twitter feed? Freakin' brilliant!"

McKenna hadn't checked the Twitter progress since she'd left for Jersey City. "Are people retweeting?"

"Oh my God. You've *totally* gone viral. Huff Post even put it on the front page of the Media section. Please tell me you've got your whole revenge plan up and ready to roll. Is it going to be like that TV show where the crazy bitch goes after a different enemy every week? You bringing a fire to their house or what?"

McKenna had always suspected that Dana's passion had nothing to do with the magazine, but she never would have guessed that the usually unanimated hipster would be so enthusiastic about a workplace scandal.

"No fires. But I do have a huge favor to ask."

"Hit it."

"Can I crash at your place? I know it's a lot to ask, but Patrick's out of town, and a reporter just showed up at my apartment wanting to talk about the Knight e-mails. I just need a break, and seeing as how I don't exactly have a salary anymore, a hotel would—"

"Just stop, okay? Of course it's fine. Not exactly the Taj Mahal, but I got a sweet daybed from CB2 that should suit you fine. When are you coming?"

"Soon. If that's okay."

"No problem. And I've got a surprise when you get here."

"Okay. Um, where am I going?" She'd never even been to the woman's home and was inviting herself over for a slumber party.

"Oh, duh." Dana gave her an address in Brooklyn. "Call me when you're out front."

# CHAPTER FORTY

**D**ana's address turned out to be for a three-story townhouse in Prospect Heights. McKenna called upstairs from the street, and Dana soon appeared at an open window on the top floor. "Catch!"

McKenna dodged to the left before the key chain hit her in the kneecaps. Upstairs, Dana was cracking up. "You can't catch for shit! Third floor. Hopefully you can walk better than you field."

At the apartment door, Dana said, "Come on in. I'll give you the tour. This is— Well, this is pretty much it." She had already opened the daybed and made it up, leaving barely enough room to walk between the open bed and the small TV stand in front of it. Beneath the window was a large desk with two laptops, a giant printer, and stacks of prints. To the side was a narrow galley kitchen.

"Oh, no. Am I taking your only bed?"

"In your dreams, McKenna. Your suppressed lesbian dreams. Nope, over here." Past the desk, she opened two sliding doors that McKenna had assumed belonged to a closet. Inside was enough space for a full-size bed and a dresser. Compact but efficient, the way a starter New York City apartment should be.

"Thanks again for letting me crash. I promise it'll just be for the night."

Dana handed her a full glass of wine from the kitchen counter. "Figured you could use this after the day you've had."

McKenna was happy to accept the offer. Dana clinked her own glass against McKenna's. "To unemployment."

The wine was awful, but McKenna said, "Mmm, nice." She hadn't known what good wine tasted like when she was twenty-five years old, either. "Word to the wise, though. Don't joke about unemployment, especially in this economy. Take it from me."

"Not just you. Me, too. I quit today."

"What?"

"Solidarity, sister." Dana held up her fist in a power salute. "Fuck the man. The way they threw you out with no notice?"

"Oh, no, no, no, no. *Please* tell me you're joking."

"No way. I'm out of there."

"You can't. Call Vance tomorrow morning and tell him you were mad and made a mistake. He'll take you back. He's a good guy."

"Yeah, right. He was really good when he was shoving a knife in your back."

"Do *not* do this for me." Dana was just a dumb kid with a degree from the New School in some kind of art thing that McKenna had never heard of. A heavily tattooed photographer wouldn't exactly be a hot ticket on the job market, and—based on her digs—she didn't seem to have a trust fund lying around. "I'll be fine. I can always go back to practice. Last time I checked, people still needed lawyers to get them out of jail and whatnot."

"I didn't do it for you. I mean, yeah, today seemed like the day to pull the trigger. But I hate it there. I only do it for the paycheck, and it's not even a good paycheck. I just want to take my weird pictures and make cool stuff that oddball people like me will want to hang on their walls."

"Yeah, but you were doing that stuff on the magazine's clock, anyway."

"Caught me. Really, though, it's fine. My friend's dad owns this huge photography studio—one of the big factories that does a ton of weddings and bar mitzvahs. He said he'll let me do assistant stuff to help pay the bills. It's better dough than the magazine, so I was already thinking about doing it. But telling Vance it was because of the way they were treating you made it seem a lot more rock-star."

McKenna could see the appeal. "All right, then. Solidarity, sister." She drank more of the wine, suppressing a wince at the paint-thinner flavor.

Dana took a seat on the unfolded bed. "Sorry, only place to sit without going in the bedroom, but, don't worry, I don't like you that much." McKenna laughed and joined her. "Now, please, please, please tell me what's going on. I know there's *no. way.* you doctored up those e-mails about Judge Knight. At first I was thinking it could have been Knight himself who set you up. Like, he heard you were running a story exposing all his courthouse crassness to the world, so he decided to discredit the messenger."

"It's a little more complicated than that." Based on Dana's comments, McKenna assumed that Vance hadn't told the magazine staff that the bogus tip had supposedly originated from McKenna's own iPad.

"Well, that's what I figured once you hijacked the magazine's Twitter feed. I hadn't heard of that Susan Hauptmann before, but I was reading up today. Sounds like it's an old cold case." Thanks to the proliferation of television procedurals, everyone with a cable box knew law enforcement lingo. "What the hell does the Knight story have to do with her?"

"I don't know. I'm still figuring it out."

Dana reached for a laptop on the floor and opened it. "You've certainly gotten people's attention. Take a look." She had opened four different windows on her Internet browser. Huffington Post. The Daily Beast. Gawker. Gothamist. It was a story ready-made for the rapid-fire, speculation-heavy world of media driven by social networking. McKenna's sudden firing from a traditional media outlet. The high-profile backstory. Her turn to Twitter to communicate with a curious public. The dangling of a "cold case" and the promise of more information to come.

The story was so weird that commenters were beginning to speculate that the entire thing was a high-concept media hoax to build buzz for *New York City* magazine.

If only that were true.

When their wineglasses were empty, Dana offered her a refill. McKenna declined. "I'm sorry. I'm just really, really tired."

"Sure, of course. I'm going to hit the hay, too. I'll see you in the morning."

Once she was alone in the living room, McKenna checked her e-mail account. She had more than a hundred new messages, almost all of them along the lines of: *Brilliant PR move. Can't wait to see what you're up to. You've got a reader for life. Who needs old-school publishing anyway?* Three media requests. A disturbing number of comments about the hotness of her publicly available head shots and the things she might have time to do with strangers now that she was unemployed.

Sometimes the Internet sucked.

She picked up her cell phone and thought again about calling Patrick, wondering what she could say. More important, she wondered what *he* could say. She wasn't ready to face the truth yet. That he had been lying to her from the minute they'd met. That he'd known more about Susan's disappearance than he'd ever let on. That he had done something terrible that they could never undo.

As long as she could tell herself that she was still looking into things, she could try to believe that everything might be okay.

She typed a new text message:

Sorry, I left the apartment because reporters were showing up trying to get a statement.

Dana had bought the story without a hitch. Hopefully Patrick would, too. Just for the night.

Felt overwhelmed and got a little hammered with a friend and fell asleep.

A friend? Nope, that wasn't going to fly. She went back and erased.

> Got a little hammered with the magazine crowd, trying to make me feel better. Fell asleep on the couch.

Whose couch? It was the kind of detail that got skipped over in the shorthand of texting, especially if she were drunk.

> Really sorry. Don't want to wake you and am too drunk to be walking around anyway. Going to crash here, but I'll see you after work tomorrow. I'm fine. You were right. Everything's going to be okay.

She turned off her phone before it could ring again.

# CHAPTER FORTY-ONE

**S**he felt the cold steel bars in her palms. She heard the clink of manacles clamping around a prisoner next door. In the distance, jail keys rattled. Then a loud beeping sound filled the block. Inmates began to yell and bang objects against bars. Something was happening. But she wasn't a prisoner. She was a guard. She opened the cell door and saw Patrick.

McKenna opened her eyes, the sound from her dream filling her head. The source of the steady staccato beeping turned out to be a work truck backing up outside Dana's building. She hadn't realized she had fallen asleep, and now it was morning already.

Dana's sliding bedroom doors were closed. McKenna stepped quietly to the bathroom, pulling the door closed gently. Her face was puffy, her eyes were red, and her mouth felt like it was coated with flour. She found Dana's toothpaste in the medicine cabinet and scrubbed her teeth with her finger.

At Dana's desk, she scribbled a quick note. *Eternal thanks for the crash pad. I'm ready to face the world again. Owe you big-time! —McK*

Dana had come through in a pinch, but her eagerness for every last detail had been a little overwhelming. McKenna didn't want to start the day with a new round of questions. She folded the sheets neatly in a corner and let herself out.

The sign outside a coffee shop on Atlantic Avenue touted free Wi-Fi. She ordered a large coffee and a breakfast sandwich. She was finally hungry. That had to be a good sign.

It was eight-forty-five. Unless Patrick were skipping work, he'd be on his bicycle. She took a chance and called his cell phone. No answer. "Hey, it's me," she said at the tone. "Sorry again about last night. They say drinking can't solve your problems, but turns out that four ginger martinis can dull the pain. A sure sign of alcoholism, huh? Anyway, I crashed at Dana's and am ready to face the world again. I'm going to see what I can find out about Judge Knight's supporters at the courthouse. My best guess is that he got wind of the questions I was asking and forged the e-mails himself in an attempt to make the entire story seem false." No mention of Susan. She was just an unemployed reporter trying to clear her name. "Hope work goes okay. Sorry I'm a lush, but I'll see you at home tonight."

That gave her about nine hours to clear or confirm her worst suspicions.

She started by calling Mallory. "It's McKenna Jordan again. We talked about that video you had of the subway rescue?"

"Yeah, sure. I just saw something on Gawker about you." The girl's flat affect made it impossible to know whether she saw McKenna's newfound fame as a good thing or utter mortification.

"I'm sorry to keep bothering you, but do you have some time this morning for a quick meeting?"

"A meeting? I sit in a cubicle all day and proofread copy for fashion auctions on the Internet. I don't exactly have a secretary keeping a calendar for me."

"I meant a few minutes to talk in person. I want to show you a picture to see if you recognize it."

"Can't you just e-mail it to me?"

McKenna wanted to make sure the girl took a close look. This was important. "It'll only be a few minutes. I'll come to you. You said something about a Starbucks near your office?"

"Yeah, I guess. Forty-fifth Street and Sixth Avenue. Call me when you're close, and I'll meet you."

McKenna hung up and made another call. She got lucky. Nicky Cervantes was at home. He remembered her. "What time do you need to be at school?" she asked.

"I don't. Teacher prep day. Got practice at one, though."

"Any chance you can meet me near Times Square? I'll make it worth your time. Twenty bucks?"

She could tell he was thinking about negotiating.

"Yeah. A'ight. Subway, too?"

"The Starbucks at Forty-fifth Street and Sixth Avenue. No problem."

Those pictures don't look right," Nicky said. "They look old or something. Like her hair and clothes and stuff."

To McKenna, ten years ago didn't seem that long ago. Sure, pictures from the 1980s? Peg-leg harem pants, Madonna bangles, and Cyndi Lauper hairdos were instant date-setters. But 2003? McKenna was certain she was wearing some of the same clothes. To a teenager like Nicky, 2003 probably looked as retro as Woodstock would have seemed to McKenna at his age.

"She'd be ten years older now," she said, pointing again at the photograph of Susan. Ten years to a teenager? Unimaginable. "She'd be my age. Could this be the woman from the subway station?"

"I don't know. She was— Damn, she was chasing me most of the time."

"You must have looked at her in the beginning, scoped her out for at least a second."

"Let me see again. Yeah, okay. I got it. Her hair's not as blond now, maybe there's more red in it or something. But the face? It could definitely be her."

"Does that mean it *could* be her, or it's *definitely* her?"

He looked at her like the question made his head hurt. "What do you *mean* what do I mean? I guess I'm saying that lady in your pictures looks a lot more like the lady on the subway than you do, or my mother, or that lady over there, or that lady, or that one. So, yeah, it could *definitely* be her."

She'd take what she could get. At least he hadn't ruled out the possibility. He grabbed the twenty-five dollars like it was the easiest money he'd ever made, even though McKenna knew it wasn't.

She called Mallory and said that she was waiting at the coffee shop. A few minutes later, a woman in her mid-twenties walked in, scanning the place with uncertainty.

"Are you Mallory?" McKenna never would have expected from the girl's voice that she'd be so attractive. She had clear alabaster skin, strawberry-blond hair, and big pool-blue eyes.

"Yeah. I didn't realize until I opened the door that I had no idea who I was looking for." Mallory took a seat at the bistro table across from McKenna. "I made the mistake of telling my friend you called again. She wants me to ask whether your whole Twitter campaign is a PR thing for the magazine. She's got some idea about doing the same kind of thing for her boyfriend's band. Like anyone would care if there was a feud between members of some band no one's ever heard of."

"It's no stunt," McKenna said. "Someone gave me a bogus tip for a story and tried to make it look like I made the whole thing up. It's complicated, but I'm starting to wonder whether the same people wanted to make sure I didn't get a lead on the subway video you shot."

"Whoa. That's intense." The woman had a way with understatement.

McKenna pulled up the photograph of Susan that she'd showed Nicky Cervantes. "It's over ten years old, so you've got to do some mental age progression. But is this the woman from the subway station?"

"Oh my gosh. I think that's her. I really think that's her."

McKenna noticed then that Mallory's coloring was close to Susan's. It made sense that she might be better able to discern among similar-looking women than Nicky. They all looked the same when "they" didn't resemble "you."

Nicky and Mallory had both seen the subway woman in person, and neither of them had ruled out a match. They were validating what McKenna had believed all along.

The real reason she'd wanted to see Mallory in person was for another photograph entirely. McKenna scrolled through her photographs until she found one of Patrick alone.

"You said you loaned your phone to a guy in the lunch line the day the subway video got erased. Could this be the man?"

Mallory took a quick look, much shorter than her inspection of Susan's picture. "Nope. Not him."

"You're sure? You told me before that you couldn't pick him out of a lineup."

"Exactly. Which is how I know this isn't the guy. This guy's pretty hot. I'd remember him. And my friend Jen? She would have found a way to give him her number. Trust me."

McKenna had never been so relieved to get a negative response. Whoever had borrowed Mallory's phone must have been the person who deleted the subway video. It stood to reason that the same person had wiped out Dana's Skybox account and fabricated the Knight e-mails sent to McKenna. Patrick had physical access to McKenna's iPad, but a decent enough computer expert could have pulled it all off virtually.

She needed to find the man who'd gotten into Mallory's phone. "You said the man borrowed the phone while you were in line somewhere? That was on Wednesday, right? Do you happen to remember the time?"

"Margon. Some of the city's best Cuban food, tucked away in that wasteland of Times Square. The lines are massive, but it's cheap. We were at the start of lunch break. It must have been between one and one-fifteen."

The man might have wiped out the video that McKenna was most interested in, but there were other cameras in the city. McKenna was going to start using that to her advantage. She was turning the tables.

# CHAPTER
# FORTY-TWO

$S$ome people would have been puzzled by Mallory's description of Times Square as a wasteland, but those people would be exposing themselves as non–New Yorkers. To non–New Yorkers—people who called the city the "Big Apple," who thought of it as stressful, a place to visit but not live, people like McKenna's mother—Times Square *was* New York City. But to people who lived here, Times Square was the place that gave their hometown a bad rap. It was like Disney World or Costco or the DMV—places you probably went but only under protest, for a very specific purpose.

A few times a year, like every good New Yorker, McKenna ventured into this combat zone for an especially lauded performance or to meet an out-of-town friend at some ghastly hotel bar. Today she had a very different reason.

It was only eleven-thirty, and a line had already formed outside Margon. As McKenna bypassed the line to the entrance, responses ranged from the passive-aggressive ("I didn't think they took reservations") to the aggressive-aggressive ("You're not that special, lady! Back of the line!").

McKenna had assumed from the restaurant's demand that it was the latest celebrity-soaked Manhattan hot spot. When she reached the front, she realized it was barely a restaurant at all. The long, narrow space was occupied primarily by a food counter with cafeteria-style service, complete with a sign reading LINE START HERE. The early birds had grabbed the few tables available for dining.

The cashier seemed as in charge as anyone. It took a few tries before he understood McKenna's request. When he finally did comprehend the question, he laughed quietly and shook his head. "No. No cameras." He gestured around like, *Look at this place.*

When McKenna walked out empty-handed, some of the line occupants gained newfound faith in karmic justice. "Yep, back of the line!"

She followed the line, scoping out businesses whose security cameras might have captured the interaction between Mallory and the man who'd borrowed her phone. Nail salon. Indian restaurant. Tattoo parlor. Three strikes.

Her next try was a parking garage. It was well past the length of the current line, but Mallory had been here during rush hour. It was worth a shot.

The entrance to the underground garage was a steep, narrow ramp. A row of cars was backed up, waiting to be worked into the Tetris-like clump of vehicles squeezed into the cramped garage. She found herself cringing in anticipation of a crunch as the parking attendant lurched a Porsche Carrera from the line. With authority. Nothing but net. It would have taken her fifteen minutes of wiggling to free that car from its knot.

She waited patiently while he retrieved cars for four customers standing nearby with claim tickets. People who needed favors couldn't be pushy. When she got his attention, he was more than happy to chat. He probably didn't get many opportunities to socialize in his profession.

"Yeah, we got cameras. A bunch of them. Two years ago, some madman pulled a woman from the street and raped her right there on the ramp. My guy was down here the whole time, but he was washing cars and listening to the radio. Didn't hear a thing. Me? If I'd heard something like that? Guy wouldn't have gotten out of here alive. Now we got a bell that rings whenever anyone sets one foot inside the ramp—you walked down here, right? Yep. I heard the bell. Knew someone was coming but didn't see a car. Works good. Plus we got cameras. A big system. Catches everything."

"What about outside the ramp? On the sidewalk?"

"Yeah, sure. I mean, not like all of midtown or whatever. But yeah, sidewalk on both sides of the garage."

"Do you have tape?"

"For fourteen days, then it cycles. Not sure I'm supposed to be showing it to anyone. No one's ever asked."

She'd heard the anger in his voice when he spoke about the madman who attacked the woman two years before. "I'm on something of an amateur sleuth venture. My little sister was waiting in line for Margon—"

"Oh, man, those rice and beans . . ."

"Well, some guy borrowed her phone, saying it was an emergency. And when she got it back, he had put these crude pictures of himself on it."

"Now, see? What the hell is wrong with people? Who does something like that?"

"That's what I'm trying to find out. The police say they can't do anything about it, since the pictures he left—they're not exactly of his face, you know? But maybe your cameras caught it on film."

"Say nothing more. I got you. We're gonna catch this fucker."

The number of drivers waiting to drop off keys continued to grow as the attendant scanned through digital video files in the back office. "Just a second, guys. I've got a big emergency here. I'll be right out. Promise!" He had queued up the feed from the camera on the west side of the garage from Wednesday, starting at one, the beginning of Mallory's lunch hour. They could see people waiting in line on the sidewalk. He played it at high speed.

"There!" McKenna saw Mallory deep in conversation with her friend. "That's my sister," she said. "Slow it down." They watched at regular speed as a man in the line said something to them. Mallory barely looked at the man before handing him her phone.

"Oh yeah." The parking attendant was now her full partner in the investigation. "There's the sicko. Yep, he's doing something. Not taking pictures but fiddling with the controls. Probably had the pictures all ready at some website to download on the phone or something."

In the video, the man handed the phone back to Mallory and stepped out of the line. "Stop!" McKenna said.

"We got him," her partner announced, pausing the screen.

McKenna had no idea who the man was.

# CHAPTER
# FORTY-THREE

**B**efore Scanlin even opened the glass front door, the two women at the reception desk of Comfort Park exchanged a glance. In that shared look, he overheard their entire unspoken conversation.

*Here he comes again.*

*We keep telling him—*

*But he doesn't listen.*

It was true. They had kept telling him. They told him Melissa didn't remember him. They told him she really was happy here; he didn't need to worry. They told him it was best to come with Jenna.

Easier said than done. Despite all of Jenna's resentment of her father for putting his work before family, she—in her words—wasn't "a morning person." It was all she "could do" to get up in time to make it to her job as a corporate accountant. Her visits to Melissa were strictly in the early evening.

Scanlin, on the other hand, was a cop with comp time that he had to use or lose. He was also the one who'd taken care of Melissa, even after everyone said she needed to move into a "facility." No one had believed him, but there were minutes back when she was home—sometimes over an hour—when she was almost normal, and it was always in the morning. She'd wake up before him and find him sleeping in Jenna's room and ask whether he wanted pancakes. Didn't she have to remember him to know that pancakes were his favorite?

"Good morning," he said. "I'm here to see Melissa Scanlin."

Comfort Park. He hated the name. It sounded like a combination of "comfort station" and "trailer park." He hated the place itself when Melissa moved in. The exaggerated attempts to make it look cheerful—flowered upholstery, flowered curtains, plastic floral centerpieces in the dining area. The dated furniture. The weird smell.

He eventually realized that his discomfort with the place was all about him, not Melissa. He wanted Melissa to be the kind of woman who would hate living here. But she wasn't. She was a woman who acted like a child due to her dementia. And much like a child, she didn't care about design or upholstery or even the people around her. She liked arts and crafts sessions, music days, and the fact that the ladies at Comfort Park constantly brought in a rotating collection of hats for her to wear.

"Of course, Detective Scanlin. I believe she's in the group room right now."

The group room was a bright, open room filled with nonmatching chairs, small tables, and activity pods for drawing, puzzling, clay molding, and reading. The woman led the way to his wife, who was sitting by herself in front of a TV tray, playing solitaire. It wasn't actually solitaire, but for some reason, the practice of placing piles of cards in seven columns and then turning over the remainder of the cards, three at once into the waste, remained a familiar pattern.

"As we talked about, Detective," the woman whispered as they approached.

"I know. Just keep her company. No reminders. No prodding."

"Exactly," she said, like he was a student who had recited the alphabet correctly for the first time.

"Not to worry. I'll act like a complete stranger."

He couldn't help himself. He recognized that the people who worked here—most of them, at least—truly cared about the patients. But at the end of the day, their jobs would be easier if the husbands and the parents and the siblings would just go away. Then they could run Comfort Park like a day-care center with giant toddlers and would not have to be reminded that the people in this room used to be adults. A woman like Melissa used to be a mother, a wife, and a kickass cook. Until she agreed to marry a cop, she liked to sneak a toke of doob. And though no one but Scanlin would ever know it, she was sexier than any porn star in the bedroom.

"Hi, there," he said. "Good game?"

"Oh, yeah. I like this a lot. I always win, too."

She *never* won, not even when she knew how to play.

"You know how to—you know." She gestured to the cards.

"I used to play. I could never win, though. Too hard."

"Doesn't seem so hard to me."

"You must be very good at it. My name's Joe. I was born in Pittsburgh. I'm a police officer, and I have a daughter named Jenna."

He'd learned that he could recite basic biographical facts without triggering a series of events ending with a staff member asking him to "come back later" with Jenna. As long as he acted like a talkative stranger, Melissa was calm, even mildly entertained. But any statements like "I'm your husband" or "We lived together for twenty-three years" or "How can you not remember?" were quickly followed by stressful pacing around the room, tears, or—the worst—accusations that he was trying to "steal" her.

"When Jenna was little," he continued, "her appendix almost burst, and we almost didn't know. Other kids yell and scream the second they get a tummyache, but all Jenna said was that she must have eaten too much pizza. She kept saying it for over an entire day"—twenty-four hours wouldn't mean anything to Melissa—"and even when the pain got really bad, she didn't scream or even moan. She said, 'Daddy, the pizza moved to the right side of my body. I think that means I need to go to the hospital.' "

There was a certain irony to the Comfort Park staff's cordial relationship with Jenna. By the time he decided to place Melissa in a home full-time, everyone they knew could barely contain their relief. *Better for both your sakes. Long time coming. Had to be done.*

Everyone but Jenna. If he could undergo a lobotomy to forget all of the hateful words that had spewed from his own daughter that night, he'd happily make the first cut.

"Does Jenna have a mommy?" Melissa asked.

He knew it. Mornings were always better for Melissa. He believed it was because the sleep refreshed her. If it were true that most people used only ten percent of brain capacity, maybe Melissa was able to use more when she was rested.

"Yes, she does. In fact, her name is Melissa. Isn't that your name?"

Melissa's brow furrowed, and he wondered whether she was about to have an episode. "That's nice that you have a—" She waved her hand in the air, the way she did when she couldn't conjure an appropriate word. "I used to have one. But he's gone now."

Melissa could not remember him, but she did seem to remember that she'd had a boyfriend at Comfort Park until he had passed away four months earlier. For her sake, he hoped she would forget. And that she'd forget the ones who were likely to come after. Melissa had long outlived the average life expectancy of patients with her diagnosis.

"It was nice talking to you, Melissa. Have a good time finishing your game."

"I always win."

He thanked the women on his way out, who gave him the sympathetic but impatient look they seemed to reserve for him.

He had an entire afternoon in front of him. He wasn't good at taking a day off. No job. No family. No hobbies.

For a while, he'd thought the Hauptmann case might become his hobby, but he'd hit a wall with Vera Hadley's notes. So maybe the nosy neighbor had heard Susan argue with a boyfriend. He still didn't know who the guy was. And he didn't know whether Susan was dead or alive.

The final straw had been the stunt McKenna Jordan pulled. Most people caught red-handed printing libelous information about a judge would lie low and take their lumps. But hauling out the name of her missing friend on Twitter to try to save herself? The woman would do anything for attention.

The thought of McKenna Jordan reminded him that he wanted to check in with his old friend Scott Macklin to make sure he had heard the news that she had imploded once again.

**M**ac's house was pretty much as Scanlin remembered it. He was never one to swear by his memory, but it was possible they had added the dormer windows to the second floor. Maybe the cedar fence around the side yard was new, too.

The door of the single-car attached garage was closed. The driveway was empty.

He rang the doorbell, expecting Josefina to greet him with that cheerful but busy voice. No answer. Another ding-dong. More silence.

The twenty-five-minute drive had seemed like nothing when he left Comfort Park. But twenty-five minutes times two was close to an hour. An hour of time wasted in the car.

He walked to the side of the house and peered into a window. If the television was on, he'd at least know they were on their way home. He could grab some McDonald's and come right back.

He tried the phone number and heard it ringing inside. No answer.

He went to his car and found an old oil-change receipt in the glove box and a pen in the console. *Hey, Scott. A voice from your past. Called yesterday. Popped in today. By next week, you'll need a stalking order. Give me a ring when you have a chance to catch up.* He scrawled his name and cell number and made his way to the porch to drop off the note.

There was no logical place to put it. No screen door to hold it in place. The bottom of the door was weather-sealed, so there was no slipping the note beneath. The mailbox had a lock on it, thanks to identity thieves.

He tried the door. If it were unlocked, he'd leave the note in the front hallway and get on his way.

It opened.

The house smelled like crispy bacon. Scanlin couldn't think of a better smell.

He bent down to place the note on the hardwood floor in the foyer. That was when he saw the bare feet protruding from the living room doorway.

# CHAPTER
# FORTY-FOUR

McKenna knew her suspicions were right the second the transit agent saw her. He recognized her. And her return trip to the video monitoring center for the subway system had him very nervous.

"Hi, Frank. Remember me? I was here last weekend looking for camera footage of that kid who fell on the tracks at Times Square."

"Yeah, sure. Sorry about the glitch. People want low taxes. Want to keep the fares down. When crap starts breaking, they act like they're all surprised."

"Back up and running again?"

"Last I heard. All set to go."

"Good. So if someone gives me a bribe on the platform down there today, you'll catch the whole thing on film?"

"Umm . . . yeah, sure, I guess. Something I can help you with?"

"I mention the possibility of a bribe being caught on film, Frank, because that's basically what happened to you."

"I think you better leave, lady. I've got work to do, and you're obviously under a mistaken—"

"Don't. Just don't, okay, Frank? That man who paid you to wipe out the footage from that day? He was an undercover reporter."

"I don't know what you're talking about—"

"He's a bit of a lowlife but fancies himself an investigative journalist. An amateur Geraldo Rivera type. He doesn't actually have the *ethics* of a legitimate reporter. See, most reporters—if they're going to do a story about corruption among low-level city employees, people like you—they actually need to *know* about the corruption first. Not Hank the Tank." No clue where the nickname came from, but she was rolling with it. "That's what he calls himself. Because he's sort of a tool. Anyway, Frank, reporters like me are pretty sick of tools like Hank running around making up stories. Not to mention that this time around, he fucked me by wiping out the subway footage I needed for my Superwoman article."

"What kind of story is he making up?"

"Well, he didn't really make it up, did he? But he did entrap you. You were just sitting here minding your own business until he came around making an offer no reasonable person could refuse. Like you said, people want low taxes. They want cheap fares. That leaves hardworking guys like you holding the bag, working more hours for less pay. He played you, Frank. He took advantage of you, paid you off, and now he's going to use you as the centerpiece of a story—like *you're* the big problem in this city."

"But that's— He can't. I'll get fired."

"And that's why I'm here, Frank. I've always suspected this hack of pulling the strings on his stories. This time I figured it out. He's already bragging that he got a city worker—on tape!—to wipe out security footage from one of the biggest terrorist targets in the world. Well, I put two and two together, and I want to reverse the sting on him. I'll show that he set you up. That he overcame your resistance by upping his price over and over until you relented. That's what happened, right?"

"*If* it happened, then yeah. But, um, does my name have to be used?"

"Nope, not at all, Frank. If everything goes to plan, my story—no names—will be the end of Hank, and that will kill his story about you."

"Okay, let's do that, then. He entrapped me. Just like you said. He came in saying that he was married to the lady in the tape. That all she was trying to do was help a person, but after the fact, she realized reporters would make a big deal out of it and everything, and she just wasn't interested. I told him there was nothing I could do, but like you said, he kept pestering me. I figured she was a hero and all. What was the harm in protecting her privacy?"

"Okay, and to be clear, Frank, this is the guy we're talking about, right?"

She showed him a still photograph from the parking garage's security camera. In her head, she had started thinking of the man as the Cleaner.

"Yeah, that's the guy, all right. Can't believe he played me like that."

"And he gave you"—she took a guess—"five thousand dollars?"

"No. It was only a grand. He's telling people *five*?"

Frank was cheaper than she would have expected. Someone needed to explain to him the value of a union job these days.

She was no closer to identifying the Cleaner, but she was now sure of two things: he was thorough, and he did not want anyone to know Susan Hauptmann was alive.

# CHAPTER
# FORTY-FIVE

Twenty-two minutes.

Scanlin knew, because after calling 911, he waited by himself on Scott Macklin's porch for what seemed like an eternity before checking his phone log to see how long it had been since he'd made the call. Then he heard the sirens. Then he saw the ambulance turn the corner.

Twenty-two minutes for someone to show up to the scene of a dead cop.

Scanlin had seen a point-blank head shot before. He wished he hadn't, but he had. He'd even seen a self-inflicted one—another cop, in fact. That image might have been what saved him when things got really bad with Melissa. He couldn't stand the thought of someone finding him like that.

But that was how he'd found Scott Macklin. His friend had been sitting in the recliner. The bloodstains on the chair and the wall behind it made that much clear. His arms had probably fallen to his lap. The gun was in his right hand. The movement of his head backward had pulled the weight of his body forward in the chair. He eventually slid onto the floor, where Scanlin discovered him.

By the time Josefina pulled up in front of the house, the ambulance had been joined by a fire engine and two marked police cars.

She recognized Scanlin standing at the curb and greeted him with a smile. She was wearing what looked like a yoga outfit. "Oh my goodness. You weren't kidding when you said you wanted to see Scott. What's all the commotion?"

"It's Scott. I'm so sorry, Josefina."

She dropped to her knees when he told her.

**S**canlin stayed with her through the entire process. The moving of the body. The questions from responding officers and detectives. The call to Tommy who now wanted to be called Thomas. The clearing of the house for entry, even as Josefina realized there was no way she was going to spend the night there.

They wound up at a Denny's, where they waited for a church friend whom she was going to stay with.

"I don't know why he'd do this." She used her fork to push the scrambled eggs of her Grand Slam to the edges of the plate. "I didn't even know he still had a gun. He seemed so happy about Tommy going to college. Maybe it was because he was out of the house? Maybe the idea of just the two of us—"

"Aw, don't start talking like that. Mac was crazy about you." Scanlin had no way of knowing whether that was still true. Hadn't the most bitter, unhappy couples been wild about each other at some point? But he couldn't imagine Mac falling out of love with the woman who had brought him to life back then. Scanlin could think of only one reason Macklin would have been so desperate, and he wasn't sure how to broach the subject with Josefina.

"I know Scott tried to protect you from the details, but I assume you know something about the shooting he was involved in before he took early retirement."

"I was a new immigrant, Joe, but I wasn't illiterate. Of course I knew the basic facts. That boy reached for a gun, and Scott had to shoot back. But the boy was black, and Scott was a white cop, and so—That's how this country still sees things. Maybe it will always be that way."

"The DA's office took it to a grand jury. The lead prosecutor was all set to steer the grand jury to uphold the shooting as justified, but then a younger prosecutor claimed that Scott had used a drop gun. That's what it's called when a police officer takes an extra gun and plants it—"

"Yes, I knew all of this. It's ancient history. They cleared Scott, but all that digging around in his past exposed other problems. People he arrested from years ago came out of the woodwork. He eventually cut a deal to leave the department and keep his retirement."

He was tainted goods by then.

"You're right," Scanlin said, "it is ancient history. Or at least it was. I called you yesterday because that same prosecutor—the one who started the whole scandal—was reviving the story for the ten-year anniversary. She's a reporter now. She wrote a big article in a magazine, trying to get attention."

"Ay, ay, ay. The reporter lady. She was out here yesterday. I come home from getting the oil changed, and there she is in my living room." Josefina was speaking more quickly now, her Mexican accent more noticeable. "I told Scott, 'What are you doing talking to some reporter?' He thinks he can be nice and charming and show her how we live a normal life, how he raised a good boy, maybe she'll leave him alone. Oh my God, do you think that's why he was so upset? Is the *reporter* the reason he would do this?"

He hadn't answered the question when he saw Josefina's attention shift to the sound of bells ringing at the Denny's entrance. A plump middle-aged woman walked in and spotted Josefina immediately. He saw tears begin to form in both women's eyes.

"That's my friend. She'll drive me to her place. I need to lie down for a while."

"Of course." He walked Josefina to her friend and waited while the two exchanged a hug. "Call me if there's anything I can do to help. Anything at all."

She nodded, but he could tell she would be more comfortable relying on people who had been a part of their lives more recently.

As the friend backed her MINI out of its parking space, he watched Josefina place her face in her hands and begin to sob.

He dropped a twenty on the table and headed to his own car. He was surprised at how hard he slammed the car door. How tight his grip was on the steering wheel. How he could almost hear the blood pounding through his veins.

A good man was dead. This wasn't right.

He found her business card crumpled in his jacket pocket. McKenna Jordan. Cell number scribbled on the back. As he listened to the rings—one, two, three—a lump formed behind his Adam's apple. He tried to swallow but felt a gasp escape from his throat. Dammit. He was not going to cry. He would *not* allow this woman to hear him cry.

# CHAPTER
# FORTY-SIX

It was amazing how much a hot shower had done to calm McKenna down. Being here, in her own apartment, surrounded by the little reminders of her everyday life—her life with Patrick—was helping, too. Patrick was gone, presumably off to work, which meant her phone calls had reassured him that everything was okay.

The contents of the box that Adam Bayne had sent over seemed to be just as she'd left them. Granted, she hadn't memorized the exact placement of every item, and she had taken the picture of Patrick and Susan that had gotten her so worked up. But if Patrick had really been as anxious as she thought he'd sounded the previous night—*Is there something in here that could be an issue?*—surely he would have torn through the belongings, searching for whatever it was he thought could be so damning.

In retrospect, it was the phone call that had set her imagination running wild. What had she really heard? She mentally replayed his side of the conversation. *She's got a bunch of your old stuff scattered all over our living room floor.*

He had said *your stuff.* She had assumed the "you" was Susan, but maybe he'd called Adam when he saw the messenger labels on the box. *Is there something in here that could be an issue?* Okay, so he didn't want her to know that he'd had a fling or whatever with

Susan. McKenna was mad—pissed—that he hadn't told her, but she could see how it would happen. They met. They liked each other. It wasn't like "Hey, I used to sleep with your friend" was a great pickup line. A lie about a past lover was nothing compared to the scenarios she'd been playing in her head.

And then there was the last part of the call: *I have it under control. Problem solved. Just take care of yourself.*

He could've meant "Fine, if she found out about me and Susan, we'll work through it." And *Just take care of yourself* could have been a jibe, as if to say "Take care of your own house and mind your own business."

Her thoughts were interrupted by the trill of her cell phone.

She didn't recognize the number. She hesitated. Every moment of the last two days had brought nothing but more horrible news. She didn't think she could take any more. She was also screening incoming tips about Susan. Maybe someone had gotten her number from the magazine.

Three rings. She had to decide. "Hello?"

"You've got blood on your hands, Jordan."

There was something familiar about the voice, but she couldn't place it. "Excuse me?"

"You're like a one-woman wrecking ball. You should come with a warning label: human destruction will follow. Do you even *stop* to think about the way your choices affect other people? Killing his job wasn't enough, was it? It's all just publicity to you, but you cost a good man his life. His *life*."

She should have known that a public call for information about a decade-old death would bring out the nut jobs. "Who is this?"

"It's Joe Scanlin. That stunt you pulled going to Macklin's house? I hope it helped you with whatever story you're trying to publish, because you pushed him over the edge. I just found him. He ate his gun."

She felt a lurch in her stomach at the imagery. "Oh my God. Scott Macklin?"

"He's dead. You pushed him over the edge. Are you happy?"

"Of course I'm not happy. He was—I *knew* him, whatever you might think of me. And I don't know what you mean by any stunt. I didn't go to his house. I haven't seen him since I left the district attorney's office." She pictured Macklin, beaming as he described the strategy he used to teach his stepson the perfect spiral football pass. That sweet man killed himself?

"His wife told me everything. She saw you there yesterday in the living room. He just wanted to be left alone. Why'd you have to—"

"She said *I* was there? I wasn't. I swear to God, Scanlin."

"I don't believe you."

"Yeah, well, I'm getting used to that these days. Did she say me specifically? Maybe it was another reporter. It's the ten-year anniversary, after all."

"She said she came home and saw a woman in the living room, and that it was a female reporter. Of course it was you. What other female reporters are going to bother a cop who left the job a decade ago?"

A woman. An unidentified woman asking questions about something that happened ten years ago. It didn't make any sense, but she could think of only one person it could have been.

"Are you there? Fucking bitch hung up—"

"No, I'm here," she said. "And it wasn't me at Scott Macklin's house yesterday. But if Scott Macklin is dead, I'm not sure it was suicide. I need you to meet me. Right now. I promise I'll tell you everything."

# CHAPTER
## FORTY-SEVEN

It's said there are certain moments in history that everyone remembers. The moon landing. The day Kennedy was shot. The night the United States elected its first African-American president. The day the towers came down.

The first reports came in right around nine A.M. on September 11. McKenna was on her way to the morning plea docket. Heading from her office to the elevator, she passed a lounge area for civilian witnesses—the most luxurious area on the floor, complete with a television set—and saw early reports of an airplane colliding with the World Trade Center. The anchors were trying to calm the worldwide audience: "The most likely scenario is that this is a private commuter plane that left its intended route. City officials are encouraging everyone to remain calm."

From there, McKenna went to the courtroom of Judge John DeWitt Gregory to accept routine guilty pleas from routine defendants on routine charges. Forty-five minutes passed without interruption. It was a different world then. It was a world without an omnipresent information stream playing constantly in the background via phones and other devices. It was also a world where the date she wrote on each of those plea agreements, September 11,

2001, was just a date. By the time she was done taking that morning's pleas, the world and America's place in it had changed.

She sensed something was wrong the minute she hit the hallway. Usually lawyers piled up outside the sluggish elevators, no matter how long the wait, because people, let's face it, are lazy. That morning, people were sprinting up and down stairs. She remembered the panic on the face of a former coworker turned defense attorney who passed her in the hallway: "We've got to get out of here. Leave downtown. Leave the city. This is really, really bad. They're saying there are eight other planes unaccounted for."

It wasn't until McKenna got to her office that she connected the frenzy in the courthouse to the television report. Her mother had left a panicked voice mail. "Kenny, we just heard the news. Aren't you right down there by the towers? I think you are, but your daddy says you're a ways away. Let us know you're safe, okay?"

By then, McKenna couldn't get a dial tone. She did manage to find a cabdriver filling up on the Lower East Side. "Stupid day to let the tank go low," he was muttering. He didn't want to take a passenger, but she begged, then offered to pay for the entire tank plus fare to go anywhere outside of Manhattan. She and the cabdriver actually argued about which route to take. Some attributes of city life were truly ingrained.

And now here she was again. It wasn't 9/11, not by a long shot, but she did feel like her life had changed forever. She'd lost her job. Susan was back, possibly tied up in a Long Island bombing. The FBI had searched McKenna's office, when she still had one. And once again, she was bickering with a freakin' cabdriver who could not accept that the best way to Forest Hills was the LIE and not the Fifty-ninth Street Bridge.

It had taken her enough work just to get Scanlin to agree to meet. Even after he relented, their conversation had turned to a geographic bartering of the metropolitan region. Surely it was easier for Scanlin in his own car to meet her in Manhattan than for her to leave the island. But he was in Forest Hills, having spent the day consoling

Scott Macklin's widow. Yep, that was the moral high ground. Scanlin got to name the spot. She was schlepping to Queens.

In retrospect, she was grateful he had a head start. By the time she met him at the Irish pub he had chosen, he was at least two Scotches in and no longer sounded like he wanted to pound her skull against concrete. She took the seat across from him in the booth. She didn't bother with introductions or even words of solace about the death of Scott Macklin.

She started with the absurd chase to determine the identity of the subway Superwoman and summarized every last detail until he called her with the news of Mac's death. The face that looked like Susan's. The missing video. The button that linked the woman to the People for the Preservation of the Planet. The bombing in Brentwood. The extremely coincidental timing of the fake tip about Frederick Knight. Even her stupid suspicions about Patrick. Everything.

"What does any of this have to do with Mac?" Scanlin asked.

"I have no idea."

"Nice."

"Hear me out. If I'm right, if Susan is alive, it means that for ten years, she was perfectly happy doing whatever it is she's been doing. But now, after a decade, she's back in New York. And look at all of the things that have happened since then." She ticked off the points on her fingers. One. "The man I call the Cleaner did not want her to be seen." Two. "Deleting the video of her is one thing, but someone also set me up with those forged e-mails from Judge Knight." Three. "Which means I no longer have a book deal about the Marcus Jones shooting, and everything I say from now on will be considered false." Four. "Now Scott Macklin is dead, and someone claiming to be a female reporter was at his house yesterday."

There was only one conclusion. "Susan being back has something to do with the fact that it's been ten years since the Jones shooting. Maybe my article triggered something."

She could tell from his expression that Scanlin didn't want to buy it.

"The timing works," she argued. "Susan disappeared not long after the Jones shooting. Look, I'm the last person who thought I'd say this. I was sure someone killed her. We all said she'd never just walk away—"

"Not *everyone*."

"Not you, of course."

"Not her sister," Scanlin said. "And not your husband."

"Patrick never thought Susan would leave. He still insists that she must be dead."

"I know you think I'm incompetent—"

"I never said you were incompetent."

"Close enough. But I'm quite sure Patrick was the one who told me that Susan had major issues with her family, hated her job, hated the pressure to work with her dad. He told me that in his gut, he thought she just started over again."

She had set aside her doubts about Patrick, and now they were back.

What had he said to her the other day? *She'd never just leave. That's what we all said. That's what we all told the police.* Yet another lie she'd caught him in.

When she looked at Scanlin, he was taking her picture with his cell phone.

"What the—"

His phone was against his ear now. "You have a picture of Susan Hauptmann on that gadget of yours?" he asked, gesturing to the iPad sticking out of her purse.

"Yes, but—"

He held up a finger to cut her off. "Josefina, this is Joe Scanlin. I'm so sorry to bother you, but it's really important. That reporter at your house yesterday? You remember what she looked like? Okay, I need you to look at a couple of pictures for me. I wouldn't ask if I didn't think it was urgent. Do you have an e-mail address?"

They sat in silence after the pictures had been sent. There was nothing more to say until they had their answer.

He picked up his phone the second it chimed. "You got the pictures? You're sure? Okay, let me see what else I can find out. Try to get some sleep." He set his phone down on the table. "Tell me everything again. From the beginning."

"What did she say?"

"That she was a hundred percent certain the woman she saw with Scott yesterday was Susan Hauptmann."

# CHAPTER FORTY-EIGHT

**C**arter should have left town. He should have gone to his safe-deposit box, pulled out his passport, and taken the first flight from JFK to Switzerland.

But some part of him—the part that had puked his guts out at the Marriott, the part that had started to reach for the pay phone yesterday, before it was too late—had kept him in New York. And the same part of him brought him to the Apple store in SoHo to search the latest local news updates.

"Good afternoon, sir." The kid who greeted him wore a black T-shirt and a giant ID badge around his neck. He looked entirely too helpful. "What can I help you find today?"

"To be honest? I'm not buying. My phone's almost dead, and I'm hoping to check some game scores."

"No problem. I hear ya. All our demos are hooked up to the Web, so have a go wherever you'd like. No pressure."

Carter picked a laptop at the far corner of the display table. Scott Macklin. Enter.

It had already happened. The suicide of a retired cop wouldn't nec-essarily be newsworthy, but reports had identified him as the police officer whose controversial shooting of Marcus Jones incited city-wide protests, widespread racial tensions, and his early retirement. Macklin's former partner was quoted as suspecting a connection between the suicide and the ten-year anniversary of the shooting.

Carter knew better. He knew because he was the one who was supposed to have killed Scott Macklin.

The story was accompanied by two pictures of Macklin with his family—one at his wedding, and one at the son's high school graduation last May. In both, the boy looked at his father like a hero.

Was it too late for Carter to be a better man?

When Carter started thinking about going private, all the work was international. That was fine. After three deployments, Carter was used to it. He would do the same job in the same hellhole and earn a hell of a lot more dough.

Then more and more people took gigs working the homeland. Now they didn't even call it the homeland. It was just home.

**P**olice were estimating that Officer Macklin had taken his life at about nine o'clock this morning. Carter had killed his cell phone at eight o'clock the night before. Even if the client had figured out immediately that Carter was off the rails, that left about thirteen hours to line up another doer. No way.

That confirmed what Carter had suspected the minute the client had changed the mission the first time. What had been a surveillance job had become an order to blow up a house in the suburbs. He was willing to do it. The woman was fair game. The rest of them were domestic terrorists, as far as he was concerned.

But the order didn't sit right with him. Carter worked best when the people giving the orders were as calm and rational and dispassionate as he was. The house explosion was about emotion. So was the order to kill Scott Macklin.

For Macklin to have died this morning without Carter pulling the trigger meant that the client had done it personally. And the client would know that Carter knew.

Carter had seen firsthand what the client's strategy was for people who knew too much. The woman. The retired cop. It was time to clean house.

It was unavoidable: Carter would be next. And he had no interest in spending the rest of his life in hiding.

Carter was a firm believer that any mission required complete knowledge of all available facts. Usually his mission was narrow—watch someone, break through a security alarm, find out a true identity. Here, it had escalated from following the woman, to planting the bomb, then taking out Scott Macklin. It was not his job to know the larger "why" behind these assignments.

Now that he was on his own, the "why" was precisely what he needed. But the two people who could have helped him were gone.

He should have called Macklin yesterday, before it was too late. He could have warned the man. Maybe it wouldn't have saved him, but it would have given him a chance to protect himself. And Carter could have asked Macklin why someone wanted him dead.

The woman might know, but Carter had no idea how to find her.

Without the woman, and without Macklin, Carter lacked the information he needed to get himself off whatever hit list the three of them shared.

He could think of only one other person who might be able to help: the man he'd seen meeting the woman on the train. Carter remembered his address.

He searched for the apartment's sales history online. Bingo. Purchased five years ago by Patrick Jordan and McKenna Wright.

He did a Google search of both names. Ah, a very nice wedding announcement in the Sunday Styles section of *The New York Times*. He was West Point, army, museum security. She was Stanford, Boalt Hall, prosecutor, writer.

Prosecutor. Carter clicked back to one of the stories he had read about Scott Macklin's suicide. *Last week* New York City *magazine published a ten-page article about the Marcus Jones shooting. The article was authored by McKenna Jordan (née Wright), the former prosecutor who initially raised doubts about Mr. Macklin's claim of self-defense.*

Interesting.

Was it too late for Carter to be a better man? He was about to start finding out.

Their phone number was listed under P. Jordan, same address.

"Hello?"

Carter was calling from a pay phone. Even if Patrick Jordan had caller ID, the number would mean nothing to him.

"You're going to be very interested in what I have to say."

"If that's a sales pitch, you need to work on it."

"Your girl is in danger," Carter said. He wanted to get this guy's attention. Patrick Jordan had to believe he needed Carter's help.

"Who is this? Do you have her?"

Huh. Carter had been hoping Patrick could lead him to the woman. Was Patrick looking for her, too?

"I'm not interested in hurting anyone. But you and I need to talk."

"We're talking now."

"In person," Carter said. He didn't know how Patrick might fit in to the picture. He didn't know where his loyalties were. He needed to meet him—alone. To read his body language. See his expressions. Figure out if they could trust each other.

"Leave McKenna out of this. She doesn't know anything."

Carter heard the break in Patrick Jordan's voice. He wasn't worried about the woman. For some reason, he was worried about his wife.

"If you care about her, you'll come," Carter said. "Trust me."

"Those two sentences don't belong together, guy."

Carter could see Forty-second Street and Lexington from the pay phone. Occupy Wall Street protestors were beginning to stream out of the 6 train exit. Others were pouring into Grand Central up Park Avenue. He'd selected the train station for the meeting because there was an unauthorized OWS flash mob scheduled to start in an hour. Big crowds. Big police presence. Big chaos. If he needed to get lost in the mob to get rid of Patrick, the protestors would provide cover.

"Grand Central Station. The north side, by the MetLife escalators. I'll come to you. One hour." He hung up, hoping that would do the trick.

He should have realized that he wasn't the only person who might be interested in the whereabouts of Patrick Jordan. Or that his attempt to get the man's attention would be so successful that Jordan would be too worried about his wife to notice he was being followed.

# CHAPTER
# FORTY-NINE

Three more drinks in, McKenna and Scanlin were hammering out wild scenarios that could connect Susan's disappearance with her reappearance and, most challenging of all, Scott Macklin's shooting of Marcus Jones.

Her phone buzzed on the table. It was Patrick. She let it go to voice mail.

"The timing between the Jones shooting and Susan's disappearance was close," she pointed out.

"I remember," he said. "That's part of the reason I hated you."

"I'd like to think I'd do things differently now."

He surprised her. "Me, too."

She was allowing herself to think aloud for the first time in two days. "The big debate was whether she left voluntarily or something bad happened to her. But if she's still alive? And if she has some kind of tie to Scott Macklin? You were the lead investigator. What do you think?"

He shook his head.

She was looking down at her gin, feeling the fatigue of the last two days. There was nothing she wasn't willing to say right now. "Look, we only got this far because I was willing to tell you that I basically saw a ghost. You have no idea how good it felt to talk about all of the insanity that has poured down in the last two days. And I'm not talking about therapy or purging or anything like that." She leaned forward intently and realized what a clichéd, intoxicated gesture it was. "But you and I are the only ones who know anything about this. You know about Susan. And Scott. We have to tell each other everything. Because you know things that I don't know. And I know things that you don't know." She was aware of the couple next to them, eavesdropping. She recognized that shared look—yep, she was wasted.

Scanlin was in the same zone. He needed to talk. To unleash. He was spinning the edge of his empty Scotch glass against the table. "After you called me last week, I asked for the cold-case files on the Hauptmann case."

She put down her gin and switched to water. "You did?"

"To tell you the truth, I wasn't my best back then. Family stuff." He waved a hand as if she'd know what he meant. "In retrospect, there were things I missed."

"See? This is what I meant. We need to work together."

"I didn't get anywhere."

"What is it they say about opting for the simplest explanation for multiple problems? Pretty much since I left the DA's office, I've lived in a world where every single day ends the same way it began. My world just happens to be falling apart at the same time Susan Hauptmann is running around on the New York City subway system wearing propaganda from a group involved in bomb-making, and when Scott Macklin just happens to decide to kill himself. There has to be a connection."

Her thoughts moved back to her husband. Patrick knew she'd been considering writing a book about the Macklin shooting. Patrick had been closer to Susan than she had ever allowed herself to recognize. But why would Susan care about the Macklin shooting? Her head was cloudy. Too much speculation. Too much gin.

Scanlin turned his glass upside down and slapped it on the table. "I got bupkes."

Her cell phone rang. It was Patrick again. She turned it off. She was on her way home. She was finally ready to talk things out in person.

"*And* I'm going home," Scanlin added. "Let me kick it around in my head some more. I'll check in with you tomorrow if you want."

"I'd like that, Detective. Thanks. And I'm really sorry to hear about Mac."

He started to throw cash on the table, but she insisted on paying.

She should have answered the phone when Patrick called. Or maybe it would have been enough had she checked her messages once she was alone in the bar. If she had, she would have called him back. He would have known she was okay—that she was on her way home, ready to talk to him. Ready to tell him that he needed to trust her with the truth. Ready to hear his side of the story and find a way to understand whatever role he had played in a ten-year lie.

But she didn't answer.

So he left a message, left their apartment, and walked into the night to meet a stranger.

It wasn't until she got back to their empty apartment that she checked her voice mail.

"Call me as soon as you can, if you can—if you're okay. Dammit." His voice cracked. "I got your message earlier and thought you were fine. But—I should have known. I should have told you. I should have—I'm so sorry. Fuck. I'm—Fuck!"

She listened to it again, and it made no more sense the second time.

She played a second message, assuming it would be from Patrick. It was Bob Vance. "McKenna, hi, it's Bob Vance. Um, I know things aren't good right now, but I thought you should know—Patrick just called me. I guess he'd been trying to get ahold of Dana with no luck, but he wanted to know whether you were out with the magazine crowd again like you were last night. I told him I didn't know what he was talking about. Dana quit, and—Sorry, the magazine's lawyers are requiring every employee to notify them about all contact with you. Anyway, I don't know what you told him about where you've been the last couple days, but I thought I should let you know he called me. I hope things work out for you. Sorry, I'm rambling. And now I guess I'll have to tell our lawyers about this stupid message. Bye."

Patrick had caught her in a lie, too. What was happening to them?

She tried his cell. Straight to voice mail. Either he had turned it off or was somewhere without reception.

She finished a quick walk through the apartment. The Susan box still open in the living room. The blankets pulled hastily over the bed, the way Patrick did it on weekdays. Not exactly hospital corners. Not exactly unmade.

Then she saw the note on the kitchen counter. *Phone call from unidentified man claiming to have my wife. Meeting him at Grand Central.* Patrick's signature, followed by today's date and the time, half an hour ago.

He had left the note behind in case he never came home.

She called Scanlin. She'd never heard her own voice sound like that before. Loud. Shrieking. Hysterical. "It's Patrick. He left. Someone said they'd kidnapped me. He's gone—a meeting at Grand Central Station. We have to find him."

"All right, just calm down. I'll call it in. They'll have someone there to look for him."

She was already out the door.

# CHAPTER FIFTY

**M**cKenna let out a groan in the backseat of the cab as the light at Thirty-fourth and Park turned red once more. She could have subwayed it faster than this. "Can we go around or something?"

"Your noises don't make the cars move any faster," the driver said.

"You don't understand. It's an emergency."

"Everyone believes everything is an emergency these days. Turn on the TV if you'd like. Some people find it makes the time pass more quickly. Or take deep breaths and count. That's what I do."

Great. She had the only yoga-practicing cabbie in New York City.

"Please. Go in the right lane. It's faster. And if you take the next turn, we can go over to Third. I'll pay you double the fare."

"You have to let me do my job. I hear it on the radio. Big protest at Grand Central. It's a traffic jam all the way around."

"Fine. I'll go on foot." She tossed him a twenty through the window of the plastic partition.

"Wait. You can't get out here. I need to pull to the curb."

She stepped out into the middle of the street, weaving her way to the sidewalk through the gridlocked, horn-blasting cars. She could jog to Grand Central in five minutes.

She noticed the first protestors on Thirty-sixth Street. She could tell from their signs. One said: HONK IF YOU'RE IN DEBT. The other was: SAY NO TO TRADE DEALS, YES TO U.S. JOBS.

By the time she hit Forty-first, protestors outnumbered regular commuters, many dressed to make their point. Union workers had come in factory and trade uniforms. Others wore red, white, and blue to emphasize patriotism. McKenna spotted one couple dressed in full business attire but with makeup to create white faces, black undereye circles, and bloody mouths. Handmade signs around their necks identified them as Corporate Zombies.

By far the most common accessories were masks. Halloween masks with dollars taped over the mouth holes. Black bags over heads to simulate images from Abu Ghraib. And the most popular staple of the Occupy crowd: the pale-faced, rosy-cheeked, soul-patched masks of Guy Fawkes from *V for Vendetta*. In typical New York City fashion, an entrepreneurial street vendor was selling the masks on the corner. Apparently the irony of purchasing a mask licensed by a multinational media conglomerate to participate in a 99-percenter protest was lost on some people.

As McKenna tried pushing her way north through the crowd, she realized that just as many protestors were trying to leave Grand Central as were heading there. As she got closer to Forty-second Street, the individual comments became more specific.

*Forget it, too crowded.*

*They've got it blockaded. That's bogus. They can't keep us from gathering in a public place.*

*This is getting crazy.*

*It's got to be the cops, man. They're probably beating on people again.*

*Holy shit. People are, like,* running *out of there.*

*I just heard there were gunshots. We've got to get out of here.*

*Oh my God, people got shot.*

*They're saying he was in a* Vendetta *mask. You know they'll try to pin this on us.*

As the words rippled through the crowd—gunfire, gunshots—a consensus built to move south. She pushed against it, turning sideways as necessary to press between protestors. She could see Forty-second Street now. She was almost there.

A wall of police officers behind barricades greeted her at the corner.

"I've got to get in there," she said to the nearest one.

"Not gonna happen."

"My husband's in there—"

"Well, he won't be for long. We're evacuating the station. You need to leave, ma'am."

"There was a shooting?" She said it like a question, then realized there was only one way she was going to get past this barrier. "I got a call that there was a shooting. It's my husband, Patrick Jordan. My husband's involved. I need to get in there. *Now!*"

The officer disconnected two of the barriers, allowing her to pass. An older officer, also in uniform, wasn't happy about the development. "Mario, what are you doing?"

"This lady says her husband's one of the guys got shot."

More than one person shot. More than one male.

The two officers led her through the press of people being cleared from the train station. She found herself praying. Please don't let it be Patrick. I'll do anything. Please not him.

The older officer seemed to be the one who knew where they should go once they were inside Grand Central, heading directly to the stream of yellow crime tape that formed a large right triangle from the west balcony staircase to the circular information booth and over to the escalators. She spotted a huddle of three people in the center of the marked-off scene. One was crouched on the ground.

She cried out when she saw the puddle of blood behind them.

The huddlers turned toward her.

"I thought we were clearing this place out." The man wore plainclothes. Badge on belt. Shoulder holster. He had to be a detective.

"This lady says she got a call. Said her husband was one of the shooting victims."

The detective walked toward her and stopped at the crime tape.

"What's your angle, lady? You with the protestors or something? Because we haven't called anyone."

"It's my husband. He got a phone call telling him to come here." She handed him the note Patrick had left in their apartment. "I think he's in danger."

The officer who originally let her through the barricades sighed. "Dammit. I'm sorry, Detectives. She told me *she* got a call. I swear to God. I should have confirmed it with you before bringing her back."

"Get her out of here," the detective said.

"My husband's name is Patrick Jordan." McKenna fumbled for her phone and showed him the screen saver—it was a picture of them together at the High Line. She was kissing his cheek. There was a rainbow over the Hudson River.

"Hold on just a second," the detective said. He walked toward the balcony staircase. She watched as he made a call. She couldn't hear the conversation, but she could imagine the words. Because she knew. She already knew. The way he looked at that picture. The way he stopped the officer from walking her out of the station. He must have recognized Patrick.

When he turned back toward her, something in his face had changed. Serious. No longer annoyed at her presence. Even sympathetic.

Oh my God. Not Patrick. Please, God, no.

# PART IV

So much past inside my present.

—Feist

# CHAPTER FIFTY-ONE

**M**cKenna's shoulders began to shake as the detective delivered the news. "Two men were rushed to the hospital with gunshot wounds. One was dead on arrival."

She felt one of the uniformed police officer's hands grab her under the arm as her knees gave out beneath her.

"Because they were rushed by ambulance," the detective continued, "we didn't have identification on either man. But I just phoned the hospital. One of the men had a wallet in his back pocket. According to his driver's license, his name is Patrick Jordan."

"No. Oh God, no."

"He's in critical condition. They're operating on him now, but he's alive. Your husband's alive."

The prayers started all over again. Prayers that surgery could save him. Prayers that she would see him again. Prayers that they would have a chance to fix whatever they'd gotten themselves into.

"We'll get you to the hospital right away."

"Thank you."

"Of course, it would help if you could answer some questions we have. You said he got a phone call instructing him to come here? Was he part of the protest?"

"Please, Detective, I need to get to the hospital. I need to be with my husband."

"Mrs. Jordan. While I sympathize with your situation, another man is dead. And we're looking at some very strange facts. The deceased victim had a gun in his waistband. We have witnesses who saw him reaching for it. And here's the thing—the reason your husband's alive and the other man is dead? Your husband came here with four thick law books strapped around his torso with duct tape, like a makeshift bulletproof vest."

She would have laughed at the ridiculousness of the image if this weren't really happening. In the ongoing negotiations that determined their household TV-watching schedule, he'd tolerated her passion for a show about a burned spy. In one episode, the main character wrapped himself in books from the law library to protect himself from a knife. Patrick had known what she was going to ask before she'd even opened her mouth. *Yes, that would work.* She couldn't imagine how desperate Patrick must have been to try something so haphazard.

"This doesn't appear to have been a random incident. We need information."

She knew now that Patrick had been lying to her. He'd known that Susan was still alive, and he'd known for perhaps the last ten years. She also knew from his note that Patrick had come here expecting to face danger. And he had come in a rush. No time to go to the museum for the gun he stored in a locker there. No time for real body armor, just stupid books. And he had done it not for Susan but for her.

Ten years. If Patrick had lied to her, to the police, to Susan's father for ten years? He must have had his reasons.

"What did you say your name was, Detective?"

"My apologies, ma'am. I'm Tim Compton."

"I hope you won't take offense at this, Detective Compton, but there's only one police officer I'm willing to talk to right now. His name's Joe Scanlin. I can give you his number if you need it. Now, are you going to help me get to the hospital, or do I have to get there myself?"

**S**he woke up on a chair in the corner of the waiting room outside the Intensive Care Unit at Lenox Hill Hospital. Someone had placed a man's sports coat over her body. She recognized it as the jacket Joe Scanlin had been wearing earlier that night.

Or was it last night? Was it morning now?

The clock above the double doors into the ICU said 6:20. Light seeped through the waiting room blinds. It was morning.

She was at the nurses' station trying to get someone's attention when Scanlin walked in with two Styrofoam cups of coffee. He handed her one. "Hope black is all right."

She nodded her appreciation and took a quick sip. "Where's Patrick? Any news?" She remembered being awake in the same waiting room chair at one-thirty in the morning, when the doctor emerged from the double doors. Patrick had two gunshot wounds. One in the torso, one in the neck. The damage was severe, but the surgery had gone well.

"What does that mean?" she'd asked. "He'll make it? When can I see him?"

Everything the surgeon had said was straight out of the bedside-manner handbook. Have to wait and see. Up to his body to determine how he responds. Not yet conscious. She wanted to punch him in the throat when he used the phrase "cautiously optimistic."

Scanlin shook his head. "Nothing new. Sorry."

"When did you get here?"

"Just a couple of hours ago. I'd passed out at home by the time Compton started calling. He said you wouldn't talk to him without me? Not a way to make friends with the police investigating your husband's case."

"Compton told me that Patrick had taped some of my law books to his body like a makeshift protective vest. He has a gun, but it stays in a locker at work. Obviously he expected danger but didn't have enough notice to get to the museum. And he didn't call the police. Patrick is the bravest person I've ever known." The kind of person you'd want in charge of the planet if it ever got invaded by aliens. *That* kind of brave. "He had to have his reasons for not call-ing the police." She suspected the reasons were related to Susan's decision to fake her own death.

Scanlin cut her off. "All right, I get it. But Compton wants some answers. And maybe you and I have reached some kind of truce, but I'm still a cop. I've got to tell him what I know."

She nodded.

"By the way," he said, "those law books you mentioned? Comp-ton says they saved your husband's life. The torso shot would have been fatal, but it was barely a puncture wound by the time it passed through all those pages. If it hadn't been for the neck shot, he would have walked away from the entire thing with nothing more than a bandage."

She remembered the surgeon telling her the same thing. How many times had Patrick asked her to throw out her old casebooks? Every time she'd moved, he'd said it was like lugging around six boxes of bricks.

The books may have protected his body, but they hadn't covered his neck. A gunshot in the neck. They were talking about it like it was something he could live through, but she could tell they were hiding the truth. Was there any part of the body that was more vul-nerable than the neck?

"Did you get any information from Compton?" she asked.

"He showed me a photo of the man who was DOA. Not just a bystander. He's the same guy who wiped out your video of Susan on the subway platform."

The Cleaner. "So who was he?"

He shook his head. "No cell phone on the body. No ID. So far his prints have come up *nada* in the databases."

"Is he the one who shot Patrick?"

"No. Based on what Compton knows for now, Patrick and the mystery man were standing in the same vicinity, which was packed with Occupy protestors. Gunshots rang out. The shooter was in the crowd wearing a Guy Fawkes mask and cape. He got lost in the ensuing chaos. I saw some video footage. Trying to track the guy on the tape was like keeping your eye on one bee in a hive."

Her husband's shooting was on tape. At some point, she would see a man in a mask walk up to her husband and put a bullet in his neck.

"I know you need to brief Compton," she said. "But he won't be any closer than we are to understanding what's happening. There has to be some connection between Susan's disappearance and Scott Macklin. There's no way around it. You worked Susan's case ten years ago. And I was the one who basically ended Macklin's career. You knew him, and I knew her. If anyone's going to figure out the connection, it's us. You said last night you had the case file on Susan's disappearance. Where is it?"

# CHAPTER FIFTY-TWO

If anyone had told McKenna a week ago that she'd be standing in Joe Scanlin's living room, she would have checked his pupils.

The house was clean but dated. An entire wall was nearly covered with framed photographs. A young Scanlin in uniform, probably right out of the academy. Scanlin in a tuxedo next to his gorgeous bride on the church steps. The young couple with their little girl in front of a muted blue background, probably at a JCPenney picture studio. She noticed that the wall-size scrapbook seemed to end abruptly. In the most recent photographs, Scanlin looked the way she remembered him from when Susan disappeared. It was as if life in this house were frozen still.

He caught her checking her cell phone again for missed calls. "I can take you back to Lenox Hill," he offered.

"No. I'm fine. They said they'd call if they had any news." Scanlin had the files from Susan's disappearance at his house. By coming here with him, she'd given them an hour's head start.

He spread the files across the table and gave her an overview. Most of it was information she'd been able to glean at the time: No blood, semen, or other physical evidence at Susan's apartment. No financial problems. No enemies. No obvious motive for anyone to want to hurt Susan Hauptmann.

Tell me again about the men," she said.

He shrugged. "Well, from what I can tell, she may have been . . . a little open with her sexuality."

McKenna looked away. It was no easier for her than for Scanlin to have this discussion. That side of Susan had always been there, but McKenna had never wanted to process the reality.

"It's like a dark side," she said. Since Susan's disappearance, Mc-Kenna had been carrying around all the best memories of her friend. Her unparalleled generosity. Her courage. Her disarming humor.

Now she was recalling another side. "She seemed like a strong, independent, self-respecting woman, but at a certain time of day, all she really wanted was the attention of a man. She hid it from me, but there were signs. I just didn't want to see them."

How many times had an exhausted McKenna left a bar alone at two in the morning, a pit in her stomach because Susan insisted on staying behind for "one last drink," almost always with some guy she'd just met. And what about all those late-night phone calls? The ones Susan would answer out of earshot, only to announce within the next few minutes that she needed to meet an old friend who was having a rough time.

Susan may have tried to hide her promiscuity from her girl-friends, but McKenna had suspected. Men, after all, weren't so dis-creet. She'd heard the talk at happy hours. McKenna knew that Susan had hooked up with at least a couple of prosecutors she had met through McKenna, including Will Getty.

"You know, it's funny," Scanlin said. "Usually when we talk about a dark side, we're talking about a man who turns all that anger and destruction against other people—his wife, his children, a stranger out of nowhere. But I used to see it back when I was in vice. These women with dark sides, they rarely turned against other people. They took it out on themselves."

Scanlin pulled out another manila folder, this one less yellowed. "A neighbor in Susan's building called in a noise report two days before she disappeared, but got the wrong apartment number. I talked to the neighbor, and it's likely that what she overheard was a fight between Susan and a man. Take a look at some of the words she wrote down." He pointed to the word "smack." "Maybe one of Susan's boyfriends had started getting physical with her, and they were arguing about it after the fact." He pointed to another word. "Important." "Maybe something like 'It's really important that you never smack me again.'"

"I think it's safe to say that Hollywood won't be calling you to write dialogue, Scanlin. Besides, if any guy raised a hand to Susan Hauptmann, he'd need a new set of teeth by the time she was done with him. But you mentioned working vice and how the prostitutes had a dark side." She realized that in giving him her rundown, she'd left out Agent Mercado asking about Pamela Morris and Greg Larson. She told him about going out to Jersey City to talk to Pamela's mother. "Susan was always trying to help lost souls. Maybe she crossed paths with Pamela. They both disappeared at the same time. Pamela Morris's mother hasn't seen her since the fall of 2003."

"Then how does she know her daughter's alive?"

"She gets letters a couple times a year. Pamela says she's married to a preacher and travels around the country. I thought maybe that was her way of describing life with the P3s."

"What does Pamela Morris look like?"

McKenna shrugged. "I've got one booking photo from 1998, and she's got on a pound of makeup and sporting a fat lip. Brown hair, dyed blond at the time. Kind of regular."

"Age? Height? Weight?"

She searched her memory for the details and saw where Scanlin was going. "Oh my God."

"A couple cards a year to Mom are a small price to pay for a stolen identity."

She remembered the fat lip lingering in Pamela's booking photo. It wasn't her first bust. She was deep into the life. And then she turned over a new leaf? That happened only in Hollywood. In real life, women who took the road chosen by Pamela Morris did not get happy endings. "You're saying that the Pamela Morris who was living with the P3s out in Brentwood was actually Susan."

"Hate to say it, but prostitutes die all the time," Scanlin said. "A lot of them are never identified. Taking a dead person's identity is one of the easiest ways in the world to get a fresh start."

Susan had been at Scott Macklin's house the day before he died. If Susan was the woman who had been living with the P3s as Pamela Morris, she must have survived the explosion on Long Island.

"But to take over Pamela's identity, Susan would have to know that she was dead."

She was looking at the papers spread across the dining room table, hoping an answer would come to her.

Then she saw it. "The neighbor. Susan's neighbor who called about the noise from the argument. You said she reported the wrong apartment. Is it possible she made other mistakes? About what she actually heard?"

"Sure. She's practically deaf now."

"Look, Scanlin. Right here." She jabbed her index finger against the page on the table. "Smack. But not *smack*. Mac! We know Susan went to Mac's house the day before he died. But if she was arguing with him—or *about* him—two days before she suddenly disappeared? There's a connection between Susan's disappearance and whatever happened on that dock between Macklin and Marcus Jones."

"And you're trying to say that the connection—whatever it may be—would somehow explain why Susan is now using Pamela Morris's name?"

He meant the statement sarcastically, but hearing him say the words out loud made all the difference. Scott Macklin. Pamela Morris. Together. Connected.

Pamela's mother told me that toward the end, before she rode off into the sunset with her knight on a white horse, she was only seeing her regulars. Harmless, lonely married guys. That kind of thing. She specifically said that one of the guys was strange-looking and slow but nice to Pamela."

Scanlin's face didn't register the point.

"Marcus Jones," she said. "The pigmentation of his face was blotchy because of a skin condition called vitiligo. And his IQ was around seventy-five, placing him at what's considered the borderline. His mother always maintained that he'd gone down to the docks to meet his girlfriend. We never found the girl, but he did have eighty dollars in his pocket."

"And the docks are a frequent cruising spot for working girls," Scanlin added.

"If Susan took over Pamela's identity, she'd have to know that Pamela wouldn't need it anymore. Maybe Marcus Jones wasn't the only person who died at the pier that night. What if Mac's shooting of Marcus Jones was bad, and Pamela Morris saw it?"

"You're saying Mac intentionally killed her to cover it up? You've *got* to be kidding me. You know, this was a bad idea. I should have known—"

"Hey, we're just talking things out, Scanlin. There are other explanations. Maybe Marcus was involved in something going down on the docks—selling stolen merchandise or something. Pamela Morris is there to meet him but sees something she's not supposed to see. Marcus, or maybe someone else, hurts her. And then Mac comes along, and Marcus pulls the gun on him."

"Mac never said anything about Marcus being with a girl, let alone someone killing her."

"You see my point, don't you? If something happened that night on the docks that we don't know about—whatever *it* might be— that would explain the timing of Pamela going off the grid. And Susan's disappearance, if she found out about it. And the fact that someone doesn't want me rehashing that night."

Scanlin was out of his chair, pacing. "Except—one—you don't even know what the 'something' that happened might be. Two—

you have no reason to think that Susan Hauptmann was connected to it. Look, no offense, but I think we've done all we can here. Compton's a good cop. He's going to look for whoever hurt your husband, and once he has some answers, maybe that will shed some light on Susan and everything else." He took a look at his watch. "I've got a shift. I'll drop you back in the city. You'll feel better once you get an update about Patrick."

The car ride was silent but for the adult contemporary radio station that Scanlin turned on to fill the void. When she thanked him as she got out at Lenox Hill, he simply nodded an acknowledgment.

The ICU was busier than when they'd left. The halls were filled with nurses and interns in scrubs. People stepped aside to make room for patients being moved on gurneys. McKenna got the attention of a nurse. There was no new information, but they had moved Patrick into a patient room, where she could sit with him if she'd like.

As long as she had known Patrick, he'd been healthy. He was just one of those people. He could pig out for four straight days over Thanksgiving and not gain a single ounce. He could stay up until two and wake at seven, looking refreshed, his eyes circle-free. If he got a cold, it came and went with a few sneezes, a couple of coughs, and a handful of over-the-counter meds. And though he had aged in their time together—the lines around his mouth, the gray hair at his temples—it wasn't in a way that made him appear weak or frail; it made him look like a man who spent time outdoors.

So when she saw him in the hospital bed, she wanted to find the nurse and explain that she'd been sent to the wrong room. The man attached to all those tubes and hoses couldn't be her husband. Just above the edge of his baby-blue polka-dotted gown was a wad of gauze taped around his neck. She knew that the gown and the gauze covered the gun wounds and surgery scars. If he managed to pull through this, those marks would be there forever, constant reminders of the events that had put him in this bed.

She looked at his pale, stubbled face beneath the oxygen mask. How could he have lost so much weight in one day? Was that possible? She wanted to see his eyes open. To watch him smile when he recognized her. To see *him*. To see him and know that they were going to be okay. That whatever secrets he may have been keeping were for all the best reasons. He would wake up and tell her everything, and then they could somehow make this right.

But he didn't open his eyes.

She felt herself starting to shut down from the inside like a child's toy whose battery had died. They'd find her body, slumped and nonresponsive, in this orange vinyl visitor's chair.

She reached out and placed her hand on Patrick's bicep, the only part of his body exposed between the blankets and the cotton gown. She tried to remember what it felt like to place her head on that exact spot as he slept, their bodies pressed together like spoons.

She never should have gone to Dana's. She should have gone home and confronted him. Torn off the bandages and learned the truth, however ugly. She hadn't, and now he was here, and she might never know why.

She leaned down and kissed his forehead. No response, not like a fairy tale, where the prince awakes. Not even a fleeting moment of comfort in which she magically knew that everything would be okay. It was just her dry lips against his warm skin.

She was not going to stay here and collapse out of helplessness. Only two weeks earlier, she had published a six-page article to commemorate the tenth anniversary of the death of Marcus Jones. Now Scott Macklin was dead. So was the man who had wiped out the videos of Susan on the subway platform. Patrick was in critical condition. And it all had something to do with the night Marcus Jones died.

She had missed something. Ten years ago, her suspicions about the gun next to Marcus Jones's body had briefly shone a light on the events that had transpired on the docks the night of October 16. But then she was disproved and the lights went dark. A decade later, with the publication of a six-page article, she had managed to lose her job, her reputation, and most important, her husband's safety. Someone wanted the lights to remain off. She was going to turn them on again.

# CHAPTER
# FIFTY-THREE

**A**s McKenna stepped off the elevator on the basement level of the courthouse, she heard two women whisper as they passed: "That's the magazine reporter who teed off on Knight." She couldn't make out the second woman's complete response, but she did hear "he had it coming" and "basically true."

That was the way the truth worked sometimes. An eyewitness might make a mistake about the color of the gunman's shirt but still pick the right man. Maybe McKenna had been wrong ten years ago when she claimed that Macklin had planted a drop gun on Marcus's body, but maybe the core of the allegation had been on the mark.

The woman at the front desk of the Supreme Court record room was reading a novel called *Criminal*.

"How about that," McKenna said. "A real, live hardcover book with pages and everything. Nice to know I'm not the only person around who likes my reading old-school."

Instead of leaving the book open with a broken spine, the woman carefully placed a Post-it note to mark her spot. "My son bought me one of those e-readers for Christmas. It was good for my summer cruise. On that tiny little machine, I took a book for every day of the trip. But there's something about turning the pages of a hefty book."

McKenna had learned the fine art of talking up administrative staff during her judicial clerkship. She could call for district court records and have pages faxed within the hour. Her coclerk, Richard, who made it clear in every call that he was a very, very impressive young lawyer working for a very, very influential appellate court judge, never understood why his requests took a week to answer. It wasn't about power or authority or official obligations. It was basic human nature: people wanted to help the nice guys and shaft the douches.

"I'm hoping you can help me out with something. I need the court file for *People* v. *Scott Macklin*. It's an old one, I'm afraid." McKenna gave the month and year for the original opening of the file.

"Oh, sure. I remember this one." The woman must have been too engrossed in her novel to have read the news about Macklin's death. "You think that's old, I had a girl in here this morning asking for a forty-year-old landlord-tenant dispute. Her building is claiming that her grandmother was evicted from a rent-controlled apartment back in the seventies, which would mean she had no right to live there now. Poor thing couldn't stop crying. I found the file, though. Turns out the eviction was never finalized. It's nice when you actually get a happy ending."

"Well, if you could find that, my file should be a cinch."

"Is there a specific document you're looking for, or do you want the whole thing? Keep in mind that photocopies are a quarter a page. And no, in case you're wondering, the money does not go to the nice lady who runs the copies."

"Wouldn't that be nice. I want the whole file, but trust me, it's a thin one."

"My favorite kind," the woman said with a smile.

Twenty minutes later, McKenna had what she needed. A twenty-minute wait at the courthouse was the equivalent of the speed of light in the rest of the world.

**M**cKenna found a bench at the far end of the basement hallway and settled in to review the file.

The stack of pages was, as expected, thin. The file was thin because there had been no charges at all. Typically there would be no documentation other than a single slip of paper with a checkmark from the grand jury, indicating that it had not true-billed the case—a fancy way of saying flushed. But the Marcus Jones shooting wasn't typical, especially after a young but respected ADA stuck her neck out and claimed that the grand jury hadn't heard all the relevant evidence.

Because of the intense public scrutiny, the district attorney had taken the extra step of filing a memorandum declining to pursue the case further, complete with a detailed justification. It was signed by the lead prosecutor who had presented the case to the grand jury, Will Getty.

She skimmed the introduction. Scott Macklin. Thirteen years with NYPD. At the seaport that night for a routine assignment pursuant to a federal-state cargo inspection program.

The report moved on to Macklin's version of the night's events. He noticed Marcus near the inland edge of the dock. Marcus appeared to be monitoring the movement of computer parts into a shipping container. Because the docks still saw the occasional snatch-and-grab, Macklin approached the teenager as a precaution. When Marcus saw Macklin heading his way, he turned and ran. Macklin pursued him, turned a corner around a shipping container, and saw Marcus reach for a weapon. He had no choice but to shoot.

The next section of the report summarized Marcus Jones's background, his mother's insistence that he did not own a gun, and McKenna's tracing of the gun back to Safe Streets, the police-sponsored gun destruction program. Only four NYPD officers had been scheduled to transport the Safe Streets guns from a locked property room to the smelter. Scott Macklin was one of them.

The report did everything it could to make McKenna's inference appear reasonable, which it would have been if not for Don Whitman. As the report went on to explain, Whitman was one of the other three Safe Streets cops. More significantly, he was convicted a few years later for being on the Crips' payroll.

When Getty realized that Whitman could have walked off with a Safe Streets gun just as easily as Macklin, he sent investigators back into Marcus's neighborhood, searching for someone who could tie Marcus to a gun slipped eight years earlier to the Crips.

The witness was James Low. The twenty-two-year-old lived in the same housing project as Marcus Jones. He testified to the grand jury that he'd sold the gun to Jones for two hundred bucks after finding it in his father's dresser following his father's death. Before his uneventful death from acute myocardial infarction, James Low, Sr., was considered a "five-star universal elite" in the New York City Crips hierarchy.

When McKenna had heard the news, only one word captured her surprise: "Un-fucking-believable."

The grand jury testimony of James Low, Jr., completed the chain from property room, to junk pile, to Officer Don Whitman, to James Low, Sr., to Jr., to Marcus Jones. In comparison, Macklin's connection to the gun was a fluke.

Or was it? McKenna had been so mortified by her rush to judgment that she had never stopped to question the alternative. She had simply assumed that Low was telling the truth.

She made her way back to the file room. The nice reading lady was back into her novel. "That was quick," she said.

"I've got another request, if you don't mind. Can you tell me whether you have any cases involving a James Low?"

The woman typed a few commands into a computer on the front desk. "I've got a few, all criminal. Starts back in 1972, looks like the most recent is 2004."

"There was a Senior and a Junior. I'm interested in the kid."

"Got it. Yes, the younger was charged as Junior. I got three cases, all resulting in convictions—theft in 1999, assault-three in 2001, and an assault-three in 2004."

McKenna already knew from the Marcus Jones case that by the time Low testified before the grand jury, he had two misdemeanor convictions—a shoplifting incident in 1999, and a misdemeanor assault in 2001 for punching a guy who spent too much time check-

ing out Low's girlfriend at a bowling alley. McKenna asked the nice
reading lady for a copy of the 2004 file.

This time McKenna didn't bother to resume her spot on the
hallway bench. She skimmed the file at the counter. The nice lady,
returning to her novel, didn't seem to mind.

According to the probable-cause affidavit filed the night of
Low's arrest, Low had been one of several men in the VIP lounge
of a hip-hop club in Chelsea. An argument broke out between
two groups of customers. The genesis of the dispute was stupid, as
usual—something about a member of the other group insulting the
ex-girlfriend of Low's cousin's friend's brother—but it culminated
in Low's side attacking the rivals with liquor bottles.

The arresting officer booked Low for felony assault. A bottle was
a weapon. Multiple perpetrators made the assault a gang attack.

McKenna knew the district attorney's filing policies. This was
definitely a felony. Low's misdemeanor assault only three years earlier would have made him an unsympathetic candidate for plea
bargaining and sentencing.

And yet.

Low pleaded to a misdemeanor. Seven days in jail, which in reality meant a night or two before early release. Instead of doing
real time in state prison, he chilled out in local for a few hours and
walked away without a felony conviction. In highbrow legal terms,
it was a sweetheart deal, and it came only a little over a year after
Low's grand jury testimony had saved New York's law enforcement
community from a scandal whose toxicity would have lingered for
a generation.

Even before she turned to the last page of the file, where the attorneys of record were listed on the final page of the conviction
order, she knew what name she would find there. For the people of
New York County: Assistant District Attorney Will Getty.

# CHAPTER FIFTY-FOUR

**S**usan had her fair share of dalliances, and Will Getty was on the list.

Neither of them flaunted that fact, but McKenna wasn't blind. She had been the one to introduce them. She remembered the night.

McKenna didn't know Getty well yet. It was about four months before the Marcus Jones shooting. He was one of the lifers, already handling major crimes. She was only four years in, handling drug cases but beginning to eye more serious assignments.

She had worked late, as usual. When she left, Getty was also heading out. It began with chitchat in the elevator.

"Not that I'm monitoring you or anything, but I'm pretty sure this is the first time I've seen you leave the office. I was starting to think you lived here."

"That's a hologram to fool people into thinking I'm actually working."

"I'll deny it if you ever tell anyone I said this, but take it easy. You don't want to burn out before you get to the fun stuff."

"Duly noted."

They stepped out on the ground floor.

"You heading to happy hour?" he asked.

"I am heading to *a* happy hour but not the *office* happy hour."

"Another piece of unsolicited advice: spend less time at your desk and more time drinking with your coworkers. Friendships matter."

"Trust me. If you knew how much I drank my first two years in this office, you'd sign me up for the liver transplant waiting list."

"Ah, but that's when you were just a baby ADA, playing with the other kids. We career guys know how it works. Most of the newbies are here for a couple years of trial experience, then jump ship to make some dough. We don't bother getting to know people until they've been around a while. Now you need to jump in with the older generation. Graduate to the lifer crowd."

"Can you seriously tell me that hanging with the lifer crowd is any different than the usual scene in this office?"

"Did you really just use the word 'scene' to describe the DA's office?"

"You know what I mean. The war stories. Who crushed which defense attorney at trial. Who hauled out the most badass line during plea negotiations. Everyone's always trying to out-macho each other."

Wincing, he started to offer a retort but stopped himself. "Yeah, that does sound familiar, doesn't it?"

"At least when I play, I do it with people who don't talk shop all night."

He looked at his watch. "They're probably all gone by now. Damn, I could use a drink. I had a cooperating codefendant retract his confession on me today. Total nightmare."

"Well, my happy hour's just getting started. You should come."

"Nah, I'd be crashing."

"No such thing." She explained the concept of Susan's monthly the-more-the-merrier gatherings. "Seriously, you should come. It's my chance to convince you that I do have a life outside this office."

She could tell he was on the fence. She pressed him. "I wouldn't ask if I didn't think you'd have fun. And you did say you needed a drink."

"Sold."

Susan had been delighted to see McKenna arrive with a guest in tow—a decent-looking male guest, to boot. Despite McKenna's assurances to Getty, she had not enjoyed much of a life beyond work recently. After a long dry spell, she had met Jason Eberly (aka Nature Boy) two weeks earlier at a city bar event, but it was nothing serious. And it never would be, because McKenna would meet Patrick at the next Bruno happy hour.

In typical Susan fashion, she wasted no time jumping into the gutter once Getty broke away to the men's room. "I knew you wanted a faster track to trying homicides, but sleeping with your boss? A bit unseemly for you, dear."

"Not funny, Bruno. That's how rumors get started."

"He's single, right?"

"To my knowledge."

"And he's not technically your boss."

"No, but he could be down the road."

Though the conversation could have ended there, Susan went on. "You're absolutely certain you're not interested? Hundred percent?"

"A hundred and ten percent. Nothing good comes from interoffice romance."

When Getty returned to the table, Susan moved her chair a hair closer to his and laughed at his jokes with a little more enthusiasm. McKenna had seen the transition before. And she could tell Getty liked it.

Four months later, Scott Macklin would shoot Marcus Jones, and Getty would select McKenna to assist with the grand jury investigation. She would wonder at the time whether she got the assignment because of her hard work or because she'd inadvertently gotten him laid.

She wouldn't really care. She had a homicide—the sexiest kind, an officer-involved shooting. Her career was finally starting. And then it ended. And Susan was gone. And now McKenna was wondering if it was all because she had bumped into Will Getty on that elevator.

Thanks anyway," McKenna said to the nice reading lady. "Thanks for everything."

The woman hadn't found any record of a conviction for the final name McKenna had asked about. There was only one person who could provide the information she needed.

McKenna couldn't get cell reception in the file room, so she took the elevator up to the ground floor of the courthouse. Gretchen answered on the third ring. "I told you I don't want to be involved."

Stupid caller ID. Given how their last encounter ended, it was a wonder that Susan's sister had picked up at all.

"It's one question, Gretchen. I promise. You said you almost got prosecuted federally when you were arrested, but you worked out a plea deal for a state conviction with rehab and probation."

"It's all ancient history, McKenna."

"You said the case was pending for a while, but you got the deal just a couple of months before Susan disappeared?" There was no record of Gretchen's conviction in New York County, which meant she had gotten her record expunged—a lenient outcome considering the severity of the initial allegations.

"Glad you were listening."

Damn, she was a bitch. "Do you know if a local prosecutor was involved?"

"Sure. My attorney did a full-court press. Finally found a guy willing to make a call to the feds—someone Susan knew. I was surprised she didn't go to you. She must not have wanted you to know."

McKenna didn't have the kind of network that a more experienced prosecutor would have. Like Getty had said, sometimes the job was about the friendships you'd made. The question was how close a friend he'd been with Susan before she disappeared.

"Was the prosecutor a guy called Will Getty?"

"My record's supposed to be clear. How did you know?"

The night Susan and Getty met couldn't have been a one-night stand if Susan had reached out to Getty for a favor four months down the road. Maybe they'd had something resembling a relationship. If Getty was involved in covering up the Marcus Jones shooting, Susan could have found out about it.

A beep-beep from her phone notified McKenna that another call was coming in. She assured Gretchen that there was no record of her drug case and ended the call.

"This is McKenna Jordan," she said.

"Ms. Jordan. My name is Mae Mauri. I'm a physician at New York Family Medical."

"Is this about Patrick?" She started rushing toward the courthouse exit, hoping he was conscious. Hoping she could finally talk to him.

"No, I'm—" She sounded confused by the question. "I hope you'll forgive the intrusion. I contacted your former employer for your number."

"I'm sorry, Doctor. I'm waiting for some very important news about the health of a family member."

"Of course. But I believe you're looking for Susan Hauptmann. I may have information you'll be interested in."

# CHAPTER FIFTY-FIVE

The receptionist at the front desk of the New York Family Medical practice greeted McKenna with a warm smile and a soft, soothing voice. "Good morning. You're here for a wellness visit?"

McKenna felt like she was checking in for a spa appointment. "I'm here to see Dr. Mauri. She's expecting me."

"Of course. Are you a new patient? I usually recognize everyone. I'll just need your insurance information."

"No, I'm not a patient. It's a different kind of appointment. Please, if you could just tell Dr. Mauri I'm here. McKenna Jordan."

"No worries. I'll let the doctor know."

*No worries.* When did that ridiculous sentence become an acceptable thing to say to another person? As far as McKenna could tell, the phrase was used most frequently when there was, in fact, a reason to worry, and almost always by the very person who was the source of the current worry. This annoying woman had no idea what worries McKenna was harboring.

The woman returned. "The doctor's ready for you," the worry-free, calming voice instructed. She led the way to the doctor's office.

Dr. Mauri rose from behind her desk to shake hands. "I'm sorry that I wasn't able to tell you more over the phone, Ms. Jordan."

"I'm sorry I was so insistent. Someone close to me is in the hospital right now. I'm— Well, let's just say I'm juggling a lot."

"I gather. At least, based on the little I know. I met my niece last night after the theater. She's an intern at *Cosmo*. She was telling me how difficult it is to make a career in print media, and as an example, she told me about your recent departure and the ensuing controversy on—is it called Twitter?"

McKenna nodded. Apparently the receptionist's insistence on a calm demeanor came from the top. The way Dr. Mauri had worded it, McKenna's professional implosion sounded like any regular day.

"In any event," the doctor continued, "my niece became quite enraptured with your story and its apparent connection to a missing woman. Then she asked me whether I remembered anything about the disappearance of Susan Hauptmann. She's nineteen years old, so for her, ten years ago is like the Ice Age. She caught me off guard with the question. I had no idea that the missing woman she kept talking about all night was Susan."

McKenna had been hoping to get more information out of the doctor in person, but so far the woman still hadn't confirmed the basics of what McKenna suspected. She tried another tack. "I was Susan's roommate and one of her closest friends. I already know she was your patient."

Dr. Mauri looked relieved. "If only all of my patients gave so much care to their own health. Annual physicals, no smoking, regular exercise. Most people insist that they eat healthy and work out, but I can tell—well, my point is: Susan was a real delight. Very gregarious, with that salty sense of humor; our conversations often went beyond the narrow confines of doctor-patient treatment. I think it's fair to say I knew her."

"You said you might know something relevant to her disappearance?"

"Given my situation, I was hoping that perhaps you had seen the police file and could confirm that anything I might know was already considered a part of the investigation."

McKenna had not seen the doctor's name in Scanlin's file, or anything related to Susan's physical health. She took a guess. "She had an appointment with you, not long before she disappeared."

The doctor smiled politely.

"Look, I know you're restricted by privacy laws, and I respect that. How about this? I'm not asking about any individual patient. I'm interested, hypothetically, in what may have happened *if* you had a patient disappear."

"Without using names, let me say that *if* I ever had a patient go missing, it was twelve weeks after she was scheduled for an office visit. I assumed when I saw her name on my calendar that she was coming in for her annual physical because she was about due for one. But my assistant alerted me that the appointment was actually forty-nine weeks after her last annual, meaning it was too early for her insurance company to cover it. They're sticklers about that. I called the patient to suggest rescheduling, but she told me it was important. I thought, well, even my healthiest patient has finally gotten sick. But when she came in, she wasn't *sick*."

But she'd been *something*. "She'd been assaulted? Victimized somehow?"

No response.

"She was pregnant?"

Dr. Mauri smiled again. "Let me just say that by the time most unmarried women come to me for a pregnancy test, they have already taken multiple home versions and are looking for a different result."

"This particular patient wouldn't have been happy about the news."

"I'm always careful not to say anything loaded when I deliver the results, because many women have no idea how they're going to feel about an unplanned pregnancy until they've had a chance to digest the reality of the situation. So I simply tell them that the test is positive and ask whether they have questions. That's usually my first indication of what direction the woman is leaning."

"And did this hypothetical patient have questions?"

Dr. Mauri pressed her lips together. McKenna had crossed whatever line the doctor had drawn for navigating this conversation.

"What types of questions do you think a single, pregnant woman might have?"

As much as she was beginning to doubt how well she'd known Susan, Susan had always made her views on the most obvious subject very clear. Susan would not terminate a pregnancy.

"Paternity," McKenna said. "She wanted to know whether you could determine paternity."

Dr. Mauri gave a small nod.

McKenna did the math in her head. She had introduced Susan to Will Getty four months before the Marcus Jones shooting, which was six weeks before Susan disappeared. Getty could have been the father.

"She would have been close to four months pregnant when she disappeared." It was only as she said the words that McKenna remembered Susan drinking club soda at a happy hour. *My thirties are gaining on me. Got to take off some L.B.s before I turn into a Fatty McFat.*

If Susan knew that Getty was involved in a cover-up, and she was pregnant with his child, that might explain why she would leave New York. Whether she liked it or not, Getty would have parental rights. She'd spend her entire life permanently connected to him.

"Did the patient happen to say anything about who she thought the father might be?"

"I've already stretched quite a bit on what I should probably say, Ms. Jordan. But when a patient asks about a paternity test—"

"It means she had multiple sexual partners. I need to know who they were."

"I don't know," the doctor said sadly.

"When Susan first went missing, you never thought to tell anyone about Susan's pregnancy?"

"Of course I did," she said. "I must have called the police three different times. But no one ever called me back. I eventually gave up, assuming that they must have already heard the news from someone else. When my niece told me you were looking for Susan, I needed to make sure it hadn't slipped through the cracks."

Scanlin had said that the police tip line had been overwhelmed with harebrained, bogus, and wackadoo calls. He'd also pretty much admitted that he had done a crappy job on the case. Dr. Mauri was making that clear.

As McKenna walked through the doctor's calming lobby back to the real world of honking cars and bus fumes, she tried to black out the images that had been flashing in her visual cortex for the last two days. Susan catching Patrick's eye with that sexy sideways smile—her go-to man-eater move. Patrick responding. Susan whispering in his ear, *McKenna doesn't feel like this, does she?*

*Stop it!* She replaced the imaginary images with a real one: Patrick in a hospital bed.

Just because Susan was unsure about the father of her unborn child didn't mean that Patrick was one of the contenders. It was as Dr. Mauri had quietly confirmed: Susan got around.

Sometimes beliefs came not from facts or proof but from faith. McKenna had always had faith in Patrick. She would choose to have faith in him now. He was going to survive. He was going to wake up, he was going to be okay, and he was going to have an explanation for everything.

In the meantime, she needed to make another trip to the courthouse.

# CHAPTER FIFTY-SIX

**M**cKenna sat on a bench at the far end of the fourth floor. She was out of the flow of traffic but had a clear view of the entrance to Judge John DeWitt Gregory's courtroom, where Will Getty was arguing against a defendant's motion to vacate a jury's guilty verdict.

McKenna had gotten lucky when she arrived to find Berta Ramos outside for one of her hourly smoke breaks. Ten years later, the woman still hadn't kicked the habit.

"Ay, Mamí," she had called out when McKenna waved at her from the sidewalk. Though their kinship had started with an un-likely shared love of *Buffy the Vampire Slayer*, Berta had become one of McKenna's better allies among the DA support staff. She barely had an accent but liked to pepper her conversation with Spanish slang. "Your ears must be burning. Lots of talk about you around here this week."

"I can only imagine."

"Don't you worry. Berta knows you wouldn't make up a story. Besides, all these people"—she used her manicured blood-red fingernail to draw a circle in the air—"they know that Judge Knight is just how you say he is. *Cerdo sucio*."

"I need to talk to Will Getty, but I'd rather not plant myself in the DA waiting room like a goat at the petting zoo."

"Don't you even worry about it. Give me your number and I'll report from inside."

Now Getty walked out of the courtroom, carrying only a single file folder. His back was straight, shoulders squared, steps even and proud. Defeating the motion clearly was a cakewalk.

McKenna pretended to be composing a text and then faked a double take in his direction. She smiled, gave a wave as an afterthought, and caught up with him.

"Bold move, being here," he said. "The courthouse staff is secretly cheering you on, but Knight's still got friends."

"I know. I thought if I came and talked to my sources, I'd figure out who burned me." *Was it you?* She searched his eyes for some sign of nervousness. "No luck yet."

"I have no doubt you'll get to the bottom of it."

"Hey, it dawned on me when I saw you that you'd be a good person to bounce some ideas off of. You have a second?"

He looked at his watch. "Sure. Gregory calendared an hour for a motion that took ten minutes."

"Coffee? My treat."

Getty opted for a Chinese bakery on Canal. Once they were settled in with a tray of roasted pork buns, Diet Cokes, and egg tarts, she continued the I'm-just-bouncing-some-ideas-off-you talk.

"Sorry if I sound a little scattered, but my thoughts are all over the place. Did you hear about Scott Macklin?"

"Fucking awful."

"I know. The first thing I thought was, Oh my God, what if this is because I was digging up the whole Marcus Jones issue again. I mean—"

Getty was shaking his head already. "You can't try to figure out why someone does that. Otherwise, everyone who ever met the guy could say, What if I had done something different? I'm sorry.

I liked Macklin, rest his soul. But what he did is on him and him alone."

"I hear you, and I appreciate that. But like I said, my mind went there. And maybe it's because I didn't want the weight to be on me, but I started thinking, No, someone doesn't shoot himself because of a magazine article or even a book. I mean, he didn't do it back when protestors were waving pictures of his face behind bars and the city was close to rioting. So, I hate to admit it, I started wondering—you know—what if it was because he thought if I looked again, I'd find something new. Something I missed. Like maybe the hammer was finally going to come down."

Getty washed down some pork bun with a big gulp of Diet Coke. "That's a lot of wondering, Wright."

"Here's the thing. I went back and took another close look at the case. It's a long story, but it turns out that a prostitute who used to meet tricks down at the piers went missing the night Mac shot Marcus Jones." McKenna glossed over the uncertainties in that part of her theory. "According to her mother, the prostitute was meeting a regular that night—someone slow and strange-looking. I think she was meeting Marcus Jones."

"Possible, I guess. Makes sense that the kid would tell his mom he was meeting a girl, not a working girl. Plus, he had cash in his pocket." Getty's lightning-quick reasoning had always been amazing. "What about it?"

"The girl never came back. I'm thinking, What if she saw something that night?"

"The shooting?"

"Or maybe she saw something *before* the shooting. And so did Marcus Jones. And they both wound up dead. You can get rid of the hooker without raising too many questions, then drop a gun next to the body of the kid with a criminal record."

Getty balled up his napkin and tossed it on the plastic tray. "I'd keep this to yourself. This on top of the Knight article? Jesus, we went through this ten years ago. You made a mistake. I thought you'd moved on."

"I know, I know. Hear me out. It was that kid James Low who saved Macklin's ass. Low's testimony put the gun right in Marcus Jones's hands. Mac's access to the gun through Safe Streets was just a coincidence."

"And yet?"

"If it weren't for the kid's testimony, it would be one major hell of a coincidence. What I want to know is, how did Low come to you? Did someone bring him in? Did he call out of the blue?"

Getty blinked; she could see him searching his memory for the details. "When you came to me about the gun coming from Safe Streets, I told you I'd look into it. And I did. I looked up the other cops in the program. Saw that one of them was on the Crips' payroll. What was his name?"

"Don Whitman."

"Right, Don Whitman. I figured a guy who took money from bangers wasn't above slipping a few guns. So I sent three DA investigators to talk to the usual suspects in East Harlem. Try to find someone from the neighborhood who knew anything about Jones and a gun. I was giving it a few days to sink in. But then you went public."

She resisted the urge to remind him that he'd locked her out of the case for two weeks before she took the evidence to Bob Vance. That was an argument they'd had ten years earlier. Getty's regret about his lack of communication was supposedly the reason he'd always defended her.

He continued, "It was a few days after the story exploded when Low showed up at the courthouse, asking who was in charge of the case. Once he got to my office, he told me he didn't want to say anything bad about Marcus, that he"—Getty let out a laugh, remembering the moment—"he *certainly* didn't want to help the cracker cop who killed him, but he didn't want to see Harlem burn." The remainder of his recitation came in clipped, just-the-facts fashion. "He asked whether I was going to arrest him if he confessed to a gun charge. I made a quick decision to give him a pass if it meant I'd get the truth. He said the gun had been his dad's, but he'd sold

it to Marcus a month before the shooting. I ran his dad. Big-time
Crip, which connected the gun back to Safe Streets through Don
Whitman."

"Did you ever think it was weird that a hard case like Low would
walk into the courthouse out of the goodness of his heart?"

"I've been doing this job a long time, Wright. Those kids don't
give a shit about themselves, but they care about their neighbor-
hoods and their mothers and their friends. Things were getting bad.
You don't think I know how the NYPD was cracking down in the
face of those kinds of protests? Yeah, I believed Low when he said
he wanted it all to stop."

"Fair enough. But here's a thought experiment, nothing more.
What if he played you? What if someone realized that Don Whitman's bust provided an alternative explanation for the gun making
it out of Safe Streets? It wouldn't be hard to find a kid who knew
Marcus Jones and had some connection to the Crips."

"And that someone would be Scott Macklin?"

McKenna shrugged. Other people might berate her for raising
such thoughts about a man who had recently died, but she knew
that after nearly a quarter of a century at the DA's office, Getty
didn't dwell on death like normal people did.

Getty said, "You know, when you first came to me, you said you
thought Mac panicked when he saw Jones reach into his pocket,
so Mac dropped a gun to cover up his mistake. Your little thought
experiment sounds a lot worse. Plus, this stuff about the prostitute.
Why would Macklin kill her?"

"Maybe the prostitute and Jones saw something they weren't supposed to see."

"It wasn't mistaken self-defense but cold-blooded murder?"

She shrugged again. "Still could have been a panic thing. Trying
to keep them from getting away. I know it's crazy. But you know
the facts of that case better than anyone. I'm just asking you to think
it through with me—as a friend, not a source. I'm not going to
quote you. But as a huge what-if, what could Jones and the girl have
seen that would make Mac panic that way?"

So far the words had come out exactly as she'd planned them. The right delivery. The right tone. Just a friend thinking out loud. If Getty blew her off because he was too busy, she wouldn't know what to think. If he became defensive or angry, she'd assume he was hiding something.

Instead of offering either of the anticipated responses, Getty surprised her. He played out the thought experiment. And damn, he was smart.

"Let me start by saying that if you *ever* try to make it sound like I *believe* any of this shit, I will drop-kick your ass back before the day I met you. But if we're really playing what-if, I'd say it was all about the pier."

"Because Mac thought Marcus was planning a grab?"

"No, because piers are where we import and export. I don't know all the details, but Macklin was on the docks that night for some kind of inspection program. If he was on the take, Marcus Jones and the hooker could have seen illegal cargo coming in. Drugs. Maybe people."

The theory was coming together even as she articulated it. "Mac heads over to make sure they're not a problem, but they're not having it. He panics, pulls his weapon . . ."

"Total fiction, if you ask me," Getty said. "But yeah, it's possible."

Depending on the role Macklin played in the cargo inspection, he could have been the one person standing in the way between seized cargo and a free pass. She remembered Macklin asking her about immigration law. The situation was complicated, he had said. She searched her memory for the specifics. Josefina had entered the country lawfully but failed to return to Mexico when her visa expired. Even worse, she had her sister bring Thomas into the country illegally when he was five years old. Macklin was pretty sure that the marriage resolved any of Josefina's immigration problems, but he was worried about Thomas getting deported. He'd said he needed money for an immigration lawyer.

Thomas, now starting college at Hofstra, obviously remained in the country. Maybe Mac had found a way to fight for his stepson.

"But once James Low stepped forward, we stopped considering the possibilities," she said. "Do you know what ever happened to him?"

"Been a long time."

McKenna knew. She'd done the research. Killed in a gang shooting two years earlier in Atlanta. "He got picked up in a bar brawl a year after he testified before the Marcus Jones grand jury."

"Sure, I know about that. I handled it, in fact. But since then? No clue."

So much for catching Getty in a lie. "I looked at the police report," she said. "It was an easy felony. Plus, he had priors. Why'd you plead it to a misdemeanor?"

"Because I have a bias against cases that are cluster fucks. There were thugs on both sides. Complete pandemonium. All the witnesses were drunk, and none of them wanted to testify. The so-called victim had a record six feet long, including multiple assaults. His lawyer—Bernadette Connor, you know her?"

McKenna nodded. Telegenic and straight-talking, Connor was her law firm's go-to person for high-profile criminal trials. Nine years ago, she was a midlevel associate at the firm but already had a reputation as a hard charger in the courtroom.

"Bernadette came to me early and made it clear the case wasn't winnable. I'd dealt with him on the Marcus Jones thing. He had a clean sheet during the year in between, and I thought he might not be a lost cause. We pleaded him out to the misdemeanor and moved on."

Getty's explanation was plausible, but it was raising questions she hadn't considered. "Did you ever wonder how a kid like James Low had enough money to hire a private lawyer? Or to get VIP bottle service in a club?"

"Not really. Club night could have been a hookup by a doorman, for all I know. And a firm like Bernadette's does a ton of pro bono."

Or James Low had been paid off to say he gave the gun to Marcus Jones.

"Speaking of pleas," McKenna said, "I saw Gretchen Hauptmann this week."

His face was blank before the name registered. "Sure, Susan's sister. How's she doing?"

"She said you helped her out of a federal drug indictment. I didn't realize you knew her."

"I didn't. I knew her sister. You're the one who introduced us, remember?"

"Sure, that one night. I didn't know you stayed in touch."

For the first time since they'd sat down, he looked offended. "Where's this coming from?"

"I just found out that Susan was pregnant when she disappeared. And I assumed from your helping Gretchen that you and Susan must have . . . connected after I introduced you. In light of the timing, I thought it was kind of weird that you never said anything to the police when she went missing."

"Look, not that I owe you an explanation, but I saw her a few times after we met at the bar. It obviously wasn't going anywhere— she had a lot going on in her life. She was looking at another deployment. By the time she disappeared, we weren't together that way. I helped her sister because she asked me to review the case and it seemed like the right thing to do."

Susan had never mentioned anything about deployment to McKenna. And she'd just seen Susan's file. Scanlin had checked with the military: Susan's service was done; she was free and clear. Was Getty lying? Or had Susan made up the deployment to break things off with him? Or had Scanlin made yet another mistake?

"Did Susan tell you she was pregnant?" she asked.

"No. Obviously not. I would have told the police."

If Getty knew more than he was letting on, she hadn't caught him. "So, you need to get back to the courthouse?"

"After the big interrogation, that's all you have to say?"

"I figured you were busy, that's all. I really appreciate the time, Will."

She could tell he wanted to say something, but he pushed the tray in her direction, shook his head, and left without a word. He let the bakery door slam behind him. So much for her last remaining ADA friend.

The meeting hadn't been a complete bust. She had been thinking so much about the gun next to Marcus Jones's body that she'd completely glossed over the reason Scott Macklin had been at the pier in the first place. She remembered the bits and pieces of the argument that Susan's neighbor had overheard. "Smack" and "important." Smack was Mac. Important? Could have been "import." If Macklin had been involved in a smuggling operation at the piers, that would explain how Marcus Jones and Pamela Morris had become a threat.

McKenna found the business card she was looking for in her purse.

"Agent Mercado, this is McKenna Jordan. I want to propose a deal."

# CHAPTER
# FIFTY-SEVEN

*I want to propose a deal.* McKenna thought the line was pretty good bait. The promise of a swap. A quid pro quo. She thought it would draw the FBI agent in.

Once again, Mercado wasn't like other FBI agents. She hung up.

At least she picked up the phone on the second try. McKenna forewent the cool pitch, trying an earnest approach. She actually said, "Cross my heart, you'll want to hear this." Combined with the desperate tone, it probably amounted to groveling. But it worked. She was back at the Federal Building and had Mercado's attention.

"I have information for you."

"Good. Let's hear it."

"Because I'm a lawyer," McKenna said, "I know I'm not obligated to turn over information out of the goodness of my heart."

"I can subpoena you to testify in front of the grand jury."

"You can. But then I'll move to quash that subpoena, and you won't be able to tell a judge what you even want to ask me. Even if you do haul me before the grand jury, once again, you don't know what to ask me."

"So, just like some scumbag codefendant invoking the Fifth Amendment, you want a deal."

"Call me what you want, Mercado, but I've seen the look of an investigator who's hot on the trail, with every piece falling into place, and it's only a matter of time before the entire thing comes together. I've also seen the opposite, where every road is a dead end, every promising tip a brick wall. You look like you've been hitting dead ends and brick walls."

Mercado held her gaze for a few seconds, then gave her a grudging smile. "What do you want? "

"The morning after the bombing in Brentwood, you asked me about four names. I know that two of them are already in custody. I assume the other two were cohorts?"

"Again, not sure why I'd tell you anything. I've heard about your brand of journalism. Not real interested."

"Fine. Just listen. I know that Greg Larson is the de facto leader of the P3s. That leaves one other name on your list—Pamela Morris. It sounded like you didn't know where Larson and Morris were or whether they died in the bombing. I have information about Pamela Morris. And I mean rock-solid information."

"Is she with Larson?"

Mercado's question meant she had not yet received confirmation that Larson or Morris had died in the explosion.

"I don't know, but—" McKenna stopped when Mercado got up to leave the conference room. "Hold on, hear me out. I know *who* she is, and her real name's not Pamela Morris. And because I know who she is, I know a context to her work with the P3s that, frankly, you're clueless about."

Finally, McKenna had gotten her interest. Jamie Mercado was not used to being called clueless.

"What do you need from me?"

"I need your word that you'll do me a favor."

Another smile, this one condescending. "You've got to understand something. *My* word? In *my* world? It actually means something. I can't give you my word when you ask for something that amorphous."

"Fine. You want specifics? Part one—I show you a photograph

of the woman you've been looking for, the woman you know as Pamela Morris. You take that to the two P3s you have in custody. They'll confirm it's her. That should earn me enough goodwill for part two: you promise to answer two questions for me—one having to do with a cargo inspection ten years ago, and one about a search of my office this week. Since I trust that you're a person of her word, once you promise me that, I'll fill in the connections. Is that specific enough for you?"

"Jesus, Jordan, you're a piece of work. Just give me the picture already."

McKenna handed her a photograph of Susan. "See if they recognize her. But tell them the picture's ten years old."

Mercado took a quick glance and dropped the print on the table. "What are you trying to pull? This is that missing woman you've been Tweeting about—Susan Hopman or whatever."

"Hauptmann. We had a deal, Agent Mercado. Show the two prisoners the picture. You'll get a match. And then I'll explain. I promise. My word means something, too."

"One of them lawyered up, but I still have the younger one hanging on by a thread. We're about to go in for another round with her, in fact."

"It'll be worth your time. I promise."

Ten minutes later, Mercado confirmed it: the woman who'd been living as Pamela Morris was Susan Hauptmann.

"Enough with all the game playing," Mercado said. "What's your angle?"

**M**cKenna told Mercado everything with the linear precision of a lawyer's narrative. Susan's disappearance. The pregnancy. The elderly neighbor hearing an argument with repeated mentions of "smack" (Mac) and "important" (import). Susan's reappearance on the subway platform, wearing a backpack tying her to the P3s, and everything that had happened since: McKenna losing her job; Scott Macklin's supposed suicide a day after Susan visited his house; the

Cleaner who wiped out the subway footage of Susan; the shooting at Grand Central Station; her suspicions about Will Getty.

"Look," Mercado said, "I'm sorry about your husband, but you've mistaken me for someone who cares about your friend's disappearance or whatever the fuck happened ten years ago between a dead kid and a former—and now dead—cop."

"Very sensitive, Agent."

"It's not my job to be sensitive. You came here with a promise of information. Tell me how this jumble of data helps me get to the bottom of a nationwide ecoterrorism organization."

"Weren't you listening?"

"Yes, and patiently, I might add."

McKenna resisted the temptation to use a condescending tone herself. "I didn't see it at first, either. But there's only one explanation for Susan Hauptmann living in that house in Brentwood. She was strictly law-and-order. A hard-core, chain-of-command, work-within-the-system type. The complete antithesis of a group like the P3s."

"So why was she there?"

"Because for ten years, she has somehow managed to support herself. I know Susan. She's industrious. She could take her military experience and talk her way into a decade of work with private security firms without revealing her true identity—the kind of firm that might not ask too many questions if an operative proved she was talented enough. The kind of outfit that might engage in the domestic surveillance you're not allowed to conduct as an agent of the government."

She saw a flicker of recognition in Mercado's face, part excitement, part frustration that she hadn't seen it earlier.

"She was hired to be there," Mercado said.

"I'd bet everything on it. No one's more motivated to bring down a gang of activists than the corporations left paying the bills from their handiwork. And those corporations can afford to hire the best. Once you know who her clients were, you can subpoena them for information. It would be illegal surveillance if it originated with the FBI, but if a private party gathered it—"

Mercado finished the thought. "It's fair game. We're regulated, but they're not. They can pose as sympathizers. Snoop in e-mails. Bug phones."

"They'll have names, locations, dates, target information. The starting point is finding Susan Hauptmann, which is where my questions come in. On October 16, 2003, NYPD Officer Scott Macklin was working on some kind of container inspection at the West Harlem piers. I'm trying to figure out the specifics. If we can tie Will Getty to it, we might have enough evidence for a wiretap. Catch his connection to Susan."

Without a word, Mercado left the conference room. She returned twenty minutes later. "Remember how, after 9/11, we figured out that however high we ramped up security at airports, we still had these gaping holes in our border because of cargo inspection? The newly formed Homeland Security Department cranked up the search requirements but didn't have the systems to keep pace. Containers were getting so backed up at the Port Authority that they literally ran out of storage space. Fancy imported food was going bad. Just a big backlog."

"The NYPD was filling in?"

"To streamline cargo inspection, a federal-state cooperative Homeland Security task force created a preapproval process for shippers and receivers." When Mercado described the program, McKenna felt a tug at the threads of her long-term memory. "Frequent importers and exporters could get prescreened to receive cargo with less rigorous inspection. Shipments could skip the usual receiving ports for spot-checking at local piers, and then the approved receivers would conduct a full search on their own and certify that they didn't receive any unauthorized items. Participants were high-volume, high-credibility entities."

Mercado was blabbing along, living up to her end of the bargain, when McKenna realized that Patrick once told her that the museum was authorized to participate in the preapproved cargo program. She remembered him working nights, inspecting art shipments.

She tried to retain control over her own thoughts. She tried to stop the images of Patrick with Susan. Without McKenna. Talking about McKenna. Enjoying the thrill of getting away with it.

She needed to focus. "Is there any way to find out which preapproved shippers were receiving cargo that night? Maybe we can find a connection to Susan."

"I'll have to reach out to Homeland Security, but I wouldn't bet on it."

"One more thing, Agent. I don't want to push my luck, but why'd you bother searching my office? What did you think you were going to find there?"

Mercado looked amused. "I only *wish* I had the time to care so much about you, Jordan. If someone searched your office, it sure as hell wasn't the Bureau."

**M**cKenna found Bob Vance on his way to Vic's Bagels. Her former editor was Rain Man–like in his consistency. Vic's was known for its multitudinous toppings. Signature menu items included the Tokyo Tel Aviv Express with wasabi and edamame, or the Vermonter with bacon, maple syrup, and cinnamon. You could make your own spread, with mix-ins as diverse as pesto, corn, or potato chips.

Bob Vance? Plain bagel, butter, lox, and tomatoes, untoasted, every day around two-thirty.

On instinct, he smiled when he spotted McKenna, but then he shook his head as reality set in. "Too soon, my dear. Get a lawyer to talk to the magazine's lawyers. Maybe they'll work something out."

"I'm not here to beg for my job, Bob. The FBI agent who searched my office. Was he this man?" She showed him a photograph of the Cleaner. His picture had not yet been released to the press after the shooting.

"Yeah, that's the one. You're not stalking an FBI agent, are you? I wouldn't mess around with that."

Yesterday she would have savored telling him he'd been duped. That his magazine's lawyers were idiots who didn't know enough about criminal law to check out their copy of the warrant, if they'd even been served with one. She would have used the infiltration as proof that someone was trying to discredit her, and she would have insisted on getting her job back.

Now she didn't really care about any of it.

"So who's the guy in the picture?" he asked.

"You'll find out soon enough."

"You should reach out to Dana. She quit in a huff about the magazine letting you go, but I saw her talking to that agent outside the building."

# CHAPTER
# FIFTY-EIGHT

In a strange way, McKenna had always been intimidated by Dana, who was younger, shorter, and less educated, but bold enough to pierce her tongue and stomp through a newsroom in a tank top with her bra straps showing. She dropped the F-bomb without mercy. And she didn't seem to care that she usually smelled like garlic.

McKenna realized now that all of the brashness was a veil. Dana pretended to place art above real-world concerns like employment, rent, and a retirement account, but she was a phony. She was for sale, no less than the corporate drones she liked to mock.

She wasn't even worth a subway ride to Brooklyn. McKenna could deal with her in a phone call.

"Hey there, M."

One night on the girl's daybed, and Dana was using a nickname that only Patrick called her.

"Do you realize that what you did amounts to wire fraud under the federal criminal code?"

"What are you talking about?"

McKenna gave her a brief tutorial in the law. As an employee, Dana owed the magazine her duty of honest services. By taking a bribe and then using the Internet to delete the magazine's intellectual property (the video of Susan) and to fabricate a false story about

Judge Knight's supposed e-mails, she had committed wire fraud. The maximum sentence was twenty years.

Dana continued to deny it.

"I'm not playing with you, Dana. You are in so far over your five-foot-tall head that you can't begin to understand the rain of hell I will bring down on you. The man who hired you? Bob Vance saw you together. He's dead now. Maybe you woke up long enough today to hear about the shooting at Grand Central? He was killed, and my husband nearly was, too."

Dana was making "oh my God" noises on the other end of the line.

"Shut up, Dana. And grow up. I am giving you one chance to do what I'm telling you. After that, I go to the U.S. attorney's office, and you take your chances with a grand jury."

"I'll do anything, McKenna. I didn't know—I thought it was just one story. Then you got fired. And oh my God, that guy's *dead*? And Patrick—"

"What did that man want from you?"

"At first I didn't know. He offered me two hundred bucks to tell him what you were working on. I told him about the Knight story—your search for a smoking gun. He paid me five grand to make it look like you manufactured your own evidence."

"I got *fired* for that, Dana." Worse. Because of Dana, McKenna had suspected her own husband of being behind the setup.

"I didn't think it would be that bad. It was a *lot* of money. That's like almost three months' pay. I was supposed to keep him updated. When you got the video of the subway lady, he gave me another grand to delete it."

"So the temper tantrum you threw about your backup being deleted was bogus."

"I didn't know you'd get fired. When I quit, it was my way of trying to make it up to you."

"Your being out of a job does absolutely nothing to help me, Dana. Nothing about your life is at all relevant to mine."

"You don't have to be such a bitch—"

"I'm pretty sure that's *exactly* what I need to be right now. Because here's what you're going to do. You're going to go to Bob Vance—in person, at *NYC* magazine—and you're going to tell him what you did. You can make whatever lame excuse you want: alcoholism, bipolar disorder, I'd probably go with a practical joke that got out of hand. You already quit, so I doubt they'll do anything more to punish you. But you *will* make it clear that you were the one who set me up on the Knight article.

"Alternatively, I will make sure the U.S. attorney's office knows that you accepted a bribe and forged e-mails under the name of a sitting New York County supreme court judge. Do I need to ask you more than once?"

**M**cKenna's pulse was just returning to normal when her cell phone rang. She recognized the general number for the district attorney's Office.

"This is McKenna."

Getty didn't bother introducing himself. "You know, Wright, I was the one person in the office who defended you when the Macklin case imploded. I felt responsible for your going public. But you know what? You proved today that my initial instincts were right. Every bad word anyone has ever said about you is right. You've got no judgment."

What comes around goes around. She had just gone off on Dana, and now Will Getty was venting at her.

"Will, you have no idea what I'm dealing with right now. I just had a few questions—"

"That's bullshit, and you know it. You were basically accusing me of knowing something about Susan's disappearance and taking perjured testimony from James Low to cover up for a bad cop. It's ridiculous. But if you want to start throwing accusations at every man who fell into Susan's bed, there's another name you should know about."

Don't say it, Will. Please don't say it.

"I told you before that things didn't work out with Susan and me. I said it was because of the deployment, because I was trying to protect your feelings. But there was something else. She told me she was in love with one of her best friends and wanted to make something work with him."

No, don't say it. Don't say it. No, no, no.

"Guess what, Wright? The friend was none other than your husband, Patrick Jordan. Maybe you better find out what he knows before you weave together your master conspiracy theory."

The line fell silent. She tasted bile in the back of her throat.

Her phone chirped again in her hand. If Getty was calling to apologize, it was too late. Some things could not be taken back.

The call was from a different number.

"This is McKenna."

"I'm calling for Dr. Gifford at Lenox Hill Hospital. We thought you'd like to know that your husband is awake. He's awake, and he's talking. He made it."

# CHAPTER
## FIFTY-NINE

The ICU was marked by the same chaos McKenna had left behind that morning. Same overcrowded hallways. Same loud, scratchy pages over the intercom system. Same weird antiseptic odor.

Patrick, though, had moved. The bed he'd occupied was now home to a twentysomething woman surrounded by balloon bouquets and teddy bears. The smocked staff had changed, too. McKenna didn't recognize any of the nurses she'd ingratiated herself with the previous night. She zeroed in on the sole woman at the nursing station who seemed to be standing in one spot for consecutive seconds.

"I'm looking for my husband, Patrick Jordan. He was in room 610, but he must have been transferred."

The woman gave her a confused look. "Mr. Jordan was moved to a room in our recovery wing. Do you mind if I check your identification?"

McKenna placed her driver's license on the counter.

"Room 640. Just through these double doors, take the first right turn, and then it's the third room on your left. And sorry about the ID check. I could've sworn another woman was just here saying she was the patient's wife, but I must have misheard her. We're a bit swamped today. Probably another member of your family."

Probably not.

For all Susan's talk about how Patrick and McKenna were soul mates, meant to be, it was obviously Susan and Patrick who shared the deep connection. Susan had probably been sneaking around with him the whole time McKenna had been falling in love. Whatever they had for each other could have been going on the entire time Susan was supposedly missing, and she had dragged him into something that had gotten him shot.

And now she had been here. With him. At his bedside, instead of her.

McKenna hated both of them.

How could Patrick ever fix this?

A pair of open eyes and a chapped-lip smile turned out to be a remarkable beginning. All of the horrible mental images she'd been carrying around disappeared. She didn't have any answers, but suddenly, it wasn't about his phone call or leaving work early one day or discouraging her from looking for Susan. Somehow she knew at a basic, cellular level that Patrick would have an explanation.

"You're here," he said. His voice was low and hoarse.

She placed a hand over her mouth and fought back tears. She rushed to him, leaning in to hug him tight, and then froze at the sight of the hoses and tubes. She settled for a palm against his temple and a kiss on his cheek. "You scared me."

"You scared me, too. I guess we're even."

When she'd decided to go to Dana's that night, it never dawned on her that he'd be worried about her safety. The fact that she'd trusted Dana over her own husband made her feel sick. Seeing him now, she knew she never should have doubted him.

"You may need to buy me some new casebooks for Christmas."

His laugh quickly turned into a cough. "Shh," she whispered. "Take it easy. I promise never to be funny ever again."

"The surgeon told me how smart I was. I had to confess I saw it on one of your TV shows. Remember?"

She nodded and wiped a tear from her cheek. "I almost lost you."

So much had changed since they'd gotten married. They had taken the plunge after a year of uninterrupted bliss had convinced them they had finally worked out all the kinks. He'd thought she was over the pain of what had happened at the DA's office. That now that she was happy in her new life as a writer, she could be happy with him. But then her second book got rejected, and she had turned into the same moody, self-centered person she'd been before. When she was unhappy, it affected the way she treated Patrick. His potty humor, once endearing, was immature. His penchant for constancy, so reliable and admirable when they met, was boring.

It was as though she'd gotten married believing he'd change, and he'd married her on the assumption that she'd always be the same. If it hadn't been for the marriage license and the apartment they'd bought together, they might have gone right back to their previous cyclical ways: on, then off, then on. She wouldn't let that happen again. Her professional life was in tatters, but all she cared about right now was Patrick.

He looked away from her. "I'm so sorry, McKenna. I—I don't know how I let this happen. There's so much I need to tell you."

"She was here, wasn't she? Susan. She was here with you."

He started to cry. In all the years she had known him, she had never seen him cry. "How did you know—"

"I know a lot, Patrick. And now I need you to tell me the rest."

**S**he e-mailed me at work last Monday. From an anonymous account." It had been two days after Susan rescued Nicky Cervantes from the subway tracks—the same day McKenna had shown Patrick the video of Susan. The same day he'd pretended the woman looked nothing like Susan. The same day he'd sat next to her on the sofa and lied to her face.

"Just out of the blue? After ten years?"

"She told me that she couldn't explain everything, but I had to trust her: I had to make sure you didn't write anything else about the Marcus Jones shooting. And she said I couldn't tell anyone she was alive. That she was in danger, and you might be, too, if I didn't keep you out of it."

"That's it?"

"Yes. I thought it was someone's sick idea of a joke, so I said I was going to call the police and tell them about her e-mail unless she agreed to see me in person. I was shocked when she sent me instructions about which train to board, which car, which seat to take. She was obviously worried about being watched."

"So you met her?"

"I'm not sure you can call it that. I handed her a flash drive with a letter on it, trying to convince her to come back. To take her life back. I didn't hear from her again until she called me two days later, wanting to know why you were posting calls for information about her on Twitter. I tried telling her that I'd done everything I could—"

"I overheard that call," McKenna confessed. "I found a picture of you together in the box Adam sent over. And then I heard you talking to her. I thought—I thought you'd been in touch with her all this time, and I left. If I had only—"

"Stop it, McKenna. If it's anyone's fault—"

"You know what? Let's not do that right now. Let's not apologize to each other or place blame or any of that. She called you, and then what?"

"I figured she had something to do with those e-mails that got you fired. She swore up and down that she didn't know anything about it, but I didn't know what to believe. All I knew was that you were supposed to be home, and you weren't, and you'd obviously been going through that box. I figured you saw something that upset you. I should have realized she'd have pictures. Jesus, I should have told you at the very beginning, when we met. Because I didn't, it always seemed too late to do it. And then the more time went by—"

"It's not important, Patrick. Not right now, at least."

She could tell he was forcing himself to move along with the facts.

"You finally called me, saying you'd gone out with the work crowd and were crashing at Dana's. I wanted to believe everything was okay, but you didn't come home the next night, either. And then I got that phone call. A guy saying he had you and to meet him at Grand Central. Susan had said that you could be in danger, so I—"

"You taped yourself up in my law books." She took his hand and kissed the inside of his wrist.

"It wasn't the guy I was meeting who shot me. It was a guy who came out of the crowd of protestors. In a mask and a cape. He shot us both."

She told him about the Cleaner. She also told him that he hadn't been as lucky as Patrick.

"Who is he?"

"They don't know yet," she said. "Part of me wondered whether he was someone you and Susan knew."

"No. I mean, when I showed up at Grand Central, I thought he might have been watching me the one time I met Susan on the PATH train. I'd never seen him before that."

"And that's it?" she asked. "You really don't know anything else?"

He shook his head, and that was all it took. She knew Patrick. She believed him.

"I saw her cold-case file," she said. "I know you told the police back then that you thought she'd left on her own. Why didn't you ever mention that to me?"

"I only suspected. I knew she had reupped her obligation to the army in 2001, right before 9/11. She'd already been deployed once, and there would obviously be more where that came from. Remember how worried you were that I'd get called up, and I wasn't even active reserves anymore."

She remembered. As she recalled it, she wasn't the only one who'd been worried. She could still picture Patrick's expression the day he'd opened a letter from the army declaring in official terms that he was "hereby recommissioned" as a captain in the army and ordering him to accept the commission by signing the enclosed documents. It was only on more careful inspection that she had

seen the small type at the bottom of the form: if he failed to accept
the commission by the stated date, the offer would expire and there
would be no guarantee that he could rejoin at his former rank.

By the time Patrick received the letter, the news was reporting
stories of the army pulling in forty-year-old officers who had been
out of the military for a decade, under a program called the Inactive
Ready Reserve. The military's position was that any officer who
retained a single benefit of military service—including a military
identification card—could be activated at will, whether duped into
signing a recommission letter or not.

"A lot of people were looking for ways to get out. We had a
classmate who hired a lawyer to make sure he had severed all possible connections to the army. Even that was enough for the crew
to write him off, like some draft dodger running to Canada. But
Susan? Given who her father was? If she didn't want to go back? Part
of me could imagine her just starting over."

According to Will Getty, Susan had been pulled back into active
duty. "Did she say anything about getting ready for another deployment?" McKenna asked.

"No. We talked about the possibility. She was headstrong about
not going back if that happened."

"If she had been activated, would pregnancy be a basis for getting
out?"

"No. Women can defer depending on the due date and the
timing, but it's just a deferral. But Susan wasn't—"

He could see from her face that Susan, in fact, had been pregnant.
Was McKenna only imagining it, or was he mentally running the
math, counting the weeks? They were still together, even then.
When, Patrick, when? Was it the entire time? But they weren't
going to talk about that. Not now. Not yet.

"She still would have owed the army her time," he said.

"Giving up her identity seems like a drastic way to get out of
service."

Then McKenna realized that she'd been looking at everything
wrong. She'd been trying to work out how Susan might have stum-

bled upon whatever happened at the docks that night. She had never seen that Susan could have been the one to make it all happen.

"Do you remember that cargo import program you told me about?" she asked. "Where the museum's shipments got spot-checked, and you were certified to do the complete inspection on your own? Did you ever mention that program to Susan?"

"Yeah, I guess I did. Some night when I had to bail on one of her parties because I was working late."

McKenna remembered the night she'd told Susan about Macklin breaking down in her office. He'd just been moved into the state-federal team working with Homeland Security.

Between the two of them, McKenna and Patrick had told Susan everything she needed to exploit a potential hole in the country's cargo inspection. By turning Macklin, she could have sneaked anything into the country.

"Is it possible Susan was involved in some kind of smuggling operation? Maybe with Gretchen's dealers?"

Patrick looked at her as if she had proposed a move to the ocean to live with the mermaids. "First of all, I think Gretchen's dealers were more corner hustlers than Pablo Escobars. Besides, Susan had her problems, but something like that? No way. She was more her dad's daughter than she wanted to admit."

He was starting to speak more slowly. She could tell he was getting tired. "I hate to ask you this," she said, brushing his hair with her fingers, "but the police want to talk to you about the shooting. Are you sure there's nothing else to tell? Because now's the time to say so. We'll hire a lawyer."

He gave her a tired smile. "I swear. There's nothing else. I'll talk to the police."

"What about today? Susan was here at the hospital?"

"I thought I dreamed that. When I first woke up, it was— God, McKenna, I thought I was dead. It was like I could see things, but then I'd fall back asleep. And I couldn't talk. I thought I saw you, too, and we were in Cinque Terre, popping open that bottle of prosecco and letting the cork fly below us to the Riviera."

She remembered the exact spot and wished they were there again. "You thought you saw Susan?"

"At one point, she was in that chair when my eyes opened. She looked relieved, and I was sure we were both dead, like she was welcoming me. But then she started crying uncontrollably and saying she was going to end this. No matter what. I thought maybe she was going to hurt herself, but I couldn't move. The next time I woke up, she was gone."

He was fading back into sleep even as he finished the sentence.

# CHAPTER SIXTY

**M**cKenna tracked down a nurse in the hallway. "He's groggy again. Does the doctor need to check on him?"

"No, that's natural. He's on a morphine drip. Your husband's very stoic, not a complainer, but he's in a lot of pain. It's better for him to rest."

Stoic. Marla Tompkins had used the same word to describe General Hauptmann's acceptance of impending death.

McKenna told the nurse she'd be in the lobby if Patrick became alert again. When she got there, she found Joe Scanlin waiting. He greeted her with a "hey," and she took the seat next to him.

"You okay?" she asked. "I should have backed off this morning. Macklin was your friend. And I didn't say enough about how sorry I am about his death. Or that you were the one to find him."

He held up a hand. "Your husband was in critical condition, and you wanted to know why. I was an ass. And I put my blinders on about Mac. I promised to see this through, and I dropped the ball."

She nodded. "You can tell Compton he can question Patrick as soon as his doctors think he's up for it."

"Compton won't need to talk to your husband."

"He needs to know about the phone call Patrick got. The Cleaner said I was in danger—"

"First of all, you don't need to call him the Cleaner anymore," Scanlin said. "We've got a name. I figured if he was connected to Susan, I'd check military fingerprints. Prints taken for military personnel before 2000 aren't in AFIS. But with the military, I got a hit. Our guy's name is Carl Buckner. Direct into army in 1995 after ROTC at Texas A&M. He put in sixteen years—military intelligence—and then quit. Honorable discharge."

She knew from Patrick's friends that twenty years of service meant retirement pay for life. "Did any of his service overlap with Susan's?"

He shook his head. "No, but I talked to his most recent supervising officer. Apparently Buckner was brilliant. And a true believer. A lot of guys entered the army in the late nineties thinking they'd never see real danger. A little UN peacekeeping here and there, with all the benefits of service. Not Buckner. When other soldiers started silently cheering on the 'bring home the troops' crowd, Buckner wanted to stay in the Middle East and finish what we started."

"And what exactly was that?"

"More than six thousand service members lost their lives for freedom, Jordan. For men like Buckner, that means something. When we decided to pull out with the job unfinished, he quit. Told his friends he'd spent sixteen years watching government contractors get rich without the sacrifices made by true soldiers. They got the impression he was moving on to the private sector, but we can't find any evidence that Buckner used his social security number to earn a single dime, or rent a house, or buy a plane ticket since the day he came home from Afghanistan."

For anyone who'd earned a reputation for brilliance among military intelligence, living off the grid for a couple of years must have been like tying shoes.

"I talked to Patrick." She gave Scanlin an abbreviated version of her husband's interactions with Susan. "He thinks he saw the Cleaner—Buckner—on the train but doesn't know anything else about him."

"I'll get the full story from him," Scanlin said. He saw the confusion register on her face. "I got the department to reassign the case to me. I told them it was connected to Susan Hauptmann's disappearance. Do I have his lawyer's permission to see him now?"

She placed a hand on his shoulder. She thought it was the most affection Scanlin could handle.

**W**hile Scanlin went in search of Patrick's doctor, McKenna placed a call to Marla Tompkins, the nurse who had taken care of George Hauptmann during his illness. Something had been bothering her about their earlier conversation, though she hadn't put her finger on it until now.

"Mrs. Tompkins, it's McKenna Jordan. I came to your apartment earlier this week."

"Of course. I remember."

"You mentioned that General Hauptmann's daughter Gretchen visited him shortly before he passed away and that you gave her his diary as a memento."

"Yes, that's correct. He was so very happy to see her. I don't think I'd ever seen him filled with that kind of joy."

"Had you met Gretchen before?"

"No, it was the first time. She was very emotional also. It was— Well, General Hauptmann came to depend upon me, and he treated me so very, very well. But his daughter—she was family. I was surprised they remained estranged after she visited. I hoped at the time that I was witnessing a thawing of the ice."

"Had you seen pictures of the Hauptmann daughters before?"

"No, ma'am. As I mentioned, he had already packed away most of his belongings, and I was told when I showed up for the home care that he found photographs of his family upsetting. Though he did have a wedding portrait of his wife right next to him on the nightstand. I saw him looking at it often."

McKenna had seen that photograph before, on Susan's bookshelf. She'd commented once on how much Susan looked like her mother.

"When Gretchen came to see her father, did you happen to notice if she looked like the late Mrs. Hauptmann?"

"Oh my goodness, yes. Isn't she just the spitting image of her mother? I couldn't stop commenting on it, but then I realized she seemed a bit uncomfortable with my remarks. My, yes, that's the woman's daughter, no question."

It was one of Mrs. Hauptmann's daughters, all right, but it hadn't been Gretchen. Just like Gretchen had said, she had left the cord to her father severed, even as he'd been dying. Susan had been the one to see her father one last time, to let him know she was alive. Susan, the same woman who told Scott Macklin's wife that she was a reporter and the Lenox Hill ICU that she was Mrs. Patrick Jordan, had told her father's nurse she was her older sister, Gretchen.

"Mrs. Tompkins, I hope you won't take my question the wrong way, but it's important that I ask. I can tell that you were a complete professional in your care of General Hauptmann, but I imagine that when you gave his daughter that diary, you had your reasons."

"I thought she would want it. That's all."

This proud woman did not want to admit there was more to the story. McKenna pressed again. "Wouldn't it be part of his treatment for you to have a sense of his mental state as he was reaching the end? Or maybe you had seen him write something about his daughters, and you wanted Gretchen to know."

"I don't snoop, if that's what you're saying."

"Of course not." What sane person sharing a house with a lonely, decaying old man—a man who'd lived a life filled with power, politics, and international travel—wouldn't sneak a peek at his journals? "But this is important, Mrs. Tompkins. Was there anything in the general's journal about his other daughter, Susan, and the end of her military service?"

"Not really. No."

"Not really" did not mean the same thing as "no." "Did Susan ask him for help getting out of active duty?"

The silence confirmed it. It was only because McKenna knew the truth that the nurse was considering putting aside her loyalty to her former patient and friend. "I cared very much for General Hauptmann, and he was a brave and good man, but I never understood the hardness he showed toward his girls. You see, that's why I read his journals. To see if there was something I could use to bring Gretchen back into his life—something he had written that he could not say to her directly. But all he wrote about was their shortcomings and his disappointment in them."

"Like Susan leaving the military?"

"Yes. According to his journal, Susan came to him and begged for help. He pulled strings for her that regular people do not have access to. He said it reminded him of the senators' sons and corporate nephews who got deferments in Vietnam. He said he had no regrets cutting off Gretchen, and now it was time to do the same with Susan. They never spoke again. He was so ashamed for helping her that he didn't tell her himself. He said that he could find no way to deliver the news without sounding like he approved of her decision. He had his business partner tell her instead. She disappeared three months later."

"Business partner? Do you mean Adam Bayne?"

"Yes, that's right. I guess that was a long time ago, but Adam was like a son to General Hauptmann. Mrs. Jordan, if you talk to Gretchen, please tell her how sorry I am for giving her that journal. I wasn't thinking about her feelings. I was thinking about the general."

McKenna's mind was racing. She didn't understand the nurse's last comment. "How were you helping General Hauptmann?"

"He was an important man, the kind of man people write about when they die. I didn't want anyone to see what a terrible father he was."

McKenna mumbled something to the nurse about being a good person and disconnected the call. Before she knew it, she was pulling up Adam Bayne on her phone and hitting dial.

"McKenna. I saw the news. They said Patrick was in critical condition. I didn't know if it was okay to call. Any updates?"

Die. Die, die, die. You shot my husband, you evil motherfucker.

"He's going to make it." The catch in her voice wasn't feigned. "He's out of the woods."

"Oh, thank God. If there's anything at all I can do—"

You can go to hell, right after you die.

"Right now it's only immediate family, but visiting hours start at six." That gave her two hours. "Patrick's asking for visitors. I think he'd really like you to come."

"Oh. Well, absolutely, then."

He was good, but she could hear the skepticism in his voice. At one point, Patrick and Adam had been close, but these days they were barely beyond holiday-cards friendship.

"In fact," she added, "you're the only person he asked me specifically to call. Maybe after that kind of danger, he just wants an old military friend to talk to."

"Of course. Anything he needs. I'll see him right at six."

Scanlin was just finishing up with Patrick when she entered the hospital room. "How soon can we get a wire set up in here?"

# CHAPTER
# SIXTY-ONE

**M**cKenna held Patrick's hand tightly in hers. "Are you sure you're willing to do this?"

He flashed her a look that revealed the ridiculousness of her question. Her plan for Patrick to coax Adam into incriminating himself was the equivalent of a luxury cruise compared to what Patrick really wanted to do to his former college buddy.

"You can't show that anger," she warned. "He'll know." She hadn't prepped a witness to wear a wire in ten years, but she remembered the basic talking points from her prosecutor days. Get the subject to talk on his own rather than merely acquiescing to your suggestions. Don't be too eager to lead. Be passive. You're the one who's scared. You're the one who's vulnerable. You're the loose cannon. Once the target feels the need to take control, he'll start talking.

She did one more test of their phones to ensure that the connection would work. Two hours' notice hadn't been enough to get NYPD approval for a recording device. McKenna had taken the situation into her own hands.

It was 5:53 P.M. She hit the call button on Patrick's phone, dialing herself, and then answered the call, activating the record function she'd installed for source interviews. "Detective Scanlin," she said, "my husband is clearly fatigued."

Patrick voiced weak protests that he was fine.

"In light of the fact that you haven't yet identified the gunman who nearly killed my husband, I assume you'll be here to frisk anyone who attempts to visit him in the hospital."

"Of course, Mrs. Jordan." Scanlin rolled his eyes, but he sounded perfectly obsequious. "I plan to stay during visitors' hours. Given the gunman's attempt to conceal his identity at Grand Central, I'd be surprised if he showed up here, but I've got two officers standing by just in case."

The real reason for the officers' presence was to back up Scanlin in the event that Adam Bayne was arrested. If Adam tried to argue later that the NYPD had orchestrated the recorded conversation with Patrick, this prologue would prove that she and Patrick had acted independent of the police.

Once she and Patrick were alone, she held his hand again and whispered in his ear. "Be careful, babe. Nothing you get Adam to say is worth the risk."

"He already shot me, M, and I'm still good. He won't be armed. I'll be fine. Now get out of here."

She paused at the door, knowing they had so much more to say to each other. But every word was being recorded, and Adam would be here any second. Patrick could see all of it on her face. *I know,* he mouthed.

Later. They would work through it later. All of the pain—Macklin's death, Patrick's shooting, even Susan's so-called disappearance— could have been avoided if people didn't always put off the problems that needed to be worked through right away.

Now it was 6:02 P.M. Adam was coming. It was time for her to go.

She played her assigned role when Adam appeared, gargantuan iris in tow. "Thank you for coming. You're such a good friend." She felt like the widow at a funeral.

Detective Scanlin played his part, too. "Sorry, sir. Routine for crime victims. Just a quick weapons check."

She stared at Scanlin as he stepped away from Adam empty-handed. As a detective, the man had missed a lot at one point in his career. But he had made a promise to her, and she'd made a decision to trust him. She had to believe he was capable of finding a weapon in a frisk. If he put Patrick in danger, she'd never forgive either one of them.

She listened to her cell phone four chairs away from Scanlin in the ICU waiting room. If Scanlin were ever asked, he could testify under oath—with no chance of contradictory evidence—that he had no idea she was eavesdropping on her husband's conversation with his friend. If something went wrong on the other end of the line, all she had to do was give Scanlin the signal, and he'd intervene.

She had one final idea. She pulled up her Twitter account on her iPad and posted a message:

Susan, you promised P you would end this. Time is NOW. We know about AB; he's here. Come to hospital. P needs you NOW.

According to Will Getty, at one point Susan had been in love with Patrick. As careful as she'd been about hiding, Susan had come to the hospital today to check on him. She had told him she was going to end this, no matter what.

McKenna had to hope that Susan was still the same person, hardwired to do the right thing.

There was nothing more to do but wait.

# CHAPTER SIXTY-TWO

**B**uddy. You look fucked up." McKenna nodded to Scanlin; she could hear Adam's voice clearly. The record function was working. "Not to rush anything, but if you die, is McKenna fair game?"

They called it the sickness, and supposedly Patrick's circle of army friends had it to a person. For someone with the sickness, nothing was off limits—profanity, incest jokes, even necrophilia jabs. It was all comedic fodder.

"You know nothing about true love," Patrick said. "It's in our vows. Promise to love, honor, obey, through sickness and health, richer or poor, and to do me, alive or in rigor mortis. Once the hard, high one wears off, that's another matter."

"What the hell happened?" Adam said. "They're saying it was some mind blow at an Occupy flash mob." The local news had made it sound like a random shooting during the Occupy protest. If McKenna's suspicions were right, Adam knew otherwise.

"Don't bother with the act, Adam. Susan told me everything. I just wanted to see you before it all went down. To try to understand how you could do this to me."

"I know we joke, but that shit's not funny, bro."

"I have a bullet hole in my neck, *bro*. You think I'm playing? It's just you and me here. For now, at least. Didn't you recognize the cop who searched you for weapons? Same guy who handled Susan's missing persons case. But Susan's back. And she knows you set her up. She's going to the feds."

"Set her up for what? Seriously, man, they may need to cut you back on the morphine—"

Scanlin looked at McKenna for an update. She shook her head. Nothing yet.

"It took ten years, Adam, but you can't keep a secret forever. Susan knows that her dad's the one who got her out of the military. Free and clear. No active duty; she could walk away."

For the first time, Adam didn't have a quippy response. That was good.

"The general couldn't bring himself to tell her. You were supposed to be the one. You didn't exactly convey the message."

She and Patrick had pieced together the theory after McKenna had spoken to General Hauptmann's nurse. If Susan had been under the mistaken impression that she was being called into active duty, it was because Adam hadn't told her that her father's intervention was successful. McKenna had been searching for a reason why Susan would have gotten involved in a smuggling operation at the piers; now they believed they'd found one.

Patrick continued to push Adam for a response. "What did you do, tell her she could satisfy her deployment by doing something closer to home? Just a few little shipments at the port? She always was a good implementer. And why shouldn't Susan have to sacrifice? She was the one who refused to save her dad's firm—the firm you'd been working your ass off in Afghanistan for. Just when you were about to cash in, the old man went and got cancer. All Susan had to do was lend her name to the enterprise—a name you'd never have, no matter how hard you tried—and she couldn't even do that."

"I don't know why you're doing this, Patrick, but I'm calling bullshit. Susan's dead. Or in the wind. Never coming back."

"You don't believe me?" Patrick asked. "Go check hospital security. She came when McKenna was out. Hospital security will have a tape of her coming in."

That was a mistake. If Adam took Patrick up on the suggestion, he'd go straight from the security office to the hospital exit, and they'd lose their shot at tripping him up. McKenna let herself breathe when she heard Adam respond. "Anyone who would disappear herself for ten years has obviously lost it. If she's making claims about me, she's got her own agenda."

Scanlin was looking at her more urgently. She shook her head again.

"Look, of all people, I get it," Patrick said. "Other guys post-9/11 were going back in, active duty, getting recommissioned—defend the homeland, get the bad guys. You know what I did? I quit the reserves. That's right. Because I knew we needed to invade someone, no matter what. And once you invade in that part of the world? You were the one who saw it firsthand. The bad guys weren't always bad. The good guys could be the most evil form of life on the planet. With the moral compass upside down, there were plenty of ways to rake in the money. And when the general got diagnosed with the big C, you realized your payday wasn't going to come, and you devised another way. But duping Susan into helping you? Setting off a house bomb to kill her? Shooting a *cop*? Coming after *me*? Taking out the guy you hired to do your dirty work?"

Despite his injuries, despite the painkillers, Patrick was yelling. In his anger, he was saying too much. They had speculated that Carl Buckner worked for Adam and then got scared off, but he also could be connected to Susan. They had wondered whether the Brentwood explosion was Adam's attempt to kill Susan, but it could have been an accidental explosion by the environmental activists Susan had infiltrated.

McKenna was sure Scanlin could see the worry on her face. Should she give the warning sign? Even without a weapon, there were ways Adam could hurt Patrick. The drip. The morphine drip. They should have asked the nurse whether it was tamper-proof.

Patrick must have realized that if he got too loud, the hospital staff would intervene. His voice was quieter, almost pleading. "I mean, Adam, who *are* you?"

"Pat, man, you've got to believe me. Yeah, okay, I got pretty screwed in the head in Afghanistan. And I got greedy. And I made— God, I made some horrible mistakes. But a house bomb? Shooting you? I have no fucking clue what you're talking about. And if Susan's telling you or the feds or anyone those kinds of things, she's lying. Believe what you want, but I'm going to go."

McKenna was shaking her head again at Scanlin. He could listen for himself once the call was over, but she knew they didn't have enough for probable cause. "I really am glad you're okay, Patrick. I mean it, and I hope one day you'll come to believe it."

They were screwed. She would have to play nicey-nice again while the man who shot her husband was allowed to walk away.

But before she saw Adam turn the corner toward the hallway from Patrick's room, she saw another familiar face. Susan's.

For days, McKenna had been convinced that Susan was alive, but she never really expected to see her again. And now here she was, twenty feet away, looking just as she had in the subway video.

Susan obviously recognized Scanlin, because she started to duck back into the elevator. McKenna ran toward her. "No, please!" The elevator doors began to close and then reopened. Susan stood at the threshold. At least she was willing to hear McKenna out.

"Adam Bayne is here but is about to leave," McKenna explained. "I can stall him. Scanlin knows everything, Susan. Just tell him so we'll have enough to arrest Adam right now."

Susan said nothing.

"You've got to do this, Susan. Or Adam gets away with everything. He'll keep coming after you for the rest of your life. And now that Patrick and I know, we're in danger, too."

McKenna could see Susan weighing the options, and for a second, it was like they were roommates again, her friend's face full of concentration as she balanced on a dining room chair to change the bulb in McKenna's closet. She had come here, hadn't she? She still cared. She was still protecting them.

"Okay, stall him," Susan said at last. "Do *not* let him leave. I have enough evidence to bury us both."

# CHAPTER SIXTY-THREE

**M**cKenna caught Adam just before he hit the double doors from the patient recovery rooms.

She put on her best tired smile. The loving wife who had spent the night next to her husband's recovery bed. The oblivious wife who didn't know yet that the hunt she'd begun for her missing friend was at an end. "Oh, no. You're done with your visit already? He seemed like he was really looking forward to seeing you."

"It was good to see him, but he's been through a lot. I don't want to push him too hard. I'll come back another time." Adam was walking away; McKenna reached gently for his forearm.

"You know, I wanted to say something. You were right—when I called you, I mean. About that old picture of Patrick and Susan. That was so many years ago, and it was stupid for me to call you that way. Something like this"—she gestured at Patrick's room—"puts things into perspective."

"That's good. I'm so happy he pulled through. I'd expect nothing less from a bruiser like your husband."

She let him hug her. The son of a bitch was actually *hugging* her. She didn't know how much more she could take.

She saw Scanlin entering the double doorways, a uniformed officer at his side. He gave her a nod. Whatever Susan had told him, he had enough.

Confusion, followed by panic, registered on Adam's face as law enforcement surrounded him. She'd never been so relieved to hear the reading of Miranda rights.

As the uniformed officer walked Adam to the lobby in handcuffs, she spotted Susan sitting in the waiting room next to the other officer awaiting Scanlin's orders. Susan's hands were in her lap, covered by a jacket.

She was in cuffs, too.

"What did you think was going to happen?" Scanlin said. "She gave it up, though. You were right. She was pregnant and had been called up to active duty again, this time for Iraq, and the army wouldn't let her out. She could defer, but she'd still be a single mother leaving behind a newborn."

McKenna knew how jaded Susan had been after her first deployment to Afghanistan. By the time she was called back in, people had figured out that the mission wasn't accomplished in Iraq. McKenna wondered if Susan had used the pregnancy as the excuse she'd never had to walk away from a life she'd taken on only for her father.

"Adam told her things had gotten even worse in Afghanistan. The military was cutting deals with opium farmers just to keep the peace. Now the farmers were crossing the line into exporting directly into the United States. He told her it was a way she could get herself out of active duty for good."

"I can't imagine she'd think that was okay."

"We didn't have time to cover all the details. She knew about the cargo inspection program from Patrick. She knew from you that Mac was assigned to the program and had an immigration problem. She put two and two together. Adam told her he got a promise that Mac's kid would be okay if he helped. It wasn't until she got her father's diary that she realized Adam had lied about the entire thing."

"It doesn't make sense," she said. "The military could fly cargo in on its own, no questions asked. And how could Adam get INS cooperation if he was acting as a free agent?"

"Again, details. We've got paper-thin probable cause based on her statements about the smuggling; plus, she says she's got recordings of both Bayne and Macklin before he died. I'm going to bring in Agent Mercado to trace the money. My guess is she'll find unexplained cash flowing to Bayne while he was in Afghanistan, not long after Susan's father found out he had cancer. From there, we'll get a search warrant for Bayne's home and office. Hopefully we'll find something tying him to Carl Buckner. Or proving that he was our shooter at Grand Central. Like I said, it's really thin."

"I know. But as long as you hold on to him, we don't have to worry about him coming after Patrick again. That's enough for now."

This was the bargain they'd struck once she had summoned Adam to the hospital. They were rushing. They had no real evidence to tie Adam to Patrick's shooting. They had to hope the police would find the gun in a search, or a drop of blood from Patrick or Carl Buckner. It was a risk she and Patrick had decided to take. If McKenna was right, Adam was so unhinged that his own Cleaner had defected, trying to turn to Patrick for help. More evidence might never come, but at least they were safe.

Scanlin started to follow the uniforms to the elevator, and then he turned around. "You're the one who made this happen. You want to come down to the precinct? Hear what your friend's been up to for the past ten years? She gave herself up to nail Adam Bayne to the wall. She could probably use the support."

McKenna had been racing from place to place, from lead to lead, for a solid week. And now Susan was alive. After all these years, and all those nightmares, she was alive, and she was in custody. There hadn't been time for a reunion, not even a handshake.

McKenna nearly followed Scanlin on autopilot. Then another instinct kicked in. "No," she said. Scanlin stopped walking, and she put a hand on his forearm. "I'm not sure I care anymore. And I mean this when I say it: I trust you to see it through. All I want is to stay here with Patrick."

The embrace Scanlin gave her was one of those big, strong hugs that certain kinds of men gave only to certain kinds of women. It was absolutely pure.

"Oh, and one more thing, Jordan. Not that it matters, but Susan says she lost the baby a month after she left New York. I got the impression that you might want to know."

**W**ords were spilling from her mouth when she walked into Patrick's hospital room. "Scanlin got him. But Susan had to give herself up. But I can't figure out—"

"Shh," he said. "Just come here."

She kept talking. "Adam told Susan they needed a domestic contact person for drug imports. Couldn't they just fly everything in themselves through the military? And then Mac got a promise about his stepson. I don't know how Adam could possibly deliver."

Patrick was smiling. He was exhausted, and nauseated from painkillers, but he was smiling. He held up his cell phone.

She realized hers was in her pocket and that she'd never disconnected their call.

"A little muffled," he said, "but I got the gist. You did it, M. You did what I couldn't do, and the NYPD couldn't do, and the FBI couldn't do. You did it all."

He patted the edge of the bed, and she managed to lie on her side next to him.

"We're going to be okay," he whispered. He kissed the top of her head and squeezed her arm. "Thank you."

*We're going to be okay.* She'd been trying to tell herself that for days, but for the first time, she actually believed it.

PART V

# PART V

# SUSAN

# CHAPTER SIXTY-FOUR

McKenna never would have thought that the best rest she'd had in a week would be on a narrow sliver of a hospital bed, listening to her husband talk between bouts of morphine-induced sleep.

His reminiscing about Susan was hard to take at first. Through the entire course of Patrick and McKenna's relationship, they had pretended—falsely, of course—that their romantic existences had begun and ended with each other. But once she got past the shock of imagining Patrick with another woman, his drug-addled memories of nights, weekends, sometimes even weeks—but never months—with Susan began to feel like period pieces. Vignettes from another time, featuring two familiar characters, but wholly unrelated to her own reality.

It had started the beginning of their third year at West Point.

Though McKenna had imagined the most passionate hypotheticals between her husband and Susan, she wanted to believe that any physical connection had been fleeting. Awkward. Meaningless.

The first time had been two days after Patrick learned his father died from an aneurysm. The commandant had him pulled from noon formation, shook his hand, and gave him the news. He also gave him the choice of taking the day off or returning to lunch. Patrick was Patrick, so he opted for the latter, then didn't say a word to anyone about the death of his father until two days later, when Susan cornered him after dinner and said she could tell he was feeling blue.

Those were Patrick's words. *She could tell I was feeling blue.* McKenna knew the Susan of ten years ago, who was only eight years older than the Susan who had been there to comfort Patrick when his father died. She had a preferred method for escaping the pains of the world, and that night she'd shared it with Patrick.

At least from his perspective, it had never been a relationship. He was twenty years old, and by that time, Susan had convinced herself that wanting sex like a man—often and without strings— was a form of female empowerment. They were never what others perceived as an official couple.

A year after graduation, Susan had taken a weekend leave from Fort Sill to find him at Fort Bragg, supposedly to escape the Oklahoma heat, though he suspected she was there for more. He told her then that he loved her as a friend, but—And she had cut him off. *As if! Dude, that's like incest.* Except maybe not, since she still wanted to sleep with him. Only for the sex. Because other guys sucked.

"We all chose to believe that was how she wanted it," he said. "We were a bunch of macho kids who thought we could have a friend who was just like us, except she was a woman who would . . . be with us." He brushed McKenna's hair back from her face. She had always known that he'd adopted the move because she'd made it clear that she liked it. "I was such an idiot then."

She'd heard enough for now. "I thought the only woman you knew before me was Ally, the big-boned girl. Frizzy red hair. Freckles and moles. Dumb as a rock."

"A real doll," he said, repeating the joke he'd made so many times when she was still trying to find out about his old girlfriends. "McKenna, I want you to know, however much—"

She shook her head. "It was a long time ago. We started over so many times, even after she was gone. And then we finally got it right." Maybe someday McKenna would press for details about the timing of the end to his hookups with Susan and the beginning of his relationship with her. Right now she didn't want them.

He saw her looking at the digital bedside clock. Susan was giving a complete videotaped debriefing this afternoon. Mercado and Scanlin had said they wanted McKenna there in case she could fill in any blanks. She suspected that Mercado was afraid she'd go public with the story if she weren't kept in the loop.

"I should go. I need to stop by the apartment first. I've been wearing the same clothes for two days straight."

"You're gross." He kissed the top of her head. "You sure you want to do this? You said they'd be fine without you."

"They would. But we're never going to understand what Susan did if we don't hear it straight from her. I'll be back as soon as it's over."

# CHAPTER SIXTY-FIVE

**M**cKenna was alone in their apartment, her first time home since she'd learned that Patrick had been shot. Susan's belongings were still scattered across the living room floor. McKenna packed them back in the box that Adam had sent over and pushed it all in a corner behind Patrick's bicycle. She didn't want to see it.

She stripped off her clothing, climbed into the hot shower, and turned her face up into the water stream. She felt the past week flow off of her. As the shampoo suds swirled into the drain beneath her, she imagined their problems carried away through the plumbing.

Adam Bayne was in custody. McKenna didn't have all the details, but Scanlin had told her this morning that he was confident they had enough to hold him for a long time. Carl Buckner—whether he'd been trying in the end to help them or hurt them—was dead. The police department was labeling Macklin's death a murder, so his family at least would be able to collect his life insurance and pension.

Tomorrow McKenna would go to see Bob Vance. By now, the editor knew that Dana had been the one who set her up. McKenna would sit down with the magazine's lawyers to make sure the retraction was sufficient to clear her name. And she would make sure they knew how much she could embarrass them with the fact that they'd allowed someone to search a journalist's office without verifying his credentials or the legitimacy of his supposed warrant. She would call the shots.

Did she even want that job?

As she turned off the shower, she let herself entertain the possibility that the district attorney's office might invite her back. Maybe she didn't want that job, either. Maybe it was time for her to write a book. Not on an agent's terms, or an acquiring editor's, but because she really had something to say.

For now, she deserved to sit on her ass for a couple of weeks. Right after she made one last visit to the Federal Building.

Tom the mailman gave her a wolf whistle when she stepped from the apartment elevator. "Take a look at the big shot. You clean up pretty good."

Her usual attire was business casual at best, but she'd hauled out her nice Hugo Boss dress, the one she'd bought when her dog-walker article had earned her a five-minute interview on CNN. (Ever stop to wonder how you know your dog got walked? That's right. You don't.)

"Thank you, Tom. I've got to look like a grown-up today."

"You've got a couple days' mail backed up here. Want me to leave it with the doorman?"

"No, I'll take it." She folded the stack in half and tucked it into her briefcase.

"I mean it, McKenna. Don't let that tough husband know I said it, but you look fantastic."

She left feeling happy about the compliment. And then she realized how pathetic she was for caring about her appearance today. She cared because she wanted to look better than Susan.

**M**ercado met McKenna in the reception area and led the way to her office, where Scanlin was waiting. "Susan spent last night at MDC," Mercado explained. "We transported her this morning to continue the debriefing we began last night."

After four sleepless years at West Point and another five in the army, Susan had always insisted on perfect sleeping conditions: room-darkening curtains, Egyptian-cotton sheets, and absolute silence. McKenna could not imagine her at the Metropolitan Detention Center.

It didn't take long for Mercado to bring McKenna up to speed. "Based on what we got from Susan, we searched Bayne's home and office. Unfortunately, as we feared, the guy is careful. No evidence yet tying him to Carl Buckner or to either Macklin's death or the Grand Central shooting. The better news is that we've got a forensic accountant examining his financial records. He's just getting started on what's going to be a long process, but he tells me he's found discrepancies already. Namely, a fifty-thousand-dollar withdrawal one day before James Low, Jr., showed up at the DA's office claiming to have sold a gun to Marcus Jones. Plus, way more deposits than reported income, and right before Susan disappeared. He used a lot of it to set up his company in New York after he left the Hauptmann firm."

The money would corroborate Susan's claim about the drug importing. The unreported income alone could send him away for a decade. It had worked on Al Capone.

"What exactly did Susan tell you?" McKenna asked.

"You're about to hear for yourself," Scanlin said.

Mercado explained the process. Susan had already been talking for hours. Now they would get a straight, clean narrative on videotape.

McKenna remembered defense attorneys' complaints about videotaped confessions. The cops never recorded the stuff that happened earlier.

"Obviously the tape will be admissible against her," Mercado said. "We'll also give it to Bayne's lawyers to put the pressure on. If he knows for sure that she's flipped and is a compelling witness, he might do the same. My guess is he has names of other private contractors who were involved on the Afghanistan side of the operation."

"How does this work? I'll watch through a one-way glass?"

Mercado nodded, but gave Scanlin a look.

"There's one catch," Scanlin said. McKenna knew they had a reason for asking her here. "Susan's the one who wanted you to come. She wants you to hear her statement—kind of like an explanation, I guess. But she wants a few minutes alone with you before she'll go on tape."

# CHAPTER SIXTY-SIX

**S**usan's orange jail scrubs were at least a size too big. They made her look like a young, waiflike girl. So did her posture—slumped in the chair, hands in her lap. Just a week ago, this same woman had outrun a high school athlete and dead-lifted his full weight.

"They told me you wanted to see me," McKenna said. It was the first time they'd been in the same room since their few minutes at the hospital prior to Susan's arrest.

Susan looked up and smiled sadly. "Of course I wanted to see you. But not to try and tell you what happened. They don't want you knowing anything other than what we're about to put on video. Undermines the evidentiary value or something."

"So why, Susan? Why am I here?" McKenna didn't try to hide the anger in her voice. She had spent the last day wondering whether she would have preferred that Susan had been murdered, as she'd always suspected. Ultimately she couldn't feel that way about anyone, but Susan had gotten people killed. And now she had to drag McKenna into the carnage of her own personal hurricane one last time.

"Because I want to tell you how sorry I am. Not just for—I mean, my God, for everything, but *personally*. I'm sorry for the harm I caused to you personally, McKenna. You'll hear soon enough why

I did what Adam wanted, and why I ran away instead of owning up to it. You can decide for yourself how you feel about that. But I am sorry. I hope someday you'll forgive me."

McKenna stared at Susan in silence. She thought about walking out but took a seat across from her at the table. "Your coming to the hospital yesterday was the beginning," she finally said. It was hard not to feel sorry for Susan. She was looking at serious prison time, and all because she'd chosen to turn herself in. "There was no other way to make sure Adam wouldn't come after Patrick again."

Susan nodded. "Don't thank me. It's only because I reached out to Patrick that he was in danger. I had to stop it."

"Patrick remembers seeing you in his hospital room. Sobbing. You still love him, don't you?"

Susan looked away.

"I know about you two. And I know you told Getty you were still in love with Patrick and wanted to be with him. Why didn't you ever tell me?"

"I almost did. That night we left Telephone Bar together, after the two of you met? I nearly told you. But I knew you'd never go out with him if I did. You'd been alone for a while, and he and I were never right together. I stole that mug for myself at first—like a memento of the night I really lost him. I gave it to you instead."

McKenna shook her head. "You didn't tell me because it would have been selfish." Typical Susan. She could have guaranteed with one sentence that she'd never have to watch the man she loved fall in love with her best friend. She could have sabotaged McKenna's relationship with Patrick before it started. But she wasn't selfish. She never was.

"My intentions weren't always pure," Susan said. "After I told Will I still had feelings for Patrick, I really was going to give it one more shot. I had this whole scene planned where I would pour my heart out, and he'd realize that he felt the same way, and maybe you'd even understand. But when I went to his apartment, all he could talk about was you. You guys had rented a paddleboat in Central Park or something. So *not* Patrick. So *completely* the kind of thing he'd usually mock. But because it was with you—anyway, I knew we were never going to happen."

"Were you pregnant then?"

She nodded.

"They told me you lost the baby. I'm sorry, Susan."

She shrugged.

"Was it Patrick's?" She regretted asking as soon as the words came out of her mouth. She'd been so careful not to press Patrick for the details. The idea of them being together after she and Patrick met had been enough to send McKenna out of their apartment after she'd found a college photograph. But now? She honestly didn't care.

Or perhaps she cared a little, because she felt relieved when Susan shook her head. "Of course not. We stopped crossing that line way before he met you. Or at least *he* stopped crossing that line. Let's just say there would have been a long list of paternity candidates."

McKenna had been idealizing her friendship with Susan, the way people do with friends who die. Now that Susan was back, McKenna realized that the personality differences she'd sensed a year into rooming together were a chasm.

McKenna placed her hands, palms up, on the table. Susan accepted the invitation. The two of them sat there, fingers entwined, in silence. It was the reunion they didn't have time for at the hospital. It wasn't much, but it was all McKenna could give. She wanted to be with her husband.

"Thank you for the apology," McKenna said, releasing Susan's hands. "And for your help exposing Adam. I imagine they'll want to start the taping soon."

"There's something else." Susan's voice dropped slightly. "So far I've been acting without a lawyer because, as you know, the best shot I have at leniency is to give complete cooperation. And I need people to understand how truly sorry I am. I didn't know— Well, again, they don't want me getting into that with you. Just the tape. I'm basically at their mercy."

"Turning yourself in and helping the government is a good start."

"I'm scared, McKenna. I don't want to spend the rest of my life behind bars. I thought about just killing myself, but then Adam would get away with what he did. I know I have no right to ask anything of you, but will you please consider writing my side of the story?"

"I don't know, Susan. I don't even have a job at this point. And Patrick nearly—"

"I know, I get it. But I'm doing everything I can to make sure Adam never gets out. That's why I'm here, probably for good. Just—just stay and listen to what I have to say. You can decide then whether you want to help me. Just listen and think about it." Susan took the lack of opposition as acquiescence. She clasped her palms together in gratitude. "Thank you, McKenna. Really."

"Whatever does happen, you eventually need a lawyer," McKenna said. "I'm sure you'll have people lined up to represent you for free, just for the publicity."

"Actually, I'm planning to hire Hester Crimstein."

The name required no further explanation. If what Susan needed was a trial by public opinion, the larger-than-life Hester was the right woman for the job. Susan's private work during her period of hiding must have been very lucrative.

"You'll be in good hands," McKenna said. "I'm going to let them know we're done here."

"Again, I'm so sorry, McKenna. For everything."

Though Susan had supposedly brought her here to apologize, she had also asked for help. McKenna felt her emotions competing again. Anger at Susan for all the harm she'd caused. The lies. The destruction. Gratitude that she'd come forward to tell the truth. Sympathy.

She would stay long enough to hear what Susan had to say for herself.

# CHAPTER SIXTY-SEVEN

It had been a long time since McKenna had watched a confession through one-way glass. She'd never thought that the person on the other side would be someone she once considered to be a close friend.

Susan looked less real than she had fifteen minutes earlier, when they'd been seated across a table from each other. She would seem less human still once she was reduced to a two-dimensional image on a screen with a digital counter ticking off time beneath her chin.

"I was pregnant. I planned to have the baby. Even though I would be doing it on my own, I was required to serve. Obviously they wouldn't force me to deliver the child during active duty, but all I could do was postpone the inevitable. I knew from a classmate that the army had activated his wife even though they had two children under the age of three, and he'd even offered to go in her place. I was desperate."

McKenna knew how this worked. The jurors who would eventually watch this tape would see an uninterrupted narrative, as if Susan were speaking spontaneously to a faceless, nameless, gender-less, identity-less biographer on the other side of the camera. It was the talk-to-the-camera format everyone had grown used to in the age of reality TV.

But this monologue—seemingly without a script, without notes—was the fruit of hours of preparation.

"I called my father." Susan provided what appeared to be an impromptu aside about her father's prominence in the military. "Three days later, his business partner—and my former West Point classmate—Adam Bayne called to tell me that I could satisfy my active-duty obligation to the army in an alternative way."

Susan took her time explaining the context surrounding the deal Adam had conveyed. By then, reports were coming out that the U.S. had lost control of both wars. Former Taliban soldiers had infiltrated the new regime in Afghanistan and were attacking from within. Women and children were being used as shields. Troops handing out water and rice had been killed by land mines. The president had declared Iraq the new central front in the war on terror, as anti-American chants and calls for resistance of the "occupation" broke out at the burial of Saddam Hussein's sons. By the time Susan disappeared, Baghdad's Green Zone would have experienced the first of many attacks when twenty-eight rockets struck the Al-Rashid Hotel.

Those were the kind of surroundings that forced governments to weigh ideology against reality. Since Adam's arrest, McKenna had done some research about that reality. After invading Afghanistan, the military largely opted to look the other way when it came to the country's thriving opium business. Opium farmers weren't friends, but they weren't enemies. They tempered local fears. They negotiated settlements. They garnered cooperation.

But they were demanding more than a blind eye, at least according to Adam. With the war impairing the usual means of export, they wanted the military to provide cover for shipments directly into the United States.

"I didn't understand," Susan explained. "I didn't want to believe that anyone in the military would strike that kind of deal, but Adam told me that soldiers' lives were at stake in the arena. It was only supposed to be a couple of shipments. They were buying a huge asset in the field, and in exchange, the influx of heroin into the United

States would tick up by one undetectable notch. It came down to a cold, hard cost-benefit calculation."

McKenna could tell that Susan was forcing herself to slow down. She could almost hear Mercado's coaching during the warm-up session. *You're talking to someone who doesn't know the background. Explain every last detail.*

"I asked him why the military, of all organizations, couldn't bring the shipment into the country on its own terms, with no inspection whatsoever. But this was quasi–off the books. Authorized and yet not. They trusted my father, and therefore they trusted me. They were funneling the job through my father's firm in order to disclaim responsibility if something went wrong. Because I was his daughter, and because I had networks in the city, they thought I was the perfect contact person within the border. This was a concrete way to save the lives of American soldiers. I know it sounds impossible now, but this was 2003—support the troops, us against them, remember the towers. I'll admit it, I didn't want to go to Iraq. This was my out. And I found a way to justify it—I felt for the soldiers who were over there, especially the ones in Afghanistan who had been left while we pursued a different agenda in another country. This was a way to increase their safety."

Adam had played her.

Susan set out the contours of the plan. The truncated cargo inspection program. A cop who needed immigration help for his new family.

"That was the hardest part to justify to myself—involving Officer Macklin. But I really did believe we were saving American lives. And just like I was getting something personally from the deal— freedom to walk away from the army—I believed, because Adam told me, that Macklin was securing citizenship for his wife and son. I realize in hindsight that Adam had no way to help Macklin. He was simply playing the odds that immigration would never come after the wife of a cop or a boy who was brought to the United States at five years old."

Susan's gaze appeared to shift in the direction of the one-way glass. "Ultimately, though, Macklin was my best asset for accomplishing the mission."

She was looking at the glass because she knew McKenna would get the message. Macklin had been the "best" asset but not the only one. Patrick, after all, was the one to mention cargo inspection to Susan. If the appeal to save soldiers' lives in exchange for a shipment or two of heroin had worked with Susan, it might have worked with Patrick, too. Yet Susan had left him out of it. Or at least she had until last week.

"Then the night of the container inspection," Susan continued, "something happened. I was at the end of the docks, watching through binoculars. There was a container filled with heroin. Some men—I don't know who they were—were unloading it into a truck. Officer Macklin spotted two individuals nearby and approached: Marcus Jones and Pamela Morris. He told me later he thought Jones was reaching for a gun, but he was probably reaching for ID, and Macklin was nervous. Jumpy. It was my fault, because I was the one who pulled him into something that had nothing to do with him. He panicked and shot them both. I rushed to the scene, but it was too late. They were both dead."

She exhaled loudly and took two slow breaths. "I'm the one who devised the plan from there. It was clear from Pamela Morris's attire that she was a prostitute. The men who took the cargo—they also took her body. I don't know where. I told Officer Macklin that he could claim mistaken self-defense: it was dark, he thought he saw a weapon. That was when Officer Macklin told me that he had an untraceable weapon, what cops call a drop gun. We placed it in Marcus Jones's hand."

She walked through the ensuing controversy over the shooting. The initial quiet murmurs in the African-American community. The church-led vigil at the piers. And then a young ADA who traced the drop gun back to Safe Streets.

"I was sure that once people began looking at the shooting, someone would start asking questions about the cargo coming in that night. Adam flew back to New York from Afghanistan and met me at my apartment. I tape-recorded that conversation and have given a copy of the recording to the FBI."

The recording was the evidence she'd said would sink both of them. The argument in her apartment. *Mac. Import.*

"Adam assured me that his contact people in the military were coming up with a plan, but I know how the world works. The whole reason the military would use private contractors, off the books, for this quasi-authorized operation was to have deniability. We were on our own. So I left everything I had and walked away. At some level, I was afraid for my life, and for my baby's, because of the secret I carried. I also saw it as an obligation to my country never to get caught."

She'd spent the last decade working private jobs, mostly overseas. She was an especially good catch for the protection market. The assumption was that a woman couldn't pull off the difficult work, let alone one attractive enough to pass for a valued asset's girlfriend or personal assistant. She never had a problem locating people who were willing to use her skills and not ask too many questions about her past.

"Three months ago, I learned it was all a lie." Her tone of voice changed. A flicker of anger registered in her eyes. "There was no *quasi* authorization. And there was no military *team*."

She described the visit to see her dying father and the relevant passages in his diary. "I was free to walk away from the army, and I never knew it. Instead, I walked away from the only life I'd ever known."

She took a job following environmental activists to the New York suburbs. They were buying small quantities of bomb-making ingredients, to locate suppliers in the event of an eventual plan to use them. She was nervous but did not believe the operation had reached a level where criminal investigators could intervene.

One day she came home and saw a fuse, something she was sure that none of the people living in that house knew how to build. She tried to grab Greg Larson, but he resisted, and there was no time. She escaped out the back window on the second floor, convinced that Adam was trying to kill everyone who might be able to expose him.

Her plan was to persuade Scott Macklin to join her in coming forward with the story. Adam would pay for what he did, and they could be free of the secrets they'd carried for a decade. Her incentive was to return to her old life. But Macklin was perfectly happy with the life he was living. He said he needed to think about it. A day later, he was dead.

"Even if it had been my own country asking this of me, it would have been wrong. We are a nation of laws. There are no exceptions. But I allowed myself to believe that we knew right from wrong in a way the general population would never understand. I bought in to the idea that there was a higher law above civil law. If I could do anything to take it back, I would. I'll pay whatever price I need to, if only for the hope that Adam Bayne is punished to the fullest extent possible."

It felt like a natural ending point, even though the moment was entirely manufactured.

Scanlin and Mercado walked out of the room together. "She did a good job," Mercado announced. "I don't know about you guys, but I'm actually rooting for a good deal from the federal prosecutor."

Scanlin patted McKenna on the back. "Your girl did good."

"She's not exactly my girl anymore, but she did. And so did you with the prep."

Despite her words, McKenna still knew Susan Hauptmann. She was the woman who'd pulled Nicky Cervantes from the train tracks when she could have simply grabbed the phone that would have led back to her assumed identity. She was the woman who'd come to the hospital when Patrick was hurt, and had returned again when it was time for her to confront Adam Bayne. McKenna even understood why Susan had never told her about the relationship with Patrick.

It had been ten years, but McKenna knew Susan at her core.

And because she knew her at her core, McKenna understood that—despite the prep, despite the video—Susan was holding back. She knew more than she was saying.

# CHAPTER
# SIXTY-EIGHT

The way her husband was shoveling ketchup-topped tuna fish straight from the can to his mouth, McKenna would have thought he was feasting on the signature dish at a five-star restaurant.

"You must be the only patient who has ever rejected hospital food in favor of something even worse than hospital food."

When they met, Patrick was still in the habit of opening a can of tuna and a deli packet of ketchup and calling it a meal. In the intervening years, most of his other disgusting culinary habits—instant iced tea, three-dollar wine, and Velveeta sandwiches—had fallen by the wayside, but he still loved tuna and ketchup.

"I wish you could go home tonight," she said. "I'd make you a proper meal."

"You mean you'd walk to Union Square Cafe and ask them to pack us up a proper meal."

Patrick's surgeon had been close to releasing him tonight, but they were still monitoring him for the risk of internal bleeding. Tomorrow, they said. No promises, but they'd reevaluate tomorrow.

"I'm getting used to it here," he said. "Adjustable bed. Free sponge baths. All the antiseptic cleanser you could possibly desire. You should go home and get some proper sleep, though. You've been through the wringer this week."

"Which of us has a frickin' bullet hole in his neck?"

"I'm going to be fine. But Susan manipulating you that way? Trying to guilt trip you into helping her? I would have expected better. She's obviously not the person she used to be."

"You weren't there, Patrick. She thought she was doing the right thing. Not just for herself. For everyone. It was almost—messianic." McKenna had conflicting emotions about Susan, but she believed Adam had been able to deceive her only by abusing her patriotism.

Patrick wasn't having it. Internal checks. Chain of command. There was no excuse for going outside the system. In her own thoughts, McKenna heard the counterargument.

The nurse who came to check on Patrick's respiratory strength made a not so subtle suggestion that he could use a night of uninterrupted sleep. Without a visitor.

McKenna kissed him on the lips. She could tell from the way he returned the kiss that he was ready to come home.

In her dream, McKenna was back at the DA's office. She had gone to Will Getty with the link between Safe Streets and the gun next to Marcus Jones. She was back to her drug cases, arriving to work each day, waiting for some word from Getty.

She walked into Getty's office. Susan was leaning over the desk, her back arched, mouth open. Adam Bayne was behind her, grabbing her hair in his fists.

McKenna's eyes opened. The room was dark.

She reached for her cell phone and checked the time.

4:14 A.M.

She wasn't used to sleeping in their bed alone. Outside of an occasional security conference, Patrick was always home at night.

She tried to fall back asleep but kept hearing Susan's voice. *I was having a baby . . . I was desperate . . . a concrete way to save the lives of American soldiers . . . support the troops, us against them, remember the towers . . . I saw it as an obligation to my country never to get caught . . . I walked away from the only life I'd ever known.*

McKenna had left the Federal Building believing that Susan was holding something back. Wasn't that natural, given the unnatural confines of the statement? In custody, on videotape, after hours of coaching? When they'd been alone, without Scanlin or Mercado or the camera, it had been like being with the old Susan. She fucked up, and now she was trying to make it right.

McKenna pulled her laptop into the bed and started to type: *My name is Susan Hauptmann, and on November 29, 2003, I walked away from my own identity.*

By the time she closed her computer, light was peering through the crack in the curtains. She had the first six thousand words of Susan Hauptmann's life as a fugitive, and they were good words. They were the kind of words that would put Susan on the *Today* show, not as a drug dealer but as a woman whose loyalty to her country had been manipulated by Adam Bayne.

What had felt like the middle of the night was now well into the morning. McKenna walked to the kitchen, hoping that caffeine would rouse her from the fog.

Her briefcase, thrown on the kitchen island, was still stuffed with the two-day overflow of mail that Tom the mailman had handed her the previous day. Con Ed bill. Bank statement. Eight furniture catalogs that Tom had been unable to squeeze into their mailbox.

Something for Patrick. Handwritten, no return address. A New York City postmark.

Seven minutes later, she placed the letter in a Ziploc freezer bag and made a phone call to Marla Tompkins.

**G**eneral Hauptmann's former nurse finally answered after six rings. She sounded tired.

"Miss Tompkins, it's McKenna Jordan. I hate to bother you again, but you mentioned that General Hauptmann was very generous to you by recognizing you in his will."

"That's correct. I didn't feel right about accepting it at first, but I prayed on it. He was a strong-willed man, and it was what he wanted."

"What about the rest of the will? How did he deal with his missing daughter, Susan?"

"I remember very well, because the estate lawyer explained it to me. It was complicated because he never was willing to accept that she was gone. He could have had her declared dead after she was gone for three years, but he never, ever did it."

"Susan was still in the will?"

"Well, yes. In a way. If she was no longer alive, her part would pass to his other descendants, but then he expressly disinherited Gretchen, so it would go to his various charities. Wounded Warriors. Special Olympics. American Cancer—"

"And what if Susan lived?" McKenna felt rude cutting the woman off, but it was the will's other contingency plan that interested her.

"That was simple: if she outlived him, she got her inheritance."

"How much was that?"

"Well, he left a quarter to me, which was just over nine hundred thousand dollars. That's mostly the value of the apartment, but I still can't believe it. Another quarter will go to the charities. The remaining half was set aside for Susan. And there was a deadline where if they didn't find out what happened to her within . . . I believe it was seven years of his death, the money would be divided among his charities."

The General had written off (and out) Gretchen, but he'd never been able to give up on Susan.

McKenna called Joe Scanlin, but got his voice-mail. She typed a text message instead:

Don't make any deals with Susan.

Susan had spent ten years on the run. Her father's death had given her more than 1.8 million reasons to come home.

# CHAPTER
# SIXTY-NINE

Scanlin placed two sunny-side eggs carefully on the plate-size pancakes. Those were the eyes. Strawberry nose. Bacon smile.

"Maple syrup on the side," he announced, positioning the plate and a small pitcher of warmed syrup in front of Jenna at the dining room table.

"You know I avoid carbs, Dad." Jenna picked at the pancake with her fork the way a crime lab analyst would handle a blood-soaked mattress.

"It's almond meal instead of flour," he explained. "Got the recipe off the Internet. Tastes like a hubcap if you ask me, but I know you're always good for eggs and bacon if all else fails."

"You got a carb-free recipe off the Internet?" she asked. "Who kidnapped my father?"

"I know you're not ten years old anymore, and this is my way of thanking you for getting up early to come here before work. It's the last time I'm going to ask you to change your schedule for me."

She gave him a confused look as she scooped up half of a runny egg.

"Your mother doesn't remember me," Scanlin said. "She recognizes me sometimes, but only when I'm with you. You have your own life and need to see her on your own schedule. So that's going to be my schedule, too."

She swallowed her food, taking in his words. "Okay."

"I've been hanging on to the past, Jenna. And simultaneously not taking responsibility for it. I've been blaming you and resenting you for giving me a hard time, without ever admitting that you've got good reason to. And without telling you how much I regret that."

"Dad, I haven't always been fair—"

He raised his hand to stop her. "Whether you have or not, that's not the point. I'm your father. And I owed you more. I owed your mother more. I even owed myself more, but mostly I owed you two. I realized that years ago, when your mother first got sick. But then somehow it became a battle between the two of us, and I was too stubborn to do what I should have done as your father—which was to put you first."

He couldn't remember the last time she'd looked at him that way. No resentment. No fatigue. Just trust. For a second, she looked like her mother.

"This pancake *totally* tastes like a hubcap." But she kept chewing.

His cell phone interrupted the moment. Jenna smiled sadly. "Go ahead, Dad."

"No, I'm not answering it."

"It's probably work."

"Absolutely not." He walked to the freezer and tossed the phone inside. "See? I can't even hear it now."

She laughed the way she usually laughed only with other people. "How am I going to feel if that's a super-secret, super-smart witness who wants to help you catch bad guys. Justice is at stake, Dad."

That was what he had always told her when he was leaving for work, despite her pleas that Daddy stay home. *Justice is at stake.*

The muffled ringing sound stopped. "Too bad," he announced. "I missed it. Justice will have to wait."

"At least take it out of the freezer." She opened the door and grabbed the phone from the top of the ice tray. "You should probably see this."

He stole a glance. One missed call, followed by a text from McKenna Jordan.

Don't make any deals with Susan. Carl Buckner sent us a letter
before he died. It changes everything.

# CHAPTER SEVENTY

McKenna met Scanlin at his detective squad. She read the letter over his shoulder, even though she'd already memorized every word.

*To Whom It May Concern:*

*My name is Carl David Buckner. Two days ago, I rigged a bomb to ignite in Brentwood, Long Island.*

*The target was a woman living there under an alias as Pamela Morris. I do not know her true identity, but I was hired to kill her.*

*Not at first. Initially, the job was to follow her and to discredit a reporter named McKenna Jordan. I paid a coworker of Jordan's to help with the latter. I then learned from Jordan's coworker that Jordan had video footage of Morris. The person who hired me asked me not only to wipe out the video but also to wipe out Morris.*

*When the woman escaped the Brentwood bombing, I was then ordered to kill Scott Macklin, a former NYPD officer. I did not comply with the order, but I also did nothing to save him.*

*It has become clear that the person who hired me is a sociopath willing to kill anyone. I am trying to stop that.*

*If this letter gets mailed (FBI, NYPD, FOX News), it's because I did not make it back to a Mail Boxes Etc. by noon the day after I wrote this, which means I am probably dead.*

*I don't know whether this will be one of those stories on the front
page for a week, or maybe no one will care (except maybe my brother). If anyone does care, I was a good person once and am trying to be
one now.*

*I know about soldiers who have come home and killed their wives
or themselves or a roomful of strangers in a mass shooting. I'm not
going to try to make excuses for myself. I crossed a line when I set that
bomb. And then I didn't do enough to make up for it.*

*I'm trying now. Is it possible to be a good person, then a bad per-
son, and then a good person again?*

*I have close to $400,000 set aside. I want ¾ to go to the family of
Scott Macklin. If possible, I want ¼ to cover college for my nephew,
Carl David Buckner III.*

*As for the person who hired me: I was contacted entirely by un-
traceable phone and e-mail. All I know is that the voice on the phone
was female.*

*Signed,*

*Carl Buckner*

*P.S. I sent a copy of this letter to a man named Patrick Jordan
because I saw him with the woman I know as Pamela Morris. He
is married to McKenna Jordan, and I believe he was trying to help
Pamela Morris. Hopefully I will see him in person before I die. I am
going to meet him now at Grand Central Station.*

Scanlin dropped the letter on his desk.

"Female," McKenna said, placing an index finger on the most
important word on the page. "The person who hired him was a
woman."

"It doesn't mean anything," he insisted. "Adam could have used
a middleman—or -woman—to hire Buckner. Or a voice distorter.
I've seen ones from spy shops for a hundred bucks that sound like
the real thing."

"You can't just ignore this," McKenna said. "Whoever shot Patrick and Buckner was wearing a mask and a cape. It could have
been Susan. She could have orchestrated the entire thing. At the

very least, the letter is exculpatory evidence as far as Adam Bayne is concerned. You'll have to turn it over to his defense attorney, who will argue that Susan was behind this from the very beginning."

"Only because you told me about it. You sure you don't want to put it in the recycle bin?" Scanlin was rereading the letter, trying to find some way to prevent it from ruining the tidy package of evidence they had put together against Adam.

"He mailed it to the NYPD, FBI, and FOX News. I just got to the mail a little faster. You said Susan had a recording of the argument she and Adam had before she ran away. Is it enough to sink Adam?"

"Yeah. It's a whole conversation about growers in Afghanistan wanting to cut out their middlemen and import directly into the United States. They talked about Macklin panicking and starting to shoot. Susan felt bad for dragging Mac into it, and Adam tried to calm her down, saying that in the end Mac was an undisciplined cop with a drop gun."

"Does the recording make clear that Adam was the one in charge? That Susan thought she was acting on behalf of the military?"

"No. If he wanted to, he could say they were in it as equal partners. No deception involved."

"If Adam can say that, maybe it's actually true. Under the terms of her father's will, Susan gets half his estate now that it's clear she's alive. You've got to ask her about this. If she's the one who hired Carl Buckner—"

"I know, Jordan. You don't have to spell it out for me. Bayne might be a smuggler, but all the blood from the last week would be on her." He took a deep breath. "Better get it over with. I'll call Mercado."

"I think I have something that might help." She handed him a document from her briefcase.

**M**cKenna was watching Susan through the one-way glass again. Mercado was seated next to McKenna, having decided to take advantage of Susan's daddy issues by letting Scanlin work solo.

Scanlin started by handing Susan a document. It was the thirty-page manuscript McKenna had hammered out on her laptop the night before. The words had flown from her as if from a wellspring. She'd always felt that the best writing required empathy. Those pages were her most empathetic attempt to tell Susan's story.

"Story" being the key word.

Susan was flipping through the pages. "I don't know what to say. Please tell McKenna how grateful I am—"

Scanlin pulled the document from her hands and began ripping the pages in half.

"What are you—"

"No one's ever going to see this. Carl Buckner left behind some evidence of his own. We've been blaming Adam for the Brentwood bombing, for Macklin's murder, for the Grand Central shooting, all because we thought he was the one who hired Buckner. It wasn't Adam who hired Buckner. It was a woman."

"But—"

"McKenna told us you were trying to go the reformed-and-repentant-female-fugitive route on us. Pretty smart, using sexism to your advantage. It's always so easy to believe that a woman is the passive underling. But it's clear that you were the one who hired Buckner, in which case I'd say this week went pretty damn well for you."

Susan miraculously escaped the bombing in Long Island, which set the stage for her to claim someone was trying to kill her. Scott Macklin died one day after she visited his house, perhaps because he refused to go along with her plan to blame the entire operation on Adam Bayne. And with the Grand Central shooting, she silenced Buckner and nearly took out the man who broke her heart.

"Here's the thing, Susan. I don't think you planned for it to go this way. Why'd you hire Buckner? For protection? To watch over you as you reemerged in New York? Make sure Adam didn't come after you? Then Nicky Cervantes stole your phone—a phone that contained incriminating calls and e-mails. You wanted that phone back, and then you did something truly selfless. You saved the kid from the tracks. Buckner managed to wipe out the video footage he knew about, but how could you be sure those were the only copies? So you had to change plans."

Her plan was to play the victim, which would allow her to claim the inheritance and hire the best criminal defense lawyer in the city to get her a deal.

Scanlin dropped a copy of George Hauptmann's will on the table. "McKenna told us you have plans to hire Hester Crimstein. I guess you're planning to pay her with your inheritance. If you'd stayed dead, you couldn't collect. But now you've got half of your dad's life savings. Pretty good time to come out of hiding."

Susan was reading the will with much greater attention than she'd given McKenna's draft article. Her lips parted. McKenna and Mercado exchanged a glance, preparing for the next wave of lies.

Instead, she pressed her lips together and flipped through the pages of the will once again. Then she started to cry. She put her head on the table, hiding her face with her arms, and sobbed.

"It's not too late to cooperate, Susan."

She managed to utter a single sentence. "I want to go back to my cell."

Susan was done telling stories. She was about to start the beginning of the next phase of her life. One that might last forever.


The hospital released Patrick that afternoon. To prepare, McKenna had propped four pillows on his side of the bed and loaded up her laptop with episodes of *Arrested Development* and *The Wire*. "I tried to roll the TV into the bedroom, but the cable cord wasn't long enough."

"It's okay. I've watched enough TV in the last two days to dull my brain for a month."

Once he was comfortable in the bed, she told him about the letter from Carl Buckner and the terms of George Hauptmann's will.

They might never prove that Susan was the masked assailant who shot Buckner and Patrick at Grand Central, but as promised, the tape of her and Adam arguing in the aftermath of the Marcus Jones shooting had been enough to sink them both.

"Do you have any questions for Scanlin or Mercado?" McKenna asked. "They were going to brief you at the hospital, but I told them you were coming home. They said to call if you—"

"You know what, M? I think we're both sick and tired of thinking about Susan Hauptmann. What do you have to say about that?"

"I say you're pretty smart for a guy with a hole in his neck."

# CHAPTER
# SEVENTY-ONE

**F**or five days, they didn't talk about her, and life got back to normal.

Normal except that neither of them was working. McKenna had an offer to go back to the magazine—higher pay, more freedom, a fancy title as a "feature columnist." She told Vance she wanted two weeks to think about it and a paycheck at the new rate while she pondered.

Patrick was using some of the eight million sick days he had accumulated after fourteen years at the museum without a single illness.

She could get used to this lifestyle.

Patrick was eyeing the cardboard box she had placed next to the front door. Susan's things. The box had been sitting in the corner next to Patrick's bicycle for nearly a week, the last visible reminder of the danger Susan had brought into their lives.

"Last chance," he said. "I'm thinking a Dumpster seems like a good idea right now."

Scanlin and Mercado had already inspected the box's contents and determined there was nothing relevant to the investigation.

"I know. But Gretchen might want this stuff someday."

"She was pretty pissed the last time we went out there."

"Maybe she's changed her mind now that she knows her sister is alive."

"Call her and find out. Oh, except then she'll tell you she doesn't want this crap, either. And you'll be stuck with it."

She smiled. He knew her too well. "Yep, it's like a hot potato. I don't care what she says. We're dumping this stuff at her house and then getting out of Dodge. No more Hauptmann sisters in our lives. I can go by myself, though. My dumb idea, my errand." She had a Zipcar waiting downstairs at the curb.

Patrick said, "I haven't been outside in a week. The car ride will be good."

She knew he wasn't going for the fresh air. Gretchen's words had been harsh. He didn't want her facing that bitterness alone. He reached down for the box and jerked back upright. It was too soon.

As hard as McKenna was working to cleanse their lives of every mark Susan had left, some of them would linger forever.

**G**retchen's Volvo sedan was in the driveway. "Looks like she's home," McKenna said.

"You could just drop the box on the front porch and run away."

"Yes, that would be a very mature way of dealing with a woman whose sister is probably going to prison for the rest of her life."

McKenna noticed as they walked to the front door that the lawn looked like it hadn't been mowed in two weeks. She balanced the box against the porch rail while Patrick gave the brass knocker a few taps.

They saw Gretchen peer out from the living room blinds. During the delay that followed, McKenna wondered whether Gretchen was simply going to ignore them.

As soon as Gretchen opened the door, McKenna stepped inside.

"Gee, McKenna, come on in."

"Sorry," she said, dropping the box to the floor. "But that's heavy. It's some of Susan's things that your father held on to. I thought you might want to have it. There are some old pictures of your mother. That kind of stuff."

Once her hands were free, McKenna noticed that the living room had changed since their last visit. The black leather recliner in the corner was gone, indentations in the carpet marking the spot where it had been. The wide-screen television above the fireplace was also missing, replaced by a smaller version on a cart against the wall. Gretchen's husband had finished moving out.

McKenna was expecting Gretchen to bawl her out for showing up at the house again without notice, but her face softened. "That was nice of you. Thanks."

They were on their way out when Gretchen stopped them. "The police were here. I know what happened. I'm glad you're okay, Patrick."

Patrick nodded.

McKenna didn't feel right, leaving without saying more. Gretchen lost her father long before his death. Her husband had left her. Now she'd rediscovered her sister only to lose her to a prison cell.

"This has to be hard on you," McKenna said. "There are support groups—for families of prisoners—if you want me to give you some names."

Gretchen's son came running through the living room, banging on the newly delivered cardboard box with a plastic sword. "I thought we were all done with the moving, Mommy."

"We are, Porter. Just give us a second, okay?"

He dropped his sword and started pushing the box down the hallway, making engine noises as he went. "I'm going to put this where Daddy's office used to be. That's where all the boxes go, right?"

Gretchen offered McKenna and Patrick an awkward smile. "We're going through some other changes around here. Figured while my husband's packing up, I might as well do some purging. You wouldn't believe how much stuff a nine-year-old kid accumulates in a lifetime." There was a crash in the next room, and she rolled her eyes. "Porter, stay out of that stuff. I told you, those old toys are going to Goodwill."

"You'll be fine." McKenna realized how hollow the words sounded.

"Mommy," Porter called out from the back room. "There're pictures of your friend in this box."

"Okay, Porter, leave it alone. I'll come see later." Gretchen moved toward the front door. "Really, thank you so much for coming."

McKenna had sorted through the entire box. The only pictures were of Susan's family and her friends from the army. There were no pictures of anyone Porter would recognize as one of his mother's friends.

McKenna remembered what Gretchen had said the last time they were here. *If you really knew my sister, you'd know that if she were alive—if she were here—she'd know exactly where I was and how I was doing. She would know about her nephew. Hell, she'd probably have Porter's schedule down to the minute.*

Gretchen knew. The whole time, Gretchen knew that Susan was alive.

"Your son knows your sister," McKenna said. "Susan stayed in touch with you. That's why you didn't want me looking for her. You knew she was alive. You knew she had her own plan for coming back to New York."

"*Moooooom.* Look what else I found."

"Porter!" Gretchen was screaming now. "Get out of there, I mean it!" Her voice returned to normal. "I obviously have my hands full here. Thank you very much for bringing her things."

They were almost to the front door. McKenna saw no point in pressing the issue. Whether Gretchen knew, whether she didn't. Whether Susan visited her nephew, whether she didn't. None of it really mattered.

They almost walked out.

And then it happened so fast that McKenna would have a hard time later describing the sequence of events.

Gretchen was shepherding them toward the front door. Porter's little feet came storming down the hallway toward them. They all turned to face the sound of his happy, bellowing voice.

"I'm a ghost," he yelled. "I'm a ghost." He ran in a circle through the living room and back down the hall, making "boo" sounds along the way.

He was wearing a black cape and a Guy Fawkes mask.

Gretchen lunged for the console table next to the front door. Patrick saw the movement and charged toward her, but he was too late. She had a gun, and now he was inches from her.

Only one thing mattered to McKenna in that moment: the gun right next to Patrick's stomach, still bandaged from the smaller of his two wounds. There were no books there to protect him this time.

McKenna jumped on Gretchen with all her weight. The three of them fell to the floor in a tangle. The gun. She heard it thud against the hardwood floor.

Six hands groping for the weapon. McKenna was so close. She felt the steel against her middle finger, but then the gun slid from her reach. She saw someone else's fingers wrapped around the grip. She felt her body tuck instinctively into a ball, trying to protect itself from the oncoming shot.

And then Patrick was on his feet. He had the gun.

Gretchen was scrambling toward him, but he took one step backward and pointed the gun directly at her head. "I'll do it, Gretchen. I swear to God, I will do it."

More footsteps toward them. "I'm a ghost, I'm a ghost."

Porter stopped dead in his tracks. He looked at them in terror.

Gretchen put on a fake smile. "Don't be scared, Porter."

He ran back down the hall.

"I'll go," McKenna said. "I'll tell him everything's okay."

She found him curled up on the floor, still in the cape, his mother's mask resting on the top of his head. The room was vacant but for a few boxes and stuffed Hefty bags. McKenna recognized the nearest box as the one she had delivered. It was open, and various pictures of Susan were scattered next to it.

McKenna knelt on the Berber carpet beside him. "Sorry we scared you. You were having so much fun playing ghost that we decided to do a make-believe game of our own. What do you think about that? Now I'm going to pretend to call the police to report the bad man in your living room." She dialed 911 on her cell and made big comic eyes at Porter while she gave the dispatcher Gretchen's address.

He looked at her and laughed. He had big dimples and a heart-shaped face. Almond-shaped eyes. She hadn't noticed it before, but he looked much more like Susan than Gretchen. More like a young, boyish version of the girls' mother than General Hauptmann. The age was right, too—a little over nine years old.

Unlike Gretchen, Susan had not been disinherited. Because she had survived her father, she was poised to come into half of his estate. McKenna had assumed that Susan had come back from exile to cash in on that provision of the will.

But that wasn't the entirety of George Hauptmann's will. As Marla Tompkins had laid it out, because the general did not know whether Susan was dead or alive, he had included an alternative. In the event she was dead by the time the estate was dispersed, her portion of the estate would go to any remaining descendants other than Gretchen.

As she looked at Porter, McKenna realized that she was looking at the person who would have inherited $1.8 million once Gretchen did what her father had never been able to do: declare Susan dead.

McKenna held her cell phone in the crook of her neck, trying to keep a calm voice while she urged the dispatcher to send a car as quickly as possible. Gretchen was crying in the living room. "It's not fair. After all this time, she was coming back and taking every-thing."

McKenna reached for the little boy beside her, wrapped him in her arms, and began removing his newfound cape.

The crime lab would need it for testing.

# CHAPTER
## SEVENTY-TWO

**M**cKenna had not been inside an attorney conference room at the Metropolitan Detention Center since her days in the drug unit.

She jerked at the sound of the door's harsh, continuous buzz as the guard led Susan in.

Susan did not look happy to see her. "I knew something was wrong when I didn't hear someone bark at the guard the instant the door opened. You are definitely *not* my defense lawyer."

McKenna smiled. "I'm not even a member of the bar anymore. Stopped paying my dues two years ago. It's time to start telling the truth, Susan."

It had been Scanlin's idea to let McKenna have the first go at Susan.

"I read what you wrote," Susan said. "That *was* the truth. My mistake was believing Adam. I had no idea how much destruction we were unleashing. When Scanlin showed me those pages, I thought you believed me."

"I do believe you. At least I believe you're telling the truth about Adam and what happened on the docks ten years ago. But I saw how you responded when Scanlin told you that it was a woman who hired Carl Buckner. I saw your expression when he showed you a copy of your father's will. You hadn't seen it, had you? Gretchen received a copy but never told you."

"This is all about my reaction to Scanlin? How would *you* respond if the police accused you of murdering two men?"

"Almost three," McKenna said. "She shot Patrick, too. You went to Scott Macklin—you wanted him to come forward—because you believed that he was fundamentally a good man who would choose to do the right thing. How can you protect the person who killed him and tried to kill Patrick?"

Susan opened her mouth, but no words came out.

"I know what you were about to say," McKenna said. "Because she's your sister. She's blood. For you, that's always come first. You spent your whole life trying to believe that your father loved you, that some part of him was proud of you, even if he couldn't say it. You risked everything to come back to New York City and see him one last time before he died. Because Gretchen's your sister, you kept a connection to her, too. She was the one person who knew you were alive."

Though Susan was shaking her head, McKenna knew her suspicions were right.

"When you saw your father and learned that Adam had lied to you about the military's involvement in the drug running, you decided you were going to get your old life back. You had a plan to have Macklin back you up. The country's immigration policies had changed. His stepson was no longer at risk of being deported. Mac could finally tell the truth without worrying about his family being sent to Mexico. And then you made the mistake of telling Gretchen. She hired Buckner to follow you. When she found out you were going through with it—contacting Mac, contacting Patrick—she tried to kill you. When that failed, she went after everyone else who knew you were alive. You figured it out when Scanlin showed you the will and told you that Buckner was working for a woman."

Susan was working her jaw as if chewing an imaginary piece of gum.

"She pulled a gun on us yesterday," McKenna said. Susan stopped chewing. "The police say it's the same weapon used to shoot Buckner and Patrick. They also found a cape and mask matching those worn by the shooter."

"So why do you need me?"

"Because she can still say you did it. She can say it's your mask, your cape, your gun. You dumped it all at her place with no explanation. She'll claim that when she heard about the shooting, she realized it was you but was too confused to know what to do. Then when we came to her house and saw the costume, she panicked and pulled your gun. She'd probably get attempted assault at best."

In McKenna's short prosecutorial career, how many jailhouse deals had she cut in these attorney conference rooms? In theory, she was rewarding those who were least responsible and most contrite in exchange for their cooperation against the most culpable offenders. Most days, it was a question of which bad guy talked first.

"Susan, you mentioned the destruction you and Adam unleashed. Look at what Gretchen did in the last week. Mistaken or not, you did it because you thought there was a higher good. You thought you were saving lives halfway across the world. And here you are, ready to pay the price for what you did, even though you already paid dearly. You lost your life for ten years. And you lost your child."

Susan looked away. "It didn't mean anything. It was just a clump of cells."

"No, it wasn't. *He* wasn't. You didn't lose your baby. Porter is your son. You couldn't be the person—the *people*—you've had to be for the past decade and also raise a child. But Gretchen could. She was clean. She got married. You're not doing this to protect Gretchen, are you? You're trying to protect Porter. How can it be good for him to be raised by a murderer? By a woman who tried to kill you so she could be the one who inherited your dad's money instead of you? Think about it, Susan: how did she hire a guy like Carl Buckner in the first place? She only knew about that kind of private work because you've been doing it for ten years. Let me guess: she probably hit you up for a lot of extra cash in the last few months. You thought you were helping her through the divorce, but you were paying your own hit man."

Susan was clenching her fists so tightly that her knuckles were white.

"Even if you try to take the fall, the police won't buy it. Gretchen will get indicted. She will go to trial. And Porter will have to testify that he found Mommy's neato mask and cape right before she pulled a gun on that nice couple who came to visit. He'll testify about mommy's friend who always brought him toys and called herself Carol—your middle name, your mother's name. He'll be cross-examined by Gretchen's lawyer. Oh, and don't forget the DNA evidence. Scanlin will get a search warrant authorizing the state to draw Porter's blood. He won't understand why a man in a white coat is poking him in the arm with a needle, but his very biology—the fact that he's your *son*, Susan, not your nephew—is proof of Gretchen's motive. She wanted the money, but she also wanted him. Some lawyer will have to explain to him that his mother is his aunt. That the father who just left his mother isn't really his father. In fact, no one knows who his father is."

Susan jolted upright. "*Stop!* Just stop, okay?" The room was silent except for the sound of her heavy breaths. "Who will take care of Porter?"

Though McKenna had been prepared to use Porter as a chip in this negotiation, she had never stopped to think about what would happen to the boy while Gretchen was serving life in prison and Susan served whatever time she got for her part in Adam's drug scheme. "Does Gretchen's husband know Porter isn't his?" she asked. "He obviously thinks of him as his son—"

"Paul?" Susan shook her head. "Gretchen met him at an N.A. meeting when she was supposedly six months pregnant, thanks to a rubber maternity bump. When she told me she'd met a guy, I wanted to shake her senseless. Faking the pregnancy got a little trickier. Fabricated doctors' appointments. Sham sonogram images. I coached her through all of it. She just had to keep him from seeing her naked for a few months. From what I understand, it's not all that hard once your gut's the size of a beach ball and the only moans you're making are from morning sickness." The momentary smile brought back memories of a younger Susan. "As far as Paul is concerned, Porter was born three weeks premature, at home in their bathtub, assisted by the doula I bribed while he was away on business. He's a decent guy—good enough to fall in love with a woman who was already knocked up. But when they got engaged, I panicked. I figured he'd want to adopt Porter, and then what would we do? In over nine years, he's never raised the subject. Being called Daddy is one thing, but being legally obligated? I need to know Porter will be taken care of. And that he might have some connection with me when I get out."

"I'll make sure of it." McKenna was hearing her own words before she'd thought them through. But they felt right. At one point in their lives, Susan had been Patrick's closest friend. Susan had been the person to introduce them. Susan had cared about them both enough to sit back and watch as they fell in love.

And now that same friend was trying to take care of a nine-year-old boy who had no one else to care for him.

McKenna saw the uncertainty in Susan's face. "I promise you that I'll work with Paul. Any man who married a woman he believed was pregnant and then spent nine years raising the boy as his own has to be a decent guy. He'll want to be part of Porter's life. And Patrick and I will help out so he won't be overwhelmed. Porter will be taken care of. And loved. When you get out—and you *will*, Susan—you'll get your life back. You'll get your son. All of this will be over."

In the silence, Susan imagined Scanlin listening to the transmission of the conversation. With nothing but audio, he would think they'd lost her, that Susan was shutting down. He could not see what was happening in the silence: Susan grasping McKenna's hands across the table. Something had changed. Porter was the key.

"It's my fault," Susan said. "I'm the one who set this in motion. Gretchen had finally gotten her life together, and I dragged her into my mess. She raised my son as her own. And when I decided I wanted to come back, I never stopped to think how much that must have terrified her. Or how much she resented me. I was the one who let my father believe I was dead, and yet he continued to hold out hope for me. He searched for me. In his mind, I became the good daughter again, even as he continued to shun the only daughter he had left. In all those years, he could never bring himself to call Gretchen and take back the horrible things he said to her when she got arrested."

"She could have picked up the phone, too."

"But she didn't. Because she never felt like she was loved. And I was just as guilty as our father. When I persuaded Getty to give her a plea bargain, I felt like she owed me, so she was the one who would keep my secret and not tell anyone I had left. When months went by and I still had no way of coming home, she was the one who would raise the baby until I figured something out. I never thought it would be ten years. Even after she got married, I still treated her like a babysitter, a placeholder. Time was frozen for me. I was in limbo. But she became Porter's mother. She *loves* him, McKenna. And she's good with him. She needs him. And now I was coming back, and I never took the time to make her feel loved enough to know that she wouldn't be left alone—no Paul, no Porter, no me. I know you think this was only about the money, but it wasn't. I did this. If I could serve her sentence for her, I would."

"You can't. You know the letter that Carl Buckner mailed before he was killed? He said he was trying to do the right thing even though he was late. He actually wrote, *Is it possible to be a good person, then a bad person, and then a good person again?* It's not too late to start making the right choices. Someone has to be there for the child you and Gretchen both love. Under the circumstances, however we got here, that has to be you, Susan. It's time to start taking care of yourself so you can take care of him."

"Give me five minutes. Then send Scanlin in."

**S**canlin was waiting in the adjacent room. He was packing up the audio equipment that had monitored her conversation with Susan. "Good job."

She nodded. Susan's testimony would help seal the case against Gretchen, but McKenna didn't feel like celebrating.

"Please tell me you were shining her on about helping out with her kid."

"Nope. Dead serious."

She allowed him a few sentences to lecture her about the seriousness of child care. The responsibility. The sacrifice. The way children can break your heart. She cut him off. "You don't know everything here."

McKenna imagined a different reality, one in which Susan was never reactivated by the military. One in which she didn't need to call her father for special treatment, and Adam Bayne never ensnared her into his scheme to squeeze every last bit of cash out of Afghanistan while he could. Susan still would have been pregnant and single, but she would have stayed in New York City, parenting a son alone. She would have had help from Uncle Patrick and Aunt McKenna.

If Susan had been here, this boy would have been part of their lives already. It wasn't too late to catch up.

# MARCH

At the beginning of this trial, you made an oath to the judge in this case—an oath that you would listen to the evidence and follow the law. And once you were sworn in as jurors, I made a vow to you, as a lawyer for the People of New York, that the evidence in this case would support every representation that I made to you in the People's opening statement."

As McKenna spoke, she made a point to look directly at each juror individually. To a person, they returned her gaze. No nervous glances at their laps. No fidgeting in their chairs.

She had this.

"You have now heard the evidence. And I know you will follow the law. I am confident that you will find I have kept my promise as well. We have played our role in the system, and now it is time for the defendant to learn that this system works. That truth prevails. And the truth is that the defendant is guilty of assault in the first degree. I am confident that your verdict will reflect that truth."

She walked solemnly to the prosecution's counsel table and took her seat. There was a time when she had tried an entire case with nothing except a Post-it note. But this was her first jury trial in ten and a half years. She had memorized that closing argument word for word.

For all she knew, those jurors would look her in the eye, lock themselves away in their little room, and then decide that Martians, not the defendant, had beaten her victim—a homeless twenty-seven-year-old whose only offense was falling asleep on the subway.

But she believed in juries. She always had.

Will Getty was waiting for her, coat draped over his arm, when she emerged from the courtroom. "I stuck my head in. Good closing. Sorry it's not the kind of case you were probably looking forward to handling."

When the district attorney himself called last month to offer her a position, he had explained that her assignment in the office would reflect her prior experience but also the fact that she had been out of practice for so long. She could tell by the cautiousness of his words that he expected her to be insulted. A year ago, maybe she would have been. Now? The events of last fall had taught her that happiness wasn't about titles or acclaim or recognition.

She had spent all those years feeling like a victim, punished for the simple act of pursuing justice. Even though her suspicions about the Marcus Jones shooting proved to be correct, her motivations weren't entirely pure. She could have pressed Getty back then to tell her more, but she used his silence as a justification to play whistle-blower. After so much grunt work, it was her chance to shine. And when her novel came out, she may have told herself that she was trying to start over, but she made a point to take her author photo on the courthouse steps. Her publicity materials talked up her prosecutorial experience, describing her as more experienced than she ever was. She had earned her former colleagues' skepticism.

Now she was just happy to be back in the only job she'd ever wanted.

"Want to walk over to the courthouse together?" She meant the federal courthouse, where Susan was scheduled to be sentenced today.

She noticed then that Will was holding not only his coat but hers as well. "I took the liberty. We need to hurry if we're going to get there on time."

**P**atrick was already in the courtroom when they arrived. McKenna took a seat next to him. Will Getty chose a spot behind them, next to Gretchen's ex-husband, Paul Henesy. So far, Susan's predictions about Paul had proved an underestimation of his resolve to remain a father to the boy he had always treated as his son. He had moved back into the family's home and was serving as Porter's primary guardian. Porter's biological father, Will Getty, was slowly easing into the boy's life. As of three weeks ago, Porter had taken to calling him Daddy Will.

Susan was wearing the borrowed suit that McKenna had given to Susan's defense lawyer, Hester Crimstein, the previous day. It was a little baggy but better than the jail's coveralls.

Crimstein set forth the conditions of the plea agreement. McKenna already knew the terms. In the five months Susan had been in custody, her attorney had managed to work out a joint deal with federal and state prosecutors. Adam and Gretchen were looking at homicide charges: Adam for setting in motion the events that led to the deaths of Pamela Morris and Marcus Jones; and Gretchen for shooting Scott Macklin and Carl Buckner. Susan would testify against them both. In exchange, she would receive immunity from the state government, serve a year in federal prison, and complete five years of closely monitored probation.

It was a good deal—so good that Susan's lawyer was worried the judge might not accept it. Every observer in the courtroom was willing to speak in support of the sentence if necessary.

The courtroom door opened, and Joe Scanlin entered with Josefina Macklin and a teenage boy McKenna recognized as her son, Tommy. To McKenna's amazement, they had come to terms with Mac's wrongdoing. Now they wanted justice—for him and for them. Learning how to forgive Susan was part of that process.

"Does the defendant have any remarks?"

Susan rose to speak. As she laid out all of the mistakes she had made, and all of the opportunities she had missed to mitigate the harm, McKenna thought about her own regrets. She had spent ten years waiting for her life to change. Waiting for something big to happen, as if she were owed something better. Waiting to be happy—someday, when things were different, when the pieces fell into place.

Susan had described her time away as limbo. McKenna had created her own limbo.

The judge announced that she was accepting the plea agreement and then banged the gavel, bringing a quick end to the proceedings. Susan threw her head back and let out a soft sigh. She was going to jail, but she was finally free.

So was McKenna. She reached next to her and took Patrick's hand in hers. Her wait for the future that would change everything was over. She had been there all along.

# ACKNOWLEDGMENTS

Ten years ago, I published my first novel with the enthusiastic support of a smart and perceptive editor named Jennifer Barth. Hitching my wagon to hers was the best non-marital decision I have ever made. She makes every book better. Thanks to her, I now also have the tremendous support of an extremely talented crew at Harper-Collins: Amy Baker, Erica Barmash, Jonathan Burnham, Heather Drucker, Mark Ferguson, Michael Morrison, Katie O'Callaghan, Kathy Schneider, Leah Wasielewski, David Watson, and Lydia Weaver.

I always struggle for words to thank my tireless agent, Philip Spitzer. He is the most loyal champion a writer could ask for. His colleagues Lukas Ortiz and Lucas Hunt round out the team. And, together with his wife, Mary, he has made his agency feel like our second home.

We also had a temporary third home this year, thanks to a storm called Sandy. Thank you, Linda and Mike, for taking us in.

Thanks as well to retired NYPD Sergeant Edward Devlin, NYPD Sergeant Lucas Miller, UC Davis law professor Rose Cuison-Villazor, and Gary Moore for answering questions along the way. Thank you to Anne-Lise Spitzer, Richard Rhorer, and Ruth Liebmann for being good friends who know a ton about publishing. And thank you to my author-friends whose work not only inspires me but sometimes makes cameo appearances in mine, like Easter eggs, to be found by the careful reader. (For this novel, those eggs come courtesy of H.C., L.C., and K.S. Did you spot them all?)

You may recognize some familiar real-life names in this novel, too. One of my beloved former students donated generously to Hofstra Law School's Public Justice Foundation to have a character named for her mother, Mae Mauri. McKenna Jordan, owner of Houston's wonderful Murder by the Book, agreed to let me use her name, because not any name would do for this particular protagonist, a fictionalized me married to my fictionalized husband.

(If reading the story behind the story is too much like knowing how sausage is made, skip the next three paragraphs.) My husband and I met despite completely non-overlapping paths to New York City. I attended a tiny hippie college in the Pacific Northwest before working as a prosecutor and then turning to teaching and writing. My husband went to West Point and served in the army before taking up security management at the Metropolitan Museum of Art. Had we not met online, we might never have met at all. No shared job. No shared friends. No shared past.

In real life, that lack of common history made it fun to get to know each other from true scratch. But as a writer, I have always wanted to find a way to mine the potential for secrecy in a relationship where either party could be lying about the past. How much do we each really know about the lives the other led before we built one together? What events and people have we chosen to filter from the present?

I also felt ready to write about the post–West Point and private security cultures that I've been privileged to learn about second-hand during my marriage. The end product is fiction, which means you won't find details on Google about most of the specific programs mentioned in the novel. However, I hope I've done justice to the cultures, institutions, and time periods depicted.

Given the backstory, I've never been so nervous to have my husband read a manuscript. In some ways, this is probably the most personal book I've written. It also, even more than the others, belongs to Sean. Thanks, mister.

# A NOTE TO READERS

I get sad every time I hear a person say, "I don't read." It's like saying "I don't learn," or "I don't laugh," or "I don't live."

I am lucky to have found readers who prove that books make you smarter, funnier, and livelier than the other bears. Writing is solitary work, but I am not a solitary creature. Getting to know readers has been an unexpected perk of publishing. Although I've met some of you personally at libraries and bookstores, I'm thankful that the Internet has made it possible for us to meet on my website, Facebook, and Twitter. I am truly thankful for the ongoing support, and always enjoy hearing from you.

Some of you have gone the extra mile and serve as an online "kitchen cabinet," weighing in on choices like character names, titles, and the funny noises kids make when they think no one is listening. You've driven long distances to serve as unofficial photographers and friendly questioners at author events. Your word of mouth support is better than any publicity machine.

Though I'm sure I'll have some omissions, I can at least try to thank you by name: Adele Sylvester, Alan Williams, Alana Kinney Amaro, Alice Wright, Allen Young, Allison Freige, Allison Russell Smith, Amanda Richards, Amber Alling, Amber Scott Guerrero, Amy Fleer, Amy Hammer, Amy Nagdeman, Amy Turner DeSelle, Amy Williams, Amy Wolf, Andrea Napier, Andrea Stacy Kirk, Andrea Wichterich, Andrew Kleeger, Andrew Morrison, Andrew

T. Kuligowski, Andy Gilham, Andy P Barker, Angie Burton, Angie
Thomas-Davis, Ann Abel, Ann Flynt, Ann Hyman, Ann Rousseau
Weiss, Ann Smith, Ann Springer Shaffer, Ann Tully, Ann Zerega,
Anna Tauzin, Anne Allen, Anne Madison, Anne Mowat, Anne
Ward, Annie Goodson Frye, Annie Noll McAvoy, Anya Rhamnu-
sia Gullino, April Smith, Archie Hoffpauir, Arllys Brooks, Art Bat-
tiste, Audrey Pink, Barb Bradley Juarez, Barb Finnigan, Barb
Kearns, Barb Lancaster, Barb Mullen Gasparac, Barbara Bogue,
Barbara Detwiler, Barbara Dux Mullally, Barbara Franklin, Barbara
Jarvie Castiglia, Barbara McPherson, Barbara O'Neal, Barbara
Rosenbloom Howell, Barbedet Philippe, Barry Allen, Barry Bruss,
Barry Knight, Barry Nisman, Basil Tydings, Baxter Legere, Bea
Wiggin, Becky Decker, Becky Prater Sullivan, Becky Rathke, Ben
Small, Bernard Payn, Bert Walker, Beth Rudetsky, Bethany L.B.,
Betsy Steele Gray, Bettie Kieffer, Betty Vaughan, Beverly Bryan,
Bill Amador, Bill Botzong, Bill Cheney, Bill Hopkins, Bill Horn,
Bill Lee, Bill Reiser, Bill Strider, Bill Taylor, Bill Tipping, Billy
Paul Craig, B.J. Van Nix, Bob Blackley, Bob Briggs, Bob Dunbar,
Bob Fontneau, Bob Horton, Bob Marquez, Bob Rudolph, Bonnie
K. Winn, Bonnie Spears, Bonny Carey Sadler, Brantley Watkins,
Brenda Curin, Brenda German, Brenda K. Gunter, Brenda LeSage,
Brian Corbishley, Brian Fingerson, Brian Highley, Brian Rosen-
wald, Brian Shrader, Bridget Munger, Bruce DeSilva, Bruce South-
worth, Bud Palmer, Bunkie Burke Rivkin, C. Michael Bailey, Cal
Thompson, Carl Christensen, Carl Fenstermacher, Carla Coffman,
Carmen E. Padilla, Carol Bennett Mason, Carol Clark, Carol John-
sen, Carol M. Boyer, Carol Mcdonnell, Carol O'Gorman, Carole
Farrar, Carole M. Sauer, Carole Schultz, Carolgene Bishop Cottle,
Caroline Garrett, Carolyn G. Manuel, Carolyn Richmond Parker,
Carolyn Schriber, Caron Legowicz Kott, Carrie Brady Lint, Carrie
Dunham-LaGree, Cassie Ane, Catherine McDonald Patterson,
Cathy Peck, Cele Deemer, Celeste Libert Mooney, Chantelle Aimée
Osman, Charlene Wigington Hulker, Charlie Armstrong, Charlie
Burton, Charlotte Creeley, Charlotte Marchand, Charnell Inglis
Sommers, Cheri Gould, Cheri Hamlett, Cheri Land, Cheryl Boyd,

Cheryl Thompson, Cheryle Meyer Stadler, Chris Austin, Chris Cooper Cahall, Chris Costelloe, Chris Denicola, Chris Hamilton, Chris Holcombe, Chris Knake, Chris La Porte, Chris Martone, Chris Morrison Dougherty, Chris Schuller, Christa D. Paulsen, Christine Jewitt, Christine McCann, Christine Sublett, Christopher Kingsley, Christopher Zell, Christy Schroeder, Chuck Bracken, Chuck Palmer, Chuck Provonchee, Chuck Stone, Cindy Current Griffin, Cindy Spring, Cindy Wexler, Cindy Whitson, Clair Leadbeater, Claire Marie Gudaitis, Clare Kelly, Clarence Davis, Claudia Meadows, Clinton Reed, Connie Camerlynck, Connie Havard Ryland, Connie Meyer, Connie Ross Ciampanelli, Connie Williams Claus, Courtney Clark, Craig Todd, Crystal Haynes Zeman, Crystal Smith Hunter, Cyndie Lamb, Cynthia Diane Gardner Marsh, Cynthia Dieterich Mooney, Cynthia Poley Parran, Dale Glenn, Damon Reynolds, Dana Lynne Johnson, Danielle Emrich, Danielle Holley-Walker, Dannii Abram, Danny Nichols, Danny Prichard, Daphne Anne Humphrey, Darren Eskind, Darryl Johnson, Daryl McGrath, Daryl Perch, Dave Bowen, Dave Densmore, Dave Hall, Dave Kinnamon, David Barnes, David Bates, David Bell, David Bolander, David Cloud, David Dobson, David Greensmith, David Hale Smith, David McMahan, David Michael Lallatin, David Miller, David P. Watson, David Stine, Dawn M. Barclay, Dawn Miller, Dean James, Deana Fruth, Deb Gravette Threadgill, Deb Sturgess, Debbie Clark Trolsen, Debbie Hartley Holladay, Debbie Hoaglin, Debbie Prude, Debbie Rati, Debbie Stier, Debi Durst, Debi Kershaw, Debi Landry, Debi Murray, Debi Sussman, Deborah Sampson, Debra Eisert, Debra Manzella, Deda Notions, Dede McManus, Dee Hamilton-Worsham, Denise Berger, Denise Sargent, Denise Shoup Andersen, Dennis Kerr, Dennis Mullally, Dennis Raders, Desney King, Diana Bosley, Diana Hurwitz, Diana Keenan, Diana Rossbach, Diane Brown, Diane DeArmond, Diane Donceel McDonald, Diane Griffiths, Diane Hilton, Diane Howell-Arp, Diane Lowery Polk, Diane Muscoreil, Diane Sholar, Diane Warrener, Dick Droese, Doc Nyto, Dolores Melton, Don Boynton, Don Lee, Don Nations, Donna Cox Trattar, Donna

McNeal Sannicandro, Donna Reed Enders, Doug Kueffler, Dru Ann L. Love, Dudley Forster, Durella Jones, Dustin Epps, Ed Caldwell, Ed Lopez, Edgar Poe, Edward Foster, Eileen Brennan Locher, El Jackson, Elaine Meehan, Elbre E. Hickerson, Elda Zenn, Elena Shapiro Wayne, Elizabeth Julia, Elizabeth Larson, Elizabeth Salisbury Anderson, Elizabeth Sheppard Cross, Elizabeth Womack, Ellen Blasi, Ellen Montroy Doe, Ellen Sattler Harpin, Ellen Wills Bailey, Ellis Vidler, Elyse Dinh, Emin Guseynov, Emmy Lunatic, Eric Dobson, Erin Alford, Erin Mitchell, Erin Sweet-Al Mehairi, Etienne Vincent, Evelyn Lavelle, Faye DeBlanc, Forrest Croce, Fran Burget, Francena Parthemore, Frank Guillouard, Fred Emerson, Fred Feaster, Fred Hobba Middle, Fred Littell, Fred Pat Heacock, Fred Vinson, Freida D Jensen, Gail Patrie, Garnett Wallace, Garry Puffer, Gary Moore, Gary Morton, Gaye Matravers, Gayle Carline, Gayle Perren Haider, Gene Ruppe, Genevieve Skorst, Geoff Moffatt, George Bennett, George Cunningham, George Reid, Georgia Whitney, Georgie Goetz, Geraldine L. Allen, Gerry Binga, Gilbert King, Glen Manry, Glenda Voelmeck, Glenn Eisenstein, Gloria Haynes, Gloria Ketcher, Gregory S. Hammer, Greta Roussos Cosby, Gretchen Gfeller, Guy Tucker, Hailey Ellen Fish, Hap Louisell, Hayden Wakeling, Heather Bowden, Heather Giles Linhart, Heather Owens Watson, Heidi Moawad, Helen Carlsson, Helen Cox, Helen Perkins, Hilary Garrett, Howard Mills, Hsin Pai, Ike Reeder, Ilene Ratcheson Ciccone, Ilene Renee Bieleski, Inga Lucans, Irene Biggins, Irwin Shaab, Jackie D'Inzillo, Jackie Denney, Jackie Schmidt Welcel, Jackiesue Roycroft Denney, Jacqo Le Bourhis, Jacqueline L. Larson, Jacqueline May, Jame A. Riley, James Amerson, James Brown, James E. Barkley, James Merideth, James R. Bradbrook, Jamie Knight, Jan Wilberg, Jana Johnson, Jane Baker Fryburg, Jane Wise Shear, Janet Brockel, Janet Lindh, Janet McClure Hammond, Janice Gable Bashman, Janie McCue Lynch, Janine Grondin Brennan, Jann Sherman-Lassman, Jay Drescher, Jean Bleyle, Jean Mirabile, Jean Spurvey, Jean-Marc Le Faou, Jeana Burke, Jeane Anderson, Jeanine Elizalde, Jeanne Adcox Lockett, Jeanne King Hendrickson, Jeanne Lese, Jeb McIntyre, Jeff Bettis,

Jeff Nowland, Jen Forbus (yep, that detective is you!), Jen Hansen, Jen Mullins Keane, Jenet Lynn Dechary, Jennifer Abelson Whitney, Jennifer B. Jacobs, Jennifer Barney, Jennifer Ellis Lindel, Jennifer Hudson, Jennifer Irvin, Jennifer Kyles, Jennifer L. Irvin, Jennifer Ledbetter, Jennifer Little Beck, Jennifer Mueller, Jennifer Murtha Kountz, Jerrica Furlong, Jerry Hooten, Jerry McCoy, Jill D'Alessio, Jill Fletcher, Jill Porter Connell, Jim Boylan, Jim Cox, Jim Lewis, Jim Mccarthy, Jim Snell, Jimbob Niven, Jimmie Montoya-Treadway, Jo Ann Nicholas, Jo Boxall, Jo Scott-Petty, Jo Trotter, Joan Hersch Schwartz, Joan Long, Joan Lumb, Joan Moore Raffety, Joan Nichols Green, JoAnn Shapiro, Joanne Benzenhafer, Joanne Comper, Joanne Kaplan, Joanne Rembac Warren, JoAnne Rosenfeld, Joe Carter, Joe Shine, JoeAnn Bruzzo, Joey Mestrow, John and Sheryl Wetmore, John Bednarz, John Buckner, John Chester, John Decker, John Elder, John F. Armstrong, John Hanley, John Jones, John K. Peterson, John Karwacki, John Ketch, John Lindermuth, John Mcdaid, John Moore, John P. Eperjesi, John Paul Farris, John Schinelli, John Thomas Bychowski, Johnny Johnson, Jolene Schlichter, Jon Schuller, Jordan Foster, Jordana Leigh, Josh Lamborn, Josh Tennille Gimm, Joyce Joyner, Joyce Marie Martinko, Joyce Wickham, Juaan Prescott Gibbs, Jude Simms, Judi Burke, Judie Warner Morton, Judith McCarrick, Judith Taylor, Judith Williams, Judy Aschenbrand, Judy Bailey, Judy Easley, Judy Gehrig, Judy Glies, Judy Jongsma Bobalik, Judy Lambert Watson, Judy Pike Smith, Judy Waren Bryan, Jules Davies-Conjoice, Jules White, Julie Bower, Julie Ebinger Hilton, Julie Fragale McGonegle, Julie Gerber, Julie Kosmata Elliott, Julie Ryan, Karen Beaulier, Karen Burke Tietz, Karen Hosman, Karen K. Stone, Karen Lavely, Karen M. Crump, Karen McNeel Meharg, Karen Mitchell Klein, Karen Montgomery, Karen Nason Abdulfattah, Karen Richardson, Karen Ross, Karen Wills Johnson, Karin Carlson, Karin Durette, Karina Cascante Zumbado, Karl Binga, Karla Davis Glessner, Kasandra Maidmentt, Kate Wood, Katherine Wheeldon, Kathi Burke, Kathleen Andrews, Kathleen Geiger, Kathleen O'Brien Blair, Kathryn Witwer, Kathy Collings, Kathy Gabrosek Walters,

Kathy Goodridge Poulin, Kathy Kiley, Kathy Pagel Carle, Kathy Sammons, Kathy Schmidt, Kathy Tidd, Kathy Vraniak Aldridge, Katie Blackmon, Kaye Wilkinson Barley, Kayla Painter, Kelly A. Gunter, Kelly Ballenger, Ken Koziol, Kenneth Johnson, Kercelia Fletcher, Kerry Souza, Kerstin Marshall, Kestrel Carroll, Kim Baines, Kim Bonnesen, Kim Hector-White, Kim Mehr, Kim Rafelson, Kim Roberts, Kimberley Stephenson, Kimberly Hatfield Deighton, Kristen Howe, Kristi Belcamino, Kristy Knox Taylor, Kylo Switzerland Keen, Lance D. Carlton, Lance McKnight, LaRaine Coy Petersen, Larry Prater, Laura Aranda, Laura Bostick, Laura Piros McCarver, Laura Pop, Laurel Haropulos Bailey, Lauren Nassimi Yaghoubi, Laurence Bolzer, Laurie Stone, Leah Cummins Guinn, Leann Collins, Lee Walton, Leigh Sanders Neely, Len Hill, Lenice Wolowiec Valsecchi, Lenny Ferguson, Les Branson, Letty Cortelyou, Liam Moloney, Lincoln Crisler, Linda Careaga, Linda Connell, Linda Ellis, Linda Flannery, Linda Gilmer, Linda Goetz Greenham, Linda Hammitt-Salmi, Linda Hanno, Linda J. Myatt, Linda Jaros, Linda L. R. Roberts, Linda Maxine Williams, Linda McIntosh, Linda Moore, Linda Napikoski, Linda Quinn, Linda Robertson Feaselman, Lisa Bergagna, Lisa Burke, Lisa Ellis Schugardt, Lisa Fowler, Lisa Keller, Lisa Mason, Lisa Minneci, Lisa Sizemore Poss, Lisa van IJzendoorn, Lisa Wilcox, Liz Patruś, Liza Kosiadou, Lloyd Woods, Lois Alter Mark, Lois Roberson, Lois Rosenstein Reibach, Lola Troy Fiur, Lori Homayon-jones, Lori Hutcheson Kwapil, Louis Brunet, Louis Dienes, Louise Maughan James, Lovada Marks Williams, Lucy Limb Edmonston, Lyle Aul, Lynda Davis, Lynda Pendley Bennett, Lynelle Russell, Lynn Ashworth Peters, Lynn Christiansen, Lynn Comeau, Lynn Hirshman, Lynn Murray, Lynne Dalton, Lynne M. Lamb, Lynne Victorine, Marc Davey, Margaret Bailey, Margaret Barnum, Margaret Franson Pruter, Margaret Louise Clarke, Margaret Overstreet, Margie Watts Iverson, Margo Underwood, Maria Aurora Riojas Jackson, Maria Lima, Marianne Wysocki, Maricarmen Romero-Vazmina, Marie Horne Jackson, Marilyn Hambrecht, Marilyn Tipton Keyes, Marion Coro, Marion Montgomery, Marion Shaw, Marjie Satten, Marjorie

Tucker, Mark Go, Mark Gould, Mark O. Hammontree, Mark Smidt, Marlyn Beebe, Martha Lyons, Martha McConnell Greer, Martha Paley Francescato, Martha Stephenson La Marche, Martin Cook, Martin Treanor, Marty White, Martyn James Lewis, Mary A. King, Mary Asbury, Mary Geary, Mary Hohulin, Mary Jo Peterson Rodriguez, Mary Moylan, Mary Parsons, Mary Phillips, Mary Steck, Mary Stenvall, Mary Thompson Bullock, Maryann Mercer, Marylou Hess, MarySue Carl, Matt Foley, Matthew Jeanmard, Matthew Wallace, Maura O'Dea Stevenson, Maureen Fink, Maureen Howard, Maureen Lennon Kastner, Maureen Liske Stavrou, Maureen O'Connor, Maureen Rice, Maureen Wiley Apfl, Mauricia Sledd Smith, Melanie Sumihiro, Melinda Martin McClung, Melissa Costa, Melissa Mitchell Tate, Melissa Simpson-Keith, Melissa Sutton Gaines, Melissa Twingstrom Tomas, Meredith Blevins, Michael Bok, Michael Charles Woodham, Michael Gallant, Michael Haskins, Michael Honeybear Cotton, Michael Ma, Michael Ridout, Michael Rigby, Michael Sladek, Michael W. Sherer, Michele Corbett, Michele Hendricks, Michele Tollie, Michelle Goad, Michelle Martin, Michelle Pabon Pharr, Michelle Phillips, Michelle Waits, Mick Drwal, Micki Fortenberry Dumke, Mike Burzan, Mike Forehand, Mike Harris, Mike Holbrook, Mike Houston, Mike Neustrom, Mike Newman, Miles Powell, Millie Ann Lowry Buck, Missie Silva, Mitch Smith, Mitt Winstead, Molly Cramer Anderson, Monica Niemi, Mysti Berry, Nancy A. Nash Coleman, Nancy Cullen, Nancy Ethier Carrod, Nancy Gillis Cawley, Nancy M. Hood, Nancy McCready, Nancy Rimel, Nancy Ryberg Key, Nancy W. Cook, Naomi Golden, Naomi Waynee, Natalie Chernow, Nathan Danger Conner, Nelda Elder, Nevin Sanli, Nic Wolff, Nils Kristian Hagen Jr, Nisha Sharma, Oliver Shirran, Otis Wayne Hale, Owen Weston, Pam Bieschke-Sebrell, Pam Hughes, Pamela Cardone, Pamela Dawn Williams Montgomery, Pamela Jarvis, Pamela Kelly, Pamela Melville, Pamela Pescosolido, Pamela Picard, Pat Mays, Pat Neveux, Pat Toups, Pat Winfield, Patricia Blackwell-Cox, Patricia Burns Porter, Patricia Eck, Patricia Hawkins, Patricia Medley, Patrick Kendrick, Patrick Riley, Patsy

Green, Patti James Anderlohr, Patti MacDonnell, Patti Neal Black-
wood, Patti O'Brien, Patty Hudson, Patty McGuire Moran
Kilkenny, Paul Deyo, Paul Hansper-Cowgill, Paul Miro, Paul
Renn, Paul Roath, Paul W Stackpole Jr, Paula Daniel Steinbacher,
Paula Friedman, Paula Rossetti, Peggy Kincaid, Penny Sansbury,
Pepper Goforth, Perry Dugger, Perry Lassiter, Pete Sandberg, Peter
Baish, Peter L. Pettinato, Peter Robertson, Peter Spowart, Phil
Messina, Philip McClung, Phillis Spike Carbone, Phyllis Browne,
R. Bruce Osmanson, Rand Hill, Rebecca Jones Woodbury, Re-
becca Roush Aikman, Rebecca S. Autrey, Rebecca Turman, Re-
becca Woodbury, Regina McCartt, Reina Schwartz, Renee Collar
Sias, Rex Bovee, Rhonda Tate McNamer, Rhonda Thompson,
Rich Maxson, Richard Fox, Richard Hurt, Richard Johnson,
Richard Sandefur, Rick Miller, Rick Reed, Robert Carotenuto,
Robert Carraher, Robert F. Klees, Robert Hartman, Robert J.
Scheeler, Robert Ray, Roberta Boe, Robin Hill Sparacio, Robyn
Alexander, Robyn Gee, Rodney E. Dodson, Roger Q. Fenn, Roger
Vaden, Ron Gilmette, Ron J. Turk, Ron Kaznowski, Ron Kramer,
Ron LaBarre, Ronald Clingenpeel, Ronda Smittle Aaron, Rose
Quaranta, Rosemary Lindsey, Rosie Richardson, Ruby Martin,
Rue Vandenbroucke, Runner Rusty Bostic, Russell Hyland, Rus-
sell Meadows, Ruth Mariampolski, Ruth Miller Blackford, Ryan
Dorn, Sabine Pilhofer, Sal Towse, Sally Channing, Sally Dorfler,
Sam Sattler, Sammi-Rexanne Huskisson-Bonneau, Samuel Perry,
Sandra Jean Krna, Sandra Sarr, Sandra Speller, Sandy Cann, Sandy
Featherstone Mosley, Sandy Holcombe Olson, Sandy Maines, Sandy
Meyer, Sandy Plummer, Sandy Schwinning Hill, Sara Baldwin,
Sara Glass Phair, Sara Gremlin, Sara Weiss, Sarah Beckett, Sarah
LaPorte Scott, Sarah Pearcy, Sarah R.H., Sarah Tobergta, Sarah Van
Zandt, Scott Bristow, Scott Irwin, Sean Neid, Sean Sharpton,
Shanna White, Shannon Kenglish, Sharon Brown, Sharon Faith
Graves, Sharon Lema Allsworth, Sharon Stewart Walden, Sharon
Woods Hopkins, Sheila Arlene Dempsey, Sheila Dawson, Sheila M.
Ross, Sheila Sanders Parker, Sheri Carlisle Horton, Sherri Caudill
Lewis, Sherri Merkousko, Sherri Young Coats, Sherrie Saint, Sher-

rie Simmons, Sherrie Whaley Frontz, Sherry Lee, Sheryl Cooper, Sheryl Ditty Hauch, Sheryl J. Dugo, Shirley Anderson Whitely, Shirley Grosor, Shirley Smith Cox Patterson, Simon Cable, Simon Lloyd, Sita Laura, Skip Booth, Skip Crawford, Skye Weber Middle, Sonnie Rix Sullivan, Soules Wanderer, Stacey Oldenburg Robb, Stacy Allen, Stan Finger, Stella Mullis, Stephanie Angulo, Stephanie Doherty Rouleau, Stephanie M. Gleave, Stephanie Smith, Stephanie Stafford Roush, Stephen Burke, Steve Downs, Steve LaVergne, Steve Shreve, Steven Parker, Stuart Spates, Sue Christensen, Sue Cipriani, Sue Hancock, Sue Hollis, Sue McLauchlan Faulkner, Sue Smith Stewart, Sue Stanisich, Susan Collins, Susan Connolly, Susan Cox, Susan Dineen Kritikos, Susan Feibush Braun, Susan Ferris, Susan Hansen Bubb, Susan Jarrett Carey, Susan Mac-Donnell, Susan Martinez, Susan Pritchett Thomas, Susie Cowan Hudson, Suzanne Abbott, Suzanne Chiles, Suzanne L. Miles, Suzanne M. Watson, Suzanne Perzy, Svend R. Nielsen, Tami Kidd Masincupp, Tammy Dewhirst, Tammy Helms Meyers, Tanya Currin Faucette, Ted Myers, Teri Bass McElhenie, Teri James, Terri Clawson Swift, Terry Butz, Terry Hill, Terry Molinari, Terry Parrish, Tetsu Ishikawa, Therman Jones, Thomas C. McCoy Jr, Tica Gibson, Timothy Daniels, Tina Lee, Tina Marie, Tirzah Goodwin, T.J. Carrell, Tom Measday, Tommye Baxter Cashin, Tonett Mattucci Wojtasik, Toni Kelich, Tony Engle, Tony Sannicandro, Tori Bullock, Tracee Forster, Tracey Edges, Tracey Paveling, Traci Boeh Wickett, Tracy Campbell, Tracy Davison, Tracy Nicol, Trena Klohe, Trish Waldbillig, Veronica Piastuch, Vick Mickunas, Vicki O'Bryant Marston, Vicki Parsons, Vicki Ray Blitenthal, Vickie M. Neyra, Vickie Parshall, Vicky Hatchel, Victoria Waller Ranallo, Viola Burg, Vivian Valtri Burgess, Wade Weeks, Wallace Clark, Wanda Brown York, Wanda Watkins, Wayne Cunnington, Wayne Curry, Wayne Ledbetter, Wendy Brown, Wendy Burd-Kinsey, Wendy Weidman, Wes Comer, Will Boyce, Will Swarts, William Bruner, William Penrose, Win Blevins, Yash Bombay, Yevon Duke, and Zita Fogarty.

Thanks for reading.

**ff**

Faber and Faber is one of the great independent publishing houses. We were established in 1929 by Geoffrey Faber with T. S. Eliot as one of our first editors. We are proud to publish award-winning fiction and non-fiction, as well as an unrivalled list of poets and playwrights. Among our list of writers we have five Booker Prize winners and twelve Nobel Laureates, and we continue to seek out the most exciting and innovative writers at work today.

**Find out more about our authors and books**
faber.co.uk

**Read our blog for insight and opinion on books and the arts**
thethoughtfox.co.uk

**Follow news and conversation**
twitter.com/faberbooks

**Watch readings and interviews**
youtube.com/faberandfaber

**Connect with other readers**
facebook.com/faberandfaber

**Explore our archive**
flickr.com/faberandfaber